ALSO BY LORI ANDREWS

Nonfiction

Future Perfect: Confronting Decisions About Genetics

*Body Bazaar: The Market for Human Tissue
in the Biotechnology Age*

*The Clone Age: Adventures in the New World of
Reproductive Technology*

*Black Power, White Blood: The Life
and Times of Johnny Spain*

*Between Strangers: Surrogate Mothers, Expectant Fathers,
and Brave New Babies*

Medical Genetics: A Legal Frontier

*New Conceptions: A Consumer's Guide to the Newest
Infertility Treatments, Including In Vitro Fertilization,
Artificial Insemination, and Surrogate Motherhood*

SEQUENCE

LORI ANDREWS

St. Martin's Paperbacks

This is a work of fiction. All of the characters, organizations and events portrayed in this novel are either products of the author's imagination or are used fictitiously.

SEQUENCE

Copyright © 2006 by Lori Andrews.
Excerpt from *The Silent Assassin* copyright © 2007 by Lori Andrews.

Cover photo © Joshua Sheldon

Library of Congress Catalog Card Number: 2006040534

ISBN: 0-312-94245-1
EAN: 978-0-312-94245-8

Printed in the United States of America

St. Martin's Press hardcover edition / June 2006
St. Martin's Paperbacks edition / April 2007

St. Martin's Paperbacks are published by St. Martin's Press, 175 Fifth Avenue, New York, NY 10010.

10 9 8 7 6 5 4 3 2 1

To Adrianne Noe and her amazing staff at the National Museum of Health and Medicine, who bring to life the past and future of science and medicine

And to the memory of Marc Lappé, a scientist and humanist of the utmost integrity who combined pathology and poetry to make the world both safer and more enchanting

SEQUENCE

CHAPTER I

THE CLICK OF THE KEY CARD EASED HIS
late-night entrance into the Wilmont Suite at the Au Contraire Resort in San Diego. Built three years earlier for the spa crowd, the castle-towered resort was now a favorite of high-end business travelers. The same discretion that attracted wealthy stars who were drying out, slimming down, or simply ducking their spouses appealed as well to deal makers who wanted to negotiate potential takeovers—or choose a new CEO—outside journalists' glare or brokers' speculation.

Wisps of moonlight illuminated the room through the beveled glass that led to the suite's private garden. He set down his faded cotton duffel bag next to her monogrammed Louis Vuitton hatbox, right inside the door. As he passed the antique coatrack, the scent of her perfume radiated from the embroidered burgundy shawl hanging from one of the pegs.

The door to the bedroom was ajar, and he stood in the entryway for a moment, tongue darting over his top lip. The tousled sheet that covered her sleeping body dipped below one breast, exposing its compact shape and tender nipple. Her short dark hair spiked in all directions, punk rock–style. Quite a contrast to the buttoned-up photo of her in last month's *Forbes*.

The hum of the ceiling fan disguised his approach. He began to pull the sheet gently back. She stirred slightly but didn't awaken. He bent over her, staring intently at her face as a tiny furrow creased her forehead. A bad dream perhaps?

He dipped his head down and lightly licked her inviting nipple. The furrow vanished. Then he raked his top teeth gently over the nipple and her eyes squinted open.

Her mouth formed a scream, but his hands were quicker. Within seconds, he slid his fingers behind her neck, thumbs positioned in front. He rocked the weight of his body forward with 180 pounds of pressure on her fragile windpipe. A small *thwack,* like the sound of a light being extinguished, signaled that he'd crushed her trachea. Her head fell violently to the side and he began to whistle.

He returned to the living room for his duffel bag, threw it on the bed next to her, and unzipped it. The Crystal Method song didn't lend itself to whistling. Few techno songs did. But he continued forming the discordant notes. Accustomed to being alone, he'd stopped noticing that his tastes were far different from most people's.

With a strong tug, he unpeeled the sheet, exposing her entire body. He looked intently over her, cataloging each slope and nook of her frame. Her wrists were exceedingly thin, he thought, and her earlobes asymmetrical.

Once he had memorized her form, he took an antibacterial wipe from the bag and cleaned off the breast he had licked.

Then he began his work.

CHAPTER 2

ON THE FIRST FLOOR OF THE ARMED FORCES institute of Pathology, the sound of the Razorbacks' latest CD blasted through the DNA lab. Alexandra Northfield Blake tapped her Western boots and wiggled her hips to the twanging surf guitar as she scraped a piece of lung tissue into a thick test tube and inserted it into the Gentra Systems Autopure LS to be centrifuged and combined with chemicals to extract the DNA. She'd then have enough viral genetic material from the corpse to analyze the DNA sequence.

Alex dotted some extra lung tissue into a series of four flat, round petri dishes, placed them on a tray, and then walked over to the gleaming silver refrigerator. As she approached, she was lost in ideas about her research and didn't give a moment's thought to her reflection in the gleaming door.

She was five seven, with a beguiling heart-shaped face and blond curly hair that flowed past her shoulders. Her trademark black turtleneck and blue jeans were nicely taut over the curves of her otherwise lean, athletic body. She wore no makeup, but the impetuous sparkle of her blue eyes attracted more men than would the application of any product from Bloomingdale's cosmetic counter.

Once the petri dishes were carefully situated on a rack, she closed the refrigerator door, which caused her 3-D fortune-teller magnet to give a brief audio prediction: "Beware of men who want to change you."

Alex rolled her eyes. "Now you tell me." She'd bought the magnet at a flea market the previous weekend because the turbanned woman resembled her mother. So far, she'd gotten better advice from the magnet than she'd ever gotten from her mom.

Alex entered her glass-walled office at the back of the lab to survey her E-mails while she waited for the DNA extraction process to take place. Her lab at AFIP was a state-of-the-art DNA testing facility. Three $300,000 gene sequencers filled one side of the room, giving her more power to explore genetic mysteries than most state crime labs or even most overcapitalized biotech companies. The room circulated its own highly purified air to ensure the best-possible growth for her tissue cultures without risk of contamination. She felt that the mix in the air also helped her think more clearly. Or maybe, after all her moving around as a child, a sleek laboratory with its dependable equipment was the one place she felt at home.

Alex had joined the AFIP eleven months earlier, a fiscal beneficiary of escalating terrorism in the years following the 9/11 disaster. After an anthrax-laden letter was delivered to a White House staffer, an undersecretary from the Department of Defense had called her. He'd read about her work trying to sequence the genome of the 1918 Spanish flu virus, which had killed more than forty million people worldwide. It was unique among flus because its victims were young, previously healthy adults. The Defense Department brass feared that terrorists could use the 1918 flu virus as the perfect bioweapon: deadly, invisible, unstoppable.

He'd offered Alex a once-in-a-career opportunity: a two-year appointment at AFIP, with as much money, equipment, staff, and resources as she needed to sequence the flu genome. Alex didn't think twice, didn't even ask for more money than she was making as an assistant professor of molecular biology at Berkeley. The AFIP had something she wanted more than riches: the recently dis-

covered body of an Inuit woman who had died of the flu
back in 1918.

Alex had tried finding the virus's DNA in hospital tissue samples from patients of that era. But she'd stumbled
down too many false paths. Some of the samples were too
deteriorated to yield any DNA. Others were mislabeled,
and the cause of death turned out to be dysentery or a different virus than the 1918 flu. The Inuit woman's body
would cut years off Alex's roundabout attempts to sequence the flu genome. Alex felt that she could persuade
that corpse, woman to woman, to yield up her genetic secrets. Despite the century between them, Alex would be
able to understand the language in the woman's cells—
that secret genetic message written in the chemical bases
of *A* (adenine), *C* (cytosine), *G* (guanine), and *T* (thymine)—the sweet, mysterious alphabet of human life.

In medical school, Alex had obsessed over the diseases
that cut down people in their prime. The college football
player who died of a heart attack on the field. The eighth-
grade computer whiz whose skinny body gave out when his
lungs gave in to cystic fibrosis. For so many of these
diseases—these ghouls that reached into healthy bodies and
squeezed the life out of them—their hideout was in the genes.

As the centrifuge churned away, Alex picked up the
box labeled "A/Brevig Mission/1/18," which encased the
Inuit sample. In 1997, D. Johan Hultin, a retired pathologist from San Francisco, had exhumed the woman's body
from permafrost in a mass grave in Brevig Mission,
Alaska. Eight decades earlier, the Spanish flu had swept
through the Alaskan woman's village in less than a week,
taking the lives of seventy-two people, almost every adult
in the town. Hultin had discovered three bodies in the
grave, but it was the woman who was best preserved.

It bothered Alex not to know the woman's name. She
thought of naming her after a talk-show host such as Ellen
DeGeneres or Rosie O'Donnell, in the hopes that she
would blab her secrets.

Yes, the name Rosie would fit. The Inuit woman was, well, to put it politely, more than a bit overweight. The two bodies on either side of her in the mass grave had turned to skeletons. But her fatty padding had insulated her body, keeping the tissue and its genetic blueprint intact. The combination of the woman's obesity and the temperature of the permafrost meant that her lungs, which were likely to have the highest concentration of the virus, looked like she had died just last week. Alex decided she would go on-line to find an Inuit name that was close to Rosie.

In her glass-walled office, Alex powered up the computer. Through picture-in-picture on the screen, she caught the opening image of a CNN broadcast, a photo of Marilyn Mayne, the wunderkind CEO of Datasmart, a software company that made Microsoft's operating system seem like something from the Stone Age. Rumor had it she was about to unveil a notebook computer that would give Apple a run for its money.

Alex turned on the sound. "The Dow Jones took a dip this afternoon after the brutalized body of Marilyn Mayne was found in a luxury suite at the Au Contraire Resort," said the male anchor. "Her locked room showed no sign of forced entry, leading to speculation that she knew her assailant."

Now the pert female anchor, half his age, could add the personal touch as photos of an elegantly dressed Mayne at various philanthropic functions filled the screen. "The glamorous billionaire kept company with some of the world's most eligible men. But in the end, she died alone, a poor little rich girl."

How vapid, thought Alex as they moved on to the next story. Nothing about Mayne's Ph.D. from MIT or her dozen patents, all of which Alex had read about in scientific journals. And what's this dying alone shit? The woman was murdered. *Somebody* was in that room with her that night.

Alex turned off the news in disgust but had no luck finding an Inuit-language Web site. She took a cursory glance at her E-mail. One from her mother, an Oberlin College professor in her fifties. Janet still dressed like a 1960s flower child and used the screen name "Wild-flower." She'd shown up for Alex's medical school graduation wearing a flowing orange-and-purple Indian sari, with little bells along the hem of the pants. Well, what do you expect from a cultural anthropologist?

Another E-mail was from an MIT microchip engineer she had met at an American Society of Human Genetics meeting. Right before she left Berkeley for the job at AFIP, she'd spent a weekend with him at an oceanfront bed-and-breakfast in Mendocino. It was a disaster. As they strolled the beach, he launched into a dissertation about the adhesive properties of grouped silicate surfaces. In their cozy room, he seemed more interested in the compressive properties of their mattress than in exploring the soft curves of the increasingly frustrated woman lying next to him. That was the problem with dating people in her field. Scientists were grounded in the physical world, constantly searching for the logical formula behind how things functioned.

In sex, love, romance, she was intrigued by the inexplicable. She had enough of her mother in her to want the razzmatazz, the whole abracadabra.

Her need for spontaneity, drama, unexpected excitement led her to people like Luke, her latest ex, who would wake in the middle of the night, hearing a new song in his head, and get out of bed to echo it on the bass guitar. Or the artist Karl, who had actually cried over a particular shade of green.

The world, however, did not reward magic. The men she dated—musicians, actors, poets, artists—were invariably short on cash. Most had short attention spans and little patience—the flip side of spontaneity, she guessed. They moved on—like surfers searching for the perfect wave—to other cities, other gigs, other women.

Luke had slipped away a month earlier. You want the magic, she told herself, you have to put up with the magician. And the risk he'll pull a disappearing act.

Alex deleted the engineer's E-mail without reading it. Now that she was working on a national security project, people didn't expect her to have time to respond to their E-mails anyway. She made the most of the national security classification. When she didn't feel like cleaning her apartment, she invoked the "national security" excuse, telling herself that dust bunnies couldn't compete with the importance of thinking about biowarfare on the way to her indispensable dark roast Starbucks.

A new E-mail popped up on the screen, with "URGENT" in the subject line. Barbara Findlay, the general counsel at AFIP and her closest friend there, issued the following warning: "Alex, if you are playing that wretched music, turn it off, comb your unruly curls, and put on that blazer I forced you to buy and keep on the back of your door. Commander Webster is about to take a VIP on a tour of our humble institution. The rumor is that this guy, Colonel Jack Wiatt, may be our next director."

CHAPTER 3

THE ALLEY WAS DESERTED EXCEPT FOR A crouching body in a bulletproof vest at the far end. A raging boom of gunfire hit the figure squarely in the chest, knocking the body against the brick wall.

"Great job," yelled a technician who didn't look to be over age twenty. Then four other white-coated figures entered the alleyway, loaded the figure onto a gurney, and transported it to the adjoining laboratory.

Colonel Jack Wiatt carefully took in the situation. The smells were all off. Sure there was the acrid hint of gunpowder, but this wasn't like any firefight he'd been in. They were in the basement of a building in D.C., for Chrissakes. These guys were playacting warfare, studying it, in a fake alley that smelled like Lysol. The body they shot had already been dead.

"This mock alley is the heart of the AFIP's military body armor lab," Commander Hal Webster, the number-two man at the AFIP, explained to Colonel Wiatt. "Researchers like Mike Dannon here analyze the injury patterns on donated corpses to design bulletproof vests."

Dannon, a young dark-haired man with the black rectangular glasses favored by brooding poets and civilian AFIP researchers, nodded at the colonel. "We're targeting urban warfare—conflicts at close quarters—in alleys, warehouses, even business districts. The battles we're fighting have moved from the jungles and deserts to the world's capitals. Americans are walking targets."

The three men moved to the lab, where the sensors of an X-ray machine were waved over the battered corpse. "Even with body armor, eighty percent of survivors need orthopedic surgery," said Dannon. "We identify the breaks and sprains, and design protective gear around that."

Dannon approached the body on the gurney. The corpse's arms were poised at improbable angles due to the breaks. Dannon put on a pair of latex gloves and ran the flat of his right hand over the corpse's shoulders, feeling for damage there.

Hal, a commander in the U.S. Navy, stood next to Colonel Wiatt, watching his reaction closely. Hal had a chiseled chin, denim blue eyes, and dark hair, which he'd already decided to darken when it turned gray. He stood an inch shy of six feet, a fact that never ceased to irk him. He blamed that missing inch—and his rural Alabama background—for keeping him from the sort of honor and recognition he deserved. He never wore his service's informal khaki uniform, only the dress blues, plus an unmilitarylike pair of Bruno Maglis. Voice lessons a decade earlier had transformed his Southern twang to a newscaster's clipped generic tones. Only when he was wildly stressed did his vowels soften and his syllables grow slow and long.

At six four, Colonel Jack Wiatt loomed over Webster. Above his heart, an array of ribbons signaling military honors punctuated his green Army jacket. To top it off, he had a full head of mahogany brown hair. With his silver-gray eyes and an easy, confident way of moving, he was a walking recruiting poster.

Wiatt watched as the white-coated crew rolled another corpse in a bulletproof vest out of the lab to be propped up for target practice. "Where do you get the bodies?" Wiatt asked.

Dannon turned away from the X-ray machine and faced him. "We've got a batch of military personnel who never saw combat," he said. "They left their bodies to us in their wills. Guess they figured they owed more to their country than being a ghost."

Wiatt grimaced. Since Vietnam, he'd led men in every war, incursion, altercation, and conflict the United States had entered. But his willingness to put his body on the line did not extend to being blasted like a crash-test dummy.

He surveyed the facility and wondered how this outfit functioned. When he was in battle, he grew tight with his men, and his unit acted like the multiarmed extension of his own mind. Back in the States, the tedium was taxing. Stateside, he couldn't control his men round the clock like he did his troops. So he commanded by distancing himself and using his physical bearing and deep voice to intimidate the recruits and noncoms alike. The distance could be chilling, as his ex-wife Clarissa had pointed out, to no avail. Jack Wiatt was nothing if not intense.

Wiatt patted his jacket pocket and heard the crinkle of the speech he'd planned to give when his old Yale roommate, President Bradley Cotter, named him to head the FBI.

But the President's chief of staff had ambushed him that morning. As Dannon and his colleagues wheeled another body into place, Wiatt replayed the conversation in his mind.

"The pollsters say the public won't accept a military man in charge of domestic investigations," Martin Enders, the chief of staff, had told him.

"You did *polls* about me?"

"Well, not about you personally, but, you know, about the idea of an Army colonel heading the FBI. It's a nonstarter. People imagine all sorts of abuses, a banana republic."

"You're going to let some spin doctors decide who heads up the Bureau?"

"Jack, it's not just the polls. We'd never get you through the Senate committee."

"Marty, the President's known me since college. I'm as clean as they come. Decorated war hero . . ."

"That's the problem. When people think of Nam, they

don't think of those sixty thousand soldiers on the Wall, they think of the women and children at My Lai, the villagers that Senator Bob Kerrey wasted. Those decorations have a way of exploding in your face."

Jack Wiatt leaned forward in his chair. "Give me a chance. Make me acting director and see how it works out."

The chief of staff shook his head. "It's not just the military taint, your special ops work. It's all those scandals at the Bureau. The President's gotta show he's serious about cleaning house."

It dawned on Wiatt that Enders had already cut a different deal. "Who's getting the job?"

Enders had hesitated, weighing whether he should disclose. Finally, he spoke. "Senator Gloria Devon. She's the chair of the Senate committee that monitors the FBI, and she's been a major critic of how it's run."

Wiatt had laughed. "She'll look good in that apron, cleaning house. But she doesn't know shit about how to command a unit of trained professionals. . . ."

"She was the DA in Denver for twelve years before she ran for office."

"Denver's not exactly Saigon or Mogadishu."

"She's the President's choice. But he's got something else for you."

Wiatt relaxed a bit. What would it be? National Security Advisor? Joint Chiefs of Staff?

"He'd like you to head the Armed Forces Institute of Pathology."

Wiatt slammed his palm down on the desk. "You've got to be fucking kidding. Instead of the FBI, I get the AFIP? Is this your idea of a joke?"

"The AFIP does good work. . . ."

"For Chrissakes, it's a goddamn museum."

"The medical museum's only a small part of the operation. They do all the forensic work for the military and the executive branch. Remember when Secretary of Commerce Ron Brown's plane went down in Croatia? The AFIP did the lab work to see if his head wound was from

a gunshot or the crash. And anytime there's a crime involving a soldier, the AFIP's on it. They've got surveillance tools and weapons that the Pentagon would piss
itself over."

Wiatt had stood up and leaned his six-four frame toward
Enders with a powerful combination of dignity and ire.
"Both you and the President know I deserve better than this."

Enders was intimidated by only one man, and that
wasn't any Army officer. "Go over there and meet the top
guys. See if you can grow the institution. The President
will back you in Congress for an appropriations increase.
If you show him you're one of the team, maybe he'll take
the terrorist investigations away from the FBI, give you
greater jurisdiction over national security."

Politicians, thought Wiatt. They can shovel more of it
than bullring custodians.

So here he was, watching dead-end soldiers shoot up
dead GIs.

"It's a tradition here," said Dannon, noticing Wiatt's dis-
dain. "When Abe Lincoln founded the facility, Army doctors came here to study limbs blown off in the Civil War."

"Think *M*A*S*H,* a hundred years earlier," said Hal.

"Have you been over to the museum yet, Colonel?"
Dannon asked. "You can see General Daniel Sickles's leg
bone, from the Battle of Gettysburg."

"I'll have to bone up on General Dan, won't I?" said
Wiatt, with pique in his voice.

Hal grinned, signaling he thought Wiatt to be a
pushover. "We're heading there next," he said.

Wiatt looked away from the corpse to face his guide.
"Commander Webster," he said. "I am not here for the Kiwanis tour of AFIP. You've got a staff of eight hundred
people and a budget of over a billion dollars. Give me a
printout of how that money is being spent and an office
where I can review it. Then I want a meeting at sixteen
hundred hours with the directors of your top projects.
You've had my ear for the past two hours, and all I've gotten is PR spin. I need to know what's really going on."

◆ ◆ ◆

THE L-SHAPED CONFERENCE ROOM WAS THE former office of the public relations staff at AFIP. The long arm of the L held a smooth mahogany conference table that could seat thirty people. The short arm housed three desks with computers, a battered couch with two overstuffed chairs, and a small refrigerator with a coffee machine on it. Unlike the typical AFIP coffeepot, this one was sleek, Italian, and made espresso as well as regular brew. An affectation, Alex guessed, of the previous denizens, the PR folks who considered themselves "artistes" and "wordsmithes," rather than company flacks.

A few years earlier, the head of AFIP's PR department had envisioned holding press briefings at the large table with the editors of *The New York Times, Washington Post, Wall Street Journal,* and other press luminaries. But she could hardly raise interest among the Army's own reporters for *Stars and Stripes.* She'd been fired, her staff reassigned. About the only part of her scheme that actually worked was the espresso machine. No one knew about the AFIP, and no one cared. If you put the acronym AFIP into any news database, you got more hits for the Antarctica Federation of Indigenous People than the Armed Forces Institute of Pathology.

Alex pressed the espresso button—no sugar, no milk. She was a caffeine mainliner, and she'd arrived a few minutes early to grease her habit. While the machine roared and sputtered, she perused the photos and posters on the walls, evidence of past AFIP triumphs. President Lincoln had established the facility when he realized that more men were dying of infections during the Civil War than of their battle wounds. He put his surgeon general in charge. Battlefield surgeons began shipping corpses and amputated limbs to the facility to advance wartime medicine, strategy, and weapons. To this day, the AFIP maintained a schizophrenic personality. On the one hand, its world-class pathology geniuses helped fight death, sending researchers to identify diseases around the world. On the other hand, its technological gurus tried to figure out ways for soldiers to kill more efficiently.

The photos in this room celebrated only the medical triumphs. Walter Reed, the institution's head in 1900, proved mosquitoes transmitted yellow fever. Army general Frederick Russell, the director a decade later, helped develop the typhoid vaccine. Alex felt a kinship with these pioneers. Her own work on Rosie was funded, like much medical research these days, under the Congressional line item of "bioterrorism control." But if she pushed the work as far as she intended, her findings could lead to an all-purpose vaccine against deadly infectious diseases.

"Checking out a spot for your own photo?" a booming Brooklyn voice asked from the doorway.

Alex turned and saw Major Dan Wilson, the AFIP's legendary forensic investigator, his eyes twinkling at her from beneath his unruly salt-and-pepper hair. Her work did not overlap his, but Alex had hit it off famously with his wife, Jillian, a headstrong, fearless photojournalist who could drink both Alex and Dan under the table. Whenever Jillian was back from assignment, the three of them would compete to find the tackiest old-time bar in which to swap stories and drink Old Weller.

"Hey! Welcome back," she said to Dan. "How'd it go?"

"Slam dunk. All four of them got life. Spanish courts don't have the death penalty."

"Ah, where's the Inquisition when you need it?" said Alex.

They were joined by Captain Grant Pringle, a muscular sandy-haired man with a buzz cut. Alex had learned recently that Grant had grown up in Vegas. Figured. With all his workouts, his physique looked as fake as that of a Sunset Strip showgirl.

Grant stood close to Alex, ignoring Dan. He was clutching a roundish rubber object with his right hand. Through his shirt, Alex could see his muscles' ridges move and shift as he squeezed. As his fingers tightened, the object changed from round to cylindrical to stringy.

He held the object up for Alex to see. "It's a BALL," he said.

"Yeah, we can see that," said Alex.

"No, a B-A-L-L, biologically astute lightweight learner. It takes measurements of the electrical impulses in my muscles and sees where they are weakest, then shapes itself to exercise those. We're testing it in boot camp in Texas."

"And just how many millions of taxpayer dollars did it take for you to develop this toy?" asked Alex.

"The boys on the Hill love it," he replied. "Every member of the Senate oversight committee wanted one."

That was Grant. The Willy Wonka of the Capitol—supplying toys instead of chocolate to the men who ran the government.

Alex was relieved when AFIP's chief pathologist, Thomas Harding, entered the room, giving her an excuse to abandon Grant, who'd been hitting on her off and on since her arrival at AFIP the previous year. Harding handed her a month-old issue of *The New England Journal of Medicine*. "There's an article about a genetic resistance to AIDS I think you'll find interesting," he said, and she nodded her thanks.

She looked down at the journal, with its stapled-on routing slip. Commander Hal Webster was in charge of the AFIP budget—a tangled web of diverse funding sources: the Defense Department, private medical organizations, foreign nations—and watched pennies in odd ways. He called it the "latte factor," saying that if a guy who bought lattes each day cut back to home brew, he'd save over two thousand dollars a year, which, if invested until retirement, would give him two million.

All Alex knew was that Hal was willing to spend big on whatever equipment she desired, then cut costs elsewhere in annoying ways. Previously, a half dozen labs at AFIP each subscribed to the journals *Science, Nature, JAMA,* and *The New England Journal of Medicine.* Hal cut back last month to one subscription to each journal for the whole institute. Since Alex had less seniority than the other lab directors, she was last in the distribution chain. Luckily, since she was just on leave from Berkeley, she could use her status there to access the journals on-line. Alex wasn't the type to hang around waiting for anything.

Alex grabbed her espresso and she, Dan, Grant, and Harding drifted to the table. They'd barely taken their seats when Jack Wiatt strode into the room, with Hal trailing in his wake.

Wiatt remained standing longer than necessary and Alex surmised that he was accustomed to using his height to intimidate the people he addressed. But then he took a seat at the side of the table, rather than at the head. So, thought Alex, he's decided to play good cop.

"Thank you all for coming on such short notice," Wiatt said. "I'm Colonel Jack Wiatt and the President has asked me to consider the position of director of AFIP." The slight scowl on Wiatt's face suggested the job was about as appealing as a stint in a Hiep Hoa prisoner-of-war cage.

"I've survived multiple combat missions," said Wiatt, gray eyes calm and probing, "by getting the best-possible intelligence in advance. That's why I ordered you here— to brief me about AFIP's strengths and weaknesses. Then, if I take the job, I'll have a shot at getting President Cotter to authorize the resources to fix any problems. If you aren't honest, and I later find that I have joined a sinking ship, you will personally be among the wreckage."

So much, thought Alex, for good cop.

Alex tuned out as Wiatt launched into a dissertation about his war experience. Vietnam. The Gulf War. Her mind wandered as she thought about how, as a teen, she was a member of the Barbie Liberation Brigade. She and her friends used their allowances to purchase talking Barbies and GI Joes from local Kmarts, switched the voice boxes, and put them back on the shelves so that unsuspecting parents would buy their kids dolls that defied the usual stereotypes. Alex gave herself credit for stimulating the economy by letting the dolls be sold twice. She was the ringleader, supplying the technical know-how—prying off the back plates, trimming the circuit boards, using a saw to sever the battery contacts, moving the capacitators, and reengineering the talk buttons. Watching Wiatt's lips move, Alex smiled as she recalled the Barbies shouting "Vengeance is mine" and "Eat lead, Cobra." She imagined Wiatt mouthing the transformed dialogue of the revamped GI Joe: "Math is hard" and "Let's plan our dream wedding."

Wiatt's lips stopped moving, and Alex realized it was time to go around the table and introduce themselves. Brownnose that he was, Grant went first.

"I'm Captain Grant Pringle." His hand pumped the oddly shaped ball and then, out of seeming respect for Wiatt, he set it out on the table. "I run Military Design and Testing—we pioneer new equipment, new weapons, new surveillance technologies, some satellite work. I understand, sir, that you watched some of my men—dead and alive—in the body armor lab."

Grant was thirty-four, young to be in charge of a division. The Peter Principle is alive and well, thought Alex. A decade earlier, Grant had been in a drab job, training marksmen at an Army boot camp in Columbia, South Carolina. He noticed that the men who played video games on their breaks shot better than those who didn't. He convinced the brass to get a computer programmer to modify the games so that the enemies looked like Saddam Hussein and his cronies. The Department of Defense awarded a huge grant for software development, and Grant found himself at AFIP, heading up the project. Video games—the gorier, the better—were soon used to enhance shooting skills, bombing skills, and even the fine motor skills of Army surgeons. Unlike so many things the Department of Defense funded, Grant's project showed tangible results. The politicians loved him. In Congressional hearings, with his buff body and offhand manner, he was a blond Rambo. When he had testified about his video games, the head of the appropriations committee in Congress asked him what he wanted to do next.

So Grant came up with a series of research projects with comic book–like titles, such as WOW (Weapons of War) and BAM (Biologically Assisted Machines). He'd spout some outrageous plan—nanotech fibers so that uniforms would dispense painkillers when someone got shot, or heat-emissions equipment that let you assess whether a vehicle six miles away was a car or a tank—and Congress would fund it. Grant's dazed staff of engineers were left to pick up the pieces, to bring to life those products that he'd just imagined.

"Problems?" demanded Wiatt. His gray eyes conveyed such power and authority that Grant jutted his chest forward in a defensive response.

"My men grouse that they make less than they would in private industry, but we don't have much turnover. Here they can work on technologies that won't be available in the private sector for another decade. For any guy who ever wanted to be 007 or even Q, my section is a wet dream." Pringle looked over at Alex, the one woman in the room. "Excuse me, ma'am," he said with mock chivalry.

"That's okay," she replied. "Women sometimes use sexual expressions, too." Yeah, dickhead, she thought.

Wiatt began quizzing Grant about weapons on the drawing board. As the men spoke, Alex brushed the fingers of her left hand against the tabletop like a classical pianist. Alex could keep long genetic sequences in her head, just as a composer could mentally call up and rearrange long strings of musical notes. Her fingertips lightly tapped out what she knew so far of Rosie's DNA sequence, with each of her four fingers representing one of the genetic letters—*A* her pinkie, *C* her ring finger, *G* her middle finger, *T* her index finger. She felt there was a certain overlap between a portion of Rosie's DNA and that of smallpox. Maybe it was some sort of clue to both diseases' interaction with the cells. She continued her silent Morse code as she thought about Rosie, her fingertips noiselessly hitting the conference table. ATGGCGTCTC . . .

"BLAKE," shouted Wiatt, and she realized that everyone was waiting for her to introduce herself. "Get your head out of last night's date and into the task at hand."

Alex's face reddened as Grant snickered at her misstep. But instantly her blue eyes locked onto Wiatt's gray ones. "I'm Alexandra Blake and I'm a civilian," she said firmly. "I was asked to join this meeting because I run a genetics laboratory geared to bioterrorism." She looked directly at Grant, who was sitting at the angle that most showed off his physique. "The Department of Defense is starting to recognize that no matter how much money they put into conventional weapons, into boys with toys, all it will take is one smallpox carrier flying into JFK on a 747 and the other 300 passengers become walking bio-bombs. My job is to sequence the genomes of potential warfare pathogens and design vaccines to ward them off."

Wiatt looked intrigued, a common reaction from soldiers when they learned that the familiar military tactics of bombs and brigades might soon be obsolete. "Who's winning, you or the bugs?" he asked.

"Easy answer," Alex replied, wondering what kind of man such flippancy concealed. "The bugs. They've got a fifty-thousand-year evolutionary head start. The main problem right now is that even though I can design a genetic vaccine to stave off smallpox or Ebola, all the enemy would have to do would be to tweak a few genetic letters in the infection's code and it could evade the vaccine."

Alex continued speaking, punctuating her words with gesturing hands raised in the air. "In the past month, I made a major breakthrough. I think I found a genetic segment that is common to two of the major killers—bubonic plague and anthrax. If I can find a similar segment in the Spanish flu and smallpox, it may just be the key to any infection's penetration of cells. Then we could develop a vaccine with a genetic lock to keep biowarfare from entering cells."

"No way the ACLU would let us use it on soldiers," said Pringle. "Look at all the shit they stirred up over the anthrax vaccine in the Gulf War."

"*Captain* Pringle," said Wiatt, "do the words *chain of command* mean anything to you? Your job, your only job, is to make this stuff work. As the *colonel* in charge, it's my job to put them in action. Understood?"

"Yes, sir," Grant snapped.

Wiatt turned to the oldest man at the table, the pathologist Thomas Harding. Given his wire-rimmed glasses, lean body, and thinning red hair, he might have been nicknamed "the Professor." Only his heavy tan, craggy sixty-year-old face, and confident manner made him a match for the stern men at the table. Like Alex, he was a civilian. Four years earlier, when his wife, Beverly, died, he'd pulled his sailboat out of Lake Michigan, sold his gracious turn-of-the-century home in the Hyde Park area of Chicago, and quit his job as chair of the Pathology Department at the University of Chicago. Everything in the Windy City reminded him of his beloved. He opted for radical surgery—a move east.

Harding had met his wife competing in a Scrabble tournament in high school. He'd thought he was unbeatable. He knew dozens of obscure terms for parts of the body, some including x's and z's and other high scoring letters. Beverly, however, knew poetic terms for the chirps of baby birds and the smell of a crackling fire. They easily beat the other competitors, tied in the final round, and when the play-off occurred, Harding found his tiles spelling out words like smitten. In college, he tiled out M-A-R-R-Y M-E, lost the game, and won his bride. When, a decade later, he bought a sailboat, he wanted to name it Beverly, and she insisted on *Scrabble*. The descendant of that boat, still named after the board game, was in a slip outside of Harding's Chesapeake Bay town house. Words continued to fascinate Harding. In the tag line of his E-mails to Alex, he would always include a new word of the day. That morning, it had been *captcha,* a computer-generated test that humans can pass but computers cannot.

"I run the pathology laboratory," Harding told Wiatt. "Since 1917, doctors and hospitals from around the world have sent samples to the AFIP for consultation in unusual cases. Each year, we get over one hundred and eight thousand tissue samples, X-rays and slides for second opinions. After we make our diagnosis, we keep the samples for historical analysis and research. We've got a tissue bank of over fifty million microscopic slides, thirty million samples in paraffin blocks, and nine million wet tissue slides from previous consultations. When the AIDS outbreak started, we were able to use the old tissue samples to pinpoint exactly when the disease had entered the country."

Harding was a topflight pathologist, who'd asked Alex for help a few times for complicated genetic diagnoses. But his clinical laboratory was way underfunded compared to the gee-whiz high-tech wing run by Pringle. Computers were scattered through the pathology section, yet inventories of the tissue samples and test results were kept in dark green ledgers, like something Al Capone's accountant might have used. There were old wooden file cabinets with dozens of tiny drawers, like an ancient library card catalog.

Initially, it had been a shock for Alex. At AFIP, hundreds of express-mail packages arrived each day, filled with slide specimens of tumors, blood samples of infectious diseases. Alex had expected a sleek modern assembly line of processing—lab techs in white jackets, computer-scannable bar codes. Instead, the express-mail packages were piled in towering heaps, each to be recorded in pen and ink in the ledger book by day workers from a nearby school for the retarded.

Wiatt glanced down at his papers about the AFIP. "It says that the administrative workforce in your department has an average IQ below ninety."

"We save a lot of money that way," interrupted Hal, the

well-dressed administrator who'd practically been single-handedly running the institution since his superior had suffered a heart attack six months earlier. "It's a win-win situation. We pay the day workers minimum wage, plus we get a portion reimbursed in grants from disability agencies."

Wiatt turned back to Harding. "Quite a nuisance compared to your last job."

"Not really," said Harding in his usual no-nonsense tone. "The inner-city aides in Chicago were sloppy and didn't care. The day workers here know their job, no matter how limited it might be, and do it with pride. They don't make the careless errors of someone bored by their work. It's a big deal for them. Integrity knows no IQ."

"Perhaps, but we're not running a halfway house," said Wiatt. "We'll revisit this issue if I come on board."

"They're doing just fine," said Alex. "Why take away their dignity?"

Wiatt seemed irked that she had spoken out of turn. "I want the best people working for me, not a bunch of grocery store baggers. A unit is only as good as its weakest link."

Grant nodded.

Miffed, Alex reached over and grabbed Grant's toy. She pumped it a few times, watched it turn into a stringy mess, then set it down. Yes indeed, thought Alex, wondering if their new boss was going to be that weak link.

Wiatt consulted the papers in front of him before turning to Major Dan Wilson, the go-to guy whom everyone from state law enforcement officials to UN human rights commissioners consulted when they wanted to know how, why, and by whom someone was murdered. As a well-decorated marine, Dan had garnered a coveted post at Eighth and I streets in D.C., the oldest Marine Corps installation in the United States, established by President Thomas Jefferson when he wanted his top soldiers "within easy marching distance of the capital."

Dan believed in the Marine Corps oath: to "support and defend the Constitution of the United States against all enemies, foreign and domestic." But after a few years in D.C., Dan felt that the United States was as threatened by crimes within the government as by terrorists from without. He switched to Quantico, went for additional law enforcement training at the Maneuver Support Center at Fort Leonard Wood, Missouri, and became a legend in military crime solving. It had been a logical promotion for him to move to AFIP five years earlier to oversee investigations not just of the military but of the federal government in general. Marines, of all the services, were known for their combat readiness. Dan applied that trait to split-second, balls-to-the-wall decisions in his forensic work. As necessary, he could call on a team of cracker-jack agents in the field—a United Nations of military expertise. Three from the Army, three from the Navy, three from the Air Force, and a half dozen from his own service, the Marines—all of whom were trained by their branch in the latest law enforcement techniques.

"Looks like you've been spending more time out of the country the past two years than here," said Wiatt, shaking his head. He consulted the file. "On loan to the government of Argentina to establish the identities of bodies found in mass graves. An investigation of corpses in Russia to determine if they were the royal family. Even deployed in the Basque country in Spain to deal with evidence in a terrorist ETA killing. What's wrong with your home base? AFIP's too second-rate for you?" Wiatt's tone indicated he shared that conclusion.

"Seems there's less need for my forensic investigations here than there used to be," said Dan. In his late forties, he dressed casually for a military man, rarely wearing his jacket, always with his sleeves rolled up, his curly salt-and-pepper hair in constant disarray. His office was a clutter of papers, journals, boxes of evidence in cases. He'd been promoted up through several layers of military hierarchy without having to make concessions. He was that good. "Technically, we've got jurisdiction over any crimes involving the military or the executive branch. But, Webster here convinced the AFIP board to hand over all but the court-martial investigations to the FBI. Now our forensic cases are a joke—an enlisted man slugs an officer and we're called in to finger the guy who threw the first . punch."

"Why give away anything to the FBI?" Wiatt asked Hal.

"We had solid financial reasons," said Hal, who looked annoyed at being second-guessed on another decision. "Captain Pringle gets us a blank check from Congress. And the molecular pathology that Dr. Blake is doing could lead to a partnership with a biotech company. There's no money in forensics."

Dan, the macho investigator, stared coldly at the administrator. "Everybody knows crime doesn't pay."

Hal's eyes narrowed. "Also, we don't have a bleeding-edge forensic DNA lab like the FBI."

The colonel ignored Hal completely. "How many cases have been diverted to the FBI?" he asked Dan.

"Three to four hundred over the past two years," said Dan.

"Jesus!" said Wiatt. "And what's their clearance rate?"

"Low, about twenty percent," said Dan.

Hal's blue eyes flashed angrily at Dan, as if he didn't like where this was going. But Alex knew that Dan was a man used to speaking his mind. Besides, Dan thought administrative jobs like Hal's were for washouts. Those who could, did. Those who couldn't, pushed papers.

"The FBI doesn't give a rat's ass about these cases, except the ones that get their boss on the news," said Dan. "A few days ago, they took a serial strangler case from us just as we were making some progress. It was one of my men who pointed out that the women were killed near military bases."

Wiatt's eyes flashed. This was the hole in the line he could run through, make some yardage. Since the AFIP job was a straight executive appointment, he could start as soon as he wanted. Gloria Devon, as a potential FBI director, would have to wade through several weeks of Senate confirmation hearings and other slap-the-back political hurdles. If she had a nanny too many in her background, he might be the next-best safe choice. And even if she got confirmed, by the time she took office, he would have gutted part of her agency and maybe even solved the serial strangler case. He would out-FBI the FBI. She wouldn't know what hit her.

"Would you like to get that case back, along with your pick of the others, Major?"

"Great to be back in the game," said Dan, a slight smile on his face as he savored the possibility.

Wiatt turned to Alex. "Can you run forensic DNA?"

Alex looked over at Hal, hoping he would stop this madman. She had Rosie to deal with. She didn't need to be sidetracked by a run-of-the-mill criminal investigation.

"When I hired Dr. Blake," said Hal, "I assured her she wouldn't have to do any forensic work. Let the boys in black handle that. Why duplicate what the FBI is set up to do?"

"Not duplicate—surpass," said Wiatt. "With their twenty percent clearance rate, that won't be difficult."

"But I'm just starting to make some real headway on a corpse who died of the Spanish flu," Alex said.

"I'm not asking you to abandon your research. Just help catch a killer or two."

Alex grabbed the ball again to pump out her annoyance. Jack Wiatt stood up, then leaned slightly forward, placing his palms on the conference table. He looked intently down the line at each person, one by one. Nobody moved. The room was completely silent.

Once he had taken each person's measure, silently convincing them that he was not a man to be trifled with, he looked at Alex and announced his decision. "Ms. Blake—"

"Dr. Blake," she said. She was egging him on. "It's kind of like the difference between colonel and captain."

"Okay, Dr. Blake, let's see if you live up to your rank. I've decided to take the President up on his offer and I'm appointing you and Captain Pringle to the serial strangler case, with Major Wilson here heading up the team."

Grant shot her a leer, licking his lips at the prospect of working with Alex. While Wiatt was turned toward Wilson, she softly raised her middle finger—representing *G* for *guanine*—at Grant. Maybe she'd coin a new expression: giving him the guanine.

This is all I need, thought Alex, working with the Testosterone Triangle: Wiatt, Pringle, and Wilson. She sighed, then said, "How about adding Barbara Findlay from the general counsel's office? She'll make sure we keep our noses clean on search and seizure."

"Makes sense," said Wiatt. "When I talk to the President, I'll secure the funds for DNA forensics so we can get the major back his cases. I'm regular Army. You don't cede territory to the enemy."

"The FBI is hardly the enemy," said Hal, shoulders tense at his realization his institute was about to be transformed.

"They are now," said Wiatt, and smiled.

CHAPTER 4

AFTER THE MEETING, ALEX TRIED TO REGAIN her composure by walking through the National Museum of Health and Medicine. Technically, it was a part of the AFIP, but her colleagues at the Institute hardly ever set foot in it. When she asked them why, they gave a variety of excuses. Outdated. Overrun with third graders. Too grotesque.

For Alex, it was a wonderful glimpse at the roots of modern medicine, of the move from shamans to scientists. She walked along the wall of microscopes, stopping to gape once again at the antique ones. Amazingly, the microscope, so central to the work of so many AFIP pathologists, was first used by rug and drapery merchants who wanted customers to see the exquisite nap of their fabrics. Then Antonie van Leeuwenhoek expanded its use, in the serendipitous, seductive way that most science proceeds: In the 1670s, the Dutchman used the microscope to look at his sperm.

Alex continued past the scopes to the heart of the museum's collection. The schoolchildren had gone for the day, and she was alone with the body parts. The leg of a man with elephantitis. A gargantuan obstructed colon. Fetuses at every stage of gestation. A display of kidney stones. A stomach-shaped hair ball from a twelve-year-old who kept chewing—and swallowing—her ponytail. This collection of medical oddities, like those in the Mütter

Museum in Philadelphia, had been the training ground for generations of doctors. Now such museums were dusty survivors. Doctors no longer learned at the macro level, seeing a whole body, but at the micro level. Your average M.D. today knew more about microscopic genes than the rest of a body's anatomy.

The museum stayed afloat with tours to grade-schoolers, who reacted with a macabre fascination. Even for that, it was past its prime. From 1888 until 1969, the museum was a tourist magnet, located on the Mall, near the Smithsonian. Then Lady Bird Johnson, the First Lady, gave their space to the new Hirshhorn art museum. The National Museum of Health and Medicine was relegated to the grounds of Walter Reed Hospital, on an out-of-the way stretch of Georgia Avenue near the Maryland border. Annual visitors dropped from 800,000 to 20,000.

Now there was talk of another move. A New Jersey Congressman wanted to transfer the collection to Ellis Island, near the Statue of Liberty, to provide a tourist destination in his district. It was well known that the Speaker of the House owed the Congressman a favor, so the move seemed likely. Alex was one of the few AFIP employees lobbying against it.

"I thought I'd find you here," Barbara Findlay said to Alex, having caught up with her at the display of pre-served fetuses. Barbara stood shoulder to shoulder with Alex, but there the similarities ended. Barbara's short black hair framed an attractive dark-skinned face. She was descended from slaves on her mother's side, and her father was a midnight-dark Jamaican. Her mother had urged Barbara's older brother to enlist in the Navy to get an education and see the world, but he'd opted for a construction job and rarely made it outside the Bronx. Instead, Barbara had taken up the call. She stood with a proud carriage, the bars on her Navy lieutenant's uniform providing a teasing contrast to the showgirl nature of her long legs.

"Walking through the aisles of cancerous lungs and obstructed colons always makes me feel better," said Alex. "Humans can survive almost anything."

"C'mon, Wiatt doesn't seem that bad."

"He's been watching too much *CSI*. He's going to set me back months while we play cops and robbers."

"He'll find out that you always manage to get your way."

"Not true. What about Luke dumping me last month?"

"Professionally, I mean. Besides, Wiatt basically told Hal to fuck off, which makes him okay in my book."

"You heard him say that?"

"Well, in a way." Barbara smiled. "I saw him."

Alex laughed. "You didn't!" Barbara read lips. But nobody at AFIP knew it besides Alex. Consequently, Barbara was a font of inside information.

Barbara also knew more than anyone in the universe about the elite in Washington. Since she was a young girl, she'd followed the activities of politicians like other women followed movie stars or British royalty. She might not know who Brad Pitt had married, but she knew the birth dates, voting records, and extramarital affairs of the entire legislative branch. To Barbara, D.C. was just one giant soap opera. And she couldn't wait to tune in each day.

The two women ambled through the museum. Barbara walked with the dramatic posture of a soldier, her body forcefully and efficiently slicing through the room. The kinetic Alex commandeered more space, gesturing with her hands as she spoke, tapping her foot when she stood.

"Did you hear that another of Strom's black children surfaced?" Barbara asked Alex. "Maybe you should test my DNA to see if I'm also related to him."

Alex stopped walking and turned to look squarely at her friend. She smiled. "I can tell you, by the powers vested in me as a geneticist, that you are about twenty shades too black to be kin of the late Senator Strom Thurmond. Besides, if I were you, I'd shoot for Jefferson's family instead. At least you'd get to be buried in Monticello."

"Instead, thanks to you, I'll be buried in search warrants."

Alex glanced down at the display case next to them. Live medical leeches, stretching and retracting like rubber bands. Then she looked up sheepishly. "I take it you heard about the Task Force."

"Yeah. Would it have killed you to be nice to Wiatt?"

"Barbara, you know I'm not nice to anyone in authority. I am an equal opportunity crank."

"I thought you liked Major Wilson," Barbara said. "And he certainly thinks the world of you since you found a Spanish geneticist to help out on the ETA killing."

"Dan's great. It's forensics that's a pain. Not to mention working with Preening Mr. Pringle." Alex assumed a stance like Popeye, flexed arms in the air, showing off muscles.

Barbara giggled, a soft feminine chuckle at odds with the severe look of her uniform. "Well, Wednesday we'll have a testosterone-free zone. You're still coming to Lana's game, aren't you?"

"Of course. I'm practicing my cheers," said Alex, moving her arms from side to side as if she were shaking pom-poms. "Give me an *L. L* . . . Give me an *A. A* . . ."

"Okay, okay," said Barbara, smiling. The two began walking again. At the museum door, Barbara waved good-bye to Alex and headed to the parking lot. As a single mom with a fourteen-year-old daughter, she left at a reasonable hour each day. Pregnant at seventeen, Barbara had caught German measles from her younger brother, causing Lana to be born deaf. When Lana was two, Barbara had joined the military to finance an engineering degree and law school, with a stint at active duty in between. A rare bird—a black female member of the JAG Corps— she'd done a bang-up job prosecuting the good old boys responsible for a Tail Hook–like incident at an American base in Germany, including court-martialing the supervising officers who tried to cover it up. She could have written her own ticket to any posting in the country. But she'd chosen the AFIP because the hours were good, she didn't face the risk of being transferred, and in a few years Lana could apply to that stellar college for the deaf, Gallaudet University, right here in D.C. But Alex knew that Barbara was way overqualified and underutilized. Maybe some funky Fourth Amendment search warrant work would be good for her.

Alex decided to wander back through an underground passage to spend a few hours with Rosie before heading home. The bowels of the Walter Reed/AFIP/medical museum complex were dark, threatening—and completely off-limits. But as a civilian, Alex told herself she was immune from the military dos and don'ts. She'd used the tunnels once before, when it was raining, and now she was fired up to explore the binding mechanism of the virus and wanted to get back to her lab as quickly as possible. She tried to remember the turns. Was it four rights and a left—or four rights and two lefts—before she should head up a staircase? She tried a stairwell after the first left, but the first-floor exit above it was locked. Damn it.

She headed back down and walked another hundred feet toward a boiler room. From out of the shadows, one of the boilers moved. Then Alex realized it was a hulk of a man charging right at her. Alex screamed, but the man barreled closer. She was about to turn and run, when the man passed under a lightbulb and she recognized him as one of the day workers.

"Wait," she said "You know me."

He stopped in his tracks, tilted his head slightly to the left, and considered the matter. He raised his giant hand to his reddened face and massaged his troubled forehead. Then he rocked back and forth, trying to decide what to do. Alex's heart leapt to her throat. She had let him get too close. She should have run when she'd had the chance.

He put his arms out to hide what was behind him. Then he started muttering. "Don't take them, don't take them, don't take them."

At first, she couldn't figure out what he was talking about. Then she peered beyond his massive form to the enclave from which he'd emerged. Every square inch was hung with pieces of posters. He'd carefully torn each poster apart and pasted the pieces on the wall according to

color. Pale yellow pieces hung next to bright yellow pieces
that were pasted next to orange pieces, and so forth.

"It's a rainbow," Alex said.

The man didn't budge. His eyes were darting about to
ensure there was no way for her to pass him.

"I won't tell," she said gently.

He relaxed for an instant.

"You must spend a lot of time down here. Can you
show me the way to my lab? Sometimes you come there
and deliver blood."

The man considered the matter, then said, "The big
machines."

"Yep, the big machines, the DNA sequencers. Can you
show me the right stairs?"

He put his hand on her shoulder as if she were a small
child to be led. He was strong and pear-shaped, with at
least 240 pounds of bulk encased in his white button-down
shirt and worn gray pants. He gripped her lightly, showing
he meant no harm. "I'm Larry," he said.

"Yes, of course you are," said Alex, feeling her body
relax with relief.

Larry was still touching her when they exited the
proper stairwell on the first floor of the AFIP, right into the
oncoming path of Captain Grant Pringle.

"Well, guys, what's so interesting downstairs?" Grant
went to open the door.

Alex didn't want Larry's sanctuary discovered because
of her. "We were just doing some scrapings down there.
Dead rodents that might have an active virus. Be sure to
glove up and put a mask on if you go down."

"Some other time," he said.

Larry descended the stairs and Alex headed toward her
lab. Grant walked alongside her for about twenty feet. He
ran his right hand over his close-cropped blond hair, then
said, "We're testing a new night-vision rifle. Wanna come
cradle my gun?"

"No, Grant," said Alex. "I'm afraid you'll have to shoot
it off alone tonight."

CHAPTER 5

ALEX WAS THRILLED TO GET BACK TO ROSIE. It seemed like years since she'd left her lab for that dreadful meeting. She walked over to the computer monitor hooked up to sequencer number two and admired the four-color quilt of rectangles on the screen. Each color represented a letter of the genetic code, signaling one of the chemicals that made up the DNA of the Spanish flu that killed the Inuit woman. Red, *A,* for *adenine.* Blue, *C,* for *cytosine.* Green, *G,* for *guanine.* Orange, *T,* for *thymine.* It was a great sequence run, the best that Rosie's tissue had offered up. Alex had almost decoded the whole genome of the flu virus. Like an old family quilt, the picture on the screen had a few tatters where the DNA had degraded and its sequence was missing. All in all, though, Rosie's DNA was holding up pretty well considering it was over one hundred years old.

I hope I look that good at your age, thought Alex.

If she ran a few more samples, each one might be degraded in a different spot, but by overlapping the images, she could construct the whole flu genome. Then she could figure out how the virus entered the cells.

At Columbia Medical School, Alex had pursued a Ph.D. in genetics while getting her M.D. If she'd entered a more traditional field, like nephrology or surgery, most of the conceptual work would have already been done and she'd have run up against a hierarchy of older males telling her what she should think. But as Alex was coming of age professionally, the federally funded Human Genome Project was just getting off the ground and needed young talent. It had been over three decades since the irreverent twenty-four-year-old James Watson and his British buddy Francis Crick had discovered the double-helix structure of DNA, deoxyribonucleic acid, the building block of life. Watson and Crick's breakthrough was based, in large part, on the uncredited work of a twenty-two-year-old female scientist, Rosalind Franklin. But when the Human Genome Project was announced in 1990—auspiciously on Alex's twentieth birthday—virtually nothing was known about the chemical makeup or function of people's genes. She was in her first year of medical school at the time and immediately volunteered to help chart the human genome. James Watson—who agreed to be the kingpin for the endeavor—predicted that it would take fifteen years to analyze the sequence of the human genome, the chemical alphabet that made people tick. But Watson had underestimated people like Alex. She and her young colleagues were the scientific equivalents of the twentysomethings who revolutionized computer hardware and software.

By February 2001, Alex and her scientific buddies at Stanford, the Whitehead Institute at MIT, Washington University in St. Louis, the private company Celera, and a few other institutions had jointly succeeded in deciphering the complete human genome sequence, a sentence three billion sweet, bright, nitrous chemical letters long. If spelled out in typeface, this genetic instruction manual for humans would fill two hundred Manhattan phone directories.

Alex's name was one of dozens on an article in the scientific journal *Nature* that described the entire human genome. The President congratulated them; Alex drank vodka shots and danced at a celebration with James Watson, then in his seventies and as impish and intimidating as ever. Geneticists around the globe started using that sequence data to figure out which letters of the genetic alphabet predisposed people to suffer from genetic diseases. Alex, high on the rush of leading the scientific pack, turned her attention to totally uncharted genetic territory: figuring out the genetic sequence of the 1918 Spanish flu. Its genetic sequence was much shorter than a human's, with eight genetic segments, rather than thirty thousand. But whenever she finished deciphering it, she could claim sole credit for a major scientific discovery—and, more importantly, help revolutionize the prevention of infectious disease.

She heard a knock at her lab door and, surprised, opened it to Commander Hal Webster, AFIP's administrative chief. He rarely came down to see what the worker bees were doing.

Hal took two steps inside. Many nonscientists were like that. They assumed that if they wandered all the way in, they might "catch" whatever infection Alex was deciphering. He didn't realize that the offending DNA was stripped down to its genetic roots and was safely ensconced in one of three gene sequencers that spanned the right wall of the laboratory.

The hooded work area where Alex actually manipulated the tissue samples was farther past the sequencers, deep in the back of the lab. On the opposite wall were shelves of chemical reagents and the refrigerator. Alex's office was a twelve-by-twelve-foot square deep in the recesses of the large rectangular lab. Two of the walls were glass, so when she was sitting at her desk in the cube, she could see she how far along the sequencers were in their routine. She had specifically located her office as far from the entrance to the lab as possible to take advantage of the fact that only highly motivated individuals, or other sanguine scientists, would run the gauntlet of the lab to get to her.

Hal was impeccably dressed, as always. His pants had a razor-sharp pleat and his crisp shirt looked like it had just come out of the package. The white gold of his Vacheron Constantin watch glistened around his wrist. With his dark hair and blue eyes, he was almost handsome. Unlike the bodybuilder Grant Pringle, he neither flirted nor preened.

"Don't worry about Colonel Wiatt disturbing your project," Hal said to Alex. "He's just passing through, looking to move up the next rung of the ladder. Humor him, do a few DNA fingerprints, and then we'll be back to business as usual."

Hal Webster had been the number-two guy—always the bridesmaid, never the bride—for the past two AFIP directors. Alex had thought he was a shoo-in for the top spot this time around, but what did she know? She'd only been there a year. She was sure that if she'd asked Barbara, her friend would have explained to her, in perfect DC-speak, who owed what favor to whom on the Hill, resulting in Colonel Jack Wiatt's appointment.

"Here's the problem," said Alex. "It takes a completely different methodology to do forensic work. Sure, the sequencing itself is the same, but we need a whole pool of reference samples. DNA forensics doesn't look at all thirty thousand genes in a person's cells. It focuses on maybe five or six. You need to know how likely it is that someone else might share those same five genes. If every Hispanic male in New York City has three of those genes in common, then you can't say for certain a given guy is the offender. I'll need to run lots of DNA samples from random individuals just to get the database for comparison. It took the FBI five years to set up their population database."

"How does it work?" He took a step backward as he spoke, peering at the sequencers from a distance rather than risking any close encounters with DNA.

"Well, say for gene one, the suspect's genetic profile matches that of the DNA left by the killer at a crime scene. If that same genetic profile is common to one in ten people, that still means that there could be a whole lot of men other than the suspect who could be the killer. If one in a hundred thousand men share the variation, then we're getting somewhere."

"Yeah, but in a city of two million—let me do the math—there would still be nineteen other men with that same profile."

"You've got it. But if each of the five genes in the test is pretty rare and they match the crime-scene DNA, then our suspect is likely to be the killer. The nineteen men with the same first gene are unlikely to have four others that match, as well."

"Unless he were the twin brother."

"Now you're thinking like a geneticist. So, it's not just a matter of looking at the killer's DNA from the crime scene and the suspect's DNA to see if they match. You also have to compare both samples to a whole bunch of DNA from regular guys."

Hal thought for a moment. "Harding gets thousands of pathology samples from hospitals each year. You could test those. Have them be—what did you call it?—the population database."

"It's a shitload of work just to let Wiatt play sheriff."

"Yeah, but I've got some other ideas. It would be easy enough to pick five or six genes that are also disease genes. You could test the samples for breast cancer, or Alzheimer's, or something like that. The analysis would do double duty. We could use them as the comparisons for forensics, but also sell the information to a biotech company I've made contact with."

"Whoa, wait a minute. That's probably not even legal."

"I've had Lieutenant Findlay check. Under the Federal Technology Transfer Act, government researchers are allowed to earn fees from outside companies."

"That's just great. I came in this morning as a biowarfare researcher. In just a few short hours, I've been asked to be an arm of law enforcement and the darling of the biotechnology industry. Any other requests? Perhaps a cooking show on a cable network?"

"Just think about it, Alex. I just don't want Wiatt's cowboy act to be a complete waste of your time."

"Hal, you're too efficient for your own good."

He left, but Alex's mood was sufficiently compromised that she decided to get out of there. She loaded up her briefcase—an old saddlebag—and went out to her car, a beat-up yellow 1963 T-Bird with a black vinyl top. For someone who spent her professional life firmly ensconced in the twenty-first century, she liked to surround herself with curios from the past.

She punched the car radio with her fist—the only way it would work—and switched back and forth between the two stations that it played. She was in the mood for music, but the public radio station was groveling for funds and the rock station was obsessing about how the dead executive Marilyn Mayne had once gone out with Eddie Vedder.

She hit the radio again, silencing it, and thought about the first time she heard Luke play. She'd met a friend for drinks at a neighborhood bar in Adams Morgan. On Thursday nights, they had a jazz combo, but that particular Thursday, the combo was off. Instead, Luke was there strumming his guitar and singing his clever acerbic lyrics. Instead of just treating him like background noise, patrons were actually listening.

Alex's friend Melanie was a linguist at American University and she insisted on inviting Luke to their table. She was interested in his use of language. Instead of repeating lines of vapid lyrics, his songs had content. "It's no big deal," said Luke. "Folk songs and country-western songs are like short stories all the time. I just do it with rock. Lots of other people have done it as well."

Melanie was hitting on Luke big-time, but he was zeroing in on Alex. When Melanie went to the ladies' room, he gave Alex his phone number and asked her to come to a concert he was doing with his band, the Cattle Prods, at a club in Dupont Circle. She became fascinated by the unruly, convoluted nighttime world of the D.C. clubs, whose smoky clutter contrasted with her pristine lab. When she ran into Grant that past spring at one of the clubs where Luke was playing, she got to use a phrase that thirtysomething M.D.s don't often utter: "I'm with the band."

Fifteen minutes after she'd left the AFIP, Alex pulled up in front of the Curl Up and Dye Beauty Salon in the Adams Morgan section of Washington. The salon had gone out of business three years earlier and had been available for rent when she'd moved to D.C. the previous year. The monthly charge for two thousand square feet was about a third of what residential property in the area was going for. When Alex first saw the interior, she fell in love with its funky potential. Her mind immediately began to design a bedroom out of the former bikini-wax suite.

Alex got out of her car and pressed a five-letter code on a keypad to slide aside the metal fencing that covered the entrance. She followed the dark hallway to another door, which she opened with a key. Inside the large linoleum-floored room, her image was reflected back from three walls of mirrors. She liked the feeling of meeting herself coming and going. The room featured four old-fashioned hair dryers attached to chairs, posters of what looked to be the latest hairstyles, circa 1960, and a revolving spindle with fifty or so nail polish bottles, with colors from Fairy Blush to Harem Red.

When she moved in, Alex hadn't touched anything in that room, other than to have a cleaning crew do some major dusting. Karl had used it as a studio for his sculptures when they were together—odd configurations of discarded metals that looked like torture devices to Alex, but which had been reviewed well in an East Village show, leading him to chase his destiny in the Big Apple. More recently, when she was with Luke, his band rehearsed there before their gigs. Over-the-top rock sounded right amid the outrageous color samples.

Compared to her other lovers, Luke was a stable guy. He cleaned up after himself and used his spare time to repaint the bedroom and office that were off of this main room. He had also been the Energizer Bunny of sex, which was fine and fun at first. But he was a mite threatened by the idea that Alex actually wanted to leave the bed in the mornings to reconnect with her work.

They'd split a month earlier, just before he'd gone on tour. The eight months they'd spent together was longer than most of her relationships. He'd walked out of her life while she was in her lab, leaving a CD he'd made, funny songs he'd created just for her. And a note. "It takes two," the note started, which surprised Alex, who thought she'd always given as much as she got. But Luke, whose spotty concert schedule left him with days and weeks free, described how he'd felt he was second fiddle ("not even second mandolin," he wrote, which was at least an instrument he admired) to her work. She'd cried as she read his closing, "Love and meteorites." She thought about how they'd made love the previous summer at an Outer Banks beach house during a meteor shower, then sat on the sand, half-dressed, and made a separate giddy wish on each of the hundreds of tiny meteors in the Perseid cloud, shards of the comet Swift-Tuttle. With so many wishes available, they'd readily blown through pleading for health and happiness for their friends and family, an end to racism and war, and a winning sports team for the District. Alex remembered the playful absurdity of their final wishes. "Love and liquor that are hangover-free," pleaded Luke, pulling her close.

"Adventure without pain, pleasure without guilt," Alex replied. "And how about a four-cup coffeemaker that doesn't just put out just a cup and a half? And comfortable high heels . . ."

"And bladders big enough for two six-packs." He'd laughed as he pressed her back into the sand with kisses.

After the tussle with Wiatt, Alex wished Luke were there to cheer her. And she wondered why, when she'd had hundreds of wishes, it had never dawned on her to wish their relationship would last.

Alex put Luke's parting CD in the player, which was always a mistake. "Unfair piling on," she said to the middle of her three reflections. Taking a bad workday and adding a maudlin night was not the prescription she needed. She was tempted to go on-line and find out if the

Cattle Prods were back in D.C. yet. No, she would not go
groveling after Luke. She remembered when a friend
from college, Callie, told her that she was going to have "a
winter of pursuit," chasing men until she found a hubby.
Alex never took that tack. Men just rained into her life. A
guy sitting next to her on an airplane, or someone assigned to some professional committee with her. The tini-
est of conversations and they showered her with attention.
So what if she was in a brief dry spell now? That was what
vibrators and a shower massager were for.

CHAPTER 6

IN THE THREE DAYS BEFORE COLONEL JACK
Wiatt officially came on board as the head of Armed
Forces Institute of Pathology, Alex worked nonstop on the
Rosie project. The only night she left before midnight was
Wednesday, for Lana's basketball game. Alex knew what
it was like to have no dad to attend school functions, and
she would never break a promise to Barbara's fourteen-
year-old daughter.

Alex was trying to decipher the remaining genetic letters from the flu in Rosie's lungs, but the code was slip-
ping through her fingers. There were too many genetic
possibilities. She related to the most recent word sent to
her by Harding. *Livelock: opposite of deadlock; a project
that never ends, because more data is constantly added.*

On Wiatt's first day, he called a meeting of the forensic
team in the former PR suite. When Alex entered the room,
she saw that Major Dan Wilson, the forensics czar, had already converted it into a work center. He'd taken down the
publicity stills and covered two walls with corkboard,
tacking up lists of evidence and leads. A large wall-
mounted Plasmavision screen reflected down on the var-
nished wood of the conference table, its images guided by
the laptop at the end of the table. Dan had taken out the
huge thirty-person table and replaced it with one that
seated a dozen. A few feet from the end of the table, at the
elbow of the L-shaped room, Dan had set up a desk for

himself and file cabinets. He'd already managed to clutter up the desk with piles of files in a disorganized heap, like a manila folder game of Jenga. From his new perch, he could peer to his left at the three desks of the data team assigned to the case. His booming voice conveyed his commands.

It didn't surprise Alex that Dan had deserted his cushy office for a seat with his troops. Dan felt most at home in the trenches of an investigation. In Argentina, she'd heard, he'd picked up a shovel and dug up graves with the locals to speed the process of identification of the dead. A long-time bachelor, he'd met his wife of three years graveside in Buenos Aires. Jillian, an Israeli photojournalist, was covering the investigation of the disappeared. They now lived in the District, with each of them jetting off on separate assignments, then coming back together with a mischievous, intoxicating passion. After covering wars on three continents, living with the chaos of Major Dan Wilson was a breeze for Jillian. Alex enjoyed Jillian, who, after a few bourbons one night, had taught Alex to cuss in six languages.

Dan smiled at Alex as she moved toward the table, then began pushing folders aside to find the one he wanted. Alex noticed three young military men standing near the coffee machine, resembling horses straining to burst out of a paddock at the beginning of a race. They looked to the major for their marching orders. He stood up from behind his desk and motioned for them to join him at the table.

Alex was still not used to working in a place peppered with men in uniforms—from every branch of service, no less. Growing up with an antiwar activist for a mom had made her distrust men who were trained to kill and whose faces seldom revealed emotion. She tried to give the soldiers at AFIP the benefit of the doubt. Her father, who'd been killed in Vietnam when she was five, had been a soldier, too. Yet she remembered the soft, loving way he'd held her and his tender smile as he treasured each of her new accomplishments—the pictures she drew for the refrigerator, the ballet pirouette she attempted clumsily, the firefly she captured in a jar.

In D.C., Alex thought of her father often, trying to recognize his facial expressions in the young military men who worked alongside her. She'd been there for eleven months, but hadn't summoned the courage to search for his chiseled name on the Vietnam Veterans Memorial. She was daunted by the thought of the black marble monument on the Mall. She feared that the crushing finality of his name on the Wall might make her feel she was losing him all over again.

When Alex was thrown into projects with the soldiers at AFIP, she would ask about their families. This was the one way she could get to see their eyes soften. In meetings like this, though, the young ones hid behind masks as foreboding and unchangeable as Japanese Kabuki actors.

Alex took a seat next to Barbara. "How's my favorite basketball player doing?" Alex asked.

Barbara pulled out a mock sports trading card with her daughter Lana's picture on it. One side showed Lana in her basketball uniform. The other had her statistics—average points per game, twenty-two—and listed her aspiration, paleontologist. Alex loved Lana's thirst to learn.

"You're so lucky," Alex said to Barbara.

"You've obviously never had to clean up after a teenager," Barbara replied. But she glanced again at the photo with a gleaming maternal pride. She slipped the card back into her jacket pocket and handed Alex a press release about their new boss just as he entered the room.

Alex read the release as Wiatt had a side conversation with Dan. Lots of combat—he was a regular fighting machine. Then she looked up at him. It must be boring to be an administrator after all that. Alex almost felt sorry for the guy for inheriting this motley crew. He probably disliked being in meetings as much as she did.

Barbara leaned close to Alex's ear. "Whatever Wiatt has on the President, it must be big," she whispered. He'd delivered all that he had promised: They had the serial-strangler case back from the FBI, along with a few dozen others, and a lab adjoining Alex's had been retrofitted with the latest in forensic DNA machinery, with a half dozen people to run the analyses. Alex would be forced to supervise this new team—a useless drain on her time, she thought.

Barbara tapped her finger on the press release and lowered her voice even further. "This much combat experience, he's got to be special ops. Watch your back, Alex. What's happening on the surface with these guys rarely reflects the real agenda."

Wiatt cleared his throat and stood at the end of the table. A dark, forbidden thought crossed her mind. Why had he come back from Vietnam, instead of her father?

"This room is your new base," Wiatt told the group. "You need to live, breathe, and fart this investigation. When Major Wilson here asks you to jump, your job is to pull a Michael Jordan."

The three young soldiers nodded with excitement, but Alex merely bristled, a fact not lost on Wiatt. One reason Alex liked science was that she was her own boss. No one told her what to do when.

Wiatt sat down and Dan took his place, standing at the end of the table. He tapped on the computer keyboard, teeing up slides on the large Plasmavision screen on the conference room wall. "Each of you has a folder in front of you with the relevant data on the three murders—pathology reports from the FBI, the interviews my men conducted over the past few days with neighbors and family members of the dead girls, cross-referenced lists of known sex offenders in each of the three jurisdictions—Galveston, Norfolk, and Beaufort. No one ended up on all three lists."

As he spoke, photos of the dead women's bodies, contorted in agony, flashed across the screen. Their corpses had been photographed from so many different directions that Alex felt she was watching a kaleidoscope of destruction.

Wiatt ended the meeting with an order. "I expect each of you to apply your area of specialty to the evidence Major Wilson's collected so far. We'll meet here tomorrow to compare notes. Let's show the FBI what military discipline and strategy can do to bring this case to a quick resolution."

Alex caught Wiatt as he was leaving the room, so she could talk to him privately. "Listen, I'm not trying to be difficult, but I wasn't kidding. I don't have time for this forensics stuff."

"If I had a better man for the job," Wiatt said, "I'd use him."

It was a subtle use of the word *man,* but she caught it just the same. Her body tensed; she was torn between letting him assume her incompetence and defending herself. "It's not a matter of capability. If I can sequence DNA out of a one-hundred-year-old corpse, I can certainly do it on a fresh body. It just seems like a waste. . . ."

He looked at her as if he understood her frustration. His voice softened a tad. "I know you're a civilian, but for the moment, you're part of my unit. The faster you get this case solved, the sooner you'll be back with your bugs."

Alex realized it was fruitless to press it further.

THE NEXT DAY, ALEX NEVER LEFT HER LAB, deciding to sneak a few more hours with Rosie before turning to the case. Music blaring, she'd floated through the afternoon in a perfect scientific choreography. She'd pulled bottles of chemicals off shelves and mixed reagents like a showy bartender. Her PCR replications went flawlessly and the latest run of the sequencer had coughed out the missing genetic letters from the Rosie sample, meaning she had the complete sequence of the Spanish flu genome. Ta-da, she said to herself, taking a bow in front of the largest piece of equipment in her lab, the Applied Biosystems 3730*xl* DNA analyzer.

She was humming, not quite focusing on the tune—one of Luke's special ditties for her. Her life with him had been like living in a musical. That constant stream of songs, in all sorts of genres. He would make taking out the garbage into a Bob Fosse number, then invent a rap song about taking a shower together. Alex smiled when she remembered the punch line of the song she was humming. Something risqué about wanting to get into her "genes."

"Well, if it isn't Alexandra Blake, formerly of the AFIP," said Barbara, walking into the lab without even a knock.

"Huh?"

"The Task Force. The serial strangler. Your precarious job. Do any of those ring a bell?"

"Oh shit, I didn't even notice the time. But," said Alex, smiling, "I made a real breakthrough today."

"You also made a real enemy. Wiatt was livid when you didn't show up at the meeting."

"I was busy. Plus, I didn't have anything to say. The killer didn't leave DNA at any of the crime scenes. I had nothing to add to the meeting."

Just then, Wiatt himself entered the lab with a pair of soldiers. "I don't care if you use DNA, feminine intuition, Tarot card readings, or divine inspiration. You are part of the team and I expect you to act like it."

The two soldiers approached the refrigerator where Rosie's samples were being stored. "Take it," Wiatt told them.

Alex watched with astonishment as one of the men unplugged the refrigerator. He and his buddy shoved it onto a handcart, knocking the fortune-teller magnet to the ground.

Alex threw her body between the refrigerator and the exit, hands outstretched to block the soldiers' ability to walk off with her research.

"Sir?" one of the men said to Wiatt, looking for direction.

Alex spoke rapidly. "I discovered something really important today," she said, waving her arms to emphasize the enormity of it.

Wiatt was not the least bit interested. "Maybe I can get a little of your attention if you don't have other things clouding up your mind."

Alex turned to Barbara, trying to gauge whether she'd been in on this. Barbara looked as surprised as she did.

"You can't do this!" Alex said. Her mouth gaped as she searched for something to say. She pointed to Barbara. "I've got my lawyer here."

Wiatt's cold expression remained unchanged. He walked over to Alex, towering over her. "In case you haven't noticed, Lieutenant Findlay is AFIP's lawyer, not yours. As your commander, I can redeploy you according to the needs of my unit."

Alex knew Wiatt was right: Barbara couldn't help her. She nervously eyed the disconnected plug dangling from the back of the refrigerator. She had only a few moments to act before the samples would start to defrost. "Okay, okay, I'll come to the meetings. I'm sorry. Please put it down."

The soldiers looked to Wiatt for their orders. His pale gray eyes stayed locked on her blue ones, making sure she understood that the future of her work was in his hands. Then he nodded at the soldiers, turned on his heels, and left. The two men put the refrigerator back in its spot, sneaking a peak at the fuming Alex.

"Son of a bitch," Alex muttered as she plugged in the cord and flung open the refrigerator to check if any of the sample vials had toppled.

"Well, things will be getting a lot more lively around here," said Barbara. "Finally someone who can give Alexandra Blake a run for her money."

After Barbara left, Alex picked up the magnet. She shook it, but it was silent. No more advice. She'd have to figure things out on her own.

CHAPTER 7

THAT SATURDAY, ALEX STALKED ACROSS THE beauty salon like a caged tiger. Pissed at Wiatt, she called Berkeley to see if she could quit AFIP and go back immediately. The provost blathered on, saying her salary wasn't in the budget this year, it was the middle of the semester, someone already was covering her courses, et cetera, et cetera. She thought about calling Johns Hopkins University; they'd been hot for her when she'd come out of medical school. Then she decided she needed to clear her head.

She wished Luke were around. He'd know exactly what to do to get her out of this funk. He'd tease her back into the bedroom and then, after they'd giddily merged, he'd lure her off to some avant-garde bit of performance art. The weekend before he split, they'd spent an afternoon following an actor in a white rabbit suit around Dupont Circle for a performance of Alice in Wonderland. Each scene took place in a different venue—art gallery, soup kitchen, day-care center, and perfume shop. As was often the case with Luke, Alex felt she'd fallen through the looking glass herself, into a magical world she'd never have imagined without him in her life. But the next morning, he'd looked disappointed and hurt when she'd rolled out of bed and headed to work.

She needed to get out of the apartment, get some fresh air, and find some un-Luke-like activity to push him—and Wiatt—out of her mind. She caught the Metro and got off at the Mall. She thought she'd wander the National Portrait Gallery, but she found herself drawn to Constitution Gardens. Maybe this was the day. Maybe she could finally bring herself to look at her father's name on the Vietnam Veterans Memorial.

She approached the Wall from the west, then veered away. She still wasn't ready to see the stark black marble, the endless list of the dead. She turned from the monument, walking a few hundred feet to the statue of a soldier dying in the arms of a female Army nurse. Somehow, she could deal more easily with this soldier. His face was not her father's. But the Wall, that was a different matter. Its polished marble seemed to reflect her father's face back to her, distorted in pain, again and again.

She circled the statue. The tableau made her wonder, as she had many times, about the last few minutes of her father's life. This much she knew: He was set to board a helicopter home the day after the war ended. The copter pilot said he'd noticed some soldiers' bodies in a clearing about ten miles away. Her father gave his seat to a corporal and told the pilot he would catch the next chopper. He wanted to collect the dog tags from the bodies. It was important to know who they were, her father had said, so their wives, children, parents, and friends wouldn't be haunted with the unfair hope that they had been captured and would one day return.

The story went that her father had approached the bodies and lifted the head of the first man to remove the chain around his neck. But the Vietcong had rigged the bodies to explode. Her father was dead within moments. Another copter was flying low enough that the pilot could see his flaming body.

The man who'd taken her dad's seat, Corporal Edward Cody of the military press corps, wrote an article about her dad's heroism for *Stars and Stripes*. Some Air Force paper pusher erroneously ruled against awarding him a Purple Heart, since technically, he had been killed in peace, not war. The bomb apparently did not know a cease-fire had been declared. Cody intervened, this time with an article in *The New York Times,* and the oversight was corrected. The Purple Heart arrived a month later, confusing the five-year-old Alex. The profile of the man on the heart, George Washington, looked nothing like her dad.

The months following her father's death, their apartment was quiet. No music. No visitors. Janet, Alex's mother, would get up and fix Alex's breakfast and pack a lunch, chatting like a mom on a TV show, but when Alex would get off the bus after school and climb the stairs to their second-floor apartment, she'd find Janet in bed, hair messed and eyes puffy.

Then one day, Alex came home from first grade and found that her mother had emerged from hibernation. Everything was packed in boxes or suitcases.

"We're moving to Ann Arbor tomorrow," Janet said. She had been accepted into the anthropology program at the University of Michigan. In a pattern that would repeat itself over the years, Janet was taking off in stealth. She didn't even give Alex a chance to say good-bye to her friends.

As an adult, Alex lost track of the number of times she'd pulled up Corporal Cody's *The New York Times* article about her father on the Internet. During her medical internship, she'd be on Medline, trying to figure out what rare disorder was eating away at the bowel of her patient. When she hit a dead end, she'd switch screens to the newspaper database and punch in her dad's name and the year 1975. She'd devour the article again—as if she didn't know it by heart—and somehow get the feeling her dad was watching over her. Then she'd go back to the medical articles.

In medical school, she'd sought the gory details of her father's last moments. In forensic and military articles, she learned the properties of the bomb that killed him. The explosion would have knocked him to the ground, showering him with pieces of the bones and bloodied organs of the corpse he'd cradled. She hoped he'd been knocked unconscious by the fall. Otherwise, he would have felt the metal shrapnel entering his body at hundreds of sites, and the scorching flames melting his face.

Alex circled the statue for perhaps the third time. She was ready to approach the Wall itself.

Of course, thought Alex, it had been designed by a woman. Wasn't it the women, like her mother and herself, who suffered most from these deaths in Vietnam? Maya Lin created the memorial when she was a twenty-one-year-old Yale architecture student taking a class in funerary architecture. Lin told the *Washington Post,* "I thought about what death is, what a loss is. A sharp pain that lessens with time, but can never quite heal over. A scar. The idea occurred to me there on the site. Take a knife and cut open the earth, and with time the grass would heal it. As if you cut open the rock and polished it."

Alex walked a few steps and stopped in front of the acrylic drawer that housed a book twice as large as the D.C. phone directory. It listed, in alphabetical order, the names of the soldiers who had died and their location on the Wall.

"Alexander Northfield Blake," she read. "Born August 21, 1946. Died May 1, 1975." He'd been twenty-eight at the time, younger than she was now. Yet she still attributed enormous powers to him. Just yesterday, after Wiatt and Barbara had left her lab, she'd pulled up the article again.

She glanced over at the ominous black scar that Maya Lin had created, then stared back at the name in the directory. A tourist bus unloaded its passengers and people started approaching the spot. She thought for a moment, then decided she couldn't go through with it. With all that was going on, she needed to talk to her father alone. Plus, what was she going to tell him? Her life was a jumble that she needed to sort out.

CHAPTER 8

ON MONDAY, ALEX POKED HER HEAD INTO commander Hal Webster's office. He motioned her to sit while he finished a phone call. Instead, she paced, looking at the altar he'd created to his ego. A photo of a younger Hal with General Colin Powell. His Naval Academy diploma. And every plaque and embossed Post-it holder ever given to him for delivering a speech.

"I've been thinking," she said when he hung up the phone. "Maybe meeting your biotech friends isn't such a bad idea."

"Not too keen on forensics, are you?"

"It's never interested me," said Alex. She walked over to his window. A group of soldiers jogged by, looking like a pack of clones with their similar buzz cuts and identical postures. The only difference among them was the color of their skin.

"Even if you do the best forensics job possible, it doesn't bring the person back," she said quietly. "Dead is still dead."

He nodded his head.

She raised her voice, speaking quickly and passionately, gesturing to punctuate the thought. "The work I'm doing with infectious disease, that will *save* people."

"I hear you, Alex. I'll make a call. Maybe buy you some independence from the forensic work."

"I just want to hear them out," she said, already wondering if she was making a big mistake.

Hal seized upon her faint twinge of interest. "Listen, there's one company I think you'd like. I heard about them because they're searching for genes associated with juvenile diabetes, and my ten-year-old daughter has it."

"Hal, I had no idea," said Alex. "How's she doing?"

"Still hates the sight of the needle," he said. "I try to make it a little game when I give her the injections. She's pretty stable now, but, as a parent, you can't help but worry about the long-term effects." He shook his head. "Possible blindness. Kidney failure."

"Knowing about the gene could lead to a cure through gene therapy."

"That's a lot more in line with your interests than playing cop."

She mulled it over. "You're right. Just give me a few days to think it over." She looked at her watch. "Are you coming to the Task Force meeting?"

He shook his head. "Somebody's got to run this place while Wiatt goes off on his hobbyhorse."

Alex continued down the hall to the conference room. Grant Pringle was the first to greet her. "Heard Rosie almost walked out on you last week." He smirked.

"Maybe she was looking for you, Grant. We all know you'll screw any woman that moves."

Alex turned on her heel and headed to the espresso machine. Wiatt was nowhere in sight. She guessed that Hal was wrong and, now that the team was operational, Wiatt would let Dan work his forensic magic. Wiatt was a man of action, with a soldier's impatient aggression. He'd be planning—or initiating—his next battle, not attending meetings.

Coffee cup in hand, Alex took a seat next to Barbara, across from three young soldiers. Alex had brought her slim folder of evidence reports to the meeting. Barbara had a stack of documents related to the case, as well as three volumes of a legal forensic text and a couple of Zip drives, whose purpose escaped Alex. Whatever that woman threw herself into, she did it with a vengeance.

Grant sat on the other side of Alex, directing her attention to his latest gadget, a sensitive digital compass that gave readouts on longitude and latitude, as well as thermal images of any humans in the area. Grant was spinning it in front of him, then clamping his hand down on it to see how quickly it recalibrated. The second time he squished it like a bug, Alex took a peek at the glowing dots representing the seven of them in the room: Dan, Grant, Barbara, Alex, and the three young soldier investigators. Seemed like an insignificant squiggle to corral a killer.

She wished Tom Harding were part of the group, as another civilian, and to bring some pathology power to the gang. But pathology wasn't so much an issue in these murders. The cause of death was obvious. The killer had strangled each woman with rope, a fanciful knot mocking each broken windpipe. Alex's expertise was more valued than Harding's in this instance because she might help identify the monster, searching the unknown killer's DNA—when they found some—for a pattern as unique as his killing style.

Dan stood at the end of the table, and Alex could tell by the economy of his movement and the intense focus of his eyes that he was in the zone, that almost psychic flow of mental currents that pushed him forward when he started making connections on a case. Alex could read that in him because she felt that way herself when she was hot on the trail of a scientific discovery. The rest of the world receded and insights flickered into consciousness like frames in an old-time movie.

"These cases were grouped together because of the MO—strangulation by rope, death, and subsequent rape—but the autopsy photos revealed another similarity," said Dan. "Tattoos."

Dan projected a photo of the waitress, Jeanette Miller, a tired-eyed woman, thirty-five or so, wearing a tight miniskirt. Then a picture of the woman's naked thigh. "She had a butterfly tattoo on her inner thigh, but that's not the one we're interested in." Another click and her prickly red nipple came into view, along with a strange insignia curving across her left breast—four wavy lines, a few millimeters apart. The assembled group started guessing about the meaning. Waves? Part of a Chinese character? A partial tattoo, where only one color and not others had been applied—perhaps indicating an interruption in the tattoo process?

Dan then clicked on an angelic-looking blonde. Grant whistled and stopped playing with his compass. "Quite a looker," he said.

"Grant!" chastised Barbara. As chief legal officer for the AFIP, Barbara had already sent Grant to sexual harassment classes twice. Growing up in Vegas had given him a warped, fanny-slapping view of what men should say and do around women.

"Cheryl Baker," said Dan. "A twenty-year-old college student at the University of Virginia. Killed on spring break, when she was visiting her mother in Norfolk." A picture of a stunning soft breast with a slight tan line. Her body naked except for a string of tiny seed pearls. On her left breast, a tattoo in the shape of a half-closed Egyptian-looking eye.

Alex stared at the fragile girl, whose panicked wide mouth was frozen in a grimace that made the dainty pearls seem breathtakingly innocent. Alex swallowed, then spoke tentatively. "Did her mother mention what the tattoo meant?"

"She claimed she didn't know her daughter had a tattoo," said Dan. "Her friends found it odd, too. Said she was the cashmere sweater and pearls type."

"What about her boyfriend?" Alex asked. "What did he know about the tattoo?" Alex recalled the rooster tattoo on her artist friend Karl's chest. It should have tipped her off about his high self-concept.

"She'd only been at college a few months, no guy yet,"

Dan responded. "The trauma to her vagina suggests she was a virgin."

He clicked again and Cheryl disappeared. The girl's life had been reduced to this, Alex thought, a memory in her mother's heart and a few seconds' image in a room full of strangers. Alex fought her instinct to ask Dan to go backward, to let Cheryl's face fill the screen a few minutes more as a silent memorial. Then she mentally chastised herself. Don't go running off half-cocked into forensics, she told herself. Don't forget about Rosie.

The next slide showed the woman who'd been killed in Beaufort, Candy Holtzman. She'd been a bank manager.

"This doesn't make sense," said Alex. "I don't know much about serial killers other than what I see in movies and newspapers. But don't they usually specialize in a certain type of woman? These victims differ in looks, age, everything. Sure, they were all strangled, but how do you know it's the same killer?"

Dan projected the next slide. "Holtzman's tattoo," he said. The indigo sketch on her left breast looked like a mirror image of the first tattoo, the four wavy lines. He put the three tattoos up at once. By putting the eye of Cheryl Baker's tattoo in the middle of the wavy lines of the other two women's tattoos, Dan created a winking winged Cyclops.

One of the clean-cut young soldiers spoke up. "Sir, we thought together they might be some sort of religious symbol. But all our consultants in Eastern religions, indigenous ceremonies, and New Age symbols were stumped as to what the meaning might be."

"Okay, guys," Dan asked the group. "What's going on here?"

This wasn't Alex's strong suit. She worked with evidence, data, DNA samples, sequencers. She asked questions rationally, not intuitively. But her scientific training had taught her to weigh data, think critically, undertake analyses. And there was something so compelling, so connected about the women. As with Rosie, she instinctively wanted to know them and help them. "Is there something about the location of the tattoo—the left breast?" she asked the group. Alex put her right hand over her left breast, as if she were pledging allegiance to the flag. "Isn't there a possible indication—hand over heart—about promise keeping, or promise breaking?"

"Are you suggesting that these women might have shared some experience?" asked Dan.

Alex shrugged her shoulders. The tattoos seemed to mean something similar, though she couldn't imagine what it was.

Then she stood abruptly and walked over to the screen. "Have you got some close-ups of the tattoos?" she asked. "Maybe from a different angle?"

Dan zoomed in on the photos, moving from whole-body shots to close-ups of the women's chests. "I've got a lead on the ink," said Dan. "It's mostly used in prisons, where inmates tattoo themselves. We thought the girls might all have gone to the same tattoo parlor, but there was no overlap in travel patterns. The Galveston woman never left the state. Neither of the other two had been to Texas."

"Hold it," said Alex. "Can you put all three up at the same time?" She traced the line of Baker's tattoo with her finger, then pointed to each of the others in turn. "We've got it all wrong" she said excitedly. "We're asking what the tattoos tell us about the women, but look at how clear these lines are. There's no aura around the tattoo marks under the microscope, so blood wasn't circulating when these women were tattooed. The tattoos won't tell us about the women. They'll tell us about the killer. He branded them after they were dead."

CHAPTER 9

ONCE ALEX DEDUCED THAT THE KILLER WAS responsible for the tattoos, they realized quickly that he would kill again. The killer was painting some sort of picture, piece by piece, on the breasts of dead women—and the picture was nowhere near complete.

"Can we warn women?" asked Alex. Then she realized the futility of what she was saying. He didn't have a victim type—like the dark-haired young women preyed upon by Son of Sam. Nor a particular locale—like the Bay Area stalkings of the Zodiac Killer. The one link between his killings was their proximity to Navy bases but, as Dan was quick to inform Alex, there were dozens of bases across the United States. How do you warn a million potential victims to take care? And what do you tell them? When Son of Sam was on a rampage, New York women dyed their hair blond, since he attacked only brunettes. Some stopped going out at night. But how could women evade this Tattoo Killer? He'd cut down three very different women as they went about their daily life. Women everywhere couldn't just put their lives on pause until Dan figured out who the hell the killer was.

Because of the military connection, Dan asked one of the young soldiers, an Army corporal from South Carolina, to stand before the group and search databases of military tattoos on the lead computer. Dan remained standing, a few steps back, as the soldier took center stage.

Corporal Chuck Lawndale's fingers glided effortlessly over the keyboard, the mouse propelling him through cyberspace. Alex had begun thinking of the three soldiers as See No Evil, Hear No Evil, Speak No Evil, since they'd hardly made any comments. But now that Chuck had been singled out, she saw he was a sweet-looking kid, twenty-two or so. A thin band of sweat on his forehead indicated how much he felt was riding on his performance.

Chuck transposed the wavy lines and closed eye over one after another of the tattoos in the databases. The tattoos flashed by on the three-foot-high screen. Some were flat pictures of tattoos alone; others were shown on the bodies of buff men. It was like a visit to a strange art gallery—flags, anchors, guns, women—all icons that warriors chose for some reason or another. To keep them safe from harm? Remind them of a mission? Advertise their power, their sexuality?

Alex thought of her mother. The day her doctor told her she was entering menopause, she went right to a tattoo parlor and had a barbed-wire design tattooed around her ankle. At the time, Alex just wrote it off as another of Janet's eccentricities. But as she watched the images on the screen strobe by, Alex pondered its meaning. Janet probably wanted to assert control over her body at a time when she felt one of its functions was failing. Alex had read about victims of breast cancer who tattooed roses over the flat impression on their chests left by a mastectomy. And the barbed wire? Alex could imagine her then fifty-three-year-old mother thinking, I'm not going to be some vulnerable old woman. I may be getting gray, but I'm still one tough cookie.

The image of an eagle appeared on the screen. When Chuck transposed the tattoo pieces over it, there was an almost complete match. But in the original tattoo, the eagle's eye was completely open. "He's dicking with us," said Grant. "He's made the goddamn eagle wink at us."

Barbara had been quiet up to this point, except for chastising Grant. She was looking at the screen quizzically. "Maybe there's a different message in it," she said. "The partially closed eye might mean that someone isn't paying enough attention to him."

As she spoke, Dan took over the mouse and started drawing lines across the eagle tattoo from the database. Chuck sat down, proud of his first contribution to the group. It took a few seconds for Alex to figure out what Dan was doing; then she realized he was creating other pieces the size of the tattoos on the three women.

Alex watched with horror as the number of sections reached twelve. Dan took a step back to consider what he'd put on the screen. "If he stays true to his pattern," he said, "he'll kill at least nine more women to finish the picture."

They all fell silent for a moment. Dan paced. "Maybe he's killed others already, but the local cops haven't made the connection," he said.

He turned to Chuck. "Put out a request through NCIC for any tattooed victims, regardless of the MO. Post this picture." He nodded at the winking eagle.

Chuck's fingers began to fly over the keys of his own laptop as he followed the order. Barbara took center stage to report on her end of the investigation. The slide of the eagle partitioned into twelve squares glowered behind her as she spoke. Through friends at the JAG office, she'd started legal proceedings to pull the employment records of all military and civilian personnel at the three bases. At first, the legal roadblocks were enormous, but Wiatt had called the heads of the bases, two of whom he knew on a first-name basis, and Zip drives of personnel had appeared on her desk within hours. The man had juice, no doubt.

Cross-checking did not identify anyone who was stationed at each base at the time of each killing. Chuck, emboldened by his recent performance, looked at Dan. "Sir," he said, "our guy has got to be in there somewhere." He pointed to the drives. "Maybe one place is his home base and he goes off to visit buddies or family in the other states. We could start with Norfolk and pull personnel records to see who has family near Galveston or Beaufort.

Check leaves from Norfolk and cross-reference flights to those other cities in the names of the guys on leave."

"Not enough time," said Dan, pointing at the eagle. "This guy's on a killing spree. And you can't just run the names of guys on leave against the airline records. The computer systems aren't compatible. We tried to compare flight manifests to passport information in the Ron Brown case and were told it would take six weeks in programmers' time alone to run a cross-check. And what's to say the guy flew? Cars, trains, it's too much to follow."

Chuck Lawndale looked dejected.

"Then what's our next move?" Barbara asked.

"I've got investigators on the ground at each of the three bases doing regular detective work," said Dan. "There's got to be a lead someplace."

Alex spoke up. "I still don't understand how he's managed to strangle and rape these women without leaving skin, sperm, or saliva."

"Gloves," said Dan.

Grant guffawed. "And used a cherry-flavored rubber."

"Who besides teenagers uses flavored condoms?" Alex asked.

Corporal Chuck Lawndale's cheeks reddened slightly, signaling a more than passing acquaintance with flavored condoms. Alex noted with amusement that the dot representing Lawndale on Grant's compass also enlarged due to the warm rush of blood to his face.

"The FBI shrink thinks that he's in his late twenties or early thirties but that some childhood trauma has him fixated mentally at an earlier age," said Dan. "But then again, that's what the shrinks always say."

"Any leads on the condoms themselves?" Barbara asked.

"Available in gas station bathrooms, so there's no way to trace the killer through that," said Dan. "It's not like those rare ticklers or emu-intestine rubbers you can only order on-line. But they're new to the market. You can only buy them in four states—California, Oregon, Washington, and Nevada."

"That's a long way from his killing fields," said Grant.

"Yeah," said Dan. He nodded to Corporal Lawndale, who had composed himself again. "It's a long shot, Corporal, but you could start cross-checking flights from each of those states to Norfolk, Galveston, and Beaufort the few days before each killing."

So much of law enforcement is data collection, thought Alex. The public visualized stakeouts and shoot-outs and sweating people in interrogation rooms, but modern law enforcement involved databases and phone calls. Son of Sam was caught because police looked at parking tickets given to cars near the killing sites. The forensic DNA work Alex would supervise—if the guy ever left DNA—would also involve painstaking details out of range of the killers: DNA prep, analysis, and database comparisons. How likely would it be that the suspect's DNA would match the killer's just by chance? How many other men might have similar DNA?

Dan turned to Alex. "I'm going to need you front and center as soon as he strikes. We haven't gotten DNA from any of the crime scenes yet. But we will. DNA's the way to break this case."

AFTER LUNCH, ALEX WALKED OUT OF AFIP, heading toward the Walter Reed Hospital, where Tom Harding wanted her opinion on a case. She saw Hal coming from the parking lot. He wore his dress shirt, despite the heat. "Alex," he said, "hold on."

She waited until he fell in step beside her. "I just had a very profitable meeting. That biotech company I mentioned wants access to DNA samples from the AFIP. They'll throw in a hefty consulting fee for you if you help with the analysis."

"Hal, I'm not really sure if that's what I want to be doing. Biotech's usually about keeping scientific information secret for commercial advantage. It goes against my gut."

"Alex, not everybody in biotech wears a black hat. At least meet with the folks at Gene-Ease."

Alex stopped. "Trevor Buckley's operation?"

"You've heard of him?"

"Hal, every geneticist knows who he is," she said, gesturing as she spoke. "He souped up the gene sequencer, letting us complete the Human Genome Project way ahead of schedule."

"We've got an open invitation to lunch, whenever you want."

Alex mulled it over. It would be interesting to meet the guy. But in her book, the business end of genetics could be pretty sleazy. "Nah," she told Hal, "I'm not ready to cross over to the dark side just yet."

"It's just lunch."

"I'll think on it."

Hal seemed annoyed, but he didn't press it. They parted company at the front entrance to Walter Reed, and Alex joined Harding in the small pediatric ward.

"How was your weekend?" she asked.

"Perfect sailing," he said, "I'm going to have to get you out there one of these days."

"I've never been on a sailboat before. I'd be like a fish out of water—or I guess it would be just the reverse. You probably know just the word for it."

"Where do you think the term *at sea* came from?" said Harding, smiling.

They entered the room of the patient Harding wanted Alex to see. The girl had been completely normal at birth, but now, at age five, her nervous system was going haywire.

The girl's green eyes twinkled and her red hair surrounded her tiny head in soft clouds of curls. Her pupils could follow Alex across the room with a glowing intelligence, but the rest of her body hung limply. She couldn't speak or control her movements. Alex sat next to the bed, rubbed the girl's arms, and was rewarded with a faint twitch of a smile, the most the little girl could muster. Then the beautiful little cherub's face convulsed in an appalling series of tremors. An alarm went off in the monitor above her bed and Alex lifted the girl's head gently so she wouldn't swallow her tongue. Harding opened a drawer and pulled out a syringe with the girl's antiseizure medication, injected it, and repositioned her on her side. Alex stayed with the girl, her face a few inches from the child's, murmuring soothing words through the bed rails that separated them, until the tiny patient fell asleep. Alex's hand lightly brushed her own knee as the girl drifted off. Her fingers were gently tapping the genetic code representing the devastating disease she was certain the girl had. TTGTAACA . . .

"Just tears you up, doesn't it?" Alex said to Harding in the hall, a light veil of moisture in her eyes. "The symptoms—seizures, loss of function, even the angelic glow—point to Canavan disease."

"But the family's not Jewish," he said. Canavan disease, extremely rare to begin with, usually struck Ashkenazi Jews from Eastern Europe. "They're Catholics whose families have lived in Louisiana for generations."

"Well, that explains it," said Alex to Harding's perplexed face. She loved the way history and medicine intertwined, which was one of the reasons she was fighting to keep the museum here at AFIP. She was afraid that if it were moved, they'd ditch the leeches and other reminders of medicine's past in favor of a glitzy, Grant-like focus on the latest gizmos. She liked the way studying the past encouraged doctors and scientists to question the assumptions of the day, and reminded them of their fallibility.

"Recently, some geneticists noticed that so-called Jewish genetic diseases were showing up among New Orleans Catholics," said Alex. "They took family histories and learned that a bunch of them had descended from one man, a German named Johann Adam Edelmeirer. He arrived by ship in 1720 but hid his Jewish origins when a law was passed requiring Jews to leave the territory within three months or be jailed. His descendants didn't know about their Jewish heritage—until genetic tests uncovered their Canavan and Tay-Sachs genes."

"Is the moral of this story that genes will out?" Harding asked her.

"You'll never hear that from me," said Alex. "I'm a firm believer that nurture matters just as much as nature. Look at Grant—he's managed to remake what otherwise might have been a puny body."

"Why, Alex, I believe that's the first kind thing I've heard you say about Grant."

"I'll have to watch it. I must be losing my edge." Then she thought about it a moment longer. "Or maybe it's only that Wiatt's begun to annoy me more."

WHEN SHE CHECKED HER MESSAGES BACK AT the lab, she listened to an urgent one from Barbara, asking her to come to Wiatt's office. Alex felt like she was being called to the principal's office. What was it that she'd done, or hadn't done, now?

She grabbed the blazer from the back of her door and put it on, then was annoyed at herself for even making that gesture. She removed it and hung it back up. They hadn't hired her for her fashion sense.

"I was at Walter Reed, consulting on a case," she said as she entered Wiatt's office. She took the accusatory open chair at the end of the row seating Dan, Grant, and Barbara, across the desk from Wiatt.

Alex looked around Wiatt's office. There were no certificates of his military achievements, nor photos of him in battle or shaking the hands of generals and politicians. The walls were covered, sparsely and tastefully, with architectural drawings by Frank Lloyd Wright. Other than a paperweight from Fort Bragg, the only indication that this was a soldier's office was the tightly wound, aggressive Colonel Wiatt himself.

Dan brought her up to speed. "San Diego responded to our NCIC request. Three days ago, they had a corpse with the blue claw of an eagle, but they didn't register it as the work of the serial strangler because the killer used his bare hands, instead of his usual rope."

"This case just got a whole lot hotter," added Grant. "The victim was Marilyn Mayne."

Alex's jaw dropped. The networks and tabloids were all over this case, dubbing it "the Locked Room Mystery." Her funeral had drawn a Who's Who of corporate leaders, a few ambassadors whose countries she had wired, even the Vice President. CNN had covered it live, as if she were Princess Di. *Hot* did not even begin to describe it.

"I was telling my soldiers," said Wiatt, referring to the uniformed Dan, Grant, and Barbara and thus making her feel like a child late for homeroom, "that the President himself is interested in the case. The victim served on his Business Advisory Council, and was a symbol throughout the world of American know-how. He's agreed to give us whatever we need to bring the case to a swift victory."

Alex knew that what the case needed, President Cotter couldn't possibly provide. Clues. Leads. DNA.

Wiatt turned to Grant. "Did you bring what I asked for?"

"Yes, sir," said Grant, reaching into a leather satchel next to his chair. He handed the commanding officer half a dozen pagerlike devices, keeping one for himself.

Wiatt passed one to Alex. "I don't want that buzzer out of your sight. When the next body is found, you're going to be on a plane, scrambling."

The conviction with which he spoke silenced even Alex.

CHAPTER 10

THAT NIGHT, ALEX COULDN'T FALL ASLEEP. she opened her eyes and stared at the beeper, its tiny green battery light winking back at her. She remained on her side in bed but reached over to grab the still-silent device. She brought it closer to her face. Seemed pretty tame for something coming out of Grant's operations. Sure, it could beep you in different musical tones, but, hell, her cell phone could do that.

She put it back on the nightstand and swung herself out of bed. She pulled a men's flannel robe around her naked body, cinched the belt around her slight waist, and used the beeper to fasten it on the side. She hadn't gotten curtains for the main room, and didn't intend to, since she loved seeing the stenciled words *Curl Up and Dye* written on the window, a seemingly magical scroll, since it was backward from her inside view. The robe was her one nod to demureness, and she'd chosen a large men's one because the sleeves hung long, even on her five-seven frame, making her feel wrapped in a safe cocoon.

She sat in one of the hair-dryer chairs and fingered the beeper. How would she feel when it finally went off? She resented Wiatt like hell for assigning her this duty, but the women's faces had begun to push his face out of her mind when she thought about the case. The media was still clamoring for vengeance for Marilyn Mayne. Some pundits were even suggesting that when the killer was caught, he should be tried first for the Galveston murder, since Texas juries readily imposed the death penalty. But much as her heart went out for *any* murder victim, she was shaken most by the death of Cheryl Baker, the delicate blonde who'd died in a strand of pearls. A college freshman, for Chrissakes. She'd never had the chance to learn the wonders of her own mind, the amazing things she was capable of. Hell, she'd never even had the chance to have sex.

Alex knew she couldn't keep up this push/pull with Wiatt. Her constant feeling of annoyance was sapping her energy, like a low-level flu. She might as well throw in the big Egyptian cotton towel and plunge into this forensic gig.

She watched the trickle of traffic outside her window as the last late-night diners cabbed home. The stillness they left in their wake comforted her. She returned to the bedroom, touched a tiny carved box on her dresser for luck, and fell into bed, suddenly too tired even to remove the robe.

THE NEXT DAY, ALEX CALLED THE SAN DIEGO coroner, just to see if he'd covered all the bases in the search for DNA. "A billionaire dies in California," he said, "I had everybody from the *Wall Street Journal* to *Entertainment Tonight* up my ass. I crippled the department for a week, with everybody searching for hairs in the carpet fibers, blood under her nails. Came up with squat. It was like a phantom reached into that room."

"Anything notable on autopsy?" asked Alex. She wasn't entirely sure what questions she should be asking, beyond her bailiwick of DNA. She made a mental note to call a former professor of hers who consulted in forensic cases.

"Can't tell much about the offender. Takes some strength to pop a trachea, but, from the dearth of defensive wounds, she was asleep until almost the last minute."

"Was she drugged?" asked Alex, feeling relieved that she'd come up with a logical question.

"Nah, the phantom just appeared and struck."

"Well, thank you for your time."

As she was about to hang up, he said, "There's one thing I didn't put in the report, something minor. Probably meaningless. He cleaned her breast with an antiseptic wipe before he tattooed it."

"Just the one breast?"

"Uh-huh. Like a surgeon before he cuts, to protect against infection."

It seemed pretty odd to be protecting a dead woman, Alex thought after she hung up. Maybe the killer was protecting himself. When they found the next corpse—she cringed at her conviction that there would be a next corpse—she'd check the breast area carefully for any trace of DNA.

A FEW MEMBERS OF CONGRESS—U.S. REPRE-sentatives David Thorne, Bob Quiller, and Sissy Clark—were due at AFIP that night. They were part of a Congressional committee to determine whether the National Museum of Health and Medicine should be moved to Ellis Island or stay at AFIP.

Military man that he was, Colonel Jack Wiatt spent the whole afternoon going from department to department at AFIP, doing a first-class inspection. When Wiatt got to Alex's lab, she half-expected him to ask her to polish her hand-tooled Justin cowboy boots.

"I didn't expect it to be so neat," he said.

"I know," said Alex. "People associate DNA with gore—blood, wounds, rape, sperm. What I work with are microscopic pieces that look like tiny bits of sugar candy."

She walked him over to the hooded workbench and inserted a slim glass pipette into a purple solution. "This has a bit of lung tissue from a corpse with Legionnaires' disease." She twisted the pipette in the liquid and then pulled it up. A shiny clear strand of material stuck to it. "Here's the man's DNA."

Wiatt looked around. "I expected more microscopes, not large computers."

Alex was surprised by his interest. No one from administration had ever bothered to find out what she actually did before.

"These computers are attached to gene sequencers." She led him over to the Applied Biosystems 3730*xl*DNA analyzer and typed in the name Rosie. "Here, take a look at one of the DNA sequences I ran this morning."

"Who's Rosie?" he asked, striding comfortably toward the sequencer.

"I like to name the samples I'm working on. It makes me remember the whole person, not get misled into thinking they are no more than the sum of their genes. She's the Inuit woman with the Spanish flu."

"How do you pick the names?"

"Usually some association for me. I'm looking for a body with a particularly gross disease to name after my last boyfriend."

Wiatt smiled and stood behind her. She could smell the soap he'd used, Irish Spring. She pressed a button and the colorful quilt of DNA hit the screen, and then, with the push of another button, the colors of DNA were changed into the letters of the genetic alphabet.

A second sequencer began to spit out results, and Wiatt walked over to its colorful screen. "What's going on here?"

"Oh, I went over to the Walter Reed pathology lab today and got some old blood samples from people who died around the same time as Rosie."

"Doesn't a person's blood get thrown out after a lab runs tests on it?"

"Nah, pathology at Walter Reed is like my grandma's attic. *Nothing* gets thrown out. I'm sifting through old DNA from people who died of other causes to find someone who was exposed to the Spanish flu but had a natural immunity. It'll help me with my vaccine work."

"How do you get DNA out of someone who's been dead a long time?" he asked.

She turned to face him, looking up into his eyes. "Any sort of preserved tissue sample will do—a drop of blood, the inner part of a bone, a hair follicle from a brush. When AIDS was first discovered, researchers here analyzed a bunch of old blood samples going back decades to see if the virus had been with us for years but people just hadn't realized what it was. Now a geneticist, Dr. Victor McKusick, wants to analyze Abe Lincoln's blood from an exhibit in our museum."

"We've got Lincoln's blood here?"

"Seems so. We've got the bloody shirt cuffs of the doctor who tried to pull the bullet out of the President."

"Why would you want to do DNA testing on a dead President?"

"McKusick's interested in whether he had a disease, Marfan syndrome. Other people want to find a supposed gene for leadership, or see if he fathered any illegitimate children, like Jefferson did."

Alex got more animated as she talked. "I can just see the next presidential race," she said. "Forget those television debates. Maybe Jesse Jackson will run his DNA profile next to Lincoln's and say, 'Vote for me. I've got more genes in common with Honest Abe.'"

"I suppose genetics is like any new technology," he said. "Applications the inventors never imagined."

"Yeah, there's even a company that makes genetically engineered pets. Put a gene from a glowing fluorescent jellyfish into a kitty and you get a combination pet and nightlight."

Wiatt laughed, his shoulders softening a bit. Even though a DNA lab was far outside his normal territory, he made himself at home there, peering at shelves, reading posted protocols. "The Lincoln thing is interesting," he said. "I thought the museum was just a collection of medical curios. I need to appoint someone to work with the Congressional committee. Are you interested?"

"Is this a trick question? Are you going to repossess my refrigerator again if I say no?"

"Nah, this one is your choice. For me, the museum is a joke. But Congress will finance the museum's development if it moves to Ellis Island. If you can think of some way to keep it here and bring it into the twenty-first century, I'd back you on keeping the museum as part of our operations."

"What would I have to do?"

"Begin with a tactical assault on the politicians at the museum tonight. There's also a trip planned to Ellis Island to look at the site; you'd need to go there."

"If I'm not 'scrambling,' as you call it."

"Smart girl—I mean doctor," he said, extending his hand for Alex to shake. "You're finally getting your priorities straight."

BARBARA AND ALEX STOOD NEXT TO THE hair ball, munching on coconut shrimp, as Barbara identified the members of Congress in the museum. Tom Harding had opted for his sailboat instead, saying he had no desire to meet the "polluticians," his word for elected officials he felt did more harm than good.

"You're like going to the Oscars with *Entertainment Weekly*," Alex said to Barbara.

"Shh, and pay attention. That's Bob Quiller, the Congressman from New Jersey who wants to move the museum to Ellis Island."

Alex looked over at the slight man. His bald head was fringed with a halo of baby-fine gray hair and he was wearing a bow tie. He didn't appear to be any taller than five six or so. "He doesn't look like too much of a powerhouse to me," said Alex.

"Think Napoléon, darling. And don't ever underestimate him. In 1998, he got the United States Supreme Court to declare that most of Ellis Island, which New York State thought it owned, really belonged to his district in New Jersey. Since then, he's been attracting money and jobs to the property. If the museum were located there and expanded in the way he wants—interactive exhibits, Web site, souvenir shop, health advisers on hand—he'd create a thousand permanent jobs and eighty million dollars a year in new revenue."

"Having the Statue of Liberty look out on his district isn't enough for him? He's got designs on the medical museum, as well?"

Barbara reached over and flicked a piece of wayward coconut off of Alex's blazer lapel. She'd managed to eat hers without any falling crumbs. "I expect he'll launch his presidential candidacy from the main building on Ellis Island. Already he's courting virtually every ethnic group who arrived in steerage there. He sponsors free Greek days, Italian days—you name it—on the island. A part of the tour is the run-down medical facility where immigrants were deloused. There's a photo of him in every room there, just like he were JFK or the Pope."

"Anybody on the committee likely to side with me?"

"The rest of the committee probably hasn't given this rinky-dink museum a moment's thought. They're part of what's called the Subcommittee on Economic Development, Public Buildings, Hazardous Materials, and Pipeline Transportation, Committee on Transportation and Infrastructure. They've got oil spills, truckers' strikes, clean-air tax breaks, and a million other things on their plate besides this."

"Why throw all those sorts of things together?"

"That's the life of the legislator. I read a study that said doctors spend an average of ten minutes with each patient. Congressmen are lucky if they get to spend ten seconds on a bill before they vote on it. They are jacks-of-all-trades, and masters of only the ones bringing moola to their districts."

Alex noticed Commander Hal Webster approaching the Congressman, a very attractive blonde in tow. They seemed to be having a bit of a tiff. "Who's the woman with Hal?"

Barbara craned her neck in the direction of the microscope display. "You've never met his wife?"

Alex shook her head.

"She's a distant Vanderbilt cousin. Got the name but not the bread."

Alex looked at her, taking in the designer suit, the large gold link necklace. "Looks pretty high-maintenance to me."

"Oh, Alex, you have no idea."

The museum door opened, and a man in a suede bomber jacket, khaki pants, and cowboy boots strode in. Alex eyed him with interest. "Know anything about the guy who just walked in?"

"Don't tell me you're upgrading your romantic profile to guys who actually work for a living?" Barbara asked.

"I'm interested in his cute ass, not what he does nine to five."

"You and half the population of the District, honey. That is Congressman David Thorne of Texas, the only genuine D.C. heartthrob."

"He's got a wild streak, showing up at an official function in cowboy boots."

Barbara threw a bemused look at Alex, who sported a similar pair on her feet. "That's not all he's got. Good looks, single, he's even smart. I like him because he had a long roll in the hay with Senator Gloria Devon, who's a good ten years older than he is. Gave me hope that once Lana is in college, I can still find a lover and become the Grandma Moses of sex."

"Barbara, you'll be only thirty-four years old then, hardly over the hill." Alex lowered her voice. "What happened to him and Senator Devon?"

"He dumped her in a very public way. Shocked the hell out of me. He seemed to be quite in love with her. Even took care of her kid. Look, he's next to your favorite exhibit."

"Well, Wiatt told me I've got to 'tactically assault' the politicians, and you know I never disobey a direct order. Want to come with me?"

"Nah, I see a genuine hero of mine, Charlene Drew

Jarvis. She used to be our D.C. councilwoman. Former neuropsychological researcher at the National Institutes of Health, she's now a politician and the president of Southeastern University. She takes multitasking to a new level." Barbara waved at Charlene, who headed over to join her. Alex made a beeline for Congressman David Thorne.

"Do you have some particular fascination with General Sickles's thighbone?" Alex asked the Congressman, who was bent over, reading the information below the bone in the display case.

"Well, I do have a fondness for thighs," he said, looking over at the front of Alex's jeans. Still bent, he was eye level with her zipper. Alex involuntarily squeezed her thighs together.

"Seems like quite a character." He continued reading. "General Daniel Sickles donated his leg bone to the museum for study. He would come to the museum to visit it each year on the anniversary of the Battle of Gettysburg, where it had been amputated."

He stood up, stuck out his hand to shake Alex's. "I'm David Thorne," he said.

"Alexandra Blake," she replied.

"You seem to know about the old geezer," he said, nodding his head toward the display case.

"That's not the half of it," replied Alex, thrusting both hands in front of her and moving them as she told the tale. "He came to Washington as a Congressman, like you. A skillful political manipulator, cunning charmer . . ."

"The parallels are mounting," David said, removing his suede bomber jacket and draping it on his arm, revealing a pale blue shirt and a yellow tie with longhorns on it.

"He cheated notoriously on his wife, including a dalliance with a wealthy prostitute, Fanny White, who funded his campaign."

"Won't cop to that, never been married." David grabbed two wineglasses from the passing waiter and handed one to Alex.

She took a sip, then continued her story. "The wife played around, too. With the U.S. Attorney, no less, Philip Barton Key—"

"The guy who wrote 'The Star-Spangled Banner'?" interjected David.

"His son. So Sickles, in broad daylight, in the center of town, shoots Key dead."

"In my home state, the great republic of Texas, that would be considered justifiable homicide."

Alex smiled. "Well then, you'll love this. Sickles pled temporary insanity—the first time the defense was ever used. And he was acquitted."

David thought about it. "Did they kick him out of Congress when it happened?"

That struck Alex as an odd question. "He didn't get to keep that gig, but President Lincoln encouraged him to lead troops in the Civil War. Sickles became a hero at Gettysburg, was named Ambassador to Spain, had a fling there with Queen Isabella the Second, and made and lost fortunes till the ripe old age of ninety-four. His biographer, W. A. Swanberg, calls him 'the most spectacularly successful failure of the century.' "

"Nice for me to have a role model. Makes my own exploits seem quite middle of the road."

The short, balding Congressman from New Jersey, Bob Quiller, joined them. "Your exploits are notorious," said Bob. He shook Alex's hand. "Nice to meet you, Dr. Blake. I could negotiate peace in the Middle East and not even get two minutes' coverage on C-SPAN. He goes underwear shopping with Cameron Diaz and it makes page one of the *Washington Post* and a spread in *People*."

David looked sheepishly at Alex. "She's a friend of my kid sister." Then he turned to Congressman Quiller. "Plus, it was the bathing suit department."

Alex looked at David conspiratorially. "A thong by any other name . . ."

"You better watch out for the gentleman from Texas," Quiller told Alex.

"Me a gentleman? Them's fighting words where I come from."

"David," said Quiller, "you've monopolized the good doctor long enough. I'm taking her over to meet the third member of our subcommittee, Sissy Clark."

"You'll love Sissy," David told Alex. "She ran for the House of Representatives in the 1970s with the campaign slogan 'A Woman's Place is in the House.' Served fifteen terms since."

Alex let herself be led over to Sissy. David was interesting, but keeping the museum in D.C. was a higher priority. Besides, she had her hands full with Rosie and the investigation.

Sissy was a sixtyish woman in a gray silk dress with a Diane Feinstein–style bow at the neck. "I visited the museum as a child, when it was on the Mall," she told Alex. "Scared the bejesus out of me, the lung black with cancer, all those body parts from the Civil War. I had no idea until tonight that the museum is linked to some major pathology work."

"Yes, and there's lots more that can be done," said Alex. "The museum started out as a working lab to prevent soldiers' infections and injuries. Now we can learn a whole lot about the evolution of infectious diseases by analyzing the bloody bandages from the Civil War soldiers, the tissue samples sent back from the guys with odd fevers during the Korean War. . . ."

"Fine, keep the wet work here," said Quiller. "But move the displays up to Ellis Island to form the tiny nucleus of a huge museum of health. We owe it to the masses to move this stuff from a place where twenty thousand tourists see it a year, tops, to Ellis Island, where we draw in more than twenty million."

Congresswoman Clark turned to him with a grin. "The masses are asses, my dear. That's why we're in office, not them. To figure out what's best and then do it. And I haven't made my mind up about whether it makes sense to move the museum or not."

Wiatt approached the podium and gave some closing remarks, saying virtually nothing about the museum but doing lots of cheerleading about AFIP. He made a promise—a bit exaggerated, Alex thought—that the serial strangler would soon be brought to justice. And he did some real lobbying for funds. Alex guessed the lawmakers were used to it. There were no free coconut shrimp in this town.

As people were leaving, David approached Alex. "I'd offer you a ride home, but my car's in the shop," he said.

"Where are you going? I'm parked in the lot, and the Metro's slow this time of night."

"Adams Morgan."

"Me, too. I'll drop you."

On the way back, Alex drove normally, which for her meant passing, feinting, and taking the corners at a supersonic pace. Barbara refused to ride with her anymore.

David was merely amused. "V-eight engine?"

"Of course," she said.

"Isn't it tough to find parts for a '63 T-Bird?"

"It's a nightmare. Not to mention that I've run through mechanics like Paris Hilton runs through boyfriends."

She passed a truck at seventy miles an hour on a two-lane road. "If the bottom falls out of the genes market, you can always get a job as a Boston cabbie," David said.

"Where in Adams Morgan are you?"

"On Adams-Mill Road."

"Ah, right next to the park."

He nodded. "When I moved here, I felt claustrophobic. I grew up on a ranch outside of Amarillo. Except for my grandparents' house, the barns, and sheds, there was nothing but land and cattle as far as I could see. Then I came to D.C., and people were penned up tighter than animals. Lawyers in pinstripes flooded the sidewalks like an overflow of the Rio Grande. My house and yard are small, but behind me is Rock Creek Park. Sometimes the Great Blue Herons come right out of the park and onto my lawn."

David directed her down the side streets to a small

wooden house, far more modest on the outside than its imposing Federal-style brick neighbors. A parking spot was open on the street in front of it.

"Well, Dr. Blake, you've gotta come in now. There's hardly ever an open spot on this block."

"So you believe in signs and omens?"

"I believe in anything that would get a bourbon in your hand on my couch."

Alex thought for a moment. She was intrigued by his contrasts. Stodgy job, but maybe a funky guy. Plus, bourbon was her drink of choice, right up there with Starbucks dark roast. "Just a quick one; then I need to head home."

She swerved the car into the tight spot with ease, then went around to open the passenger door, which was missing its handle on the inside. "Nice trick to keep your men right where you want them," he said as he climbed out.

She assessed him quietly under the porch light as he inserted his key. She'd have to pump Barbara for more dish about him tomorrow.

The inside of David's Cape Cod was painted in masculine dark hues—maroon, hunter green. But the rest of the decor was a surprise. He had neither the Dave Barry–style trappings of early bachelorhood or the hunting-scene prints of the stereotypical successful man. Instead, a set of whimsical track lights hung down—a tiny man on a bicycle, with the bulb flashing out of his bike light; a fair maiden with the bulb as the gem on her necklace; a lighthouse with the bulb as its fog light.

"They're great, aren't they? A ten-year-old friend of mine helped me pick them out," he said. Alex saw a photo on an end table of a beaming brunette with braces. She must be the one, Alex realized.

Alex nodded, then took a few steps down the hallway to admire a series of black-and-white photos. "A four-by-five camera?"

"How'd you know?"

"An artist friend uses one." Alex thought about Skip, one of her exes, who used such a camera. She had one of his photos above her bed—a beautiful nude portrait of the back of an Asian woman. He'd left Alex for an affair with the model. But the photo was so striking, Alex hadn't thought twice about bringing it with her to D.C.

Alex was enchanted by the way the photographer played with light. They were landscapes, but the way the light hit them conveyed multiple other meanings. Each one seemed to be a picture within a picture within a picture. Mountains around cloud formations around a woman's face.

"He's really good," Alex told David as he handed her a bourbon.

David took a bow, nearly spilling his drink.

"They're yours?"

"You bet, double major in political science—or 'pitiful science,' as my dad used to say—and fine arts at the University of Texas. I wouldn't even mention what my dad used to say about the son of a wrangler being an art major. If I hadn't also been head of the rifle team, he'd have questioned my sexual orientation."

Alex looked at one of the photographs more closely. It looked like a river with a building in it, with a hand grenade inside that. "Triple exposure?"

David stood close behind Alex. "None of these employs any tricks of the camera or the darkroom. It's all a matter of lying in wait until the light hits the subject in the most extraordinary way."

He touched her elbow to steer her to the couch in front of the fireplace. She sat down and he sat next to her. He put his drink on the hammered-copper table in front of them and lightly traced a circle on her jeans, just above her knees. She moved his hand away. She was interested, but she had no desire to become a perk of his job.

He let it pass but stared intently into her eyes. "Photography taught me two things. First, never believe your eyes."

"And the second?"

He took the bourbon out of her hand and set it next to his. "With enough patience you can get anything you want."

Just as he leaned toward her, the doorbell sounded.

David slumped back against the couch cushion. "Oh shit, I forgot about Lil."

"You forgot you had a date?"

"No, it's not what you think. Lil's my chief of staff."

Alex could hear a key in the lock and then a cheery redhead in her mid-forties came into the room. "Don't tell me you forgot your after-dinner talk tonight at the Century Twenty-one convention," said Lil. "They're the second-biggest employer in your district."

"Don't worry, Lil. I've got my speech down pat. 'Four score and seven mortgage points ago . . .'"

Lil turned to Alex. "This man is going to be the death of me."

David stood up and gave Lil a big hug. "She lives to serve me," he told Alex. "Lillian Koniak, meet Dr. Alexandra Blake. She's the new liaison from the National Museum of Health and Medicine." Alex stood as well and stuck out her hand.

"Have you got a card, Dr. Blake? I'm the staff person who schedules the committee meetings."

Alex unzipped her leather fanny pack and handed her one.

"I don't do a thing without Lil's help and permission."

"If that were true, you wouldn't have gone underwear shopping," Lil teased him.

"It was bathing suits," said Alex.

David walked Alex to the door. "Thanks for the lift. Perhaps another time?"

"Sure. I need some underwear, too." Her smile turned into a tease, and she headed out the door.

CHAPTER II

THE NEXT DAY AT WORK, ALEX RECEIVED A messengered packet from Lil. It included the transcript of a previous Congressional hearing about the museum relocation, the agenda for a committee meeting the following Monday, a pass to get her in the Capitol Building, and a first-class Amtrak ticket to Jersey City for a week hence. There was a hotel reservation, a ticket on the ferry to Ellis Island, and a sheet to fax back about her food preferences and any food allergies. Alex was impressed by Lil's efficiency. No wonder David's turned his life over to her, thought Alex. I could use a Lil of my own.

A few minutes before noon, Barbara walked into the lab. "Did I see the Adonis of government get into the Thunderbird with you last night?"

Alex nodded.

"Was he as scrumptious in bed as he looked?"

"Honestly, Barbara, what you must think of me. I just met the man."

"Am I talking to the same woman who made it with Luke in the cloakroom of the White House during a Saturday-morning tour?"

"That was in my frivolous youth."

"Alex, that was last summer."

Alex rolled her eyes. "He had to give a speech last night. Plus, he's not my usual type."

"A point in his favor, as far as I'm concerned."

Alex smiled and grabbed her gym bag and they headed out of the lab. Alex had played racquetball in college, but when she arrived at AFIP, Barbara had tutored her in handball, a faster, tougher, more exhausting alternative. This was a man's game. They were the only two women who ever used the courts.

It was a glorious May day outside, with the faint smell of cherry blossoms in the air. "How about bagging the game for a jog instead?" Alex asked.

"Alex," said Barbara, "you know what a battle it is to get these courts. I don't want to go to the back of the line again. But more on your date. Are you going to see him again?"

"I admit I'm intrigued. What do you know about him? You've always got much juicier stuff than the *Washington Post.*"

Barbara had seen politicians up close when, her first year in service, she was part of a U.S. Navy Color Guard that stood with flags at White House events. She'd kidded Alex about how she hadn't progressed much from the days when her ancestors were maids. There she was, in uniform, standing around in a white guy's big mansion. And the politicians said things in front of her, as if she were invisible.

"In my stint with the Color Guard, in the early days of his relationship with Gloria Devon, I saw them at the White House, pretending like they weren't together."

"Why the act?"

"He was a brand-new Congressman from Texas, assigned to her committee on water rights. There were sparks, but she was fifty, he was thirty-nine."

"So? Men date younger women all the time."

"You know women don't get the same breaks. The other Senators whooped it up when seventy-four-year-old Strom Thurmond got his thirty-year-old wife pregnant. But they just freaked at the thought of Gloria with a younger man. With the amount of angst they felt, you would have thought she had done a Senate page in the cloakroom."

Alex chuckled at the picture of the elegant, diminutive Gloria Devon going at it with an intern. "After the Clinton mess, wouldn't that have qualified her for the presidency?"

"It would have been okay if it had just been a matter of hazing by fellow Senators, but then the press got hold of it. There was some blowup between David and Gloria's ex that made the *Washington Post.* Probably David wanted to make news based on his legislative accomplishments, rather than as a boy toy."

"Well, he's the older man in my case."

"Quite a change for you. I swear, some of those guys you hang with act about fifteen."

"Barbara, you've got to get out more. Men today are in touch with their inner child."

"One child's quite enough for me, honey. And before we lose you to this new romantic venture, how about having dinner with Lana and me tonight?"

"I'd love to see Lana, but I just got three volumes of reports about the museum to read before my first committee meeting. How about over the weekend?"

Barbara nodded. "You're still adamant about keeping the museum here?" she asked.

Alex nodded.

Barbara asked, "It's not just the collection, is it?"

"I think it's important to keep the museum right under our noses. We've got a huge responsibility at AFIP. Tom Harding's second-opinion program keeps hospital patients from death's door. Dan Wilson's forensic tests determine if someone walks free or gets the death penalty. The museum reminds us of our fallibility. It shows not just what science and medicine do right but also what they do wrong."

"Like the leeches still on display," said Barbara.

"Yeah. And did you see the exhibit last summer about unethical experimentation on women?"

Barbara nodded. "But sometimes the exhibits are so lame. Look at the one on deafness going on now. Some of the displays are articles taped on poster board. Lana and her friends do better work than that for science class. They make videos, PowerPoints, 3-D animations. . . ."

"Well, maybe Lana and her high school friends should be in charge of the museum."

"I can just see the first exhibit: 'How Many Is Too Many? The Medical Implications of Multiple Earlobe Piercing.'"

"Seriously, Barbara. The museum needs money, not a move."

They opened the door to the fitness center and a whoosh of air-conditioned air enveloped their bodies. They passed the weight room and noticed Grant pumping iron. In the women's locker room, they changed in four minutes flat and were on the court a minute later.

When they came off the court, Alex's gray sleeveless T-shirt, covered in sweat, was sticking to her breasts. She and Barbara passed Corporal Chuck Lawndale, the young data cruncher who was part of the Tattoo Killer team. He stared just a little too long at them in their short, tight, wet clothes, then saluted Barbara. Alex doubled over in laughter at the gesture. But Barbara remained professional, despite the sweat rolling down her forehead. "At ease," she said.

THAT AFTERNOON, DAN ARRIVED BACK FROM San Diego after reworking the Mayne scene. He'd learned that Mayne's personal secretary had made her reservations for the $1,500-a-day suite, and that it was not uncommon for Mayne to go away to a spa for a few days to collect herself before she made a major business announcement. Her whereabouts were guarded like a state secret. The secretary provided a huge list of people who might have been angry at Mayne—business competitors, former suitors—and Dan had dutifully interviewed them all. Most were alibied for the night and the few who weren't just didn't feel right for it. He pressed the secretary for information about whether the woman might have had a secret lover, maybe someone beneath her in stature, who didn't go with her public image. "I knew more about her than anyone else on earth," said the secretary. "I picked up her birth-control pills, remembered her lovers' birthdays, paid a few men off when she got tired of them. If she had been meeting someone in San Diego, I would have known about it."

Over a quick dinner of burgers in the AFIP cafeteria, Dan told Alex he had gone to the Au Contraire Resort to double-check whether anyone had seen anything unusual that night. Security at the place was tight, and people swore it had been equally efficient the night of the killing.

"So, how'd he get into a locked suite?" Alex asked. "The report says Mayne's door showed no sign of forced entry."

"Turns out someone had drifted behind the desk when the night clerk was off taking a leak. He or she just programmed an extra key card to get into Mayne's room. When the night clerk returned, he saw the box with the key cards was not in its usual spot."

Alex thought about how quickly hotels made her a new electronic key whenever she lost one. Now women travelers had to worry about some pervert cloning their key. "Why didn't this come out earlier?"

"Clerk told the manager, but the head honcho didn't want to reveal how easily their security could be breached. Those $1,500-a-night rooms aren't quite so appealing if guests can be killed as they sleep. Asshole manager told me he hadn't mentioned it because he didn't want Mayne's family suing him for wrongful death."

Alex could imagine that provoked a colorful reaction from Dan. "So what's next?"

He pointed to the beeper on her belt and narrowed his eyes in frustration. "We just wait."

CHAPTER 12

THE NEXT DAY, ALEX TOOK A CAB TO THE
Rayburn House Office Building. She showed her committee consultant pass, with its embossed gold seal, to the security guard, who merely yawned and motioned for her to
put her leather portfolio, fanny pack, and boots on the
conveyor belt that ran through the X-ray machine. Then
she stepped through the metal detector and a female atten-
dant called her aside, wanded her, and patted her down.
Alex noticed that all the women in business suits got to
skip this last step. Her own outfit—the jeans and the
blazer—must fit the terrorist profile. Alex was more
amused than annoyed. What could be more all-American
than a blonde in blue jeans? And here they were, acting as
if she were on a mission from Al Qaeda.

Once she was cleared, she started down the impressive
wide hallway to the hearing room. There was a hush to the
building, as if regal and important events were taking
place. Every so often, one of the intricately carved
wooden doors swung open, a gateway into the legislative
equivalent of a religious temple. A group of people would
emerge, after paying their respects and asking for miracles
from their elected demigods. Some of the people were
smiling; some were tense. Not everybody got what they
wanted.

Alex found Room 2203 and gave her name to the
young man at an imposing wooden table outside the door.

His ID tag indicated he was an aide to the chair of the sub-committee, the ranking Democrat, Tiger Vance of Florida, a sixty-five-year-old former professional linebacker.

The aide signed Alex in and told her they were running about a half hour late. This was a full meeting of the Sub-committee on Economic Development, Public Buildings, Hazardous Materials, and Pipeline Transportation. They were dealing with hazardous-waste issues now, but the museum would be next on the agenda. He opened the heavy door to the hearing room, put his finger to his mouth to shush Alex, and whispered that she should take a seat in the last row of the audience.

The room was divided into two parts. On a raised dais, covering about one-third of the room, sat nine members of Congress. They had plush chairs and pitchers of ice tea and water spaced along the long ornate table in front of them. Every few moments, two or more of them would check their watches, remove themselves from their chairs, go off to the main chamber of the House of Representa-tives, and vote on an issue of interest to their constituents. At other times, aides would come and whisper something into the ear of a Congressman or Congresswoman and get a whispered response back. Alex found the whole tableau fascinating. The Congressional side of the room was a buzz of activity. On the side of the room she occupied, the supplicant side, as she thought of it, people were silently jammed together on folding chairs, acting as quiet, sober, and respectful as if they were in Sunday school.

Her side had a long rectangular table where people were called to testify—with a three-minute limit—about their issue. Judging by the actions of the members of Congress—tapping fingers, leaning over to colleagues to whisper comments, signaling to staff people at the side of the room—three minutes was probably the max of these guys' attention spans.

The night before, drafting her comments, Alex had worked hard to jam her testimony into the requisite time limit. All the while, she had thought about the process. No matter what the issue—the scourge of AIDS, the abuse of prisoners, the decision of whether the nation should go to war—three minutes was all that was allowed. It was like the old days of being at a pay phone; you were just about to say something important, when your quarter ran out.

Alex looked at Congressman Vance, seated in the middle of the legislators' table. He was a beefy man, a former football player who didn't exercise enough, whose muscles had turned to fat. He was barely listening to the speaker, the general counsel of the Environmental Protection Agency. Vance's chair was tipped slightly back and Alex thought he might just fall asleep.

After the EPA man finished his three minutes, David started in on him with questions. Sitting on Vance's left, David certainly looked like Congressman Thorne today. Gray suit, red power tie. A slight nodding of the head when the man was speaking. Alex didn't know him well enough to tell whether it was a sincere indication he was listening or just a show for the C-SPAN camera, Thorne's equivalent of Bill Clinton's "I feel your pain" look.

David was on a roll now. He gestured to an aide, who came forward with a chart. "According to this data, your agency is letting people get away with environmental discrimination." He paused for emphasis and looked away from the witness to the C-SPAN cameraman. "The last six hazardous-waste sites have been located in minority neighborhoods, often closer to inhabited areas than the regs allow."

The EPA man stuttered a feeble excuse, something about neighborhood patterns changing in an unexpected way, throwing off projections. David cut him off. "I want you here in two weeks with a full report on what you are going to do to remedy this." Then he dismissed the speaker.

The subcommittee chair, Congressman Vance, called Marvin Cooper to the witness table, and Alex, too. Cooper, the director of tourism for New Jersey, gave a glowing two-minute-and-fifty-nine-second report about how it would benefit the museum and the American people to move the museum to New Jersey. He had obviously done this sort of thing before.

Then it was Alex's turn, and she was surprised at how nervous she felt. She'd had no trouble giving speeches to audiences in the thousands at national scientific meetings. But the hot C-SPAN lights and the eyes of the other supplicants behind her boring into her back—not to mention the strangeness of appearing before David on oddly unequal terms—made her voice catch a little when she started to speak. Once she got going, though, she made a strong case for the museum staying at AFIP, and she could see Congresswoman Sissy Clark nodding sincerely as she spoke. Her basic message was that it was dangerous to separate the wet work from the dry work. The museum should remain at the AFIP because there was so much that contemporary medicine could learn from the exhibits. And to glean as much as one could from those old body parts and tissue samples, the museum needed to be next door to a first-class pathology lab, not stuck off on some tourist island.

None of the Congresspeople had questions. The museum just wasn't that big an issue for them. Before moving on to the next topic, though, David asked if she had one sentence that summarized her main concern.

Alex wasn't used to talking in sound bites, but she plunged ahead anyway. "Don't separate the past from the present. It's never a good thing."

The New Jersey Congressman pushing for the move then addressed Cooper. "Do you have anything to say about that?"

The tourism guru responded, "Sometimes it's better to move on, lay the past to rest."

Alex opened her mouth to comment further, but the rules of legislative engagement did not allow it. Vance dismissed her and Cooper and they were on to the next topic, something about the Alaska Pipeline.

As Alex left the room, David whispered something to

the lawmaker sitting next to him and slipped out of the room, as well.

In the hallway, he told Alex, "You did fine."

"Thanks. It didn't feel that way."

"We had to give Quiller the chance to present his best case for the move. Just remember, though, Cooper isn't on the advisory committee; you are. There'll be a private session with just you, me, Sissy, Quiller, and the other two advisors on Monday. Then you'll have the chance to make your real case."

Alex relaxed a little and thought back to the more casual David, sitting on his living room couch. Taking in his gray suit, she said, "You've got a real Dr. Jekyll/Congressman Hyde thing going on here. Where are the cowboy boots?"

"I'm a *politician*," he said playfully, as if he were revealing some snazzy secret. "For everything I do, I've got to think, How is this going to affect my career?"

He walked her back toward the building's entrance, then smiled and shook her hand. He leaned close to her ear. "I hope you'll consider dinner sometime."

She smiled. "Hmm, how might that affect your career?"

"Wait a minute, let's think." He looked her up and down. "Feisty, beautiful, brilliant? I go out with you, people are going to think I'm a lot smarter than I am."

ON THEIR WAY BACK FROM HANDBALL THAT afternoon, Barbara asked Alex, "Any chance you can pick up Lana from practice around seven P.M. tonight?"

"No problem. What's up?"

"Wiatt's brought in a slew of auditors from the Government Accounting Office. My office is overseeing them rather than Hal's because Wiatt wants to double-check all the financial reports."

Alex shook her head. "Hal must be livid."

Barbara nodded. "When I told him they needed access to his computer password, he nearly went postal."

"Am I missing something here?"

"Well, let's just say Wiatt and Hal aren't exactly doing any male bonding. Rumor has it that Wiatt wants to bring in his own financial guy."

Alex whistled under her breath.

"That's not all," said Barbara. "I just processed papers for a Sergeant Major Derek Lander, a Special Forces guy from Wiatt's old unit, to come on as Wiatt's right-hand guy. Hal's not going to like having someone between him and the CO."

Alex was shocked. Sure, Hal could be annoying at times, and a little secretive about what was going on, but, to her, Hal *was* the AFIP. He acted like a good medical school dean—raised money, ran interference with the politicians, left the researchers alone. "Don't tell me we're going to get a new layer of bureaucracy here," said Alex. "It'll be like, like . . ."

Barbara smiled, "Like working for the government?"

Alex laughed. At heart, she didn't care who was in charge, as long as she got to continue her work with Rosie. And for that, Hal was a much better bet.

"Any rules for Lana tonight? Homework only, or can I take her to dinner?"

"If you took her for deep-dish pizza in Georgetown, I'd be forever in your debt." Barbara constantly worried about her weight. "I could live a long time without meeting any more pepperoni."

When they entered the AFIP, Barbara hugged her friend in thanks, then rushed off to mediate between Hal and the accountants.

ALEX HAD PLANNED TO WORK ON ROSIE UN-til the wee hours, but the prospect of dinner with Lana was a welcome diversion. Still, she knew that once the beeper beckoned, Wiatt would want her full-time on the Tattoo Killer case. He'd been willing to threaten her research by removing her refrigerator. Who knew what he'd try if there was a break in the case? Alex didn't want to jeopardize everything she'd worked on, so she spent about an hour that afternoon photocopying her lab notebooks. She thought of Gary Hodgen, a researcher at the National Institutes of Health, whose promising work on a morning-after pill had been thwarted some years back when a pro-life administration took office. When she'd met Hodgen at a scientific meeting after he'd quit his government job, he'd told her the chilling tale of how government officials had entered his lab at NIH and confiscated all his scientific notes, even the handwritten ones. Years of grueling experiments and observations, gone in a political heartbeat.

Wiatt was burning with his own political agenda, and Alex wanted to make sure that her work on Rosie did not get sacrificed to that fire. She made backup copies of her scientific notes, as well as a CD-ROM of the findings she'd entered into her computer.

At 6:00 P.M., she was struggling to carry two boxes of papers and books to her car when Larry, the day worker, offered his help. "Nice," he said when he saw her yellow T-Bird. Lots of men had that reaction upon seeing her classic car. She constantly got approving looks at stoplights from men in the next lane. She always assumed it was a response to the T-Bird. It never dawned on her that the classic beauty they admired was her.

While Larry held the boxes, Alex started the car in the feeble hope that she might summon a response from the fickle air conditioner, cooling the car while she rearranged the trunk to fit all that paper. The engine coughed in a new way and Alex fretted that it was nearing time for her to find yet another mechanic. She got out of the car to grab the boxes from Larry, but in the exchange of the heavy containers, she accidentally knocked the car door shut, locking her keys inside the coughing vehicle.

"Shit," she said. She looked at her watch. The last thing she wanted was to be late for Lana. There wasn't enough time to call AAA.

Alex knew that slim jims—those long, thin pieces of metal with an indention in the end to cover just this situation—were illegal in some counties. She didn't know if D.C. had outlawed them, and she wondered if she should go in to ask the guy at the desk if he had one. She hated to leave her car running like this, but wasn't sure if Larry would understand if she told him to ask the guard for a slim jim.

"Larry," she said. But he had put the two boxes on the ground and was rooting around inside them. She couldn't imagine what he was doing. She was about to chastise him for messing up her files, when he pulled the metal strip out of a green Pendaflex folder. He inserted the strip into the small opening where the window came out of the door and then pushed it down hard. The notch at the end of the metal strip touched the mechanical bar that connected the door-lock knob to the actual lock. Larry jiggled the metal strip, and a few seconds later, Alex heard a satisfying click. "You're a genius," she said to Larry. She gave him a hug, stuck the boxes in the backseat, and drove off to meet Lana.

"CAN I GET MY EARS PIERCED AFTER DIN-ner?" lana asked.

Alex opened her eyes wide and said, "Are you crazy? Your mom would kill me."

Lana giggled. She'd known it was a long shot, that there was almost no chance Alex would let it occur on her watch, but she liked to try out on Alex things that she wasn't ready to tell her mom.

"I'll tell you what," said Alex. "I'll take you to the store and we'll pick out ones that look pierced, even though they're not. Then it's up to Lieutenant Mom whether you can go all the way. Chain of command, you know."

At the store, Lana ran into a girl she knew from school and they chatted animatedly. Alex was heartened to see that Lana's deafness was not getting in the way of junior high girl talk. Alex gave them a bit of privacy and wandered the jewelry department. Alex's mother had a birthday in a few weeks; maybe she'd buy earrings for her, too.

Alex fingered the earrings that were the most shimmery, the brightest, the ones that dangled or twinkled or jingled. Ah, Janet, she thought. Her mother could sparkle like that, too. But for Janet, everything was alchemy—contingent, changeable. Alex wished her mom was more like her father, someone she could count on. Then she thought how unfair she was being. She could count on her father because he never changed. Made it difficult for her mother—or, for that matter, the men in her life—to compete with him.

Moved, in part, by guilt, Alex chose a pair of earrings that cost more than she had intended to spend. They were a dazzling combination of amethyst and turquoise. She could picture them sparkling through the long, tousled curls of her mother's dark hair. When she conjured up her mother's face, she smiled, and felt strangely comforted.

She went to the main jewelry counter to pay for the hoops that Lana picked out and the earrings for her mother. After she handed her credit card to the clerk, she noticed a necklace of small seed pearls, like Cheryl Baker was wearing on the night of her murder. Hastily, Alex purchased that, as well. She wore it out of the store, tucked underneath her black turtleneck. In the days that followed, she would touch the tiny beads through the fabric of her turtleneck as a talisman to bring her luck.

CHAPTER 13

JACK WIATT PACED THE CONFERENCE ROOM. The rage emanating from his body seemed almost visible, like heat radiating from fireplace flames. Corporal Chuck Lawndale shifted uncomfortably in his seat. Alex and Barbara looked at each other quizzically. Grant jutted out his chest as if preparing for blows. Only Dan Wilson, the veteran of so many of these investigations, seemed calm and unperturbed. Everyone was waiting to hear what Wiatt had to say, why he'd called them in on a Saturday.

"Bitch," said Wiatt. He stopped pacing and faced the group. They all knew exactly who he was talking about. The incoming chief of the FBI, Senator Gloria Devon.

The evening before, ABC aired a one-hour special on the life and death of Marilyn Mayne. Afterward, on *Nightline,* Devon, soon to be head of the FBI, was asked why the Bureau hadn't solved the case yet. She smiled generously and said it wasn't part of the FBI portfolio. With a shrug that made it seem like she'd be arresting the killer that second if it had been left to her, she explained in an exasperated tone how the case had been turned over to a certain Colonel Jack Wiatt.

Wiatt turned to the assembled team and demanded to be brought up-to-date on the progress of the investigation. "The President himself called me for an explanation for our foot-dragging." That was the term Devon had used in a follow-up interview with the *Washington Post.*

"The problem isn't on our end," said Dan, defending his team. "We've been kicking ass on the bases, but we weren't there to work the scenes when they were hot." Dan's gang was no closer to the Tattoo Killer, but their investigations had uncovered other transgressions. A petty officer boosting items from the Norfolk PX and selling them on eBay. Two cases of date rape out of the San Diego base. Alex marveled at how entwined deviance was in normal life, like dust bunnies under the bed. Shine a flashlight and all sorts of things come into focus.

Dan continued. "What's key is not what happened before—we've milked that for all it's worth. What's important is what happens next." He pointed toward a large calendar on the wall showing the killer's chilling pattern. A murder every eighteen days. It was now day fourteen. There were just a few days before he was due to strike again.

"Captain Pringle," said Wiatt, and Grant snapped to attention. "I don't care what your men are working on now. I want half of them switched to forensics. Anything that's useful for crime-scene analysis, I want your guys on it, ramping up its capability. The next crime scene, it's all-out war."

BACK IN HER LABORATORY, ALEX COULDN'T get the calendar out of her mind. Sure, she'd imagined there would be other victims, but she hadn't focused on the timetable. Right now, the killer could be stalking, choosing, maybe even exchanging a kind word with his next victim.

Would he be overweight and suburban-looking like John Wayne Gacy or a handsome man like Ted Bundy? Would there have been some incident in his past that made him kill, or was it all a matter of biology, neurotransmitters gone haywire?

Alex felt the beeper on her belt loop. She turned down the Razorbacks CD she was listening to, so that she would be sure to hear the beep when it occurred. Then she fretted that maybe the beeper wouldn't work. She'd never actually tested it.

She dialed Barbara in the legal office and asked her friend to beep her. Barbara understood immediately. "I was spooked by the calendar, too," said Barbara, "the inevitability of it."

"You read the abstract crime statistics—rapes, murders in the District," said Alex. "But this is different. This is one particular woman, and we're her only hope. Right now, she's just like us, probably at work. . . ."

"Maybe even talking to a friend . . ."

"And soon she'll be dead." There, she'd said it, that nightmarish thought that was in her mind, in all its perverted finality. "I can't stand the way Wiatt is looking at this next death as an *opportunity,* instead of a tragedy."

"Alex, don't be so harsh on him. You didn't have a Senator piss all over you on network TV last night. He's doing the best he can, just like we are."

She realized Barbara was right. "Okay," she said, and sighed. "Beep me while we're on the line, so I can tell you if it works."

A few seconds later, the cheesy notes of Paul Anka's "Having My Baby" chirped out of Alex's beeper. Alex surmised that Grant had picked this antifeminist pap just to annoy her.

"Dare we see what's on mine?" Barbara asked.

Alex beeped her and was shocked to hear the music from a black exploitation movie tinkle out of her African-American friend's beeper.

Barbara just laughed. "I've always liked the theme from *Shaft.* Maybe I'll get myself a pimp hat."

Alex laughed at the image of her well-turned-out friend in a fedora rather than her trim lieutenant's cap. "What would we do without Grant, that familiar figure of fun?"

When they hung up, Alex returned to her work on Rosie. She wondered what she would do if she didn't have Barbara to talk to.

FOR THE REST OF THE WEEKEND, THE BEEPER on the belt loop of her jeans remained eerily silent. The charged energy she felt waiting for the killer to strike next, she applied to her work with Rosie. She worked manically until the wee hours of the morning, running experiment after experiment to determine which part of the Spanish flu's genetic sequence coded for the receptor. That would be the secret to how the flu entered a healthy person's cells. A word Harding sent to her last week floated through her mind: *fugacious.* Evasive. Elusive. Untouchable. She wondered if the stress of the strangler case was too distracting, perhaps causing her to overlook a clue to the infection's trigger.

Congressman David Thorne called her on her cell phone near 11:00 P.M. on Sunday, interrupting her exasperation. "I wanted to remind you of the meeting tomorrow."

"Isn't that what you have Lil for?"

He was quiet for a moment. "Busted. I just wanted to hear your voice, try to figure out when we might get together. I hope I didn't wake you."

"Sheesh, no. In fact, I'm still at work."

"Me, too," he said. "Aren't we a pair?"

There was something about the comfortable way he said "pair" that flattered her.

"What's keeping you so late?"

"Fillibuster on the new energy bill."

"By your side or the other guy's?"

"You obviously didn't read the editorial in the *Post* this morning."

"I'm a tad busy to waste time with the political hoopla. My friend Barbara tells me it takes an average of five years to pass a bill. Think of all the time I can save by not reading any legislative articles except the ones that discuss what's actually been enacted."

David laughed. "It's refreshing to talk to a woman who isn't in my business. A breath of normality."

Now it was Alex's turn to laugh. "No one's ever said that about me before."

He asked what was keeping her so late and she explained a little about the Rosie project. He expressed the same interest in it that he'd shown in each new topic in the hearing she'd attended. Alex guessed that if your job was to help run the country, nothing was too big or small to think about.

"What will happen when you figure out the receptor?" he asked.

"Before or after I get the Nobel Prize?"

"It's that important?"

"Nah, that's just the phrase we scientists repeat as a mantra to motivate us to work long hours for little pay. But the research could revolutionize vaccine work." Alex chided herself mentally for using the word *revolutionize*. That was just the sort of thing she criticized biotech companies for—using exaggerated words to hype their work. She realized that she was doing a lame job of flirting, trying to attract him through her work. Maybe she should just invite him to dinner or something.

"I'd love to hear more about it," he said. "Would you consider dinner with me in New Jersey when the advisory committee goes up to Ellis Island?"

"Why, my dear Congressman, I thought you'd never ask."

AT THE HOUR-LONG MUSEUM COMMITTEE meeting at the Rayburn House Office Building the next day, Alex was discouraged to see how far along planning for the move was. Congressman Bob Quiller showed architectural drawings of the proposed building and recited projections for revenue from a prospective gift shop. Alex continued to press for the museum to remain in D.C. She also spent a lot of time looking at David. His jacket was off and his sleeves rolled up as he gave serious thought to all the data being presented, pro and con.

There were just six of them in the small conference room off of David's office, the three members of Congress and the three advisors. David had to keep excusing himself and leaving the room to deal with other issues that his staff brought up.

Congresswoman Sissy Clark, who was sitting next to

Alex, whispered to her, "He's not perfect, but you could do a lot worse."

Alex turned to her. "Is it that obvious?"

"No more obvious than the way he looks at you."

Alex concentrated hard to hold back a smile at the thought.

"Plus," continued Sissy, "he's been wandering around like a whupped puppy since he and Gloria split. I'm his friend and I'd like to see him happy."

DAVID CALLED AGAIN THAT EVENING, AND caught Alex in a meeting of the Task Force.

"You're on the serial-strangler case?" he asked when he learned why she couldn't talk long. "What's that got to do with infectious disease?"

What indeed, Alex thought as she walked out of the conference room into the hallway to grant herself a little privacy. "I sort of got dragged into it, to do the forensic DNA work. It's crazy, but now the case is the first thing I think about in the morning and the last thing I think about at night."

"Well, Dr. Blake, I'd love to change that. Perhaps get you thinking about a certain Texas lawmaker."

CHAPTER 14

THAT WEDNESDAY WHEN ALEX REPORTED TO Dan's conference room, there were laptops at every position on the conference table. Today was the day—eighteen days since the murder of Marilyn Mayne—when the Tattoo Killer was expected to strike. Dan was tethered to the phone, conveying assignments to men in the field.

As the other members of the team each claimed a spot at the table, Grant proudly explained what was up with the computers.

"Each one shows a map detailing a two-mile radius around several different Navy bases."

Alex looked at hers. The legend on the bottom read "Whidbey Island, Washington, Naval Air Station; Newport, Rhode Island, Naval Station; and Earle, New Jersey, Naval Weapons Station."

Grant stood behind her, touching her shoulder with his right hand. She was too entranced by the map to move it. But Barbara shot him a dirty look, and, possibly to avoid another session of sexual harassment training, he removed his hand and started explaining what would be expected of them.

"These computers are linked in real time to law enforcement headquarters near each of the thirty-eight Navy bases across the country," Grant said. "When a murder of any sort occurs, a red dot will light up to show the location of the crime."

Each person squinted at his or her screen, trying to imagine a bloody dot.

"What about attempted murder?" Barbara asked.

"Way too much data," said Grant. "Do you know how many people try to knock off other people every day in America? More people get killed each year in the United States than were killed during Kosovo's ethnic cleansing during the 1999 war. If I included attempted murders, it'd swamp this system."

"But," he continued, "I've set it up so that if the attempted murder involved strangulation, a blue dot will appear."

God bless America, thought Alex, home of the brave and land of the violent. She recalled her first day in the ER at Columbia-Presbyterian Hospital when she was a fourth-year medical student. A young Hispanic woman was brought in with rope burns around her wrists from where her boyfriend had tied her to a chair and a concussion from his hitting her with a baseball bat. Alex had been shocked to learn that the ER had fact sheets in thirteen languages about follow-up care for rope burns. Plus a support group for women whose boyfriends had hit them with sports equipment—Louisville Sluggers, titanium golf clubs, and, in one case, a Heisman Trophy.

Alex was studying genetics at the time and wondered, like many in her field, whether there was a gene for violence and whether the American melting pot had somehow bred more of it. *U.S. News & World Report* certainly thought so. They ran a cover with a baby in prison stripes with the headline BORN BAD, reporting on a gene mutation related to monoamine oxidase deficiency, which supposedly caused criminal aggression.

Stephen Mobley, a Georgia man convicted of killing a twenty-four-year-old Domino's pizza manager, asked to be tested for the errant gene. He wanted to argue "My genes made me do it."

Mobley was hardly a sympathetic character—he'd proudly tattooed the word *Domino* on his back and deco-

rated his cell with a pizza box from the chain. He wanted
to convince the judge that the aggression gene ran in his
family, since his relatives were divided between successful
businessmen and men of violence, two sides of the same
genetic coin. It was the same with disease genes: They
brought both good and bad. If you inherited one copy of
the sickle cell anemia gene, you were protected against
malaria. If you got two copies—one from each parent—
you suffered from the potentially devastating disease,
sickle cell anemia. Mobley never got to make his genetic
defense. Since the successful businessmen side of the
family were paying his legal fees, the last thing they
wanted was someone snooping around in the family genes.

"Fish on the line," yelled Chuck Lawndale. Grant
moved to his side and told him to click his mouse on the
icon of a phone. The image from Chuck's screen was
transmitted to the large screen on the wall for all to see. A
red dot near one of the Texas bases. Chuck was hooked
via phone to police headquarters in Ingleside, Texas, near
the Navy base there.

Dan hung up his call and joined Grant behind Chuck just
as the speaker on Chuck's laptop relayed the phone connection from Ingleside. Dan talked to the dispatcher there.
"What have you got?" he asked after a brief introduction.

"Man shot his wife," she said.

Dan got off the line and looked at Grant in frustration.
Then he turned to the team at the table. "Okay, listen up.
You each will take over the prelims on the calls. Pull me in
only if it seems linked to our guy."

Over the next hour, a dozen red dots appeared. For
eight of them, a friend or relative was implicated. "You
only hurt the ones you love," Grant said, deadpan.

Barbara quoted the national crime statistics. "Only one
in five murders is done by a stranger."

Two more murders were reported over the next two
hours, but neither matched the serial strangler's MO. It
was early yet. The four murders he'd committed so far had
all occurred later in the evening.

Time passed and they continued in this convoluted, depressing variation of bingo. Alex got the first blue dot at 10:00 P.M. "Hey, I've got something indicating strangulation here," she said.

She clicked on the phone icon and reached the chief of police for Oak Harbor, Washington, where the Whidbey base was located. She asked him about the details of the crime. "Victim was admitted to intensive care about an hour ago with rope burns around the neck."

"Did the victim give a description of the assailant?"

"The vic's still unconscious. He was found by the landlord."

"Did you say *he*?"

"Yes, ma'am," said the young Oak Harbor police officer with embarrassment in his voice. "Doctor says it was some sort of, uh, autosomething sex thing."

"Autoerotic asphyxia?"

"Yeah."

Definitely not their guy.

The dots continued to pepper the screen well through the night. Dan told the team at midnight that he'd bring in a fresh set of eyes, if anyone wanted to leave. But no one did. They were drawn to their screens with a macabre fascination. With the frustration of gamblers laying down more chips on the assumption their luck would change, each one thought the next dot would help them catch the killer.

THE NEXT MORNING, THE RAGGED BUZZ OF Alex's alarm clock seemed more piercing and angry than usual. Her heart flopped oddly as she awoke, a familiar quirk of her body when she hadn't gotten enough sleep. She'd left the AFIP at 5:00 A.M. The flashing lights had finally slowed down around then, indicating that even murderers and stranglers needed some rest.

She'd gotten just three hours' worth herself. A faint purple shadow arced under each eye. When she saw it in the mirror, she started riffling through the cabinet under her bathroom sink for makeup that she'd tossed there a few months earlier, the last time she'd dressed up.

She groomed with extra care, combing her hair down in waves over the shoulders of a silk blouse, then made her way to the Rayburn House Office Building.

Sissy could read her disappointment as she looked around the conference room and saw that David was not there. "He's doing an interview with NPR. They're interviewing him about Sheila."

Alex must have looked startled.

"The hurricane, honey," said Sissy. "The one that is crossing the Gulf of Mexico to strike Texas."

Between Rosie and the Task Force, Alex had been too busy to keep up on meteorological forecasts. But later that afternoon, David called her at the AFIP. She described the chilling way that she'd spent the evening and how a different set of watchers were manning the laptops tonight. "We've got so little on the killer," she told him. "We'd all deluded ourselves that at least we had his pattern. That all we'd have to do is wait out the eighteen days and then we'd somehow be able to nab him."

On previous nights, Alex and David had fallen into an easy combination of chatter and flirtation. Now, her tone was weary and discouraged, and David's matched it. "It looks like it is going to be a direct hit on Galveston," he said. "The governor's asked me to come back and walk the area with him after it touches down."

"When are you leaving?" Alex asked, disappointed that he might miss their trip to Ellis Island. She felt that a reprieve from the case would allow her to see something in the killer's pattern that she was currently missing. Not to mention wanting the chance to be with David outside of his overscheduled life in the District.

"Tonight. I'll try to make it back for the trip to New Jersey. I'm desperate to spend some time with you."

He went on to describe the chaos that would occur if Galveston was hit. "The main hospital for the region is there, University of Texas at Galveston. If that's struck, we're going to have a helluva time getting medical care to the injured. No other facility in the area has enough of a supply of painkillers and antibiotics."

Alex thought about it. "I've got some friends at the CDC. They keep emergency reserves for epidemics of infectious disease. I could ask them if they'd ship a supply from Atlanta tonight."

"You would do that?"

"Of course. Just have Lil let me know where to send it."

After she hung up, she wandered down the hall back to the conference room, unable to stay away. Three hours of sleep or not, she wanted to do anything she could to move the investigation along.

CHAPTER 15

ALEX TOOK HER DESIGNATED SEAT IN AN empty first-class compartment of the Metroliner. She pulled a copy of the British journal *Nature Genetics* out of her saddlebag, pulled off her cowboy boots, and put her stocking feet up on the seat across from her. Just as the train was about to pull out of the station, Congressman David Thorne pushed open the sliding doors of the compartment and joined her. She smiled broadly.

He seemed to relax instantly, as if he'd finally come to the end of a long journey. He bent down and kissed her cheek.

"The CDC came through, just like you promised," he said, setting a red shopping bag down on an empty seat and placing his briefcase on the rack. "Painkillers, antibiotics. The governor's in your debt."

"Glad to help," she said.

He sat down on the plush seat next to hers. She noticed that his eyes seemed dulled, encircled in a tired darkness.

"I heard the death toll's over a hundred," said Alex.

He nodded somberly. "Including the woman who ran my Amarillo office. She was in Galveston on vacation."

"Oh no. In the hotel that collapsed?"

He nodded. "I went to the funeral in Fort Worth this morning, then raced to the airport. I'd done all I could down there . . . and I didn't want to miss this chance with you."

Alex was touched. She listened to the hum of the train

and felt the frisson of sexual tension between them. The train moved along, making a few stops on the outskirts of D.C.

"It's amazing we've still got the compartment to ourselves," she said.

"Not that amazing." He pulled a wad of train tickets out of the pocket of his navy blue blazer. "I bought out the whole car."

Alex tried to suppress a smile. "I hope the government auditors don't find out."

"Not a dime of the taxpayers' money. That's one good thing about Papa owning a ranch the size of Rhode Island. I'm one of the few legislators who can't be bought. And once in awhile, I give myself a big splurge."

"So you're used to getting whatever you want?"

"Nah, I'm used to earning it. It irritated the hell out of me when I was a teenager, but my parents didn't believe in spoiling us. I worked every aspect of the business, from typing invoices to cleaning the slaughterhouse, before I finished college. Even now, I live entirely on the salary I make in Congress. Figure I can't represent people in my district if I can't identify with them. Have to know what it's like to make ends meet when the roof starts to leak."

"Whoa," said Alex. "Didn't you guys just vote yourself a pay raise? A hundred and fifty thousand dollars buys a pile of roof tiles."

"Busted," said David. He shook his head and smiled. "I know it sounds like a lot, but you've never had to open an office in your home state."

No, thought Alex, I don't even have a home state. She'd never lived anywhere more than a few years.

"Honestly, I don't know what I'd do if I wasn't in office," he said almost to himself.

"How can you keep 'em down on the farm after they've seen D.C.?"

David smiled and reached into the red shopping bag and pulled out sandwiches wrapped in tinfoil.

"Don't tell me your arts degree included the culinary arts, as well?" said Alex.

"No, I do cook—but these babies I picked up this morning at Bryant's BBQ in Fort Worth." He held one of the dripping sandwiches up to her mouth. "They've got a great Cajun sauce."

"Yikes," she said as she bit into it. "Spicy but heavenly."

She took another bite, and then he put the sandwich on a plastic plate and started unwrapping a few others.

"Did you see your parents when you were back?"

"Ouch, you know how to push those guilt buttons, don't you? That's always a conflict for me. My staff stacks me up with so many appearances—and truth be told, I love that part of the job. I've got a particular penchant for visiting train stations and bowling alleys."

"An odd combination."

"Yeah, Lil says I'm a kid who's never grown up. An eighth grader who shadowed me for one day for a school project told his class I get to goof off all day."

"I've seen you be mighty serious and get things done."

"Yeah, it's a schizophrenic job." David put the plate of sandwiches down and shifted in his seat until he faced her. "You hardly ever talk about your family. Where'd you grow up?"

"Oh, here and there," she said, reaching for more BBQ.

He pulled the plate of sandwiches out of her reach, shaking his head. "I pour out my hard-luck life from bullshit to business, practically right down to my grandma's grits and blueberry pancakes, and that's all you cough up in return? C'mon, we've got hours to go."

He waved the plate under her nose, bribing her to talk.

Alex hesitated. She looked out the window. Trees whizzed by in a slight blur, an Impressionist painting. Then she looked at David's handsome face.

"Well, nearly everyone has seen a photo of my mom. She was the flower child in a 1968 AP wire photo, handing a canister of tear gas back to a Chicago cop at the Democratic National Convention."

David nodded with interest. "It's as famous a photo as the student next to the body at Kent State."

He reached up and moved Alex's curls to the side. He looked at her face, comparing it to his memory of the famous picture. "The girl in the photo had long dark hair, if I remember right," he said.

"My dad was the blond, Sergeant Alexander Northfield Blake, U.S. Air Force."

"The protestor and the pilot? A modern-day Romeo and Juliet?"

Alex nodded. "When Janet—that's my mom—and her antiwar buddies marched on the Pentagon, Sergeant Blake had the guts to join her on the dais to dispute her facts."

"If she was anything like you, I can understand the chemistry."

"Apparently they were hot. A month later, she married him, much to the chagrin of her activist friends."

Alex rewarded herself with a bite of BBQ.

"And then they added a spunky little girl to the equation," he said.

She smiled. "My first memories are a blur of music and incense. Lots of my mom's friends would stay with her and me, sleeping on the floor of our Cleveland apartment while my dad was away in the war. Instead of coloring books, I filled in reds and blues of block-lettered placards: 'Hell no, we won't go.' 'Impeach Nixon.' I was outside a lot, at concerts and rallies. I was happy."

"Are they still together?"

Alex had forgotten that he didn't know the end of the story. She shook her head. "I was five when the war ended. Dad was supposed to come home for a month before his next assignment. We decorated the apartment with streamers. One of my mother's friends added a photo of my folks to a 'Make Love, Not War' poster. A bunch of them came over to welcome him back.

"Then the telegram arrived. I didn't understand at first. People huddled around my mother and nobody seemed to notice when the music ended and the reel-to-reel tape kept circling, with a little *pfft* each time the last two inches of it hit the other reel. I just watched it. I was too scared to move into that quivering hub of people around my mom.

"The telegram said he'd been killed in Vietnam, the day after the war officially ended."

"God, Alex, I'm so sorry."

Alex's body grew stiff, her eyes distant as she remembered the aftermath. "After he died, my mother slept constantly. I could hardly fall asleep at all. In the middle of the night, I'd open the bathroom cabinet and sniff my dad's Old Spice."

She turned to David, her nose close to his neck, inhaling his aftershave.

David put his arms around her, leaned her head against his shoulder, and they just listened to the muffled clatter of the train.

Alex wondered what had come over her. She never talked about that day when she was five, not even to Barbara or Luke. And here she was, spilling her guts to some guy she barely knew. No, not just some guy, David. Someone who seemed more real, more capable of commitment than the men who'd previously made pit stops in her life.

The train stopped abruptly, bringing Alex back to the present. She tilted her head back and let David kiss her.

CHAPTER 16

IT WAS AROUND 7:00 P.M. WHEN THEY AR-
rived in Jersey City. When they checked into the Hyatt Re-
gency, they were assigned neighboring rooms. "Did you
get Lil to do this, too?" Alex asked.

"Wish I'd thought of it, but it was just chance."

They left their bags with the bellman and went off to
explore the city. David chose a seafood restaurant looking
out at Lady Liberty.

"Are you sure you don't have some speech you'll have
to run off to tonight?" Alex asked teasingly once they
were seated.

"Actually, three. I was supposed to be the cocktail
speaker at an ACLU fund-raiser, the dinner host at a Kiwanis meeting, and the after-dinner raconteur for the
steamfitters' union. The typical life of a lawmaker. I
thought it was more important to get to know you."

"How'd you clear it with Lil?"

"A little horse trading. Sissy's going to do the ACLU
and Kiwanis gigs. Few groups actually want to hear me.
They just want some token member of Congress so they
can go home to Kansas or Montana and say they were
hobnobbing with some government official."

"So you're all interchangeable?"

"Not all of us. Nobody takes Gloria Devon's place. If
she's booked for a speech, there are no substitutes."

Great, thought Alex. Is it some rule of the universe that

the first time you go to dinner with a man, he has to talk about an ex? Gloria Devon had ticked off Wiatt big-time, but Alex had to give the woman credit for her political instincts. "I watched her Senate confirmation hearing a few weeks ago. No matter how the Republicans tried to trip her up, she gave just as well as she got."

"Yeah, I knew she'd sail through the committee the second I saw her shoes."

"Her shoes?"

He chuckled. "She was wearing her red high heels. Calls them her lady luck shoes."

Their appetizers arrived and the waiter made a show of explaining the background of each dish. Alex was a little surprised at the sting she had felt about his easy intimacy with the Senator. God, she barely knew the man. What was happening to that famed Alexandra Blake cool?

"What about the steamfitters' speech?" she asked, changing the subject.

"A certain blond actress friend of mine is in the play *The Violet Hour* at the Kennedy Center. She'll make an after-dinner appearance and everyone will wonder why they'd invited me in the first place."

AFTER THEY ATE, THEY WALKED ALONG THE waterfront. "I didn't realize Ellis Island was so close," said Alex.

"Thirteen hundred feet. I know because Congressman Quiller is lobbying for the feds to build a bridge from here to there." David leapt up on a park bench and began a Quiller-style oration: "A monument with the heritage and history of Ellis Island shouldn't be held hostage to the ferryboat monopoly."

David jumped down and continued. "He's actually got a point. My instincts tell me he's lobbying to move the museum just so we'll give him his bridge."

Alex faced the water once again, enjoying the breathtaking view of the Statue of Liberty in moonlight. She turned to David. "I feel guilty about taking this time for

myself. I keep thinking there's a woman out there, somebody's daughter, somebody's wife . . ."

David held her, calming her in mid-sentence. "One day
away won't make a difference. From what I see in the papers, there are a helluva lot of investigators on the case."

"It's odd. My research on infectious diseases deals
with death, too, but for murder, the timetable seems more
urgent."

He gently took her hand as they walked back to the hotel and retrieved their bags. When they reached the ninth
floor, David walked up to his door and Alex to hers. Then
he dropped his overstuffed briefcase on the floor, strode
over to her side, and took her in his arms for a sizzling kiss.

The elevator dinged and the couple who got off applauded them.

Alex smiled. "Grab your bag," she said.

She backed into the room, and he followed, face to
hers, his hanging briefcase slung over his back. They remained inches from each other until she backed onto the
bed and he lay down next to her, his head propped on his
hand, elbow on the bed. Alex's blond curls were fanned
out around her head in a halo. David still had his bag attached to his side. He kissed her gently on the forehead,
then got up, neatly moved their bags to the side of the
room, and put his blazer on the back of a chair. He returned to the bed. She was lying on her back, her legs dangling over the side. He pulled off her cowboy boots in one
fluid motion.

"The steamfitters don't know what they're missing,"
she said.

She unbuttoned his shirt and he took it off, dropping it
on the floor alongside the bed. She stripped down to her
black turtleneck and black bikini underpants. And then he
began to help her. He gently pulled the shirt over her head,
caressing her hair back into place after the whoosh of the
turtleneck had fanned it out wildly. Then he tackled the
bikinis with considerably more lust.

She reached over and unzipped his khaki slacks. He removed his remaining clothes, covered her body with his, and gave her a bouquet of kisses—light kisses on the forehead, teasing licks on the neck, slippery long circles around her nipples, feathery touches on the inside of her thighs. Then he sat her on the edge of the bed and his tongue began an excruciatingly delightful journey until she was almost begging to be brought to a climax.

She pulled away from him and invited him to lie on the bed. She mounted him, and, grabbing on to the headboard, moved back and forth with him inside her. He got harder and harder, and she pulled back, knelt over him, and teased the tip of his cock with her tongue. When he was groaning with pleasure, she put him back inside of her. He flipped them both over, and they moved together to a shattering orgasm.

"If I'd known that committee meetings could be such fun," she said, her breath still coming in quick bursts. "I might have volunteered for public service long before this."

He let out a satisfied moan. "You're much too good for government work," he said. He kissed the tip of her nose and then pulled her up against him, her head nestled on his shoulder. They dozed briefly in that comfortable, comforting position.

His cell phone woke them about 11:30 P.M. He hesitated answering it. He checked the caller's phone number and seemed surprised. "Hello," he said in a whisper. And then walked into the bathroom to take the call in private.

Alex wondered who would be calling at that hour. If it had been Lil, he'd have taken the call in front of her. Perhaps the blond actress was reporting in. Alex hated herself for the tinge of jealousy. She was still sticky inside, and he was already on the phone with someone else. In her bathroom, no less. Plus, she had to pee.

Alex laughed at herself. She could imagine the *Cosmopolitan* magazine quiz about it: "How to tell if the government official you barely know is cheating on you: (A) He takes personal calls in the bathroom. (B) He comes home with a new tattoo, which says Thelma."

She hadn't yet gotten to *C* when David came out of the bathroom and started putting on his clothes. When he noticed she was awake, he sat on the side of the bed and stroked her hair. "I'm so sorry, Alex. Something's come up. I need to go."

"Let me guess, a speech to the Nocturnal Order of Police?"

"Don't make light of us. I'd like nothing more than to stay. Get some rest. We're going to take a boat ride past that interesting lady with the torch in the morning."

The door closed behind him a few minutes later. Alex briefly toyed with getting out of bed to hook the latch on the door and do a little work on her laptop. But she just rolled over instead. The world was made of two types of men, she told herself. Those who stay and those who go. She always found herself with those who go.

CHAPTER 17

ALEX AWOKE, ALONE IN BED, TO A STRANGE sound of creaking and rolling wheels in the hallway outside of her door. A knock. "Room service," a voice said.

"I didn't order any," she yelled from the bed.

She heard the electronic pop of a key opening the door, and sat up, frozen in fear. The autopsy photo of Marilyn Mayne popped into her mind.

A rolling table nosed its way into the room and Alex leapt out of bed and grabbed the lamp. Behind the table stood a man.

David.

He looked at her defensive pose—warriorlike, hand around the lamp base—and laughed. The tension in her eyes eased and she said, in mock annoyance, "You scared the hell out of me."

He smiled. "It was worth it. I got to see your naked Statue of Liberty impression."

He moved a chair next to the table. "Let me make it up to you," he said. With a flourish, he pulled the silver lid off a plate. "Seafood crepes."

She wrapped the sheet around herself and sat in the chair. He stood next to her and drew her close to him, smoothing her hair with comforting strokes. "Sorry," he said. "I sometimes get carried away."

"It's just . . . this case."

"Of course."

She pointed to the tray. "How'd you pull this off?"

"I flashed my voting record down in the kitchen. Said I'd voted to increase the minimum wage."

ON THE FERRY RIDE TO ELLIS ISLAND, ALEX and David were surrounded by New Jersey lobbyists and constituents who were pushing to have the medical museum moved to the island. A cute tawny-haired woman from a consumer medical-supply company envisioned a sales booth at the new museum. Several owners of construction companies wanted the contract to build the new facility. A member of the New Jersey teachers' union thought schools should hold classes there. Alex didn't know how David could live in a world of that many people sucking up to him. The lobbyists nodded or winked at their local Congressman, Bob Quiller, but didn't bother talking to him. They already had Quiller's vote to move the museum from Washington to Ellis Island.

Alex had never felt so, well, invisible. If Pamela Anderson had waltzed in and removed her clothes, none of these guys would have glanced her way. If you didn't have the legislative juice, you just didn't exist.

Quiller saw that Alex had been shut out of the circle around David, and he joined her next to the rail. He was wearing a brown suit and his trademark bow tie. He was an inch shorter than Alex, which made her wonder how he'd gotten elected. Didn't the taller guy always win? But there was something about his wiry energy that overcame his short stature and balding head. She'd been reading about his background and knew that, though they clashed on the museum issue, he meant well. He'd done a lot for his district, particularly for immigrants. He'd seeded social programs for Ukranians, Cambodians, and Syrians, following each new wave of settlers.

Quiller nodded over at the crowd surrounding David. "That sort of raw adulation makes us all think we are far more interesting than we really are," Quiller said to her. "It can also make some politicians think they're invulnerable."

"Like Gary Hart," said Alex.

"What a moron!" replied Quiller. "A reporter suggests Hart might be cheating on his wife, and Hart has the audacity to deny it and challenge the reporter to tail him."

"I remember the photo of him with Donna Rice, who was wearing some skimpy outfit and sitting on his lap. Hello reporters, good-bye presidency."

"And what about my colleague Dan Rostenkowski?" Quiller said, shaking his head. "Thirty-six years in Congress, chairman of the powerful Ways and Means Committee, and he couldn't keep his hand out of the public cookie jar. Spent seventeen months in prison on a felony conviction. You would think those of us who make the laws would be a little more careful to avoid breaking them."

The north end of Ellis Island came into sight. Quiller pointed to a dramatic Beaux Arts structure. "As many as seven thousand immigrants a day passed through that building, hoping to be admitted to a new life," he said. "Then in 1954, with changing immigration patterns and fewer people arriving by ship, the center was closed. The feds just came in and turned off the lights."

"I thought Lee Iacocca changed that during the Bicentennial."

"He raised funds to renovate the north side. But there are more than thirty buildings on the south side—most of them former medical buildings that are just rotting away."

A half hour later, Alex saw what Quiller meant when he led the advisory committee, lobbyists, and constituents on a tour of the main hospital building. The exterior was covered with shrubs and vines, and weeds grew in the gutters. Inside, water was seeping in, rusting and rotting anything in its path.

"In 1997, the National Trust for Historic Preservation put this building on its list of America's Eleven Most Endangered Places," Quiller said to the group. He and David were standing on a raised platform with Sissy, who'd arrived on an earlier ferry.

"These buildings are an important part of our heritage

and clearly need protecting," David said. "But why use them as a medical museum?"

"Because the great U.S. Public Health Service started right on this island," said Quiller. "When the immigrants climbed the stairs in the main building, the medical exam began. Doctors eyeballed the immigrants and put a chalk mark on the backs of people with possible problems, *E* if you had a problem with your eyes, *P* for lungs, *Ct* for trachoma, *L* for lameness."

"That hardly sounds like a medical system that you want to celebrate," said Sissy. Then she used some of the information Alex had briefed her with during an earlier meeting. "A six-second exam would mean the difference between getting into America or making the grueling trip back. And weren't the boat companies charged a fee if the people they brought over weren't healthy?"

"You're right that people with incurable or dangerous diseases were sent back, but only two percent of the people were ruled out," said Quiller. "In five times that many cases, the people were treated in one of the dozen buildings here and then allowed to enter the country."

While Quiller droned on about the need for a museum, Alex went to the window to look at the other medical buildings. She stared out at what had been the contagious disease buildings—stucco over brick, with rotting red clay tiles. A verandalike corridor linked those buildings, its wide spaces reflecting the state-of-the-art thinking of the 1930s about how to prevent transmission of infectious diseases.

Alex recalled the saga of her great-grandmother Ava, who had come from Hungary when she was fifteen. She had a slight limp, and a doctor had chalked the letter *L* on the back of her jacket, along with the letter *B*, indicating she should be returned to Eastern Europe. But Ava had not come this close to Lady Liberty to give it all up and return. She'd nervously turned her coat inside out so the letters didn't show. Then she'd waited in terror to see if she would be discovered and denied the chance to enter America.

Alex's mother said Ava's passage had cost three hundred dollars. But Alex knew there was no way to measure the real cost. Giving up her friends in Hungary. Even giving up her last name, which had too many syllables for the immigration officials to manage. She was reinvented as Ava Heller.

Perhaps a willingness to remake oneself ran in the genes. In all their moves, Alex's mother had tried on new identities. There was even that fling with her dead husband's best buddy. But the nightmare of memories that relationship had evoked proved to be too much for both of them.

And what about Alex? Who would she ultimately be? She'd flitted from internship to fellowship to a brief stint of teaching, and now a two-year commitment to the AFIP. Did the lettering of her base pairs spell out a predisposition to wanderlust? Or had she just not found the right spot yet?

Alex noticed that David was speaking again, and she moved closer to the platform to hear him. It was odd to think this handsome man in a gray suit had been inside her twelve hours earlier. She was reliving that moment when she felt a flutter below her waist. At first, she thought her sexual urges were a little more vivid than usual. Then she realized it was her new pager, the one for the Tattoo Killer. She had put it on vibrate.

Major Dan Wilson answered when she dialed the glowing number with her cell phone. "I'm on a Lear out of Andrews. There's a chopper to La Guardia waiting for you at the Southport terminal. They'll hold United flight 679 for you to Chicago."

"He's killed again?"

"A librarian on the Great Lakes Naval Base itself. They've closed off the crime scene until we get there."

She didn't wait for the next ferry, or even to say a proper good-bye to David. She hitched a ride on a police boat. The deserted medical buildings were disturbing. Like her great-grandmother, she was glad to get off the island.

C H A P T E R   1 8

GREAT LAKES NAVAL BASE, WITH ITS POPU-
lation of twenty-five thousand, was larger than the
Chicago suburb abutting it. As her limo rolled onto the
grounds, Alex saw a hospital, churches, restaurants, a
child-care center, even a television station. Great Lakes
not only served as the primary boot camp for the Navy; it
also offered its enlistees college courses from five local
universities. The base was a world of its own.

Captain Grant Pringle met her at the entrance to the
education center. Alex wondered if he stood in his pecu-
liar way, leaning one shoulder forward, to show off the results of his workouts. He reminded her of the old-time Mr.
Universes, always posing in a way to make their muscles
ripple.

"Dan's inside," Grant said. "He's managed to piss off
the entire chain of command by closing off the library until you got here."

Alex didn't need Barbara's lipreading power to get the
gist of what was going on two hundred feet down the hall
as Dan and a Great Lakes officer sparred. As she got
closer, she could hear the officer arguing that he was in
charge of the building and expected his own men to work
the case.

Dan introduced Alex to the red-faced officer, Chief
Warrant Officer Doug Mitchell, who rolled his eyes at the
indignity of having had to wait for some *girl*. The officer

said to Alex, "Are you sure you can handle this? There's a lot of gore in there."

"I worked the ER when I was at Columbia Medical School. We had one gang fight where a guy's testicles were cut off and shoved up his nose."

The warrant officer grimaced, his hand involuntarily moving to protect his manhood. Ah, thought Alex, the universal gesture of male panic.

"Well, Doc," he said bitterly, "let's see what you make of our body."

Chief Warrant Officer Mitchell opened a pair of heavy mahogany doors and led Alex, Dan, and Grant into what looked like the library of a small college. The books had a different focus, though. Books on battles and boats, guns and cannons, strategy and spying. Grant stopped to look in a glass case with a hefty book open inside. "They've got a first edition Francis Dawson," Grant said. Alex looked at the title, *Reminiscences of Confederate Service, 1861–1865*.

"It's worth at least ten grand, easy," he said to Alex as they rounded the next set of stacks and the body came into view.

Unlike the other women, Madeline James had fought hard. He'd beaten her badly, sliced her all over the body. Blood streamed out of her in every direction.

Mitchell looked at Alex to see how she'd react. She merely knelt next to the woman and wriggled latex gloves onto her hands. Grant Pringle, though, took one look at the mangled corpse, walked briskly to the circulation desk, and threw up in a garbage can.

Dan knelt next to Alex, rolled up the sleeves of his wrinkled shirt, and pulled gloves on his hands, as well.

"You've got to love a guy like Grant," Alex said to Dan. "He can design a weapon to wipe out a village from a thousand miles away, but he can't stomach one bloody corpse close-up."

Dan pointed out that the killer had cleared away the blood from her left breast to stencil on the tattoo. Alex sniffed the antibacterial smell on that breast, just as the San Diego pathologist had mentioned. Dan reached into his jacket pocket and removed the printout of the twelve pieces of the imagined complete tattoo. "We've got the part from the lower-right quadrant, more claws of the bird."

"She fought back, so there's bound to be DNA under her fingernails," Alex said.

Dan gently lifted her right arm from the pool of blood. The hands had been cut off at the wrist.

Something sparkled in the mire of muscle and bone that used to be her wrist. Dan carefully extracted the gold object. A charm bracelet.

He stood up and addressed Mitchell. "Let me get this straight, Officer," Dan said. "A guy waltzes in, spends, I would guess, forty or fifty minutes cutting up and tattooing a woman without anyone hearing her scream, and then he waltzes out covered in blood with a doggie bag of extremities. What kind of operation are you running?"

A more composed Grant joined them. "The library has soundproof walls," he pointed out. "Probably so people can study here."

The officer nodded. "With military cutbacks, we needed funds from the state to maintain the library. They made it a state repository. Any citizen has to be allowed access."

Dan slowly turned, taking in the space around him, assessing doors and windows, trying to feel the presence of the killer. "The guy would have come in at a busy time and hid out until she was alone and closing up," he said.

Officer Mitchell thought for a moment. "He could have left during the three A.M. shift change. There are fewer people securing the perimeter then."

A stocky photographer from base security finished taking pictures of the body and photographed the slashed and tattered slacks and shirt the killer had removed from the woman. They were covered in blood, no more than mere rags at this point, but the killer had folded them neatly and placed them to one side.

Grant used one of the new props his team had created in the wake of Wiatt's urging: a handheld computerized hair and fiber analyzer. "The woman's got a cat, that's for sure. The fibers on the back of her clothes are the same as on the front, and they're pretty uniform. On what used to be the seat of her pants, I've found fibers that match her chair here, some other upholstery fabric that probably matches her home, the cat hair, and her own. I don't see any hair that could have come from a man."

"Short military cut, then?" Dan asked. "Or maybe shaved bald? He would have stuck out with a stocking cap or nylon over his head."

Alex watched Grant flood the body with blue iridescent light. Then he aimed the light in increasing wide circles around the body, but no telltale pattern of semen emerged.

"Try around her left breast," said Alex. "I think he cleans up after himself. Maybe saliva, maybe semen."

Grant stood above the woman's body and the blue light danced over every centimeter of the librarian's body, but still no sperm or saliva. Alex crossed her fingers that the flood of blood around the woman contained some blood of the killer, too. She doubted it. There were no telltale blood spots tracing his exit from the room. A phantom indeed.

"Dan, may I clean the other breast?" she asked.

Dan nodded, indicating the photographer had finished his work. Alex cleansed the right breast and then compared the two. She was grateful that the crime scene had made even Grant somber. She had no idea what she'd do if he'd made a crack about the woman's breasts.

Alex looked closely, comparing the right and left breasts, and noticed the tattooed one had a little ridge that the right one didn't. She gestured excitedly to Dan to look. "I think we have some teeth marks here."

Dan called the autopsy suite at AFIP, telling them to have the plaster ready for an impression at the three o'clock mark on the left breast. Madeline James would be flown there for her last medical work-up.

Alex put her head close to the bruised and bloody

vaginal area of the woman. She sniffed. "Another cherry condom."

"I guess you came a long way for nothing," Grant said to her.

Alex stood up and turned to Officer Mitchell. "If he hid until closing time and then didn't leave until three A.M., he was perched somewhere. He probably took a leak. Where's the bathroom?"

He nodded over toward the way they'd entered.

"Too public, too close to the circulation desk," Dan said. "Where else have you got one?"

"There's one near the stairs in the third-floor stacks."

Alex, Grant, and Dan followed him. She noticed wooden tables and chairs scattered around the third-floor stacks. One of the tables had a book on it, open about a third of the way through.

She looked at the shelves near the table. Two of them were filled with fiction—novels by Lee Child, Tom Clancy, Clive Cussler, Ian Fleming.

"Dust the book," she said to Grant, feeling the flush of the hunt.

Grant reached into the kit he was carrying and used a camel-hair brush to put a thin layer of a black dust over the volume. "No fresh prints, but lots of smudges, like the guy was wearing gloves."

He continued working the scene, focusing on the area the killer's feet would have touched. "I want any shoe prints, any soil or grass that he might have stepped in," Dan said to him.

Alex waited until they were done with the book. Then she took her gloved hand and moved it slightly so she could read the title. Pat Conroy's *The Great Santini*.

She led the way to the bathroom.

"Gloves on him, there aren't going to be any prints here, either," said Grant.

Alex had another plan. "Let's assume he kept the gloves on to take a leak. He held his penis, shook it, and a microscopic bit of skin might have flecked off. Find that for me and I'll tell you his DNA type."

♦ ♦ ♦

ALEX LOOKED OVER THE ASSEMBLED NAVY personnel, the twenty-three men who had used the library the previous evening. Mostly young, in their early twenties, mostly black. Serial killers were almost always white. But Alex was going to take DNA from all of them to compare to any DNA later identified as the murderer's. At that moment, people were searching these soldiers' rooms on the base, but it was unlikely the killer was a local.

All of the men described everyone they'd seen in the library, but it just looped around to others in this room. No one had been to the third-floor stacks. No one had seen a stranger.

Under the forensic DNA protocol, Alex was required to ask permission before taking a blood sample from each of the men because she did not have probable cause to suspect anyone individually. As she walked down the rows of the men standing tall, she got little resistance, not even a question as they stuck out their arms. Most people thought of soldiers as programmed to kill, but they were also programmed to obey. Look at the flash, the Army had told the soldiers at Los Alamos when they detonated the bomb. And they had.

The oldest man in the group, Lieutenant Tim Wieger, did not extend his arm. "I'm not willing to undergo a DNA test. I'm not a suspect."

"You were in the library, weren't you?" Dan asked him.

"Far as I can tell, reading *Newsweek* is not yet a federal offense."

Dan dismissed the other soldiers after they'd been sampled. He led Lieutenant Wieger into a room, gave him a cup of coffee, and ordered him to wait while he got a warrant.

Dan and Alex phoned Wiatt from the warrant officer's desk. He patched in Barbara. "He's right," Barbara said. "You don't have enough to make him give a blood sample if he refuses. It would violate the Fourth Amendment, no probable cause. Here's how the U.S. Supreme Court views it: The body is a temple; you don't mess with someone's body unless you have a very good reason."

"I thought that's what you might say," Dan responded. "So I gave him some coffee. When he leaves the room, we'll have his saliva on the cup. What's the legality of testing that?"

"Wait a minute," said Alex. "That's not how I do business." She respected Dan and it pained her to go up against him.

"What do you mean?" Dan asked.

"If it becomes legal to test DNA in that way, think what would happen. Employers would offer you a drink, then run your DNA and refuse to hire you if you had the gene for a disease that would show up later and increase their health-care costs."

Wiatt's voice crackled across the phone line, sounding annoyed. "This is a criminal investigation. You know how much is riding on it."

"He's not a real suspect," said Alex. "He's too old for the psychological profile, he's got too much hair for the crime scene evidence, why go there?"

Barbara piped up. "I'm sorry, Alex, but the case law's against you. Once he leaves the room, that saliva is considered garbage. Anybody can do anything they want with it. I'm willing to go to court on this one. It's a no-brainer."

"That's how we tracked down the Unabomber," said Dan. "DNA testing of his saliva from a postage stamp."

"Let me try to talk to Weiger first," said Alex. "Maybe he's got some legitimate reason for not letting us peek at his DNA."

"Yeah," said Grant, who had been listening in on their conversation. "Like he's the killer."

ALEX AND GRANT WALKED INTO THE CON ference room where Weiger was waiting. "I'm Dr. Alexandra Blake, and you've already met Captain Grant Pringle," she said to the lieutenant. "Now tell us, why is it that you don't want to give blood?"

"Just think of me as a DNA conscientious objector. I've been to the Gulf, Afghanistan. I've done my twenty-five years and I'm getting out in three months. The government's gotten its pound of flesh; they don't need my blood, too."

"That doesn't make sense," she said. "You've got a great record. Why make waves now, just as you are leaving?"

"You some sort of shrink?"

"No, an M.D., a geneticist."

Weiger turned to Grant. "I want to talk to her alone."

Grant shook his head. "I'm not leaving a murder suspect alone with a civilian woman."

Alex intervened. "I'll be all right. He's already been searched, and if he gets up from that chair, I'll yell and you can come—"

"And shoot him," said Grant, smiling. He turned and left the room.

Alex felt certain Weiger was not the killer, so certain, in fact, that she sat on the corner of the table right next to his chair. She looked down at the lieutenant. "Why me and not him?"

"I figure you're a doctor, so any information I give you is confidential."

Alex thought for a moment. "I'm willing to make that deal, so long as you're not concealing evidence of a crime."

The lieutenant looked down at the table. "I'm gay and the Navy hasn't found out. You know how they are—I could be kicked out with a dishonorable discharge. I hear you can tell if a guy's gay from his genes. I don't want you snooping in mine."

He looked back up, challenging Alex with his eyes.

"I can understand," she said. "But you don't have to worry about that. The forensic DNA fingerprint just looks at five segments of your DNA, none of them linked to homosexuality. I promise you I'll run your blood myself, and I won't let anyone else at it."

He hesitated, then nodded. She took a syringe out of

her fanny pack and stuck his arm, drawing his blood up into a plastic tube. With a pen, she labeled the tube with his name and added "Destroy after analysis."

"Thank you, Lieutenant," she said.

She waved the blood-filled tube at Dan and Grant when she came out of the room. She put it next to the other twenty-two samples in a biological shipper filled with dry ice. Her driver was waiting to speed her back to O'Hare.

"Wait a minute," she said, handing the driver the container, which resembled a three-foot-tall thermos bottle. She strode back into the library, where Madeline James's body still lay. She knelt next to the woman, whose battered corpse formed a portrait in agony. The photos of the other women haunted Alex, but their impact was nothing like this, the smell and heft and crush of death.

Alex stared closely at Madeline, thinking of how the woman had set her hair the previous morning and clasped on her charm bracelet. The librarian's day had started like any other—but ended in devastation and death.

Alex reached over and smoothed the woman's hair. "I'm so sorry."

CHAPTER 19

BACK AT AFIP THE NEXT DAY, ALEX STOOD before the Plasmavision screen. She pointed to the image of five strings of DNA code. "This is the DNA fingerprint of our guy."

"How can you be sure the DNA belonged to the killer?" asked Dan. "A lot of people were in the library." Dan looked like he'd slept in his clothes, if he'd slept at all. He'd worked the scene at Great Lakes all night, then taken a 6:00 A.M. flight back to D.C. that morning.

"Actually, not that many after the three P.M. cleaning crew. None of the twenty-three we questioned made it to the third floor."

"But still, how did you figure it was his?"

"Fleck of skin from the men's room had powder on it, from a latex glove. Cleaning crew uses rubber, not latex."

"Nice job," Dan said.

"Well, that was the good news," she continued. "The bad news is that he's not in CODIS, the FBI's database of convicted felons, and his genetic profile doesn't match that of any of the men whose DNA was collected on the spot."

With this break in the case, Wiatt himself was sitting in on the meeting. He'd even pulled in Hal Webster, whose spotless white shirt, spit-and-polish maroon Bruno Magli shoes, and well-tailored dress uniform sharply contrasted with the wrinkled, careless fashions of the tired men and women chasing the clues.

Now that they had a fresh crime scene, Wiatt wanted a big push. The Wharton School of Business at the University of Pennsylvania was dedicating a new facility in Marilyn Mayne's honor in two weeks. The White House was expected to send the keynote speaker, possibly the Vice President. And the last thing he wanted was an embarrassing question about why his administration had not solved the case.

"Okay," said Dan, taking Alex's place at the laptop. Alex sat down between Hal and Barbara. "Here's what we know," he said. "He's probably got short hair or a shaved head, and Alex says the DNA is consistent with that of a white guy. We found a partial print of his shoe near the third-floor library carrel—size-ten work boot, the kind you can buy at any Wal-Mart. Makes him about five nine or so. We're checking rental-car records from O'Hare and Midway to see if anything jumps out. But there are a million other ways he could have gotten there. You know, flight to Milwaukee, train from Des Moines.

"Plus, we have no idea how much time he spent in the area before the kill. His previous kills were eighteen days apart. This one was twenty days after Marilyn Mayne's murder, possibly because of the difficulty of committing the murder on a guarded base. He could have hung around Great Lakes a couple of weeks while he selected his victim."

"I think he knew exactly who he was after," Wiatt said. "You don't risk a crime at a Navy installation unless you've locked onto a particular target."

"He could have some connection with the base, that's true," said Dan.

"Check past employees of Great Lakes, people who've been stationed there," said Wiatt. "Check their DNA."

Alex was astonished. "You can't just bleed thousands of people. It would cost a fortune to track them down, meet them, and take their blood samples. Besides, the killer might not step up and volunteer to be tested. And we've got even less probable cause for some guy who was stationed there five years ago than we did for the men who were in the library that night."

"There's a way around that," Hal Webster said as he doodled pentagons with his Mont Blanc pen.

Alex turned, surprised that he'd joined the conversation. He never asked her about the case, only about whether she was ready to meet with Trevor Buckley and the folks at Gene-Ease.

Hal paused for a moment, relishing the attention of all eyes focused on him. Then he continued. "The Department of Defense DNA Registry. Every recruit has to give blood when he enters the military. That way, his remains can be identified from his DNA."

"'No more Tomb of the Unknown Soldier,'" said Barbara. "That's what my first CO told me when he made me give a blood sample." Alex noticed that the pile of materials Barbara brought to the meetings kept growing. Today, two pillars of folders framed her face.

"We could run DNA tests from the bank on every man who's ever been stationed at Great Lakes and the other four bases," said Hal.

Alex shot him an annoyed glance. "That's a huge invasion of people's privacy," she said, "especially if those soldiers were told the samples would only be used to identify their bodies if they were killed at war."

"We're in a war against the Tattoo Killer," Wiatt boomed at Alex. "I didn't grab this case back from the FBI to let some civilian tell us what to do." He turned to Barbara. "Lieutenant Findlay, who's in charge of the Department of Defense DNA Registry, anyway?"

Barbara avoided looking at Alex, knowing she wouldn't like the answer. "The bank is administered by AFIP. So, technically, sir, you are."

CHAPTER 20

LIEUTENANT COLONEL FRANK MIDDLETON escorted Alex down the corridor of the ultrasecure Maryland facility that housed the Department of Defense's DNA bank, which was full of saliva or blood samples from everyone who served in the military. Middleton had day-to-day responsibility for oversight of the bank. "This is highly irregular," he said. "We've never had a request in conjunction with a criminal investigation before. There's nothing in our manual about how to handle it."

"Same procedure as with any potential evidence," said Alex. "The key is chain of custody. You sign a set of forms that indicate that the samples are labeled with the proper identification numbers and were collected in the normal course of Department of Defense business. I watch them each get loaded into the liquid nitrogen tanks so that I can later testify in court that no one screwed up and mixed up John Doe's with Colin Powell's."

Alex was no happier about the situation than Middleton. Barbara had waved in front of her a copy of a Homeland Security law, allowing searches of the DOD DNA bank in criminal cases. It might be legal—technically—for Wiatt to order this, but to Alex, that still didn't make it ethical. It just wasn't right to analyze people's DNA without their consent unless there was a specific reason to suspect them. Plus, analyzing thousands of samples would be a big fat waste of time. Wiatt was grasping at straws, ordering her to run not just the DNA of men who were stationed at the bases when the murders occurred but DNA from any man who'd ever been deployed at Galveston, Norfolk, Beaufort, San Diego, or Great Lakes. And forcing her to do the scut work of picking up the DNA samples and transferring them to the lab seemed to be a punishment by Wiatt for daring to oppose him.

They were approaching the inner sanctum of the DNA bank. Middleton tapped in a code, inserted his badge, and then placed his finger on a scanner so that it could read his fingerprint. Satisfied that the visitors were legit, the door popped open for the two of them. Alex involuntarily shivered as she walked into the sixteen-by-thirty-one-foot freezer room that housed over two million saliva or blood samples from people affiliated with the military. Five thousand more were added each day, making this the largest DNA repository in the world.

It had taken thirty-six hours to generate a list of all the men who'd served at the four bases, then half a day to link the code numbers on their samples to the proper locations in the freezer. Alex was overseeing the withdrawal of one of the two vials of samples that were stored from each of the soldiers. It was a complicated task. Men moved from base to base with the frequency that she switched boyfriends.

Alex initially thought she could just pull the first set of samples out of the bank and put them in the dozen liquid nitrogen tanks she'd packed in the AFIP van. But the military was as bad as dealing with a union. There were rules about who could handle what when. And apparently, she wasn't on the list. Middleton showed her the room; then his own team of men started locating the samples and showing each of them to Middleton one by one. This was going to make her crazy.

Middleton sent a man to the van for the tanks and told Alex to wait in the reception area. She felt it would be useless to protest. Besides, she was shivering from the chill of the room and was glad to get back to the security desk in the reception area, where at least she could watch CNN on the security guard's television. Out of the corner of her eye, Alex saw Gloria Devon on the screen, giving her first press conference as the new FBI director. She'd fired the number-three guy and shifted hundreds of agents to new assignments. Alex wondered if Gloria knew what she was doing. She doubted it was a good idea to piss off a bunch of guys with guns.

As the press conference ended, Alex could see that Gloria was wearing her lucky red shoes. Alex wondered if they'd been lucky for David, too. They certainly looked like fuck-me high heels to Alex.

By the time the first set of a thousand samples was ready, Alex had seen all the top CNN stories repeat at least three times. Next time she came to this bank for a withdrawal, she would bring her laptop so she could work while Middleton slowly made his way through a morass of procedure.

ALEX COMMANDEERED A DOUBLE-SHELVED equipment cart from the loading dock at the AFIP, loaded it up with the liquid nitrogen tanks, and wheeled them into the new forensic lab next door to her lab. She greeted the AFIP lab technicians who were waiting for her and welcomed the ten additional techs that the Maryland State Police had loaned AFIP for the forensic analysis of this massive collection of DNA. The Maryland folks were keyed up, excited. Here was the chance to be in on a case of a lifetime. The AFIP guys—and, of course, they were all guys—were their usual stone-faced selves.

Colonel Wiatt came down to the lab and gave them a little pep talk about the case. As he left, Alex followed him into the hall. "I got the samples, like you requested," she said. "But *inside* the lab, I run the show. No cutting corners. No leaks of information. No meddling."

Wiatt was not used to being challenged, but he could relate to a commander's need to control his—or her—troops. "Understood."

"And I'd like Larry Davenport assigned to the lab."

"What unit is he with? I'll put through a transfer of duties."

Alex's gaze pierced Wiatt's own. "He's not with a unit. He's one of the day workers."

Wiatt held her stare as he processed the request. He was still considering the possibility of eliminating the day workers entirely, but Alex and Thomas Harding continued to advocate on their behalf. "Fine. Just make sure you get results."

Alex returned to the lab and welcomed the team, *her* team. She explained how DNA forensics had changed greatly since the British geneticist Alex Jeffreys first introduced DNA fingerprinting in 1985. In the earlier days, technicians were given the print of DNA from the crime scene—a series of banded lines, like a hazy, out-of-focus bar code—and then were given a suspect's DNA print, equally fuzzy, and asked to eyeball them to see whether they matched. The cops often went to the technicians, saying, "We got the horrible sexual pervert." The technicians felt pressured to find a match. Sometimes they declared a match even when there were slight differences in the DNA, indicating they might have come from two different men. Innocent men were sent to prison.

Nobel laureate Kary Mullis, who invented the polymerase chain reaction technique that allowed forensic DNA tests to be undertaken more quickly, had pointed out the unfairness of that approach. "It's like holding a one-man lineup," he'd said.

Alex ran her lab more fairly. Each of the techs was assigned fifty people's DNA to analyze, but they weren't given the sequence of the DNA from the Great Lakes killer—in order not to bias their analyses. They then inputted their results into a computer program that already had the killer's pattern in it. The computer, through exacting comparisons, declared whether or not there was a match. Nobody had any information about the identity of the DNA that they were testing. For privacy reasons, the samples from the Department of Defense DNA bank did not indicate the person's name, just a code number. Despite the power Wiatt claimed he had over the DOD bank, Alex wanted to protect the privacy of those men as much as possible. If one of the technicians got a match, it would be up to Alex to use the code number to break confidentiality and see whose DNA it was.

WHEN LARRY ARRIVED AT THE LAB, HIS bulky body was clothed in a clean button-down oxford-cloth shirt and well-worn but neat gray pants. Since their encounters in the basement and the parking lot, he'd been quietly protective of Alex. Sometimes he stood silently at the side of the new lab, his eyes following Alex's every move. He showed the Maryland techs where the bathrooms and coffee room were, and shuttled chemical reagents for the tests from the supply closets. He wasn't any good at figuring out change, so Alex sent him for sandwiches at the deli where they had an account.

The group's optimism, which had been so apparent on Tuesday, was beginning to ebb by Wednesday afternoon. They'd run over 250 samples using a nearly developed five-gene sequence analysis, and there were a few with vague similarities, but not close enough to be declared a match. The process wasn't helped by the fact that the killer's DNA had been degraded. The cleaning chemicals used on the bathroom floor had made the code even more difficult to read. The computer program compensated for it by filling in what the sequences of the five target genes most likely looked like, but there was room for error. They might not have the guy's DNA code exactly right. Perhaps they were missing a match that should have been declared.

At the Thursday Task Force meeting, Alex reported they had struck out so far on the DNA. Dan, though, was following another lead. "The spatter pattern around the body indicated that there was some blood bounce back. We knew the guy was wearing a plastic coverall, like a cape. We found it."

He showed a slide of a cheap rain poncho, covered with a dark substance. "A homeless guy in a suburb near the base was using it as a tent. We had to give him ten bucks to buy it from him. He showed us the garbage can it came from, and then we found these." The slide changed to one of surgical-like booties.

"We wondered how he got out without dripping blood all over. He must put these things on for the kill, take them off afterward, carry them out in some dripproof bag, and then ditch the contents. But he didn't ditch the bag.

"The poncho was a wash as far as prints, fabric, and so forth. Filth from the tent guy and rain killed our chances there. But the booties are a different story."

He showed a slide of a piece of khaki green thread under a microscope. "It's a U.S. Navy–issue material, not used on civilian goods, but here's where we got even luckier. They stopped making it in 1979. Duffel bags are real popular. Most army-navy stores don't carry inventory from that long ago, so chances are the bag was originally issued to him or to someone he knows.

"So now we know we are looking for a guy who's five-nine or so, probably shaved bald, carrying a U.S. Navy duffel bag large enough for protective outerwear and a set of tools. That's going to make getting eyewitness information a lot easier."

"What have you got on the victim?" asked Grant, who was sitting with his body slightly angled, posturing as usual.

"She'd been at the library only a few months," said Barbara, queen of the employee records. "The previous librarian had retired down to Boca Raton after twenty years—couldn't take another Chicago winter."

"Let me guess: The new gal was from Norfolk, Galveston, Beaufort, or San Diego," said Grant.

"No such luck," said Dan. "We can't link her to any of the locales of the previous kills."

After the meeting, Alex walked Barbara back to her office to grab a Butterfinger bar from the candy dish on her desk. "I'm preparing for a long night," Alex said.

Barbara pointed to a yogurt on her credenza. "Me, too. This audit is turning out to be more complicated than we thought. Right now, there's a two-hundred-and-fifty-thousand-dollar shortfall no one can explain. Wiatt's ready to blame Hal, but it may just be a fluke. There are so many different Congressional appropriations going in and out, so many different suppliers. We're trying to line up the military budget with the one we get from the VA."

"Is Lana set for the night?"

"Yeah, she's sleeping over at a friend's. At least someone's going to have fun tonight."

"I'M ON STRIKE," CONGRESSMAN DAVID THORNE said when he called Alex later that evening. "I'm taking the night off from canned remarks and rubber chicken. Can I take you for Thai food?"

Alex found some appeal in a night away from forensic DNA work. "As long we can do it late. Some of my chemical reagents aren't behaving right. I'm mixing a new set and won't be out of here until at least nine P.M."

"Great, I'll meet you at Beau Thai at nine-thirty."

"Sounds wonderful. I'm dying to get away from forensics."

At dinner, he quizzed her about the men in her life. She answered vaguely, but he kept pressing. Finally, she began to open up a little.

"You might expect me to want a father figure, since my dad died when I was young," she said. She was proud that she hadn't fallen into that trap. Instead, she explained to him, she dated artistic men her age or younger, not stable daddies.

"Ah, but you do date people like your father. Men who don't stay around to take care of you."

Alex was taken aback, but she hardly missed a beat. "Well then I guess I've come to the right place. From what I've heard, you dumped Gloria Devon big-time."

He sat back in his chair, tensing his shoulders. "It wasn't like that at all. Gloria was a big part of my life, but she was the one who called it off"

Alex used a fork to shift the pad thai on her plate. She was beginning to regret wading into this conversation. He sensed her discomfort and reached over to hold her hand across the table.

"It was a mutual decision," he said, correcting himself. "It's really best for her daughter, Rayna."

"She was jealous of the time you were spending with her mother?"

"No, that we could have dealt with. The problem was with Ted."

They were wandering into serious territory, which made Alex vaguely uncomfortable. "The new United Airlines plane?" she quipped.

"No," said David, smiling. "Ted Devon, the evil ex-husband."

"How did that affect you?"

"He wanted me out of the picture. Here was a guy who, in the six years since the divorce, had bothered to claim only a week a year of his supposed joint custody. And that was a week that he mainly dumped Rayna on her grandmother in Boca Raton while he chased coeds in bikinis.

"Once he got wind that I was in the picture, he was livid. He may not have been willing to play the role of dad, but he was damn well not going to let someone else do it. He still lived in Colorado, but when he found out about me, he rented a corporate apartment in Reston, Virginia, so that he could insist on playing a larger role in Rayna's life. Gloria got wind through the legal community in Denver that Ted wanted to challenge her custody by claiming she was an unfit mom."

"Doesn't sound like he'd have a chance if he was as distant a dad as you make out."

"At first, Gloria brushed off the rumors," David said. "Rayna was nine years old, doing great in school, an adorable sprite of a girl. But that was before the *Nutcracker* incident."

"The nutcracker incident?"

David explained how Ted arranged to take Rayna to an early December performance of the *Nutcracker* ballet at the Kennedy Center. Gloria had no idea why Ted had thought of it. He had no abiding interest in either his daughter or ballet. Perhaps he'd read about it in one of those divorced dads' rights manuals.

The night of the performance, Gloria couldn't drop Rayna at the theater because of a last-minute Senate vote. At that point, she and David had been together for nearly two years. Rayna treated him like a stepdad, and it was the most natural thing in the world for Gloria to ask David to drop Rayna off.

Virtually all of D.C. was watching when Ted went ballistic at the handoff. He threatened David, referred to Gloria as a whore. Not only did his scene delay the start of the ballet but a photo of Ted, David, and Rayna made it into the *Washington Post* the next day. Gloria's low-key, homey relationship with Congressman David Thorne was the talk of D.C. Reporters had even managed to dig up a Nordstrom's clerk to comment on the type of lingerie she was buying of late.

"You've got to understand, nothing means more to Gloria than her daughter," said David. "And Ted was a master of dirty tactics. He told her he was going to challenge custody and claim that I was sexually abusing Rayna."

A profound sadness clouded David's eyes. "Of course it wasn't true, but we just didn't want to put Rayna through it. Gloria told me it was just too complex having me in her life. I honored her request to stay away. Since then, I've been with a lot of women, but I couldn't put her out of mind."

He reached over and touched Alex's cheek. "Now I've found someone who's occupying my thoughts more and more."

He paid the check and they wandered back to the Curl Up and Dye. It was a bit much for some men, but he got into the spirit of it right away. He insisted on hearing what was in her CD player at the moment. She skipped over Luke's CD and went for disc two, the Razorbacks.

She felt awkward. She'd never given a second thought to playing exactly what she wanted, but she found herself worrying about what David might think of the music.

He started playing air guitar, then reached over and swung the lazy Susan of nail polishes around, making the colors turn into a blur. He stopped its motion abruptly, then started reading the names of the colors. "Candy Pink, that's definitely not you," he said. "Hmm, Red Roar, that's more like it."

He sat her down on a hair-dryer chair and bent down to kiss her full on the lips; then he kissed her down her body through her clothes. Light kisses down her turtleneck, a big smack on the zipper of her jeans. He lifted her left leg and kissed the side of her knee. Then he took off her boots and her socks. He shook the nail polish bottle like a pro, opened it, and began to layer Red Roar on the nail of her baby toe.

"Wait," she said, "I'm not that type of girl."

"Never had a pedicure?" he asked.

Alex shook her head.

"Then you're in for a real treat."

He sat on the floor and applied the red coat neatly and quickly to the toenails of her right foot.

She looked down at her foot and swiveled her ankle around. "I love a man who can color between the lines."

He asked her about the amp in the corner.

"Belonged to an old boyfriend," she said.

"Not too much dust on it, couldn't have been gone that long. Miss him?"

She sat down on the floor next to him. "Not right this minute."

He reached up and turned off the lamp. Then they began to make love on the floor. Their playful thrashing smudged the hell out of her Red Roar.

CHAPTER 21

LARRY HAD JUST LUMBERED BACK FROM HIS deli run for the team when a woman from the Maryland crew noticed that sample number 5650 was lighting up. It was a partial match, not a complete twin of the crime-scene DNA. Alex couldn't tell whether it was a false positive—close, but not the guy—or whether it was a real match that wasn't perfect because of the degradation of the DNA from the Great Lakes bathroom.

Alex logged on to the secure computer in the forensic sequencing lab, the one with the confidential link to the identities from the Department of Defense database. Once she found the identity of the sample, she walked down the hall to see Dan.

He was behind his paper-piled desk, on two phones at once, tracking leads, trying to make connections. His face lit up when he saw her. She wasn't the sort of person who would take up his time unless she had something.

"It's suggestive, not definitive," she told him when he hung up the phone.

He yelled over to Chuck Lawndale to start searching databases for more information about the soldier whose DNA seemed similar to the skin fleck the Tattoo Killer had left at Great Lakes. Then he paged the whole group to come to the conference room.

Within minutes, Alex was explaining her finding to

Dan, Barbara, Grant, and Dan's backup team. As a scientist, she wasn't used to having so much riding on a single test, a single speck of tissue. With Rosie, she could just slice off more lung tissue and run test after test to double-check her work.

"I can't be sure," she explained. "I'd need fresh blood from the suspect to get a better idea."

The file of the soldier flicked up on the screen, courtesy of Corporal Chuck Lawndale, the computer guru. Admiral Kenneth Mason, fifty-two years old. "That's why it took us so long to get to him," said Alex. "I was going with the psychological profile of a younger offender and ran the DNA in reverse order of birth.

"His was one of the oldest men, as well as one of the earliest samples put into the DOD database. They did some of them with saliva then. I definitely need blood to be sure."

Chuck scrolled down to see where Mason was posted. The list looked familiar. His first five postings had been at the following bases: Galveston, Norfolk, Beaufort, San Diego, and Great Lakes.

"He's our guy. I can feel it," said Grant. He shifted in his seat in excitement.

Dan, the veteran forensics chief, was not so quick to leap. "Where's he stationed now?" he asked.

"Left the military two years ago," said Chuck.

"He's looking better and better for this," said Grant, bouncing his leg.

"We can't link him to it on DNA," Alex explained again. "The match isn't conclusive."

"If we can find the son of a bitch," said Grant, "the order of postings and the partial match will be enough to get a warrant to do another test. We can sort it out then."

Chuck's fingers were flying across the keyboard. "Sir," he said to Dan, "the admiral had twelve military postings altogether. The same as the number of pieces of tattoo. And the killings so far have occurred in the order of the places he was at."

Grant pumped his right arm, "Yes!" His confidence was contagious. Even Alex was beginning to waiver a little. "Well, even though it isn't perfect, there is considerable overlap in the DNA prints."

Dan was more skeptical. "What's the connection? He was at all of those bases years ago, before any of the murders took place."

He mulled it over, tipping his head back and forth as he thought about it. "What was his last-known address?" he asked Chuck.

"Chevy Chase. He got an apartment there when he worked at the Pentagon, posting seven, and then hung on to it when he got posted briefly in Maine."

"Is it still good?" Dan asked.

The young soldier flicked a few more keys. "Driver's license still lists that address. Same with the phone book."

"Let's go in," said Grant.

Dan thought for a moment. "All right, but let's do it by the book. Scope him out. He's an admiral, for Chissakes."

"Former admiral," said Grant. "How about we skip the local cops? I've got a team of men and the latest in SWAT gear. Barbara can cadge a warrant from Judge Kline while we're on our way."

"Whoa, down boy," said Dan. "It's five-thirty in the afternoon. What makes you think the admiral is even at home now? We'll put surveillance on the house and move in when it's clear he's there."

"I wanna pull first shift," said Grant.

Dan rolled his eyes. "Okay, take the van and get out there. But nobody moves until I'm on the scene."

Grant saluted—an infrequent gesture around the building—and charged out of the room. Barbara followed closely on his heels to start drafting the warrant.

The underlings scattered, too, and Chuck, Dan, and Alex were left at the table.

"Want me to find the admiral, sir?" asked Chuck.

Alex and Dan looked at the young soldier as if he were crazy. Chuck explained. "He drives a Mercedes SL. Since

2003, they've had a GPS in each car so people can get computerized directions to where they want to go. We can use the same technology to find the car."

"You've got access to that database?" Alex asked.

Chuck nodded as he entered a series of numbers into the computer. "Since September eleventh, we practically have access to his underwear."

Alex shook her head and congratulated herself again on her choice of cars. Nineteen sixty-three was long before Big Brother started watching. No fancy positioning devices then. Just glowing chrome and a lot of horsepower.

While Chuck pulled the identification number of the car from the Mercedes dealer's mandatory filing with the government, Dan settled back in at his desk to read new reports from the bases. Alex sat on the outside corner of Dan's desk, swinging her legs while they waited.

Dan looked up from his reading. "What's the likelihood he's the guy?"

"Not a hundred percent, by any means. But well worth doing some follow-up testing."

"Okay, we'll play it low-key, then."

"Are you going to call Wiatt?"

"Not until I'm sure this isn't some wild-goose chase."

Alex stopped swinging her legs when a map of D.C. flashed up on the wall screen.

"His car's stopped in Rock Creek Park," Chuck said.

"You mean parked?" asked Dan.

"No, he's on a little dogleg of a road, off of Potomac Parkway, just pausing."

The three of them watched as the dot representing the car started to move.

They watched it curve up Calvert Street, then get on Connecticut.

"Doesn't Connecticut lead to Chevy Chase?" asked Alex.

"Yeah," said Dan, opening a locked drawer and removing his gun and shoulder holster. He put them on, then threw his jacket on over them. "Come with me. Our guy's headed home."

Since the AFIP was closer to Chevy Chase than the park, they beat the admiral there. Dan pulled the AFIP Ford Escort behind Grant's white truck, which was designed to look like an air-conditioning repair van. Dan and the men in the van were armed, but Alex was not. In her ever-present fanny pack, she carried a needle and syringe. Dan wanted her on hand to bleed the admiral for a DNA sample as soon as they found him.

The house was Tudor-style, probably four bedrooms, sitting on about an acre of land. The inside was completely dark. After about fifteen minutes, a black Mercedes pulled up, a man and young woman inside. The plates matched Mason's car registration. The woman got out first, before he'd even opened his door. Grant rushed the car, gun in hand.

When Mason saw the weapon-brandishing bodybuilder, he put the car in reverse and tore off, leaving the woman standing in his driveway.

Grant jumped back in the van, revved the engine, and started chasing the Mercedes. Lights popped on in houses all down the lane as the noisy entourage flew by.

Dan had his gun aimed at the attractive brunette as soon as he was out of the car. She looked young, maybe nineteen, tops. She was wearing a tank top, hot pants, and fishnet stockings. Her purse had a print of a poodle on it, outlined in sequins.

"Are you Vice?" she said, throwing her hands in the air. "I didn't get the money yet. You can't charge me."

Dan kept the gun focused and approached the young woman.

"I can do you, you know," she said to him. "Then we can forget all about this, can't we, honey?" She jiggled her breast a little, showing off the merchandise.

Dan asked Alex to give him the girl's purse and pat her down. "Nothing fancy," he said, "just check if she's armed."

Alex found it awkward. As a doctor, she was used to touching other people's bodies. But all those people had come to her seeking medical advice. There was something vaguely disturbing about touching this woman, who'd probably done nothing more than get in a car with the wrong guy.

When Alex indicated that everything was fine, Dan lowered his gun and asked the girl about the admiral.

She spoke slowly, in a breathy Marilyn Monroe wannabe voice. "I don't know much, honey. We only just met."

The questioning was going nowhere, when, five minutes later, they heard sirens and a chopper. A Channel 2 news helicopter flew by overhead.

The van returned with a Maryland police car escort. Grant had run the Mercedes into a tree and then pulled Mason out of the wreck. The handcuffed admiral was in the back of the van.

Dan approached the Maryland patrol car and flashed a military investigator's badge. The young cop rolled down his window.

"Thanks for your help, Officer. I'll take it from here. It's a military matter."

The cop looked disappointed. True crime didn't often hit this upscale neighborhood. "Are you sure there's nothin' I can do?"

"Why don't you escort the admiral's, uhm, niece home?" Dan suggested, handing the cop her purse.

The cop looked over at Little Miss Hot Pants and she fluttered her fingers in a wave at him. He wasn't buying the niece bit, but this wouldn't be the toughest duty he'd ever pulled, either.

He got out of the car, motioned the girl over, and opened the passenger door for her, as if they were going on a date. She smiled at Dan and Alex, realizing that if she wasn't sitting in back, she wasn't being arrested.

After the cop and the girl drove off, Grant shoved the handcuffed man out of the back of the van. Alex studied Admiral Kenneth Mason. For a man in a lot of trouble, he looked awfully relaxed, almost cocky. Tanned face, relaxed smile. Twinkly Richard Gere eyes. He wore civilian clothes, a well-tailored beige suit, gold cuff links.

Three of Grant's men got out of the van and surrounded the admiral. Dan took Grant aside. "By the book, I said. What happened?"

Grant said, "We've got him now; let's do the Miranda dance."

"Okay, but you went outside the bounds of what I authorized. Don't blow it here."

Dan stepped back in front of the admiral and began. "You have the right to remain silent. . . ."

Grant's cell phone rang. Barbara was calling to say Judge Kline had approved the search warrant. Grant jingled the key ring he'd recovered from the wrecked Mercedes, explained the state of play to Dan and the admiral, and then stepped up to the door of the house.

The house had a security system that a nuclear bomb–storage facility would envy. Grant returned to the admiral. "You're locked up pretty tight," he said. "What are you trying to hide?"

The Channel 2 news chopper hovered overhead.

"Get my attorney on the phone. I have no idea what you're after."

"You sure took off like you were guilty," said Grant.

"Guy with a gun shows up in an unmarked vehicle, so would you."

"We're going in," said Grant.

"I wouldn't do that if I were you. The inner door is set up to shock anyone who hasn't got the code."

"Well then we'll just have to get it," said Grant.

The admiral jutted his chin forward, steeling himself for Grant's blows, but Grant grinned instead and said, "Who ya gonna call? Codebusters!" He returned to the van and grabbed an electronic device about the size of a package of cigarettes.

"Tu casa es mi casa," he said to Mason, raising the device in the air as he passed him on the way back to the house.

Forty-five seconds later, the inner door was disarmed.

Dan called over to Grant. "You help Alex with the blood draw. I'll take the men in for the search."

Alex walked over to the admiral. Even cuffed, he radiated power. She expected him to take charge at any moment and start issuing orders. There was something about that raw confidence that was mesmerizing.

"Admiral Mason," she said. "We've got a warrant that covers your property and your person. I'm going to need you to provide a blood sample."

He looked at her calmly. "There's no need for the cuffs," he said.

"Grant, can you take them off? It's hard to find a vein with the arm in this position."

"I don't care if you take it out of his dick," said Grant. "He's too dangerous to let loose."

Mason continued staring at Alex. "I haven't done anything wrong."

Alex found herself almost believing him. Maybe that was how he got close enough to the women to kill them.

"Nothing wrong?" Grant said. "Isn't solicitation for prostitution still a crime? Not to mention five bodies in five states?"

The admiral tensed a bit. "What are you talking about?"

One of Dan's men came out of the house. He showed a duffel bag to Alex. "We found this in an upstairs closet. It's got blood on the inside."

"I use it for deer hunting," said the admiral, who had regained his bravado.

Alex took the soldier aside and peeked into the duffel bag. She wasn't about to discuss evidence in front of a suspect. "If the spattered poncho had been in it," she said to the soldier, "there would have been a helluva lot more blood."

"Alex," Grant said, signaling her back over. "Are you going to jab this prick—or I am going to have to give him a bloody nose and get my own sample?"

Alex walked up to the admiral. "Yes, Alex," he said in a deep, calming voice, "what are you going to do?"

She fingered the seed pearls beneath her black turtle-neck, while Grant focused a gun on the admiral and made him walk toward the van. Grant opened the handcuffs on the admiral's right wrist and chained him to the handle of the van door. "Don't move a muscle," he told the admiral. "She'll do what she needs to."

Alex stood in front of Mason while he looked her up and down with a bemused smile. He was cuffed to the van, with one arm hanging free along his left side. She gently removed a gold cuff link from his shirt. It had a nice weight to it, solid gold, in the shape of a twisted knot. She slipped it in the pocket of his beige tailored jacket so it wouldn't get lost. She pushed up the sleeve of his jacket, then rolled back the soft fabric of his shirt, curling it up until his inner arm was exposed.

"Make a fist, Admiral," she said.

"Anything you say, Alex." He flexed his arm muscle in a slow, sinuous rolling motion.

Alex felt she was doing something almost erotic when she bent his arm up, tied on a tourniquet, and plunged the syringe into his vein. She could feel his eyes burning into the top of her head as she pulled the needle back out.

The minute she capped the vial, Grant intervened. "Okay, Admiral, you're all mine now," he said.

"It's been a real pleasure, Alex," the admiral said as she turned to find Dan. She retrieved the car keys from him and drove the blood back to the lab.

It was nearly 7:00 P.M. by the time she arrived back at the AFIP. The forensic DNA techs had left for the night. As Alex ran the admiral's DNA sample, she thought about the raw energy of the man. Positioned in front of a matched pair of computer sequencers, she felt like she was at a Las Vegas slot machine. If the five genes of the murderer on screen one matched the five from the admiral's blood on screen two, she would have nabbed the killer.

The two screens flickered, and the genetic alphabet

started filling in. Gene one matched perfectly. Alex felt her heart racing a bit. Forensics evoked an adrenaline rush that didn't accompany her normal work.

Gene two glowed on both screens—also a perfect match. Then gene three.

Three cherries, thought Alex. C'mon, baby. . . .

The fourth ones lit up. Alex gasped. They were radically dissimilar. She hung her head and thought about how to break it to Dan.

She walked to the interrogation room just as Barbara was approaching it from the other direction. They knocked and Dan came out of the room for an update.

"I'm really sorry," said Alex. "I double-checked the sample to see if a fresh one would be any closer than his stored sample. Three of the five genes are identical, but the other two aren't. It's clear it's not him."

"And the blood in the duffel bag?" Dan asked.

"Deer, just like he said."

Dan steeled himself for Barbara's report.

"Worse news," said Barbara. "His alibi for the night of the Great Lakes kill is airtight. You're not going to like what his new job is."

Dan looked at her inquisitively. "How much worse can it get?"

Barbara grimaced in reply. "He was detailed to the Office of Homeland Security. He was in the Justice Department with the attorney general the night of the Great Lakes murder."

It didn't help that the Channel 2 copter had captured the chase on film. The story ran at the top of the hour for the next three days. Little-known, out-of-control federal agency terrorizes upstanding government official. The little strumpet was conveniently left out. They ran old footage of Admiral Mason with the Secretary of State, then photos of the smoldering Mercedes.

Martin Enders, the President's chief of staff, called Colonel Jack Wiatt with a terse message, which he passed along to his team. "When we told you to put AFIP on the map, this isn't what we had in mind. You've embarrassed the administration. You'd better arrest the real Tattoo Killer pronto, or your career is in the crapper."

CHAPTER 22

WHEN ALEX WALKED INTO THE CONFERENCE room for the next Task Force meeting, Wiatt himself was there. "So, Miss Blake," he said to her, dropping her down several levels from her title of doctor, "what exactly were you thinking when you prompted this entire team to chase after an innocent man?"

Alex opened her mouth to respond, but Dan intervened. "I'm the senior officer on this," he said. "I'll accept full responsibility."

Wiatt wasn't buying. "A commander is only as good as the information he gets." He glared at Alex. "The admiral's threatened to sue."

"Colonel," interjected Barbara, "he's just blowing smoke. We had a valid search warrant."

"We can't afford an enemy like him," said Wiatt. He pointed at Alex. "You," he said, "are off the case."

Alex's mouth dropped open. "I'm not the one who ran him into a tree. Why dump me?"

"Captain Pringle was only acting on your erroneous information," said Wiatt.

"I urged caution," she said. "I was clear it wasn't a complete match."

"She's right, sir," said Grant, starting to come to Alex's defense. Alex looked at the beefy bodybuilder, giving him a silent nod of gratitude, but Wiatt cut him off.

Wiatt tipped his head toward the door. "Out," he said to Alex. "We don't need the kind of help you're offering."

Later that day, Alex paced across a rug with the seal of Texas in the reception area of David's Congressional office, waiting for him to finish a photo op with a group of Texas dairy farmers. She was dying to talk to him about the Admiral Mason fiasco. Wiatt had put her in the penalty box big-time. A few weeks earlier, she'd been trying everything she could to stay out of the forensic business. But she was invested now. What about Cheryl Baker and the Great Lakes librarian? What about the acid taste of failure in her mouth?

She'd normally talk to Barbara about her feelings, but Barbara was buried in legal motions, trying to stave off a full-scale attack from the admiral. So here she was, trying to get in to see David, and being treated like some dumb lobbyist or a visitor from his district. She was supposed to be the current woman in his life.

She twisted her wrist for what seemed like the hundredth time to check her watch. Then she sat down. She'd worked her way through three back issues of *Texas Monthly* before David appeared and gave her a great smile. Lil immediately interceded, though, and reminded him of a committee meeting that he was already late for. He had only enough time to tell Alex that he would meet her at the Meskerem, an Ethiopian restaurant, at 8:00 P.M. that night.

At 8:10 P.M., she was sitting in a corner booth when her cell phone rang. She saw that it was David's office number. For the first time all day, she smiled. "Hey, handsome," she said.

There was an awkward silence on the other end. Then Lil said, "He said to apologize. He's running about twenty minutes late."

"Oh," said Alex.

The disappointment in her voice must have been palpable. "He would have called you himself," explained Lil, "but he's doing an interview with a *National Journal* reporter in the cab on the way over to the restaurant."

About fifteen minutes later, David arrived at the restaurant, reporter still in tow. She was in her mid-twenties, perky-looking, with her brown hair in a fashionable flip. She wore a pink linen dress and ballet-type flats. She was hanging on David's every word, looking at him as if the amendment to the patent code he was discussing was the most fascinating issue in the world.

David hugged Alex and whispered in her ear, "Do you mind?"

Alex stiffened. She did mind, but there wasn't much she could say, since Brenda Starr, girl reporter, had already taken a seat at their table.

The girl stayed for the entire meal, finally getting into a cab as David and Alex started walking back to the Curl Up and Dye. When they got to her house, all the lights were on and there was music blaring through the door.

"Did you leave the stereo on?" David asked her.

When she opened the door, they could see a man in Calvin Klein underwear and a Cattle Prods World Tour T-shirt. The man was strumming an electric guitar, his long hair bouncing up and down as his head kept time to the music.

"Luke," she yelled. "How did you get in here?"

He stopped strumming. "Same as before. Keypad on the gate, then I used my key."

She turned to David apologetically. "We broke up a few months ago. I thought he was still on tour."

Luke turned to David. "I assume you've heard the old joke, 'What do you call a bass player who broke up with his girlfriend?'"

David shook his head.

Luke smiled. "Homeless." He emphasized this punch line by a slide on the guitar, then started playing a magical, sweet tune.

Alex closed her eyes and listened. She'd missed his

music at the Curl Up and Dye. She opened her eyes and shook her head.

"Luke," she said, "you can't stay here."

"Where will I go?" he asked, putting down his guitar and moving toward her with the familiar steps of a man who would often sweep her off her feet in a hug.

Alex took a halfhearted step away from him. "YMCA? Greyhound terminal?" she said. "Some other one-star accommodation?"

"Alex, honey, you've got one of my CDs in your stereo. You must miss me. And I wrote a new song for you."

Alex looked at the two men. Their images were reflected dozens of times in the three walls of mirrors. The tanned Texan and the lean longhair from Detroit. Great, she thought, a righteous end to a perfectly screwed-up day.

The men glared at each other, then looked to Alex, expecting her to choose.

"Listen, guys, I've had a helluva day. Could you just take it outside? Now that I think about it, I'd like to spend the evening alone."

David put his arm around her and kissed her lightly on the top of her head. "Whatever you need, Alex. I'll call you later in the week and we can try this again."

She nodded at David, then watched as Luke climbed back into a pair of jeans, repacked his guitar, and grabbed his suitcase. As the two men left the Curl Up and Dye, Alex could hear Luke saying to David, "You don't happen to have a spare room, do you?"

CHAPTER 2 3

OVER THE NEXT FEW DAYS, DAVID WORKED from his home office in Texas and only had time to call her once. Luke reached her answering machine, playing his new song and telling her he'd leave her a phone number once he got one. Alex spent most of her time working on the Rosie project. She was close to identifying the genetic lock-and-key mechanism—the receptor—that had let the Spanish flu enter Rosie's cells. Alex wanted to test her theory on the other bodies from the Brevig dig. Not all of them were in as good shape as Rosie's. She could barely get DNA out of the skeletons of most of them. She had started with the adults and now was working on the skeleton of what appeared to be an eight-year-old boy.

She had found a bit of tissue in his cartilage. His infection was the same as Rosie's, and the receptor functioned in the same way. Further tests showed a remarkable similarity between the nucleic DNA of the two corpses, as well. Then it dawned on Alex. This was Rosie's son.

She caught Dan at his desk in the conference room. "We need to get into Mason's personnel files. Has Mason got a brother or a son?"

"Brother died in combat. It was a big deal. Friendly fire in Afghanistan, don't you remember?" asked Dan. His eyes clouded over as he thought about the incident.

Alex's life was not dominated by the military like her colleagues'. Sadly, the names of the dead never stuck in her head. To her, it was like asking someone who read a newspaper that morning to remember who had written the article on page fifty-two. Your perspective in the world colors how you organize all the information that assaults you each day. She felt guilty, though. After all, her father had been one of those men.

"What about a son? That would fit the age of the original psychological profile."

"When we searched the house, there was no sign anyone lived with Mason. No photos up, either." Dan yelled over to Chuck Lawndale to run the name Mason through the Maryland driver's license database.

"Lots of hits for the name Mason," he reported, "but no one in the right age range."

"Mom might have remarried and given the son a new last name, or the guy might live someplace else," said Alex.

Just then, Dan's phone rang. He picked it up, barked a hello, then put his hand over the mouthpiece. "I'm going to take this call, but I'll give your theory some thought."

Alex left the room and walked down the corridor to Barbara's office. She sat in the cozy chair across Barbara's desk from where the lawyer was working. She popped a handful of M&M's from a cut-glass bowl on the edge of the desk. Barbara always said the bowl served two purposes. When Lana was little, she would actually ask to come to the office on Saturdays to see what sort of candy her mom was offering. And during the week, Barbara enhanced her information sources with soldiers and secretaries dropping in for their chocolate fix.

"I need to pull Admiral Mason's medical records to see if he has a son," Alex said to Barbara.

"Alex, you can be so exasperating. Do you hear yourself? First, you argue for genetic privacy; now you want to nose around in his most intimate files? The Justice Department will be all over us if they find out."

Alex explained why she thought the son was involved. "I can't okay it," replied Barbara. "The federal law about medical records—HIPAA—protects his privacy except when he is an active suspect. Your own DNA test ruled him out. We can't go there."

"But the DNA could easily be that of a relative. . . ."

Barbara shook her head. "You said yourself that the crime-scene sample was degraded. Besides, you're off that case."

"Don't you Wiatt me," said Alex, wagging her finger at Barbara.

"Listen," Barbara said, "the case is making everyone crazy. How about dinner with Lana and me tonight? We've all been under a lot of pressure."

Alex nodded, grabbed a handful of M&M's to go, and returned to her office. But even Rosie and her son seemed less interesting at the moment. She powered up her computer, went on the newspaper database, and read through the articles about her dad, the one from *The New York Times,* and then one from 1974 that she hadn't seen before. She looked at the tag line. Now that she was an AFIP employee, she had access to the military publications, too. She put in a search query: "Kenneth Mason and son." Up popped an article from ten years earlier from the Great Lakes Naval Base newspaper. Mrs. Kenneth Mason, the former Elizabeth Davis, had died at the age of thirty-four. She was survived by her husband and her thirteen-year-old son, Francis. The photo of the graveside service showed Mason saluting. Looking at him with absolute hate in his eyes was a teenage boy in a school uniform.

She paced her lab for a few minutes, then locked the laboratory door from the inside, something she rarely did when she was working there. Feeling a little rush of excitement, she dialed the private boys school near Great Lakes for information about Admiral Mason's son. They had no idea what he was doing now. "You know those military kids," the registrar said; "they go to so many schools before they're eighteen, hardly anyone has a full picture of them. But one of his teachers is still here. I could transfer you."

When Dick Leavitt picked up, Alex explained. "I'm

trying to get some information on a student you had ten years ago, Francis Mason."

"Doesn't ring a bell."

"His mother died the year he was in your class."

"Oh, of course. At school, he wanted us to call him by his middle name, Sam. He thought Francis sounded too much like a girl."

"So what was, uh, Sam like?"

"Sad case. Father was away a lot. Mother came to the parent-teacher conferences alone and a little tipsy, if you know what I mean."

Alex processed that bit of information for a moment. She tried to imagine the sort of woman who had lived with the admiral. Then she probed further about the boy. "Did he get into any trouble at school?"

"Some skirmishes with the other boys, the usual. One girl accused him of stealing from her locker, but nothing was ever proven."

"Anything else unusual?"

There was a pause on the other end while the teacher thought about it. "He missed classes a lot, and then transferred after the funeral. I think he had some job or something in the base library."

Alex thanked him, hung up, then opened the file on the Great Lakes kill. Dan had mentioned a former librarian. Claire Hilton, her name was. Alex called her.

"You want to know about Francis Mason?" the woman said. "Is he in trouble?"

"We're not sure."

"Well, there's not much I can tell you," said the librarian, but Alex could tell from the hesitation in her voice that she was holding something back.

"I understand that he spent a lot of time at the library."

"Uh-huh."

Alex could hear a television in the background. Some game show.

"Mainly, I remember him as a lonely kid. Could you hold on a minute? I'll pick this up in the other room."

After she picked up the extension, Claire yelled to her husband to hang up the phone. Alex could hear Claire lighting up a cigarette, then puffing.

There had been a wisp of affection in the woman's voice. Alex tried to play on that. "He may need some help; we're trying to find him. Anything you can tell me about his interests or his friends might help."

"Sweet boy," the librarian said quietly, as if she were talking to herself. "Spent hours and hours talking to me about his science project and the books he read. Helped me, too. He'd stay late and help me reshelve books."

"Sounds like you really cared about him."

"I did." She sighed. "And he thought I was his special friend."

Claire paused again, inhaled, and puffed.

Alex was excited. "Have you kept in touch?"

"Oh, gosh no. When he found out I was seeing his dad, he almost went berserk."

Alex was stunned. "You were with Mason?"

"His wife, God rest her soul, was so drunk most of the time, I think she was relieved she didn't have to deal with him."

"I see. Mason was unhappy for a long time?"

"Yes. It's not like I was the first. Ken was a total charmer. He even stayed friends with some of his former lovers, visited them when he went back to their cities. He'd get investment tips from one of them. Bought me some silver bracelets when his Intel stock went through the roof."

Alex could hear a tinkly sound as the librarian jingled the bracelets.

"How did he, um, end your affair?"

"Actually, I did. When his poor wife drank herself to death, I didn't want to be wife number two and find myself wondering who he was seeing in Dallas. Married a nice divorced guy, helped him raise his two kids, retired down here when the second one got into college."

Claire puffed and continued, a heavy sadness in her voice. "I tried to protect the boy. Ken expected so much of him. Made him practice tying sailors' knots until his fingers bled." She fell silent again.

"Do you have any idea where Francis might be living or what he might be doing?" Alex asked.

"One thing for sure, he won't be near the water. Hated it after all that pressure. Ken pretty much gave up on the boy when he found out that he wasn't going to raise a Navy SEAL."

"Well, thanks a lot, Claire. This has been really helpful."

Claire puffed again, not ready to end the conversation. Her voice caught as she spoke. "If you see Francis, tell him I still think about him."

"Of course," said Alex. She heard a last quiet tinkle of the bracelets as Claire hung up the phone.

Alex put down the receiver. A faint, sad picture of Francis formed in her mind—a young boy trying unsuccessfully to please his father, then blaming him for his mother's death. Were those experiences enough to seed a killer? She wondered how she could find out more about Francis Samuel Mason.

LANA WAS RADIANT WHEN ALEX ARRIVED AT the house that night. She had just made the varsity basketball team at her high school. Lana was now pressing her mom to let her attend the residential summer program at Gallaudet University. She wanted to spend a few weeks in June living there, just like a college student.

"She's too young," said Barbara as she leaned over and kissed Lana's head.

"What, Mom?" Lana asked. She was sitting at the kitchen table in their small flat and her mother had been standing behind her, outside of her line of vision. She couldn't read her mom's lips.

Barbara knelt in front of her. Since Alex didn't know sign language, Barbara and Lana tried to stick to speech when she was there. "I said I'm not ready to be an empty nester yet. I get a gnawing in the pit of my stomach when I think of you being off on your own already."

"Maybe the gnawing is from too much dessert," Alex said.

She'd felt guilty about not seeing Barbara and Lana for such a long time. What with David, Rosie, and the Tattoo Killer, she'd been busy most nights. So when she stopped at the bakery, she had picked out a mango cheesecake, some cannoli—and a pound of chocolate dot cookies, for good measure. They had tried everything she'd brought. Several times.

Lana headed into her bedroom to do her homework. Alex and Barbara took their coffees into the living room.

"The son theory doesn't make any sense," said Barbara. "What sort of beef did he have with the woman in the library? Think like Dan for just a minute and ask yourself, What was the motive? So far, all you've got is a lonely kid who hates his dad."

"Francis lived at all those bases."

"When he was a *kid.*"

"But the DNA—"

"The sample from the scene was a mess."

"If I'm right, the next murder will take place at the next place Mason was posted—in Connecticut."

"I'll tell you what. I'll do what I can to alert security there with the potential description of our suspect. But I think the bases are a coincidence. Hell, I've been stationed at three of them myself."

Barbara's voice softened. "Listen, you said yourself that forensics wasn't your game when Wiatt first pulled you into this. You can do a lot more for the world if you work on Rosie and her clan."

"Maybe you're right," said Alex. "Who am I to think I can find something Dan missed?"

They sat in silence for a minute, sipping and thinking. "Tell me what's new with Rosie," Barbara said.

"I think I'm onto something about how infections enter the body's cells. And I'm exploring ways to do more research on genetic diseases. I've decided to talk to a scientist at a company, Gene-Ease. Hal's going to make an introduction."

"I've got some good news, too. The auditors are finally out of my hair."

"What about the missing money?"

"Hal showed them right where it was, an account they had overlooked. He was gloating around Wiatt today, but that new sergeant major is still insisting something fishy is going on."

"Is Wiatt going to fire Hal?"

"Hard to tell. One thing's for sure: Wiatt and that special ops guy he brought in seem to be planning something."

IT WAS 11:00 P.M. WHEN ALEX GOT BACK TO the Curl Up and Dye. There were five lottery tickets pasted on her door, plus a note from David. "Take a chance on me." She called him when she got inside.

"Where were you?" he asked. "I've been back in town for hours."

"Went to dinner with Barbara and Lana."

"I've got a great idea for dessert."

"I'm over the top on cheesecake already."

"This kind doesn't have any calories."

Forty-five minutes later, his cowboy boots were in the bedroom, lying next to hers.

CHAPTER 24

THE NEXT DAY, HAL WEBSTER MET ALEX IN the lobby of the AFIP at noon. He was wearing a dressier uniform than usual, almost regal. His shoes glistened. They walked out to the parking lot.

"Let's take my car," Alex said.

He took a long look at the pale yellow Thunderbird with its black vinyl top, its backseat brimming with papers and medical journals. "For God's sake, Alex, we are going to visit the Bill Gates of biology. We can't drive up looking like the Beverly Hillbillies."

"It's a vintage car," she said.

"It's a dinosaur."

He motioned her into his BMW 740i, showing off a dozen of the sixty-four functions of the computer on the dash.

"Go ahead," he said. "Type in the address of Gene-Ease and it will figure the best route."

Alex had to admit it, the car was impressive. Walnut trim, a built-in voice-activated phone, parallel-parking sensor. DVD monitors on the backs of the front seats so that Hal's daughters could watch movies. "Your kids must think it's the greatest," she said.

"I've only taken them in it once," he said. "The last thing I need is Cheerios and juice box stains on the leather seats."

On the drive, Alex asked Hal to use his clout to get her back on the Task Force.

"A few weeks ago, you wanted me to do everything in my power to keep you out of forensics," said Hal. "Fickleness, thy name is woman."

"I'm convinced Mason's son is the killer. He's going to strike again."

"Dan's already following that lead. But if this meeting goes well today, you'll be plenty busy advising Gene-Ease. And you'll be able to afford to drive whatever you want."

"The T-Bird *is* what I want."

"Suit yourself."

In the passenger seat, Alex moved her feet against the floor as if she were driving. She could never understand anyone who actually followed the speed limit.

An hour earlier, Alex had tried calling David to discuss her qualms about visiting a biotech company. The receptionist wouldn't put her through, saying he had a full schedule of meetings. Alex was pissed. She'd seen him duck out of those meetings without a thought to take a call from the *Washington Post* or probably even the *East Armpit Daily News.* As the Maryland scenery sped by, Alex remembered how Luke had always been available to listen, to puzzle through what was bothering her. David could be attentive, sure, but it was always on *his* schedule.

The Rockville, Maryland, office of Gene-Ease looked deceptively unassuming from the outside, like a U-shaped two-story nursing home. Inside, though, the reception area was like nothing Alex had ever seen. Lush, colorful plants, with a hint of a gardenia scent. The receptionist sat in front of an aviary of dainty hummingbirds. She barely focused on Alex, but she gave a big smile to Hal. Well, the man *was* attractive—dark hair, perfectly fine body—but he'd always struck Alex as uninteresting. Too much of an administrator sort for her, not to mention, he was married.

"Watch this," Hal said. "Can you dim the lights, Farrah?"

The reception area went black, but the birds glowed a luminous green.

"GFP protein?" Alex asked.

The receptionist nodded. "They've been genetically engineered with the green fluorescent protein gene from a bioluminescent jellyfish."

"The venture capitalists go crazy for it," said Hal. "And wait until you see the boardroom."

He walked Alex down the hallway to the right. The walls were covered with paintings, photographs, and sculptures by the hot new breed of artists who used genetics as their theme—Eduardo Kac, Suzanne Anker, Bradley Rubenstein. Serious dough had gone into this collection.

As they entered the boardroom, Alex wondered how Hal knew so much about the company, and why he was given free rein to wander the halls. She took a seat at a large square glass-top table. The table alone was the size of her kitchen. She gasped when she saw what was underneath the glass table—an entire aquarium of predatory fish: piranhas, snakefish. But rather than being their natural drab browns and grays, they were wildly colorful.

Just then Trevor Buckley entered the room, and Hal stood up quickly. Trevor shook Alex's hand. He was slightly older than Alex, maybe thirty-eight or so, nicely lean and tan, with sandy-colored hair. He wore beige pants and a peach-colored blazer. He actually looked a little like Bill Gates, thought Alex. She also remembered her mother's admonition, "Never trust a man with bangs."

"Amazing, aren't they?" he said about the fish.

"But now they've lost their evolutionary advantage," said Alex. "Can hardly sneak up on their prey when they are wearing the fish equivalent of a loud Hawaiian shirt."

Trevor motioned Hal to sit back down, then brought over a silver ice bucket with a Spanish cava and placed champagne glasses in front of Alex and Hal.

"You're not having any?" Alex asked as Trevor eased himself into the chair next to hers.

He shook his head. "I sequenced my own genes and found I've got a genetic propensity for liver failure. I changed my diet accordingly."

A butler arrived and set a china plate in front of her that had a sketch of a genie's lamp on it.

"Gene-Ease, I get it," said Alex.

The waiter served crab cakes with a side of polenta. Alex put a bit of the flaky seafood in her mouth, then turned to Trevor. "Let me guess: You used your magic to genetically engineer these to be richer in taste."

"Actually, there are some things—beautiful women, for example—that just can't be improved upon," he said. "I caught these in crab traps off the dock in front of my Cheasapeake Bay house."

It must be a trip to have so many homes you have to identify them with adjectives. My weekend home. My island home. My home on the bay. "About the only thing you can catch in front of my house is the Number Three bus," said Alex.

During dessert—a pomegranate crème brûlée—Trevor described how he founded the company. "The media calls me an 'accidental millionaire,' " he said. "I was working at the Centers for Disease Control, in their metabolic screening section, when I found a way to sequence genes more quickly."

"The Buckley advantage," said Alex. "All the new gene sequencers use it." She had worked her way through her own luscious dessert and was reaching down the table to nab a bit of Hal's. He was apparently watching his weight.

"I don't consider myself a genius in the field. I'm not like Kary Mullis or Craig Venter or Leroy Hood," continued Trevor. "They're the genetic-sequencing pioneers, like Ben Franklin discovering electricity. I'm more like Henry Ford, a guy who applied assembly-line techniques to make the whole game more streamlined."

"And more profitable," added Hal, pushing his dessert closer to Alex, obviously perturbed at her lack of table manners.

"I went to the head of my department at the Centers for Disease Control and explained my approach," said Trevor. His face darkened a bit and he went on to explain. "He told me stick to what was in my job description."

Alex rolled her eyes. "Bosses," she said, looking at Hal.

"I would have just set the idea aside, but at my college reunion, I talked to a venture capitalist buddy. He lured me away from government, we cofounded the company, and the rest, as they say, is—"

"IPOs and stock options," said Alex.

"You've got it," replied Trevor. "I'd have given the invention for free to the government and the CDC. Instead, I now have stock options worth as much as the whole CDC budget."

After their lunch, the waiter came back in with a silver tray of food for the fish. Alex watched a three-foot-long snakefish, its scales the bright orange of a punk rocker's hair, eat a whole stuffed quail.

"The Burmese people think snakefish are reincarnated sinners," Trevor said.

"Just goes to show that crime must pay," said Alex. "Sinner in the last lifetime, spoiled gourmand in this one."

"Would you like to see the sequencing center?" Trevor asked, lightly touching her arm while he spoke.

"Of course," she said.

Hal stood first, not wanting to miss anything. She had agreed out of courtesy. She didn't expect to be impressed; after all, she had three sequencers in her lab. And most biotech companies had more going on paper than in reality. To her, the corporate biotech world was just one big Ponzi scheme.

So she was unprepared for what she saw when they entered Trevor's lab. Rather than the three sequencers, which were more than most companies had, Trevor had thirty. It was like opening someone's garage and expecting to see a Mercedes but finding out he drove the space shuttle.

Even more shocking than the plethora of machines was

the paucity of people. Two men in white lab coats, and three babushkaed cleaning women chattering to each other in Polish. "This is Gene-Ease?" she asked.

Trevor nodded. "Automation has been the key. Robotic arms drip DNA into these grids and then insert them into one of the sequencers. The machine then creates a file of the genetic sequence, which is bipped up to the second floor and compared, by supercomputer, with the sequences of all known genes. That way, we can predict what the gene we have sequenced probably does."

"Homology," said Alex.

"Exactly," Trevor replied, shooing the cleaning women out of the room so he could show off his equipment in peace. "If the human gene we sequence is similar to a known sequence that causes asthma in a rat or dog, we probably have the human asthma gene."

"This is the reverse of what I am doing," Alex explained to Hal. "I start out knowing the function of a gene—like that it causes the Spanish flu—and I try to determine its sequence."

"And we learn the sequence and use computer databases to try to figure out the function," said Trevor.

Alex moved to one of the computer screens and eyed the analysis in progress, watching as the genetic letters filled the screen. Hal stood next to her and watched as the letters *CAG* repeated over and over without changing. "Hey," he said to Trevor, "this one is skipping like a broken record."

Trevor stood behind the two of them and Alex responded to Hal. "Some diseases do this," she said. "Looks like this patient had Huntington's disease."

Alex stole a glance at Trevor, who nodded, then smiled as if their mutual knowledge was some personal secret.

"My way is how science has been done forever," said Alex. "Start with a problem and try to find a solution. You have a wealth of solutions for which you are trying to find problems. Isn't that like looking for a needle in a haystack? You're going to sequence a lot of worthless genes before you hit the lottery and find one that causes heart disease or cancer."

"Precisely. And that's where the AFIP comes in. You've got a couple million haystacks there that we can use."

It dawned on Alex what he was after. "The Department of Defense DNA Repository," she said quietly.

"Largest collection of DNA in the world," said Hal, beaming like a proud papa. "A veritable gold mine of genetic information."

"Gene-Ease is prepared to ante up for access to that DNA," said Trevor. "With the dollars I'm talking about, your pal Hal's consulting fee would skyrocket. He could become an accidental millionaire himself. And you'd get paid as the AFIP liaison who prepares the samples for sequencing."

"It can't be legal to sell people's DNA to a biotech company," said Alex in astonishment.

Hal raised his brow with a look of superiority toward Alex. "Don't you remember? Whoever controls the AFIP controls the DNA bank."

"Everybody does it," said Trevor. "Duke and Harvard both made deals with one of our competitors, supplying blood samples from their hospital patients to a company called Ardais."

"Colonel Wiatt wouldn't allow it," said Alex. "He's not about to do something that controversial, especially now. Even if it's legal, it smells bad."

A cloud of anger again passed over Trevor's face. "From what I read in the papers, Wiatt might not last that long. I'm betting on a different horse."

Hal's face relaxed and he gestured broadly at the astonishing room around him. "From what I can see," he said to Trevor, "your bets always pay off."

Trevor walked them back to the reception area. Alex noticed that Farrah, the receptionist, seemed to blossom like one of those night-blooming plants when Trevor came into view. The woman was wearing nail polish to match the glowing green birds and a skirt with a side slit that reached almost to her waist. My, my, thought Alex, she's angling to marry the boss, just like Melinda Gates married hers. But Melinda flaunted her MBA, not her T and A. Alex shook her head. Too bad, Farrah. Trevor would probably marry up, not down.

"You've got an amazing operation here," she told him.

Trevor smiled. "I'm only as good as my next discovery." He stopped just short of the door.

"Our methods may be different, but, in the end, our goals are the same," he said. "Wipe out disease, make people's lives more comfortable."

He opened the door for her, while Farrah gave Alex an envious stare. "And just so you know, we *are* genies," he said to Alex. "So give some thought to your personal three wishes."

C H A P T E R   2 5

ALEX WAS ATTENDING HER FIRST OFFICIAL
function as David's date that evening. The Boys and Girls
Club of America were giving him an award for a charity
he'd started back in Texas. About three o'clock that afternoon, a box from Nordstrom's was delivered to her office.
She was surprised to see it was a purple power suit, a St.
John knit. Gawd, she thought, even my grandmother
doesn't dress like this. It looked like Hillary Clinton on
the campaign trail or Supreme Court Justice Sandra Day
O'Connor at her farewell party. A typed note on David's
Congressional stationery read, "Thought you might like a
little something for the event tonight."

So this was how it started, the route to become a politician's perfect companion, the Stepford wife who puts her
needs aside for the legislator's image. The sort of woman
who could talk to a brick wall and make it appear charm-
ing and interesting. It made Alex want to get her nose and
tongue pierced for that evening's gala.

Instead, she dumped the lilac Nordstrom's box, suit and
all, into a Hefty bag. Her concession for the evening's
event was to put on black stovepipe slacks instead of blue
jeans, and a gold turtleneck along with her black blazer.
She let her long blond hair sway loose and curly. She
turned heads at the Mayflower Hotel as she walked past the
bar to the ballroom where the reception was taking place.

When she saw Lil, she gave her the trash bag. "This has your name written all over it," said Alex.

David came over to see what the fuss was all about. He kissed Alex on the temple and told her she looked fabulous. Lil looked sheepish and David disavowed any knowledge of the suit. He whispered in her ear, "A red teddy is more my wish for you."

David seemed genuinely surprised, but who could tell? Barbara had pointed out that politicians tended to roll in whatever direction seemed most likely to benefit them at the moment, often sending up trial balloons they later disavowed, just to see which ideas would sell. And legislative assistants were notorious for taking the heat for their bosses. But Alex decided she wouldn't let it ruin her evening.

Rather than having the three honorees give speeches, the Boys and Girls Club had asked high school students to talk about the charities. An African-American boy in hip-hop pants who looked to be about sixteen mentioned David's program, one that took inner-city kids out of D.C., Chicago, New York, and Los Angeles and offered them three weeks on ranches in the Southwest. "Congressman Thorne was the first person to tell me there were black cowboys on the old frontier, like James Kelly, the Ebony Gun." While the boy talked, a silent slide show ran in the background. In one, the boy and David were sitting around a campfire. The ravine in the background was familiar from one of David's photographs.

The event was an odd experience for Alex. It made her admire David, but she felt queasy around the other politicians at her table, who spoke less about important social issues—like poverty or racial discrimination—than your typical college student at a coffeehouse. Instead, they talked about their latest opinion-poll rankings. Congressmen ran for office every two years and were constantly campaigning. Once you were in office, the best way to stay in office was not to offend anyone. No wonder government policies were so stagnant.

Alex felt herself missing the funny little events she went to with Luke. The musicians, the rhymers at the poetry slams, and the wanna-be novelists who made up his circle of friends might not have had much money but they were richly passionate about their beliefs. There was something searing and electrifying about being that close to other people's cores. Here, the people seemed distant and protected, wrapped in plastic coverings like the living room furniture in Grandma Blake's bungalow.

"How do you stand it?" Alex asked David later that night, before they drifted off to sleep. "The people are so fake." She had made love to him fiercely, almost as if trying to prove they were both still alive.

"Some of them mean well; they're just scared about their future," said David. "I figure if a Congressman does one good deed a week with his power, that still puts him above the average Joe."

David got up to use the bathroom. On the way back to bed, he ran his fingers through his hair in front of the dresser mirror, an unconscious gesture from primping for public appearances and television interviews. As she watched from her position under the sheet, Alex found his motion slightly unsettling. Who combs his hair to go to sleep? she wondered.

David picked up a small carved box on the dresser, a two-inch circle of dark wood with intricate inlay. He reached toward its cover with his other hand.

"Don't open it," Alex said vehemently.

He put it down abruptly and sat next to her on the edge of the bed.

"It's from my father," she said, embarrassed by her reaction and feeling the need to explain. "I was only four when he gave it to me, and I didn't really understand his being away. But he told me he put zillions of kisses in it, so that when I missed him, I could open it up and get one."

Alex thought about how hard it had been when he'd first left for Vietnam. Every night, she'd expected him to come home and read a story, like he'd always done. She must have opened that little box ten times a day.

Her eyes moistened. "He'd fill it up with new kisses whenever he was home on leave. That final time, when he was supposed to come home for good, I put a kiss in there for him."

They sat silently for a moment. She added quietly, "I haven't opened it since."

David pulled back the covers and lay down beside her. "I'll be here for you. Whenever you need kisses, I'm your man." He started a gentle series of kisses across her forehead and on her cheeks. Then he held her and they fell asleep.

In the morning, she and David jogged through Rock Creek Park. They picked up bagels and coffee on the way back. As they were sitting across from each other in her kitchen, savoring their Saturday together, he said, "I have a really personal question to ask you."

She hesitated a few seconds, then said, "Shoot."

"Where's the manual for your outside keypad?"

She laughed. "*That's* your personal question?"

"I think it is time you changed the code."

"Is this the high-tech equivalent of asking me to go steady?"

"Something like that."

She got the manual and took her coffee outside, admiring this handsome man in jeans and a Waylon Jennings T-shirt as he worked on the alarm.

"What's the alarm code that you have now?"

"P-R-O-D-S," she said. "Luke's band used to practice here, and I had to pick something the drummer could remember."

"It says here you can have a string of letters from as few as four up to fifty," he said.

With the manual in his left hand, he reset the code. N . . . J . . . D . . . C . . .

"Huh?" she said. "How am I supposed to remember that?"

"It's the two places we've made love. With forty-six other characters available, we can add lots of other states. . . ."

CHAPTER 26

GRANT SAT DOWN NEXT TO ALEX IN THE
cafeteria the following Monday at lunch. He was clearly
protein loading. His tray contained two steaks, a hunk of
cheese, and scrambled eggs. He reached into his shirt
pocket and fetched a ring with a strange black stone and
put in on Alex's finger.

"It's a lie detector," he said.

"Well, ask away," replied Alex.

"Still mad at me?"

"Yes," said Alex vehemently.

The stone turned a bright red.

"You're lying," he said.

She nodded. "It's not your fault I'm off the case; it's
Wiatt's." She thought for a moment and then, smiling,
said, "Now ask me if I think you're a sexist pig."

"Hell no," said Grant. "I know the answer to that one."

Alex held her hand in front of her and admired the
ring. "So what was the development budget for this new
device?"

"Nine-ninety-five," he said.

Alex whistled. "Nine hundred and ninety-five thousand
dollars?"

"No, nine dollars and ninety-five cents," said Grant.
"Some guy was selling them last week at the Metro stop.
So far, it's beating the pants off all our lie detectors. I've
had one of my engineers at the stop the past two days,

hoping the guy will come back so we can find out where he got it."

"I can just see it now. You've sweating out some Middle Eastern terrorist in a hovel in Afghanistan and you ask him, 'Would you prefer the ring, tie tack, or shall we just electrocute your testicles like we used to do?'"

Grant put on a fake look of exasperation. "Alex, I wish you would take my work more seriously. I'm trying to be a kinder, gentler torturer."

She fingered the ring. "Will it work if I ask a question of myself?" she asked him.

"For sure."

She closed her eyes and asked herself, Is David right for me? She nodded her head, then opened her eyes and looked at the ring.

"Wow," said Grant, "I've never seen that before."

The ring was glowing bright yellow. "What does that mean?" asked Alex.

"Damned if I know." Grant smiled. "But I bet the Senate committee would cough up a few hundred thousand for us to find out."

"Don't bother," she said, handing him the ring back. "I'll muddle through on my own."

THAT AFTERNOON, WIATT'S AIDE-DE-CAMP, Sergeant Major Derek Lander, called Alex and asked her to report to the auditorium at 4:00 P.M. "What's up?" Alex asked.

He snorted at Alex's informality and presumptiveness. The sergeant major said, "Just follow the orders." Then he hung up.

Nazi, thought Alex. She dialed Barbara's number. "What's up in the auditorium this afternoon?" she asked.

"Apparently, Wiatt's gathering everybody who has ever worked on the Tattoo Killer case. From what I hear, there might be some reassignments."

"How did you get that out of Lurch?" asked Alex, using their nickname for the sergeant major whom Wiatt had brought on board from his old combat unit. After just a few weeks, the AFIP staff had discovered that the man shared the television character's brutish, humorless demeanor.

"Even the Addams Family liked chocolate," said Barbara.

At four o'clock, Alex and Barbara joined about sixty other people in the auditorium. Onstage, Wiatt and Dan were seated behind a table with a third man, who, to the horror of many in the audience, was smoking a cigar. Dan did not look happy.

Barbara gasped. "That's President Cotter's chief of staff," she whispered to Alex. People of that stature rarely visited the AFIP.

The lights dimmed, a screen came down behind them, and a video began to play. It showed Marilyn Mayne, the computer company CEO who had been killed in her room at the Au Contraire Resort. It included still photos of her with other pillars of American business and ended on a shot of her with the President. Her death was described as "a loss to the country."

When lights came back up, Wiatt spoke. "Datasmart will begin running that ad across the country tonight, offering a million-dollar reward for information that leads to the arrest of Marilyn Mayne's killer," he said. "The President himself will make a plea for information on *Nightline*. Martin Enders, the President's chief of staff, has asked for the opportunity to address us today about the investigation."

The toadlike man took a heavy puff of the cigar and then began to speak. "Colonel Wiatt requested this case back from the FBI," said Enders. "Since then, the President has given you every resource you needed—money, equipment, staffing. Now he has asked me to come to you with something else—a deadline."

Alex knew Dan well enough to read his thoughts about this asshole. What did Enders think, they'd all just been twiddling their thumbs?

Enders continued: "You have one more week to solve the case, or it is going back to the FBI."

Alex saw the painful expression on Wiatt's usually calm face. She turned around to see how the folks behind her were reacting. She noticed a camera crew in the rear, the reporters from Channel 2 who had skewered them about Admiral Mason. Enders must have brought the crew with him, she realized. Wiatt would never have let them in otherwise. Enders was setting them up, covering the President's ass. If Mayne's killer was not found soon, the AFIP would take the heat. What did Barbara call it when she talked about the games people played in Washington? "Plausible deniability." Passing the buck.

Enders left with a flourish, camera crew at his heels. Wiatt addressed the stunned audience. "Okay, soldiers, here's what we are going to do. First, a dozen of you will be assigned to field the calls that come in once the ads start running. That operation will go twenty-four/seven. And we are going to pull all the field officers off the investigations of the other victims and put them on tracking down anything we can find out about Marilyn Mayne. . . ."

Dan opened his mouth to protest, but Wiatt silenced him with an angry look. "Any man so much as looked at Mayne at any point in her life, we're going to find out where he was on the night she got killed."

Dan shook his head at the wrongheadedness of this approach. Alex's hand reached up to touch her pearls. What about Cheryl Baker, the college student? Didn't her life matter?

ALEX HAD AGREED TO MEET DAVID AT HIS house that night at 11:00 P.M., after he finished his last appearance. When he opened the door, he scooped her up in a hug, but rather than whisk her off to the bedroom as she'd fantasized, he plunked her down in front of the television. He was hooked on the evening news, trying to ascertain which way the political winds were blowing, which events might allow him to push his agenda along more quickly.

At 11:20 P.M., the ad about Marilyn Mayne ran. "Isn't that the case you were working on?" he asked.

The anchorman was moving on to the weather, so David was willing to talk again. Congressmen didn't have to worry about the weather at all. Staffers would hold umbrellas over their head or drive them around in the rain. In fact, that layer of governmental manservants isolated members of Congress from all everyday worries, including picking up their cleaning and remembering their anniversary.

"Yeah," said Alex. "Some idiot named Enders showed up today. . . ."

"Martin Enders?" asked David, his voice lilting in surprise.

"Uh-huh. He put pressure on Wiatt, and now Wiatt has some cockamamy idea that we should pull our investigators off Cheryl Baker, the college student who got killed, and three of the other victims, and move them all to Marilyn Mayne's case."

"This could be great for your career. You could do worse than having a friend in the White House."

"Are you listening to me? Enders is an asshole. Politicians shouldn't be running this investigation."

David spoke to her as if she were a child. "Alex, this is Washington—politicians run everything. It wouldn't hurt for you to be a little political yourself from time to time. The lone cowgirl approach went out with Annie Oakley."

Alex stiffened, but she decided she wouldn't let this spoil her time with him. "I know it's hard for you to understand, but scientists are a different breed than politicians. We try to get at the truth. Nobody ever got a Nobel Prize in science for following orders."

David touched her cheek. "You're good at what you do—incredible, in fact—but sometimes you've got to go with the organizational flow. I want you to be able to stay in D.C. I like having you close."

He moved toward her and wrapped his arms around her. Then he turned his head sharply as Ted Koppel announced that evening's guest, the President of the United States.

Having lost his attention to the Commander in Chief, Alex got up, grabbed her saddlebag briefcase, and moved into his kitchen. She made herself a cup of mango tea and took a file out of her bag. She stared at a photo of Cheryl Baker, then started copying down names and addresses. The weatherman had predicted sunny skies the next day. Perfect for a drive to Norfolk.

CHAPTER 27

SYLVIA BAKER SAT ON THE COUCH, HAND-
ing photos of her daughter across the cocktail table to
Alex. This was much harder than Alex had expected. She
glanced down at the picture of six-year-old Cheryl Baker
in footie pajamas, white-blond hair streaming past her
shoulders, beaming smile despite a missing front tooth.
Then Alex glanced up at Sylvia, who reminded her of her
own mother in the months after her father's death. Sylvia
showed the same gaunt face, perpetually red eyes, and
nervous gestures that had haunted Janet.

Sylvia was recounting the high points of Cheryl's early
life. Alex did not want to interrupt, even though she knew
that stories of Cheryl's role in the second-grade play
wouldn't advance the investigation. Alex had enough of a
healer in her to realize that Sylvia was soothing herself
with the perfume of the past.

"Mrs. Baker," Alex said when Sylvia stopped to wipe a
tear from her face, "we now think we have something of a
description of the killer. . . ."

Alex saw Sylvia's face contort at that horrible word,
and Alex immediately wondered if there was a less brutal
way to refer to the man, one that did not so vividly conjure
up her daughter's torture and death.

"We're wondering if you saw her with—or heard her
talk about—a man who was around five nine, with a bald

head or really short hair. He might have been carrying a U.S. Navy duffel bag."

Sylvia flinched. The description of the man forced her again to visualize the tragic incident. Her voice was quiet. "No," she said. "I already told one of the other investigators that she didn't mention anyone like that."

"Who did she spend time with when she came home for spring break?"

"She mostly stayed at home with me, helping me sort through some old things of her dad's."

Oh God, Alex thought. She'd forgotten that Cheryl's dad had died a month before she was killed. This poor woman.

Alex thought for a moment. "What did you do with his things?"

"I just wanted to throw them out, but Cheryl insisted on taking them to a place where they train street kids to apply for white-collar jobs and give them suits so that they can go to interviews."

"Do you remember the name of the organization?"

She shook her head.

"How did Cheryl find out about it?"

Sylvia thought for a moment. Her eyes brightened, eager to help. "An article in the local paper the Sunday of spring break."

Then the fatigue and loss turned her face gray again. She opened her mouth to speak, then shut it. Then she tried again. "You don't think that her death is somehow related to that, do you?"

Alex knew what she was really asking was whether she had somehow contributed to her daughter's death. Alex recognized that fearful expression from her medical school days of dealing with the parents of children who'd died. The parents dwelled on every action they had taken in the weeks leading to the death. Had they tempted fate in some way? Was there a different path they could have chosen? Was there any way possible that God would let them rewind the tape?

"No, I don't think her death was related to that in any way," said Alex. But it wouldn't hurt to interview those people, she thought, and retrace Cheryl's steps the day before she died.

GOING THROUGH NEWSPAPERS AT THE LOCAL public library, Alex read about the opening of "Up Yours," the combination pool hall/job-training center run by a former gang leader with a Harvard M.B.A. Mickey was a short African-American in his late twenties, who'd sold a successful business and now put his energies into opening up opportunities for other folks in his hood. His "business establishment," as he called it, was twenty minutes outside of Norfolk. Hip-hop music provided an odd musical score for the PowerPoint presentation that Mickey was making when Alex entered. Mickey was telling a bunch of nineteen-year-old toughs what they needed in order to move "Up" in the world (the operative word in the center's title). When he finished the session, he took Alex into his office. He knew exactly whom she was talking about when she described Cheryl.

"Man, I thought we had a guardian angel when she walked in the door," he said, leaning back in his ergonomically designed desk chair. "The newspaper had jumped the gun. The article came out the week before we were scheduled to open. It was just me and the electrician. The clothes I was planning to give out were still in storage. And in floats this woman in pearls with a Hefty bag full of eight suits and two dozen ties. When guys started dropping in later that night, we could say we were open for business."

"Do you remember anybody hanging around outside, paying particular attention to her?"

"Nah, she was here at ten or so in the morning; none of the homeboys are up that early."

"And this electrician, can you give me his name?"

He shook his head. "Guy just responded to an ad I put up at the grocery store down the street. I only needed an hour's work, getting my office rewired so that I could position the desk by the window. I was on the phone most of the time he was here."

"What did he look like?"

Mickey thought for a moment. "Skinhead, medium height. Looked like he might be one of those neo-Nazi types, so what he said when he left surprised me."

Alex gave him a quizzical look.

"He thanked me for helping *him* and gave me my first donation to the center." Mickey tipped his head toward a five-dollar bill that he had tacked up to the wall.

"Did he seem interested in the girl?"

"Who wouldn't be!"

"Did he talk to her?"

"Not here, but he left just a few minutes after she did. Maybe he caught her outside."

THREE HOURS LATER, BACK AT AFIP, ALEX entered the Task Force room. The people working there were a caffeinated jangle. If the Tattoo Killer followed his earlier pattern of killing every eighteen days, they would be identifying a new body the next day. If he went for twenty days again, the kill would occur sometime Thursday night. The laptops were already in place.

Alex handed the evidence envelope with the five-dollar bill to Dan Wilson so he could try to lift prints. In its place, Alex had left a twenty-dollar donation. And she promised she'd send all her male friends an E-mail to let them know where they could donate their used business clothes.

CHAPTER 28

LATE THAT AFTERNOON, WIATT CALLED ALEX, asking her to report to his office. She had expected to see the chairs in front of his desk filled, but she was the only one who had been summoned. Even Lurch had already left.

He slammed down the phone as she entered. His eyes held a repressed rage. She couldn't tell if it was directed at the caller or at her. She wasn't sure she wanted to find out.

"I'll get right to the point," he said. "You are in serious danger of blowing your career."

She felt her pulse quickening. She wasn't sure what he was talking about. Sure, Wiatt had pulled her off the Tattoo Killer case, but how could he know she'd been poking around Norfolk? Dan wouldn't have ratted her out.

She leaned forward in her chair and prepared to take him on. But before she could explain, he handed her a piece of paper. A disclosure form, like that required before any government employee did any outside consulting. She looked at it closely. Commander Hal Webster was disclosing that he and she might be doing some consulting for Gene-Ease. Her cheeks reddened. She was miffed at Hal for filling in the form without asking her.

The colonel stared at her for a long time before he spoke. "As long as you and Commander Webster work for me, I don't want to hear that you're poking your noses in places they shouldn't be. The interests of the AFIP have to come first."

Alex shivered at the way he delivered the words. "Sir," she began.

His phone rang again. He flicked his hand, dismissing her. Then his expression softened a little and he covered the mouthpiece and said, "Dr. Blake, I don't know you well, but this doesn't sound like you. Be careful."

ALEX STORMED DOWN THE HALLWAY AND swung open Hal's door without even knocking. "What do you mean filling my name in on a consulting form without asking me?"

Hal's initial look of anger softened. "Calm down, Alex. I didn't mean any harm. You know how the government is, slow as molasses. I didn't want to close off any possibilities. I wanted everything to be in place if you made up your mind to go ahead with it."

Alex stopped fuming. What he was saying made sense. Kinda. "Well, next time—"

Hal nodded. "Next time, I'll talk to you first."

BACK IN HER LAB, ALEX REVIEWED HER WORK with Rosie. She'd hit a dead end. She'd figured out how the infection entered the cells, but despite all her attempts, she couldn't find a way to defuse this genetic bomb. She decided that she'd move from the genetic analysis to experiments with the proteins the genes created. She spent a few hours creating a computer program to simulate a 3-D image of the way the proteins created by the Spanish flu gene interacted. She'd let the program run overnight to see whether the resulting image triggered any new ideas.

At 7:00 P.M., Alex picked Lana up after basketball practice. Barbara was at a meeting at the D.C. Bar Association, and Alex was taking Lana to the Pentagon Mall to find a birthday present for her mom. After her chilling encounter with Wiatt, Alex was glad for the exuberance of a fourteen-year-old companion.

They went into the shop Made in America, and Lana picked out a set of towels and a toothbrush with the emblem of the White House's Lincoln Bedroom on it. "She'll love these," said Lana. "Mom's such a D.C. celebrity fanatic."

Lana insisted on having dinner at the food court. No accounting for a fourteen-year-old's taste. Once they were seated with a cheddar burger for Lana and a Middle Eastern wrap for Alex, Lana's face turned more serious. "Promise you'll help me," she said to Alex.

Alex felt a wrench in her gut. Was she going to ask for advice with boys? Alex was hardly in a position to give it. If she were ever a mom, she would be one of those "Do as I say, not as I do" types.

Lana's face screwed up like she was having trouble finding the words. Her hands flitted about, not quite signing, because Alex wouldn't understand it. But the tremors of Lana's hands were an indication she had something troubling to say.

Alex panicked. What could be bothering Lana so much? Alex couldn't bear the thought of anything bad happening to this magical girl.

"What is it, sweetie?"

Lana crossed her arms in front of her, as if she were summoning up her courage. "I really want to go to the summer sleepover camp at Gallaudet."

"That's it?" asked Alex.

Lana looked hurt that Alex didn't immediately understand. Her lower lip quivered.

"Your mom just worries about you, honey," said Alex.

"She treats me like a baby and acts like I can't take care of myself. It's because of this." Lana pointed to her ears.

Alex nodded. Why deny it? Lana's deafness did put her at risk. What if she walked out in front of a car? Or someone sneaked up behind her and hurt her?

"Your mother's just worried that you might be less safe because of your disab—uh, difference."

"It's *not* a disability! Do you know how much junk hearing people deal with each day? I mean, sure I might miss something cool, like music. But how much time do you really spend listening to Mozart or one of those guys? Most of the time, you hear the stupid commercials on television, or car horns in traffic, or your boss yelling at you. I wouldn't change anything. I like having more time with my own thoughts."

Alex felt affection well up in her as she watched this dear girl and heard the passion in her voice. "I've never thought about it that way."

"People think we can't take care of ourselves. But, Alex, kids like me grow up faster."

Alex assessed Lana, who was tall for a high school sophomore, almost a mirror image of her mom. But while Barbara favored skirts and her crisp U.S. Navy uniform, Alex didn't think Lana owned girl clothes. Tonight, she wore baggy hip-hop shorts and a zip-up hooded sweatshirt despite the heat, perhaps to hide the contours of womanhood that had recently remolded her body. She lived and breathed basketball, spending most evenings perfecting her jump shots on the court of the apartment building where she lived with her mom. In her coed gym class, boys and girls alike lobbied to have her on their team.

"You're only fourteen, Lana."

"I wanna be on my own for a little while. I love my mom, but we've been together practically every single day since I was born."

"When do you have to let Gallaudet know?"

"Next Friday."

"I'll see what I can do."

Lana seemed surprised to have won Alex over. She leaned across the table and gave Alex a big hug. As she squeezed Alex, she whispered a phrase into Alex's ear: "Ice cream." Then she leaned back and counted the crumpled dollars in her pockets.

She's a great kid, thought Alex, watching Lana dart over to the ice-cream line to get them each cones. Now how am I going to pitch this to Barbara? Alex decided that the water-torture approach would be best. Talking about it bit by bit over the next few days. Barbara wasn't the type you could spring things on all at once.

ON THE DRIVE HOME, ALEX FIDDLED WITH the T-Bird's air-conditioning, trying to will it back to life, then gave up and opened the windows. She thought about Lana's desire to go to camp. Alex's childhood experience had been much different—she'd felt that being sent to camp was some sort of punishment. In the summer of 1981, Alex's mom was researching her dissertation. She'd moved Alex to the University of Michigan, then Arizona State, then Santa Clara College, until she finally settled in at the University of Chicago. That summer, she needed to work long hours in the University of Chicago library, but what could she do with eleven-year-old Alex? Janet's solution was to enroll Alex in one camp after another. June brought two weeks at the Young Artists Camp at the Art Institute of Chicago. There, Alex sketched among the budding Rembrandts. While she tried her best to draw the outline of a daisy, the boy next to her brought to life a snorting horse caught in mid-stride. The girl on the other side of Alex drew spritely fairies who fluttered as if they could fly off the page. Alex realized her pictures were lame, but each night, Janet would dutifully tape Alex's drawings to the refrigerator door.

The next two weeks were an away camp for magicians. Alex was bored. Each trick was so *obvious*. She almost got expelled the day she hid Wizard Bob's pointy hat. ("If you're so magical, why don't you just make it reappear?" she asked him.) He sent her to her cabin for the rest of the day, which suited her just fine. She spent the afternoon filling out a math-puzzles book her mother had sent with her. Years later, Alex realized that her mother's odd gifts reflected her pattern of buying everything at the university bookstore.

The last camp that summer was a six-week soccer camp in Minnesota. Alex thought it would be like Young Artists Camp all over again. But it was a million times worse. The other girls ran and kicked with grace and determination. She'd never even held a soccer ball before. Her first day there, she just tried to stay away from the ball as much as possible, acting as if it were a ticking bomb. When her whole team ran after the ball, she let the bodies wash past her like a brook flows past a pebble.

Near the end of the last soccer match of the day, the ball rolled right to the tip of Alex's shoes. She kicked, but the ball veered left and missed the goal entirely. Her team lost the game.

"Are you a complete idiot?" asked a hefty brunette, whose face was contorted in anger. Without warning, she threw the ball directly at Alex's head. Alex ducked just as the coach turned around and caught wind of what was going on. The woman blew her whistle. "Emily, you're benched for tomorrow morning's match."

The girl walked past Alex, whispered, "Die, scum," and moved on. When she got a few feet past Alex, she turned her head and looked back. "It was worth it," the thick-legged brunette said to Alex.

Alex felt tears well up in her eyes. I want to go home, she thought.

A tall, pale blonde appeared next to her. Pamela reached down, picked up the ball, and started walking back to the cabins alongside Alex. "I hated it at first, too," Pamela said. She dropped the ball to the ground and absentmindedly kicked it from side to side as she walked. "My mom had a soccer scholarship to Brown. She practically made me play when I was coming down the birth canal."

Alex was too busy holding back tears to respond to Pamela's overture. Then Pamela's face got animated. "Do you want to see something really neat?" she asked.

Alex nodded and Pamela retrieved the ball, then diverted them to an overgrown path through the woods, heading to a clearing near a stream. There was a huge field of dandelions, all fluffy and white. Pamela picked one and blew the soft wisps at Alex. Alex bent down, picked her own, and blew back.

Pamela started spinning the ball on the tip of her finger. The she stopped it abruptly, looked seriously at Alex, and said, "Do you want to learn to play?"

By the time the camp ended, with Alex returning to Chicago and Pamela to Minneapolis, they were best friends. They wrote to each other all during the school year. For every holiday, Alex asked her mom and grandparents for stationery, and the boxes piled up on top of her dresser. Pale blue with a navy *A* for Alex, long sheets with Peter Max faces, postcards with rows of kittens. Alex kept a list of which stationery she used when, so she wouldn't send Pamela the same type twice in a row.

Spurred on by Pamela's example, Alex joined a Park District soccer team. She was a natural athlete and soon became the captain of the team. Janet was delighted. Now Alex had something to do after school while Janet sat at their kitchen table, typing her dissertation.

The next summer at soccer camp, Alex and Pamela were inseparable. In the fall, their letters continued, at least twice a month. Alex wrote about her classes, and how her math teacher looked like television's Mork but was totally cool. Pamela wrote about her younger brother, who was totally not.

That year, Alex led her local team to the city championships. It wasn't that difficult—the Chicago Park District wasn't exactly a hotbed of soccer activity; sixteen-inch softball was the favored local game.

In March, Alex was involved in a science-fair project and didn't answer one of Pamela's letters for three weeks. She thought Pamela was punishing her when, after Alex finally responded, she heard nothing from Minneapolis. Alex wrote her again. She used her new round stationery.

Starting in the middle, Alex wrote the entire letter in a spiral, with each line circling the next. Weeks passed. Still no response. Oh well, thought Alex, she'd see Pamela soon enough at camp.

Alex hopped out of her mother's car when they got to camp, running off to the main hall to read the list to see if she and Pamela were in the same cabin. She read down the list four or five times for "Stewart, Pamela," but she couldn't find the name.

"Where's Pamela?" she asked the coach. The coach's cheeks turned slightly pink; then she told Alex to wait there a moment while she talked to her mother. Alex watched as the two women spoke. Janet's eyes grew wide and she raised her hand to cover her mouth. Then she looked sadly at Alex.

The two women came over to Alex. Janet held her close, stroking her hair. "Pamela's not coming back," she told Alex. "She's sick and in a coma." The coach said something like "such a wonderful girl" and "brain tumor," and so forth, but to Alex, it was like they were talking to her from underwater. Alex broke away from them and ran, toward the cabins and then down the path, past pines and fences, until she got to the stream and the field of dandelions. She broke off one and blew, and then another, and another, dozens and dozens, until she was out of breath and dizzy and needed to lie down. How could this have happened? How could her friend be dying and she, Alexandra Blake, be just fine?

When Janet found her twenty minutes later, Alex had only one request: "I want to go home."

Janet didn't say a word. She didn't start speaking in that singsongy voice she sometimes used when she was saying something "for Alex's own good." Instead, she nodded, helped Alex get up, and held her hand all the way back to the car.

Alex spent the five-hour drive home lying prone and silent on the backseat of her mom's beat-up Impala. She tried to imagine what it was like to be in a coma. Were

Pamela's eyes open or closed? She tried it both ways, first looking up at the dome light above her in the car, then closing her eyes. She hoped Pamela's eyes were closed. It would be too scary if they were open. She'd be able to see her family but not talk to them or tell them how she felt. That would be terrible. Yes, it would be better if Pamela's eyes were closed. Then she could be dreaming. What was it her Spanish teacher had taught them—*Sueña con los angeles,* "Sleep with the angels." Yes, maybe Pamela could sleep with the angels or dream with the fairies, those lovely delicate fairies who seemed to fly off her neighbor's sketch pad at the Art Institute.

When they got home, Alex took her new soccer ball and thunked it into the trash bin outside their apartment. Janet didn't even scold her, even though it had cost a lot of money. Even though Janet had to make a special trip to Sportmart to get it because they didn't sell soccer balls at the University of Chicago bookstore.

That summer while Janet finished her dissertation, Alex would sleep late, have a quick lunch at home (always the same—a peanut butter and banana sandwich), and then walk six blocks to the Museum of Science and Industry. She would sit in front of the exhibit that showed forty-one preserved human fetuses, from day six of development to nine months of gestation. She would look and look and try to figure out when the tumor had developed. On day fifteen? Month eight? Or did it develop during March of Pamela's eighth-grade year, when Alex had failed to write to her for three whole weeks?

One day, the curator of the science exhibit asked Alex if she'd like to help. She was putting some chicken eggs into the incubator so that the schoolkids could watch them hatch. Alex held the incubator top open while the woman, Eliza Fenton, gently placed the eggs inside. Fenton was a biologist. In the following weeks, Alex helped her with odd jobs around the museum. Then Alex got the courage to ask her when a brain tumor starts.

Eliza was recording the characteristics of each of the

eggs from which the chicks emerged—color, size, consistency, amount of fluid left inside. She was trying to correlate those variables with the level of alertness in the emerging birds. She answered Alex absently. "Sometimes it starts at the moment of conception. Sometimes the problem is in the genes."

Eliza went on to explain about Mendel's peas and the rules of inheritance. But Alex was only half-listening.

She was going to find diseases in genes. And she was going to stop them.

AT HOME AFTER HER SHOPPING TRIP WITH Lana, Alex caught up on her E-mail. All the mother-daughter talk at dinner, and her recollections on the drive home, had inspired her to write a long note to her own mom. She was deciding whether to offer to visit, when the doorbell buzzed.

David entered and handed her a T-shirt. Alex unfolded it and smiled at the image of Annie Oakley, six-shooters in each hand.

"I'm sorry about what I said the other night," said David.

Alex thanked him and led him to the kitchen, where she offered him a drink. She noticed his sly glance at the kitchen clock. Then it dawned on her. It was almost time for the news.

"C'mon," she said, taking his hand and leading him to the bedroom. Her apartment was not set up as well as his for viewing television. The dryer chairs in the living room weren't positioned in a way that she could figure out where to put a television set. But she had a small set across from her bed.

She turned it on, and they sat at the foot of the bed, her head resting on his shoulder as they caught the last few minutes of a *CSI* spin-off. They started kissing. With her body pressed against his, she reached for the remote to douse the image. But then the newscaster said, "Gloria Devon."

When Alex looked up at the screen, the girl standing

next to Gloria caught her attention. Alex recognized her as the girl whose photo she'd seen in David's house. Gloria Devon's little girl. Figured.

Then she saw the smiling face of her lover—on the screen. He was a younger-looking David, in a tuxedo, smiling at Gloria Devon during a White House party. That image was replaced by a black-and-white newspaper shot of an angry David, the young girl in holiday finest clinging to him while another man yelled at them both. The *Nutcracker* incident.

David pulled away from her and knelt on the floor next to the set, as if that would give him a better understanding of what was going on. There was a scene of a body being taken out of an apartment building. Alex figured that CBS was on to the next story. But then she saw some footage of her boss. Wiatt was explaining that Devon's ex-husband had been found dead. Because Gloria Devon, the FBI's new head, was too close to the situation, the AFIP would be handling the case.

David stood abruptly, a panicked look on his face. "I'm sorry," he said to Alex. "I've got to go."

CHAPTER 29

ALEX HAD NEVER SEEN WIATT LOOK THIS EX-cited. his body was practically vibrating behind his desk. He was nervously clicking his ballpoint pen.

"Ah, um, Colonel," Barbara said, motioning toward the pen. Wiatt straightened his back and stopped making the little click noises. His excitement seemed to have distracted him from his anger at Alex. He looked around his office and smiled at the group he'd called together—Dan, Grant, Barbara, and Alex.

"Well, folks, we've just been handed a second chance," Wiatt said. "Ted Devon. This is probably the most highly charged political murder since JFK's. We are going to go strictly by the book on this one." He looked right at Alex. "No screwups this time. I am going to be in the loop every step of the way."

"What do we know so far?" asked Grant. He was clenching and unclenching his fist at the side of his chair, showing off the muscles in his lower arm.

"I took a look at what the D.C. cops had before they turned the case over," said Dan. The creases in his face seemed a little deeper than usual, as if the frustrations of his investigations were eating away at him. The interrogations of men who'd known Marilyn Mayne had produced zip so far. The electrician who might have followed Cheryl Baker had vanished, and the five-dollar bill Alex had retrieved was too smudged to yield prints. The evidence on the Devon case didn't look much better. "All I can say is that we're starting from a sinkhole," said Dan. "Guy's been dead for over two weeks. The air conditioner was cranked way up, so the body didn't decompose that quickly, but eventually the neighbor in the next condo complained about a smell. Thought maybe there was a dead rat in the wall."

"This guy sounds like dead rat," said Barbara as she glanced over the file. "Shady real estate deals in Colorado, ex-wife got a restraining order against him when they were first divorced. . . ."

Grant interrupted. "Ex-wife's a former district attorney turned U.S. Senator. She might just have been dicking with him, making a case for sole custody. It's easy enough for a woman to cry wolf about violence and get some judge to freeze the guy out."

Grant's bitterness revealed some familiarity with the battle of the exes. It was no secret that he and his ex-wife were still not on civil terms. His animosity got in the way of his getting serious with someone new.

"Why wasn't I called to collect the DNA at the scene?" asked Alex.

"When the D.C. police went in, they had no idea whom they were dealing with," Dan said. "Their own forensic guys worked the scene yesterday morning. They're messengering the evidence here as we speak."

"Cause of death?" asked Grant.

"Might have passed as a heart attack, but his skin showed marks of being shocked by a Taser, so the coroner listed it as a murder. We're checking for a poison," said Dan.

"That's certainly got woman stamped all over it," said Grant. "Men cut and shoot. Women are more devious."

"Forced entry?" asked Barbara.

"Nope. Whoever it was, they had a key or he let them in," said Dan. "Body was pretty decayed by the time he was found, but the D.C. coroner was able to pin down the date of death as late on the night of May 19."

The date was etched in Alex's mind. The day she had gone to New Jersey with David. The day before she saw Madeline James's mutilated body in the Great Lakes library.

"Did the doorman or a neighbor see anyone go into the apartment?" Barbara asked.

Dan had already started interviewing building residents. "His ten-year-old daughter went there after school. Baby-sitter dropped her off for a couple of hours, but the sitter herself didn't go in. After the daughter left, he had Mexican food delivered—service for one—and then he had a late-night visitor."

"A woman?" asked Grant.

"No, a man," said Dan. "The witness was vague about the time. She thinks maybe eleven P.M. She was up with the stomach flu and just looked out her peephole on one of her trips to the bathroom. Couldn't give much of a description. 'Kennedyesque,' she said."

"Hard to tell what that means anymore," said Grant, a broad smile rearranging his features. "The good-looking Kennedys are dead—JFK and John junior. Teddy looks more and more like the Pillsbury Doughboy. It's like a witness saying he looked like Elvis. You need to know, the skinny Elvis or the fat one?"

"I'm sure she meant the skinny one, Grant," said Barbara. "When women say 'Kennedyesque,' they mean it as a compliment."

"How does the man's visit relate to the time of death?" asked Alex.

"That's going to be a tough one," explained Dan. "Two weeks in a D.C. heat wave and that body's going to be rotting like nobody's business. Coroner would be lucky to pin it down to a seven-hour window."

"You're right," said Wiatt, whose gaze had been focused on Dan during the entire conversation. "They're saying between nine P.M. and four A.M."

Dan leafed further in the file. "The later end seems more likely. At a little after eleven P.M., a call was placed from his condo. Unless he was communicating from the grave, he was still alive then."

Everyone turned to that page in their files. Next to the number on the phone record, the D.C. police had written the name Gloria Devon.

"The night before she is sworn in to her new job, Gloria Devon gets a call from her ex-husband?" asked Barbara. "It's too late for him to be calling to talk to the daughter. And it's unlikely he's called to wish her well. From what the papers say, they were in a state of unholy acrimony."

"Could he have been blackmailing her in some way?" asked Alex. "Maybe she'd been involved in a shady property scam with him, their own version of the Clintons' Whitewater. Or maybe she was clean but the revelation of his problems would have gotten in the way of her career— like Geraldine Ferraro being gypped out of a Senate seat because of her husband's real estate deals."

"Lots of reasons why she might want the ex neatly out of the way," said Grant.

"Wait a minute, buddy," said Dan. "You seem to be running off half-cocked. We haven't even got the evidence in hand and you're ready to string up Gloria Devon. Why don't we all read the files, have Alex work a little magic on the DNA samples they send over, and try to get more of a handle on our late-night visitor? We can meet in the Task Force conference room at noon."

"That won't be necessary, Major," said Wiatt. "You still need all your wits on the Tattoo Killer. The White House is all over us on that one. I want Grant and Alex on the evidence for the Devon case. I'll pull you in if it turns out to be complicated."

Dan looked miffed, but Wiatt hadn't left any room to maneuver. Dan got up and headed to the door. "You know where to find me," he said.

C H A P T E R   3 0

WHILE WAITING FOR THE EVIDENCE FROM
the D.C. police, Alex enlarged the computer renderings of
deadly protein created by the Spanish flu and posted them
on the wall above the sequencers. She thought maybe
they'd filter into her unconsciousness while she was working on the more pressing task of a new forensic case.

When the evidence arrived, Alex began the painstaking
job of categorizing the DNA from hair, dandruff, blood,
and skin cells found at Ted Devon's apartment. So far,
she'd come up with three males and four females. One of
her Maryland techs was out at the apartment complex,
getting samples from Devon's landlord and his cleaning
lady in order to rule out people who were in the apartment
routinely for legitimate reasons.

By the middle of the afternoon, Alex had determined
that most of the DNA samples came from Male One, the
dead man himself. There were a few from the landlord,
mainly collected in the kitchen, where a pipe had broken
the previous week. The landlord, Male Two, also served as
a handyman. Male Three was a mystery. Alex ran the third
male sample through the CODIS databank, the national
DNA profile bank of previous offenders. Male Three had
a clean nose. He wasn't in the system.

She then started in on the women. D.C. police had confiscated the bedroom sheets, and Alex now scraped samples from several places. The semen matched that of the

dead guy. The vaginal secretions were from two different women. Asshole doesn't even change his sheets between sex partners, Alex thought. The sheets weren't terribly wrinkled. They couldn't have been on the bed too long. Could Lady A have found about Lady B and killed Ted in a jealous rage? She paged Grant immediately so his men could start asking neighbors about whom Ted had been seeing.

Alex then moved on to the female hair samples from the living room. One of the females was the victim's daughter; half the DNA bands were identical to Ted's. Alex presumed the hair came from Ted and Gloria's daughter, Rayna, but after the fiasco surrounding DNA in the Tattoo Killer case, she wasn't going to leap to any conclusions. You couldn't tell the age of a person from a DNA sample. For all she knew, this particular DNA was from another child of his. As she analyzed the other samples, she looked for one bearing the DNA sequence of that child's mother. But she didn't find any indicating that the mother had been there.

Maybe that meant the kid was Rayna after all. Gloria Devon had told the D.C. police she had never been in her ex's apartment. There was only one way to check: Alex would have to do a DNA test on Rayna. But testing a minor was going to be tricky.

AT 5:00 P.M., ALEX AND GRANT MET WIATT in his office to update him on what they'd found. Alex sat on the side of a small conference table that faced a sketch that Frank Lloyd Wright had done for the Fallingwater house. Wright had superbly designed buildings to fit into their natural settings. Over the recent weeks, Alex had gotten the feeling that Wiatt, too, took careful measure of his surroundings before taking any action. And that whatever action Wiatt took would be as big and dramatic as Fallingwater itself.

Grant covered the table with the papers and printouts their team had produced about the Devon case.

"We've gone through Ted Devon's recent credit-card bills to track down Ladies A and B," Grant reported. "Turns out he eats quite a bit at the Persimmon, a few blocks from his apartment. We turned up one of the women that way. He goes there with a girl called Linda Lake. Sometimes she pays, so we're tracking her through her credit-card number. No answer on her phone or at home, but we've got men waiting outside her house."

"We're investigating the possibility of poison. The killer hadn't doctored the wine or the food," said Alex. "When I leave here, I'm stopping by the morgue. Maybe the body itself will provide a clue."

"Where did the receipt say the Mexican food was from?" Wiatt asked. "Maybe the deliveryman saw something strange."

"We've got someone on that," said Grant.

Barbara came into the room, holding her briefcase. "I'm just back from court. Turned out to be harder than I thought."

Barbara rustled through her papers as she talked. "We know Ted called Gloria around eleven P.M., so I subpoenaed her records to see if she called anyone right before or after that."

"Seems straightforward enough," said Wiatt. "You've pulled a lot of phone records in the Tattoo Killer case."

"Turns out it is not so simple to get phone records from the sitting director of the FBI," says Barbara. "The goddamn Justice Department intervened on her behalf, saying that it would hurt law enforcement if such a subpoena were allowed, since the head of the FBI might be talking to informants."

"No way," said Grant, his nostrils flaring in indignation. "The Queen of the Fibbies isn't going to be getting her manicure dirty doing street investigations."

"You don't know Judge Kline," said Barbara. "He gets his mind made up on a particular theory, and you can't dislodge it from his thoughts. I argued that this was the day before she was sworn in, so it was unlikely the calls were from informants. Then I asked him to authorize a limited revelation of her records, in his chambers. I requested any phone numbers that she called in the twelve hours after Ted's call. He told Director Devon that if she swore it was an informant, he could quarantine the number and not pass it on to us. I figured that would at least start you guys out with something while I appealed Kline's ruling to a higher court.

"So here's what we've got. There were five calls between eight A.M. and nine A.M., probably related to getting the daughter to school and Gloria to work. But . . ."

Barbara pointed to another number with her finger. "There was a single call right after Ted called her. At around eleven thirty P.M., Gloria called a local number."

Grant took the paper and said, "I'll get on it right away."

But looking over Grant's shoulder, Alex knew what he was going to find. The number written there, 202-555-5151, was one she called all the time. It was the cell-phone number for Congressman David Thorne. It was the call he had received in their hotel room.

CHAPTER 31

ALEX SWERVED HER T-BIRD TO AVOID AN ambulance racing toward the Walter Reed emergency room just as she was leaving the AFIP lot. She'd been dazed by Barbara's disturbing news. When David had talked about Gloria at dinner in New Jersey, he'd said quite adamantly that he never spoke to her anymore. Yet that very night he'd been on the phone with her at the hotel. And he'd left Alex's room shortly after. Ted Devon had been alive at 11:00 P.M. that night. The next time Alex had seen David, at 9:00 A.M. or so the next morning, Ted was dead.

Could he have gotten to D.C. and back in that short a time? Alex felt guilty even asking herself that question. A series of comforting images of David went through her mind—the concern in his eyes as she'd recounted her father's death, his suggestive smile as he'd changed the access code in her entryway, on and on. But then other images intruded. She thought of the door closing behind him as he left her hotel room in the wake of Gloria's call.

From the car, she dialed Amtrak. She needed some way to banish that dark image. There was a train that could have gotten him to D.C. within the time frame that Ted had been killed, but no train that could have delivered him back in time in the morning. Alex breathed a sigh of relief. Whatever David was up to that night, he wasn't killing Ted Devon.

At the morgue, Jeanie Nash, an assistant coroner in her mid-fifties, unveiled Ted's body. "We've been up to our eyebrows in dead bodies. We usually don't get this volume of murders till the dog days of summer."

"Thanks for finding time to see me," Alex said.

"My pleasure. We're grateful you took the case off our hands. Want a few more? I can give you a deal on a baker's dozen."

Alex put on a pair of latex gloves and looked the man up and down. She picked up the corpse's right hand, where she could see an evenly distributed bit of blood under each of the nails. "Your report said there was blood under all five nails of the right hand but not the left."

"Yeah, struck me as odd. Most everyone with defensive wounds lashes out at the killer with both hands."

"Any evidence the left arm was restrained in any way?"

The coroner shook her head. "No rope burns, handcuff marks, or contusions."

Alex looked at Ted's left arm. It was completely normal, except for a tiny but visible needle mark. "Why wasn't this in the report?" Alex asked.

"His medical record showed a recent physical, including a blood test. We didn't think the needle stick here indicated any foul play."

Alex got excited. "We're checking on the possibility of a poison. The killer could have used this entry spot for a lethal injection." Alex reached for a scalpel and cut off a piece of skin around the mark. "We can run it for traces of a toxin at the site of entry."

Back at the AFIP, Alex asked Thomas Harding to run a toxicology screen on the skin from the injection site. Then she entered the forensic lab to interrogate the DNA from under Ted Devon's nails.

It was nearly midnight when she finished her work. She posted the printouts of the DNA sequence on the wall of the forensic DNA lab. The DNA was from a female, but it did not match Lady A or B, the two who'd had sex with Ted. However, it had 50 percent of its genes in common with Ted's child. On the night of his death, Ted had scratched the kid's mother.

CHAPTER 32

ALEX, GRANT, BARBARA, AND WIATT WERE sitting solemnly around the table in Wiatt's office. "We need to be enormously careful about how we take this next step," said Barbara.

"Here's what we know," said Alex. "Ted Devon called Gloria at eleven P.M. Between that time and the next morning, he was knocked out with some sort of Taser and—according to Harding—killed with potassium chloride injected into an existing body site."

"Isn't that what they use for the death penalty?" asked Grant. He was wearing a wide belt that looked like a cummerbund. But Alex was so involved in the case, she didn't ask him anything about the properties of this latest toy.

"Yep," said Alex, "that's the lethal injection of choice on death row. Fast and bloodless."

"How easy is it to get potassium chloride?" Wiatt asked Alex. "Maybe we can use purchase receipts to track the killer."

"It's too common," Alex replied. "Our killer probably just dissolved some salt substitute in water and injected it. You can get it at any grocery store."

"If it's that easy," said Barbara, "why aren't more people killed that way?"

"The killer's got to know how to give a shot. Plus, it's hard to get a murder victim to sit quietly while you inject him. Even with a Taser, you have to act fast, or the victim will fight back.

"In this case," Alex told the group, "Ted Devon had time to take a swipe at someone."

Alex pulled up a DNA profile on the screen of her laptop. "He had blood under the nails of his right hand. The chromosomes showed XX."

"A woman?" asked Wiatt in surprise.

"Yes, he must have scratched her shortly before he died. If he'd washed his hands after scratching her, we wouldn't have had such an abundant sample under each nail."

Alex flashed the next genetic profile, that of Ted's daughter, identified through hairs in the living room and spare bedroom. She circled the similarities between the two. "The woman is the mother of Ted's child."

"So let's arrest Gloria Devon. What's the big deal?" asked Grant.

"Well, for one thing, her being scratched doesn't mean she killed him," said Barbara.

"Give me a break, Barbara," said Grant, letting out a deep breath in exasperation. "Why do women always stick up for one another? If it was a corpse with some *guy's* DNA on his hands, we'd arrest in a New York minute."

"Here's the problem," said Alex. "We don't have anything to compare the mother's and daughter's samples to. We would need to get a blood sample from Gloria Devon to be sure that it was her, not the mother of some other child of his."

"Can you broads listen to yourselves?" said Grant. "There is nothing at all in the record to even suggest he had another daughter. Let's move on Devon."

"To prove our case, we'd need to get the FBI director's DNA type," said Barbara. "Given the trouble we had even getting her phone records, there's no chance Kline is going to okay it. We haven't got anything to link her to the poisoning."

"We may not need *her* DNA," said Alex. "It's perfectly legit to ask for DNA from Rayna in order to rule out certain hairs at the scene so we don't think they belong to the suspect. If Rayna did leave the daughter DNA, the mother DNA under the nails definitely would be Gloria's."

Grant reported on interviews with neighbors and girl-friends while Barbara left the room to call Gloria's lawyer and the judge.

"Did anyone ever see Gloria go into the apartment?" Wiatt asked.

"No," said Grant, "but neighbors often saw the daughter open his apartment door with her own key. It would have been the easiest thing in the world for Gloria to go over there when her kid was sleeping and put Daddy into a nice long sleep himself."

While Alex and Wiatt were mulling that over, Barbara walked back into the room. "It went much easier than I thought," she said. "Gloria okayed the DNA test on her daughter without our having to go to court—on two con-ditions. One, that the blood draw be done at her house so the daughter isn't scared."

Barbara looked directly at Alex. "And two, that Alex do the draw."

GLORIA DEVON ANSWERED THE DOORBELL herself. In jeans and flat shoes, she looked much younger than her fifty-three years. And much softer than she had in the televised hearings and press conferences. In fact, thought Alex, she looked quite beautiful. Not tired or ner-vous, just gracious. Alex felt a sudden pang of jealousy, wondering what role Gloria was currently playing in David's life.

Gloria led Alex into Rayna's room, where the girl was reading at her desk. Alex noticed that the light hanging over-head was a bicyclist, just like the one on David's track light.

"Mom says that you're a doctor," Rayna said. "That's what I want to be when I grow up. It's between that and an artist. That's why I like this book."

She closed the book she was reading, *Gray's Anatomy*. "I'm learning about the circulatory system."

"When I was her age," Gloria said to Alex, "I thought all women could do was be a nurse, schoolteacher, or a backup dancer on *The Dean Martin Show*."

"I thought I'd bend it like Beckham," said Alex, wistfully remembering her two summers of soccer . . . and of having a best friend.

Alex asked Rayna to extend her arm and point out a vein. She put out her right arm. "There's one right here," said Rayna, using her left hand to point to the underside of her right wrist.

"You're left-handed?"

Rayna nodded. "Like my dad." Her nose twitched like she was going to cry, and she reached over to her mom's arm. Gloria stepped closer and wrapped her arms around her daughter in a comforting embrace.

"I'm really sorry about your dad," said Alex. "This will help get the guy who murdered him." Guy or girl, thought Alex, sneaking a peak at Gloria out of the corner of her eye.

Alex gently took Rayna's right hand and pointed to the vein inside her elbow. "I'd like to put a tiny needle in your vein here."

Rayna nodded bravely from inside Gloria's embrace. "Mom already told me what you were going to do."

"Why don't you look over at the bicyclist?" said Gloria. "We'll make up a story about him."

Rayna looked in that direction and Gloria started whispering a story in her ear. Alex unzipped her fanny pack and used an alcohol wipe to cleanse the skin. She next took out a syringe, pricked the girl, and got her sample.

"You're a very brave girl," Alex said to Rayna. "You're gonna be a great doctor." Rayna beamed with pride, then went back to her book.

Gloria kissed her daughter on the head before she left the girl's room.

"Would you like some tea before you leave?" she asked Alex.

"I'd love some," said Alex. Isn't that what Dan would

teach her in Murder 101? Get close to the suspect. She wondered, though, whether accepting a drink from a potential poisoner was going above and beyond the call of duty.

Alex followed Gloria into the kitchen, responding to the siren sound of the whistling teapot. The pot was shaped like a parrot, with the steam coming out of his beak. "My Mother's Day gift from Rayna," Gloria said.

They sat at the table with their cups, silent for a moment. Then Gloria said, "I appreciate your coming. Rayna's already been through so much."

"I can understand you wanting the blood drawn here," said Alex. "But why ask for me?"

Gloria looked down at her teacup, then back up at Alex. "David speaks highly of your integrity. That's not a word one hears often in this town."

Alex held Gloria's gaze, trying to calm her racing jealous pulse from the easy, casual way Gloria had mouthed the name of her—no, their—lover.

Gloria, ever the astute politician, read the look on Alex's face. "No, it's not what you think."

Alex couldn't help herself. "How is it, then?"

"David came here the other night when the news broke. It was less about me than about Rayna. He wanted to make sure she was all right."

It didn't set right with Alex. David not telling her about Gloria's call the night of the murder. Then dashing out of her apartment after seeing Gloria on the news. She had three messages on her cell phone from David, asking her to call him, but she wasn't ready to talk to him just yet. She wasn't sure how she felt.

Alex changed the subject. "I thought you were amazing in the confirmation hearings."

Gloria smiled and tossed her head back. "There I was, being raked over the coals by my own colleagues in the Senate. People I'd worked with for a decade, whose kids I knew by name, were treating me as if they'd never met me.

"And the Republicans!" She rolled her eyes. "The same guys who'd loved my work on the crime-control bill sprouted fangs and claws at the thought of my running the FBI."

"But other people were out there rooting for you," Alex said. "I saw the ad in *The New York Times* where the cops' union and the national association of district attorneys threw you their support."

"That was all great, but it was the smaller things that mattered more. Like my friends in the Women's Caucus, whose shoulders I could cry on in the middle of the night."

Well, thought Alex, why didn't you call one of *them* the night your ex-husband was murdered?

"What's it like to be head of the FBI?" she asked. "Everybody must ask you that."

"Actually, only the women."

"Because you're blazing a path."

"I guess it's like what you faced when you went to medical school, or I encountered when I first joined the Senate. A lot of hard work and quite a few men who want to see you fail. But it's great fun getting into that kiddie playhouse marked 'No girls allowed.'"

Gloria thought about it further. Then she added, "There are some days, though, when I wish I'd chosen backup dancer."

CHAPTER 33

WHEN ALEX FLASHED HER ID CARD AT THE
guard at the AFIP reception desk, he told her, "Colonel
Wiatt wants you in his office at once." It wasn't a suggestion, but a command.

"I'm just going to drop these samples off in the lab,"
she said.

"He said immediately." There was a young private
standing by to walk her directly there.

The private left as soon as he'd accomplished the handoff. Wiatt and Grant were waiting for her. They didn't even
give her the chance to sit down before addressing her.

"Why didn't you tell us?" Wiatt asked.

Alex was silent. She stood quietly, waiting to see how
much they knew.

"Alex, for Chrissakes," said Grant. "You were fuckin' a
suspect. A desk clerk remembers the two of you checking
in together and two other guests from that floor saw you
two"—he opened his notebook and quoted, " 'making out
in the hallway and then disappearing into a room.' "

Alex folded her arms defensively in front of her. "He
wasn't a suspect at the time," she said.

Wiatt's gray eyes engaged hers. "But now you've got a
serious conflict," he said. "I don't want you anywhere near
the evidence." He looked down at the plastic container,
about the size of a lunch box, that she'd brought back with
Rayna's blood in it. "I've asked Rick Baer from the Mary-

land techs to handle the analysis. He'll run the forensic genetics for this operation."

"You're shutting me out?" asked Alex, grasping the case with the blood sample close to her body. She felt foolish now, but it had never dawned on her that her personal life would merge into her work life. She'd always managed to live in two completely different spheres.

"The last thing we need is having our case thrown out because of your involvement with the Congressman," said Wiatt.

Grant joined in. "We'd be chum in the water for those defense piranhas. If the DNA showed Gloria did it, they'd say you were just some bitch in heat trying to eliminate the competition."

"Plus," said Wiatt, "there's the distinct possibility that the Congressman is an accessory, maybe even the killer."

"He couldn't have done it," said Alex.

"See?" said Grant, looking over at Wiatt. "That kind of magical thinking could compromise the whole investigation."

Alex faced her colleague. "I'm a professional, Grant, just like you. Judging by the amount of time the Congressman was with me, and the Amtrak schedule, I'm convinced he wasn't in D.C. that night."

Then she took two angry steps toward Wiatt's desk and carefully placed the case squarely in front of him. She put her palms on the desk and leaned forward, invading his space. "I can do my job just fine, no matter what the circumstances. I don't see how putting me off in Siberia, like you did with Dan, is going to strengthen your investigation."

But there was no changing Wiatt's mind. He moved the sample case toward him, thanked her coldly for doing the blood draw, and dismissed her.

She left the room, off to join the caribou on the permafrost.

ALEX STORMED DOWN THE HALLWAY TO HER laboratory just as Rick Baer was coming out of the lab next door, presumably on his way to pick up the samples that Wiatt had taken from her. Here was a guy who couldn't find the supply closet two weeks ago and now he was running DNA on a case that was on the front page of the *Washington Post* every morning.

He walked past her, then turned around and came back. "Dr. Blake," he said quietly. "I'm not sure what politics put me in the center of the Devon case, but I want you to know I wasn't angling for the job. I'll try my best to do it with excellence, just like you taught us."

"Thanks, Rick," she said. "I appreciate that you're not treating me like a leper right now." She opened the door to her lab.

"There's one other thing," he said, embarrassed. "They changed the locks on the forensic lab while you were out today. Your key's not going to work anymore."

"Was it Grant or Wiatt who came up with that little twist?"

"I'm not sure. Some building-manager type came over. If there's anything you need from there, though, just let me know."

She nodded and entered her lab. She closed the door behind her, then took the position of all-city champion soccer striker. With her right foot, she kicked a wheeled stool down the length of the lab, past all three sequencers. Amazingly, it landed under the hooded lab shelf. If it had veered off course and hit any of the machines, it would have wrecked thousands of dollars' worth of equipment.

Alex sat on the floor. Maybe Grant was right. Maybe her judgment was impaired. She stayed there, trying to figure out what to do. After a few minutes of breathing the purified lab air, she felt slightly better.

She got up and sat at her desk, powered up her laptop, and pulled up the files she'd used when she presented evidence about the case to Wiatt and Grant. The blood samples from the scene were in the forensic lab next door, *terra prohibida* at the moment. She was at a dead end as far as figuring out whether Gloria's blood was under Ted's nails. But for the other question that was nagging at her, she didn't need the actual samples, because she had the completed DNA profiles from the scene on her laptop, and a binder with the police reports on her desk.

She opened the computer file labeled "Male Three." The man had been in Ted's apartment between the time the maid had cleaned on a Tuesday and the time Ted had been killed on a Friday.

She probably could narrow the time frame even more. Four hairs belonging to Male Three had been collected. She leafed through the binder until she found the list of evidence and the photos from the scene. Her attention fell on the photo of the room where the second hair follicle from Male Three—evidence piece number 202—was found. There had been two hairs on top of each other at that site. Her DNA analysis showed they were from two different people. But which one had been on top? She went back through the notes of the D.C. forensic guy who had collected the evidence. Of course, there was no mention of so trivial a detail. But, thought Alex, the numbering of samples could provide a clue. If she were putting samples of evidence into bags, she would have put the top sample into a bag first, wouldn't she? Male Three was 202, which meant that the female sample 203 was under it. Since 203 belonged to the daughter, the man had visited the apartment after the girl had.

She thought about the phone call from Gloria to David. Was he the man?

She tried to think back to the trip to New Jersey and the morning on Ellis Island. Something about the train tickets flashed into her mind. She remembered him putting the return tickets into his blazer pocket. But then he couldn't find them the next morning.

Why was that nagging at her?

Then she visualized him on the dais, giving his speech. He wasn't wearing a blazer. He had changed into a suit.

Where had he gotten a suit? All he'd been carrying on the Metroliner was a briefcase with an extra shirt and underwear.

Had she been wrong when she assumed that he hadn't gone back to D.C.? Was he the guy in Ted's apartment the night he died?

Be calm, thought Alex. If he killed Ted because he blamed him for the breakup, why wait a year?

Why not?

He'd certainly be less of a suspect a year later, especially after all that public affection with another woman. Alex.

When David had described his photography, hadn't he talked about how he'd learned to lie in wait for just the right moment?

But then how to explain the phone call? If Gloria and David had been secretly planning to off her ex-spouse, why that bit of incriminating evidence? Unless, of course, Ted had threatened Gloria with something that would have prevented her from being sworn in the next day.

Alex's curiosity was swelling. She wanted so badly to believe that David was who he seemed. But in some dark recess of her brain, she worried that she'd been the dupe all along.

She started pacing the length of her lab. She could picture Ted threatening Gloria and David taking charge, heading over there and warning Ted to lay off. But she couldn't picture the next step—David killing Ted.

Was David at the apartment that night? Was he Male Three? Alex realized that she could easily find out. Unlike Monica Lewinsky, she didn't have an infamous blue dress. But she did have a toothbrush that David used at her apartment.

C H A P T E R   34

"PLANNING A SLEEPOVER?" DAN ASKED ALEX as she came down the hall of the AFIP later that day after a brief trip to her apartment.

She realized it did look a little odd, racing along with a toothbrush sticking out of a brown paper bag. "Proper dental hygiene has changed my life," she said. "Anything new on the Tattoo case?"

"We've got a pool of about eighty potential suspects," said Dan. "Every woman jilted by a sailor has phoned our office to claim her guy must be the Tattoo Killer."

"What about Admiral Mason's son?"

"I haven't forgotten about him. We've talked to people who knew him as a kid. Guess how he learned about his dad's affairs?"

"The admiral brought the women home?"

"Nope, kid tapped the phone line. Starting at age twelve. Read a book about it in a base library. We're looking for a drifter in related industries—telephone companies, cell-phone makers, electronics. Ties in with your theory about the electrician in Norfolk. So far, the only break we've caught on the son is a copy of his 1998 driver's license out of Nevada."

"That's at least something," said Alex as they walked. "Hey, wasn't that one of the states with the cherry condoms?"

"Good memory," said Dan.

Then she thought about the librarian in Great Lakes. "Did you try to match the bite cast with any dental records?"

Dan nodded. "No luck there. Barbara's told us we can't ask the admiral about the kid's dentist. Doesn't strike me as a family that keeps in touch, anyway."

"Let me know if I can help," she said. "As you might have heard, I've suddenly got a lot of time on my hands."

Dan smiled, the first time Alex had seen him do so in quite awhile. "Don't tell me you're actually beginning to enjoy forensics."

She thought about it for a moment. "It's not really that different from my disease research, lots of dead ends, and a lot riding on it."

In her lab, Alex scraped residue off the toothbrush and put it in the centrifuge. She inserted the pipette and tried to extract some DNA.

Nothing. She was sleeping with the only guy in America who rinsed his toothbrush off thoroughly after he brushed his teeth. If she wanted DNA, she would have to collect it herself.

"I WAS WORRIED WHEN YOU DIDN'T RETURN my calls yesterday," David said as he sat in one of the dryer chairs in her living room, sipping a glass of red wine after dinner at Meskerem, the Ethiopian place a few blocks from her house. "There's something I really need to talk to you about. . . ."

He put down his wineglass and moved over to Alex's chair. He sat down at her feet, like he had done the night he'd painted her toenails. "The forensics people assume I was with you all night in New Jersey. What are you going to tell them if they ask you?"

Alex was surprised. "You want me to alibi you?"

"I know it's a lot—"

"A lot!" she snapped. She got out of the chair and started pacing. "It could be a career breaker for me. Ugly words like *perjury* and *misrepresentation* come to mind."

"I didn't do it, Alex. Neither did Gloria."

"Then prove it."

"How?"

"Explain to me exactly what did go down that night, starting with when your supposedly *former* lover interrupted our lovemaking?"

He reached up to take her hand, but she pulled it away.

"Honest to God, I hadn't heard from Gloria for nearly a year before that call. But she was crazy with grief. Ted was threatening blackmail."

"What did he have on her?"

David hesitated for a moment, still protecting Gloria. He stood up and walked to the window. Alex walked over and stood next to him.

David watched a taxi drop an elderly man off at the building next door. His gaze followed the man's cane as he tapped his way to the stoop, fumbled in his pockets for a key, then let himself into the adjoining building. Alex's impatient shoe tapping diverted David's attention back to her.

"She'd prosecuted a case as a young lawyer," he said, "low-level mob guy. Made a few mistakes that a more seasoned DA wouldn't have made. The guy walked."

"So?" She sat on the windowsill, determined to not have her movements or gestures give any clue to what she was thinking.

"When Ted called that night, he told Gloria he had an affidavit from the mob guy that he was going to release. It said that Gloria had thrown his case in exchange for five thousand dollars."

"Who would believe him? The word of a criminal against that of a U.S. Senator?"

"Think about it from Gloria's standpoint. Whether or not he was telling the truth, she would look bad. She either took a bribe—or she had to admit her incompetence. Either way, the President would have pulled her as FBI director.

"And there was more. With Ted's work, there was always cash going in and out of their joint checking account. The affidavit says the five thousand dollars was paid on a certain day. It was a day, back in 1983, when precisely that amount showed up in the account."

"Sounds like a perfect reason for her to get rid of Ted. Maybe even to ask for help from her lover. . . ."

"Ex-lover."

She got up and focused on his eyes, her moving arms punctuating her speech. "Ex-lover only because old Ted got in the way. Just tell me one thing. Were you in Ted's apartment that night?"

"You've got to believe me, no."

"Did you go back to D.C.?"

He hesitated, then spoke slowly. "This is how much I trust you, Alex. I'm going to tell you something that could ruin my career if the media got hold of it."

Alex fumed. "You're always about your career," she said, waving her hands. "This is about us, our relationship."

He walked over to the nail polish holder and started spinning it absentmindedly.

"Well?" said Alex, hands on her hips.

David looked at her, a pained expression on his face. "Gloria sounded so distraught when she called me that night, ready to give up everything she'd worked for. I walked out of our hotel and paid cash for a ticket on the last train to D.C. I went to her house in Georgetown, calmed her down, and helped her write a press release to counter what Ted was going to say. I told her to stick it out, the country needed her."

"Did you go to bed with her?"

"Alex!" he said, taking a few steps until he was directly in front of her. "Of course not. I'd just made love to you." He bent over and kissed the top of her hair.

Alex stood there for a moment, and they held each other, their bodies swaying slightly, a gentle rock, calming each other. Then Alex broke away.

"It doesn't make sense. Why would Ted go after her like that?"

"What makes anyone do what they do? Maybe he never forgave her for the divorce, for topping him professionally, for Rayna loving her more. Who knows what goes through the mind of a guy like him?"

Alex thought for a moment. "How did you get back to New Jersey in time?"

"I borrowed Gloria's car, drove home, showered, and composed myself. Then I drove to Jersey City. I was planning to take the train back with you. Gloria said she'd send a staffer up to drive the car back down."

"Why didn't you tell me about it?"

"You took off from Ellis Island without a word. Remember? When I saw you next, the whole thing had blown over, Gloria was back out of my life, and I wanted you. Simple as that."

"How convenient for Gloria that old Ted was offed that very night."

"I admit it's kind of unbelievable, but pursuing me and Gloria isn't going to get you any closer to the real killer."

Alex wondered how much she should tell him. She was willing to bet one of her $300,000 sequencers that it was Gloria's blood under Ted's nails. But that didn't mean David was in on it. She knew herself how easy it was to trust a lover who might not be all that you thought.

"A man was in Ted's apartment that night. We haven't been able to figure out who it was."

David was quiet. "You've got DNA?" he asked after a moment.

She nodded.

"And you think it might be me?"

She grimaced, not sure how he'd react.

David's eyes looked relieved rather than hurt. He stuck out his arm to give a sample. But her kit was now in Rick's hands. "Take me to your sequencer," he said.

CHAPTER 35

ON THE DRIVE TO THE AFIP, ALEX REALIZED that she could hardly waltz a murder suspect past the guard, especially when Wiatt had ordered her off this case. So she dropped David off about two blocks from the entrance and told him where to meet her and when.

Fifteen minutes later, she was opening the door of the National Museum of Health and Medicine. The security at AFIP rivaled that of the White House, but the catacomb of underground tunnels led her to the museum, where she easily let him in the unguarded front door.

"Memory Lane," he said as they hurried past General Sickles's amputated leg bone.

Alex was in no mood for a romantic tour through their past. She steered him down into the tunnels. Four rights, then two lefts, up the stairs, a few steps down the hall, and they were in her laboratory. She took a syringe out of the drawer. "Time for you to put out," she said.

He extended his arm and she took some blood. She poured it into a fat test tube and inserted it into the Gentra Systems Autopure LS, where it was centrifuged and combined with chemicals. At the end of the process, the test tube had nothing left in it but a small dollop of David's DNA. Alex transferred the clear, syrupy DNA to the sequencer. She programmed the computer to compare David's DNA to that taken from the scene of the crime. In fifteen minutes, the sequence of five genes from his blood would flash up next to the DNA sequence of Male Three.

This time, it was the opposite of a slot machine. If the cherries matched, she would be standing alone in her lab with a killer.

David was standing in the middle of the lab, trying not to touch anything. That was a common reaction of nonscientists. They didn't want to disrupt something that might be important. But now Alex began to panic at her rash decision to bring David here. She was in her lab with a possible killer. Was he just trying not to leave fingerprints?

He was talking about something, but Alex wasn't listening. No one knew he was here with her. They hadn't passed anyone on the street leaving her apartment nor in the halls here. If he were to kill her, who would suspect him?

He realized she wasn't listening, so he started wandering around the room. He looked at the CD rack next to her stereo. He walked over to a shelf and picked up her letter opener, a heavy brass one with an intricate design, which her mother had bought in India. He held it in front of him and took a step toward her.

"Stay where you are," she said.

He looked shocked. Just then, the sequencer spit out its results. They both looked at the screen. Congressman David Thorne was not a match to Male Three.

CHAPTER 36

THAT SEARING MOMENT OF DISTRUST IN HER laboratory drove a painful wedge between David and her. He fumed silently as they retraced their steps through the museum. They got into the T-Bird, but she didn't start the car. Instead, she leaned toward him over the stick shift. "I'm really sorry. It's just . . . the way you took off to Gloria's when you heard the news, I didn't know what to think, what to believe."

He faced her, opened his mouth to speak, and then shut it without a word. His brow was rigid and his mouth a frown. He'd aged a decade since the evening began.

She reached over to touch his cheek but pulled her hand away when he stiffened. He spoke quietly, "How could you?" Then he turned away from her, rolled down the car window, reached outside, and opened his door. He got out.

She braced herself for him to say something brutally final, like "Have a nice life." But he just looked at her sadly, closed the door gently behind him, and walked to the Metro stop.

When she got home, she opened a bottle of tequila and took it into the living room. She sat down in one of the dryer chairs to drink, but she was overcome by the memory of David painting her toenails there. She got up abruptly and took the tequila into her bedroom.

This is a new low, she thought. Drinking in bed. She

pumped Jose Cuervo into her system as she mentally listed all the things she was screwing up. Men. Work. Even family. She hadn't called her mother in a month. Over the next half hour, she berated herself for virtually every slip she'd made her entire adult life. Then she pulled herself out of bed, still fully clothed, went out the front door, and got into the car.

When she got to David's house, she could see his silhouette in the window. He was sitting in his living room, most of the lights off.

She knocked quietly and he answered the door, a drink in his hand. "You look as bad as I feel," he said to her.

They sat down on the couch, both slumping back, legs up on the copper cocktail table. They were silent for a few minutes. Then David turned to her and said, "I keep seeing that look of terror in your eyes."

"I know, I know. I'm sorry."

"How could you not trust me?" he said, a hint of anger in his voice now.

Alex was annoyed. This seemed so unfair. "Well, you didn't trust me. Why didn't you tell me what was going on?"

"I promised Gloria I wouldn't say anything."

Alex got up. "I'm sick of Gloria and how you're protecting her. I wish she'd just click her red shoes and go back to Oz."

"Alex, Gloria doesn't have anything to do with us. You're the one who's been pushing me away. You're not ready for a grown-up relationship."

Alex had the urge to fling his drink in his face, but that would be proving his case. Instead, she gave him an angry glare. "Forgive me for not following you around like a puppy dog, like those reporters and staffers. You don't want grown-up, you want suck-up."

David got up and started pacing. "I know politics isn't the real world. But I've never felt you respected what I did."

Alex was stunned. A Congressman needing her respect?

He continued, "My colleagues may not be as exciting as your artist and musician friends. But at least they're willing to commit to something."

"Puh-leese," said Alex, "spare me Civics 101. I'm not an eighth grader visiting you on my class trip."

David fell silent for a moment. "See what I mean? You don't respect me. And you can't commit to someone unless you feel respect and trust. In fact, I don't know if you're capable of committing to anything at all."

Alex was angry. "I came over here to apologize, and you're turning this all around. What do you know about relationships? You're the guy who has his chief of staff call me when he's going to be late."

Alex got up and strode out of the house, slamming the door after her.

Tears filled her eyes on the way home. Now she'd screwed this up, too. Maybe David was right. Maybe she couldn't commit. She liked teaching because you got different students each year. If you made a mistake one year, you could start over with a new crop. She was past thirty and had no five-year plan. She didn't have a fire in her belly to go back to Berkeley. She had no idea what she would do after her two-year fellowship at AFIP ended.

Her only commitment that night was to the bottle of Jose Cuervo.

THE NEXT MORNING, ALEX FELT COMPLETELY spent. She made some espresso and turned on the television in her bedroom while she drank the coffee standing up. CNN, the other networks—everybody was carrying the story.

Gloria Devon, the director of the FBI, had been arrested for murder. Rick's analysis of Rayna's sample had provided probable cause to get a DNA sample from Gloria. The blood under Ted's nails proved to be hers.

Even though Alex had seen this coming, something about it did not ring true. She'd seen how much Gloria doted on Rayna. She couldn't imagine her leaving a ten-year-old alone at home to go kill her ex. Even Janet, at her most distraught, had never left Alex alone as a kid.

And there was something nagging at her about the

blood under the nails. She put her left arm in front of her, made a claw with her right, and scratched. She saw how the nails hit. The epicenter for each nail was just a little different. The nail of the thumb hit at the oddest angle of all. Yet the blood under Ted's fingernails was uniformly distributed.

She then realized there was an even bigger problem. The blood was under the nails of Ted's right hand. Ted, like Rayna, had been left-handed.

GRANT, WIATT, AND BARBARA SAT AT WIATT'S conference table and listened to what Alex had to say.

"It's definitely *Brady* material," said Barbara. "If we have evidence that could exculpate Gloria, we have to turn it over."

Barbara turned to Alex to explain. "There's a U.S. Supreme Court case, the *Brady* case, which requires prosecutors to give defendants any exculpatory evidence they turn up. The idea is to level the playing field."

Grant countered, "This isn't evidence. It's just Alex's interpretation. The report says the blood is from the right hand. Gloria Devon can figure out herself that the guy she lived with all that time was left-handed."

"You may have a point there," said Barbara.

"Plus," said Grant, waving a piece of paper in Barbara's direction, "look what we found in Ted's desk drawer."

He showed the group an affidavit alleging that Gloria had thrown a case in exchange for money. "It's got motive written all over it," said Grant. "If old Ted took a swipe at her with his other arm, what does it matter? Maybe he was holding a drink or a copy of this in his left hand."

Wiatt turned to Alex. "Are you saying that there is no way that the blood pattern under the nails could have occurred naturally?"

"It would be highly unlikely."

"Alex," said Grant, "think about what you are saying. Who would want to frame Devon for this?"

"There's still an unidentified male on the scene."

"Sure," said Grant, "and he must have been a vampire. Where else would he have gotten her blood to leave at the scene? Can you explain that away, too?"

Alex hadn't quite thought that far. She shook her head.

Wiatt thought for a moment. Then he turned to Grant. "Have Rick Baer pull all our past forensic cases where there was blood under the nails. If the pattern here is truly unique, we'll report it to Devon's attorney."

Then he turned to Alex. "I like to win, but I like to win fair."

Grant frowned at having lost the argument. Alex pondered how she might play on Wiatt's reasonableness to argue her way back into the Devon case.

"Colonel," she said calmly, but before she could finish her sentence, Dan Wilson barged into Wiatt's office, paying no heed to the menacing protests of Lurch, the assistant.

"The Tattoo Killer's scored a new victim," Dan announced. "She's a floater, just washed up. The body is too bloated to be identified just yet. But she's got the right tattoo."

"Near a base?" asked Barbara.

"It's been pretty stormy in the Northeast, so the body could have traveled quite some distance. The nearest base is Groton."

Connecticut. Just as Alex had predicted.

CHAPTER 37

THREE HOURS LATER, THE WATERLOGGED body arrived at andrews Air Force Base, where an ambulance raced it to the AFIP. Grant and Alex were already suited up in the autopsy suite. Dan had fought hard with Wiatt to get her back on the Tattoo Killer team. Since this was the first break that they'd caught in weeks, Wiatt was willing to say yes to whatever Dan wanted. But he would only allow Alex to collect the DNA. Someone else would be in charge of analyzing it.

Thomas Harding would conduct the autopsy. Back in Chicago, he'd autopsied a couple of gang members whose bodies had floated up in the Calumet-Sag Channel of the Chicago River. The morgue at AFIP was perfect for a drowning victim. The Navy had funded Grant's team to create computer visualizations based on bone structure to show what drowned sailors actually looked like. Between bloating and being eaten away by predatory fish, some drowning victims had features distorted beyond recognition. The Navy didn't want to be in the position of having one of its ships sunk by the enemy and then not be able to identify the bodies.

The Connecticut police chief hadn't been happy that his new corpse was being dissected someplace else. But Dan Wilson was such a legend in the forensics community that the chief stopped protesting once he'd extracted a promise that Dan would speak at the next annual meeting

of state police. While the corpse was being flown to Andrews, Dan was flying to Groton. He was on the ground
there now, waiting for clues from the autopsy to jump-
start the search.

Nobody had any idea who the woman was. She was
wearing a T-shirt and shorts, which had been tattered and
slashed by the rough ocean rocks. There was no purse, no
ID, no jewelry, no distinguishing scars. The only unusual
thing was a three-foot-long piece of electrical wire wound
around her neck and tied in an intricate knot. The shape
meant nothing to Alex, but Harding recognized it. "It's a
Flemish eight," he said. "Sailors use it because it doesn't
fray the rope as much as an overhand knot."

Corporal Chuck Lawndale, Dan Wilson's computer
aide, entered the room and eyed the corpse with curiosity.
The cause of death was obvious, but the autopsy was necessary for clues about the identity of the woman and her
assailant.

"Looks like she spent around two days in the water,"
said Harding. That meant that the killer was back with his
pattern, killing eighteen days after the Great Lakes murder. "She's bloated, but not too badly decomposed."

Harding snipped away the T-shirt on the woman, revealing her muscular upper arms and a lovely set of breasts,
marred only by the shaky indigo tattoo of an open eye.

"She worked out," said Grant.

"Not likely," said Harding. "All of her musculature
is in the upper part of the body. Her legs are much less
developed."

As the autopsy proceeded, Harding started reading various measurements of the distance between bones, esti-
mated the angles of the muscles, and relayed those figures
to Chuck. Grant showed Chuck how to enter them into the
computer program to create a rough image of the drowned
woman's appearance, without the bloating.

Alex scraped under the corpse's fingernails for DNA, a
long shot, since the salt water would have washed away almost everything. "What do you make of the marks on her

hands?" Alex asked Harding. She lifted the corpse's hand and moved it toward Harding. It had an eerie effect, as if the corpse were waving.

"Superficially, they look like defensive wounds," Harding said. He then used a thin knife to peel back a layer of skin. "Nah, she shows a lot of repetitive injury to this area, like she's been struck repeatedly across time with a blunt instrument."

"Violent husband?" asked Grant. Now that he'd shown off his 3-D program, he returned to the body.

"Probably not married," said Alex. "She's pretty tan and there's no white mark where a ring would be." Alex stepped back to survey the whole body. "The tan itself is odd. Her legs and lower arms are dark brown, but the rest of the body is untouched by the sun. Most women avoid that sort of tan. You look like an idiot, then, if you wear a low-cut dress."

"Like golfers in a bathing suit," said Grant.

Harding was gingerly cutting the cord from around her neck. Alex noticed the color there. "She's sunburned, not tan, on the neck. She must have been outside recently, after a haircut."

Alex looked at the woman's hands again. The injuries were mainly on the top of the left hand, particularly on the finger closest to the thumb. Alex thought about how she had suffered a similar blow when she was nailing up a picture hanger. Then it dawned on her. "She works construction."

SINCE GROTON WAS IN THE NORTHEASTERN Rust Belt, construction projects weren't exactly plentiful. It was easy for Dan to find one where a female worker had gone missing a few days earlier. More importantly, one of the guys on the job had disappeared at the same time. The missing man was around five nine, with a buzz cut. He'd shown up at the site, knew everything there was to know about wiring, and worked effortlessly and well for about a week before his disappearance. "He was like some kinda electrical genius," the construction foreman told Dan. "He just sorta dropped out of the sky. It didn't surprise me when he left, because, his kinda talent, he could work anywhere."

Once Dan had located the warehouse construction site, Alex had been put on an Air Force jet to the nearby corporate airfield. Now she was pacing around the half-built warehouse, trying to figure out where the killer might have left his DNA. This wasn't like the Navy base library. Too much time had passed. The area had been swept by rain and high winds earlier that week. From the beer bottles and condoms in a corner, Alex could tell that teens had discovered the building and used it after hours. And the construction workers had poured concrete over the floor and put up drywall, sealing away any evidence the killer might have left.

Dan and three of his investigators were interviewing other workers, trying to get some sort of picture of the guy. The magical electrician certainly fit the profile. Loner. Tense.

He'd given his name as Ben Meecham, but no one had checked ID. The construction site was strictly a cash-and-carry operation.

"That name seems familiar," Dan said to Alex. "I'm trying to figure out if he's wanted on some other case I've worked on."

Then it dawned on him. "Shit. He's not a person. He's the character of the son in *The Great Santini*."

Once the other construction workers realized that the drifter might have killed their friend Kelly, they were willing to do anything to help. In fact, a lynch-mob mentality was beginning to brew. Dan tried to steer them to think about information, not revenge.

"How did he get to work?" Dan asked the group. "Did he drive?"

No one could remember him having a car at the job site. One guy, though, remembered him getting on a bus in front of the Buddy's Bar, heading north. A buzz went through the team that Dan had brought with him. Finally, something useful.

Dan walked over to his men. "I want you to find out where that bus goes and what cheap motels it leads to. I don't think he was here long enough to rent an apartment."

One of the construction guys, a tanned thirtysomething with curly dark hair and paint-spattered jeans, eyed Alex like a carnivore eyeing baby-back ribs. Rather than ignore him, she sought him out. "So tell me what this electrical guy was like."

"Queer." He laughed.

"What do you mean? He brought his boyfriend to the warehouse? He sang the Village People's 'Macho Man'? He tried to get it on with you?"

He squinted his eyes in disgust at the idea. "No, he wore work gloves all the time. What a pussy."

Fuck, thought Alex, can the DNA beat get any worse here? "I hear his work was pretty good, though."

"Yeah," the guy said begrudgingly. "Especially the central wires."

Alex's eyes lit up and she joined Dan and told him her plan. They rejoined the head of the construction crew.

"She needs you to break down the wall in front of the most complicated electric work," Dan said.

The beefy foreman looked like he was going to explode. "No way. That'll slow us down and put us in overtime."

The local police chief spoke up. Since Dan's arrival, the chief had been trailing Dan like a puppy. "Mr. Masters," he said, "if you don't do exactly what this man says, I'll have your ass as an accessory to murder."

In anger, the foreman took a sledgehammer and knocked out a section of drywall. Alex gasped in shock as the dust spilled inside, compromising any evidence. Then the foreman got control of himself and instructed one of his men to cut away a section of the ceiling where Kelly's killer had brought together the essential wiring. The wall pounding had just been a show.

Alex trudged up a ladder and looked into the hole. The wiring looked like some sort of beautiful weaving. The killer was scrupulous and artistic. But to put something together that complex, the guy would have left some sign of himself.

Alex shone the UV light on a complicated section of wire in which many strands had been brought together, but without any loose angles or irregular end lengths. If there was DNA here, the light would cause it to fluoresce. She mentally urged the light to provoke a glow. But she came up blank.

She was admiring the handiwork at the juncture of the wiring and a wall when she used the tip of her light to move the wiring slightly. On the underside of the braided cord, there was a smudged fingerprint. Hallelujah, she thought. He had taken off his gloves to coax the wires into this masterpiece.

Dan ascended next and applied Dual Contrast Powder with a camel-hair brush to enhance resolution of the fingerprint. He photographed it and then cut the three feet of wire around it to take back to AFIP for further analysis.

When the foreman saw what Dan was doing, he looked like he was going to cry. "That'll set us back weeks!" the construction boss moaned.

"Think of it this way," said Dan. "You construction guys always run late and over budget. At least now you've got an excuse."

Alex was about to head back to the airport with the section of wiring. Then Dan got a call that one of his men had struck gold. At the Cleaver Inn, a fleabag motel near the bus line, a guy had paid in cash for a month's worth of time. The manager, if you could call a guy in a dirty sleeveless T-shirt that, hadn't seen him for a week, but the room was as he'd left it.

When Alex and Dan arrived at the motel, they realized that the manager wasn't kidding. Nobody had gone into the room lately, certainly no maid. There were no clothes or personal belongings in the room. But the killer had left signs of himself. A full set of five fingerprints ringed the television remote. In the bathroom, Alex found some short blond hairs in the shower drain and saliva on the many paper cups in the wastepaper basket. The cups also bore a name on them—that of a nearby Internet café.

Their next stop was the café itself, a computer-gaming paradise with a few workstations for going on the Internet or typing résumés. The clerk there, a college kid, remembered a man matching the killer's description. The guy had paid cash, which was unusual. Most of the people who came to the computer center were game addicts with prepaid plastic cards they inserted into the computers.

The clerk recalled the last day the man had been there, a Tuesday. "I could study for an exam, 'cause there were just a few customers. Saturday nights, with all-night gamers, I'm busy all the time."

"What time was he here?"

"I'll check the digital logs; they show the times guys sign off or on, and he was probably the only one who paid cash."

The clerk changed screens on the computer he was using behind the counter. "He was on-line from ten P.M. until ten-forty-five P.M. I remember now that I thought it was odd he didn't finish out his whole hour."

"Which machine was he using?" Dan asked.

The clerk took him over to a particular PC. Dan dialed up Chuck Lawndale's computer at AFIP from that PC and asked Chuck to work his magic and trace everything that had come in or out of that computer during the forty-five-minute period the previous Tuesday.

By the time Alex flew back to AFIP and dropped off the saliva and hair samples in Rick Baer's lab, Chuck had his results. The suspect had been looking at bus and train schedules. He wanted to go from Hartford to Washington, D.C.

CHAPTER 38

THE NEXT DAY, ALEX PACED HER LAB, FEEL-
ing a vague unease. She'd liked the thrill of being back
on the investigation, but now the saliva from the cups was
being analyzed next door, out of her control. She was fuming as she ran some samples of DNA of infectious diseases. She had picture-in-picture blaring on the computer
monitor. The case was just now being covered on CNN.
The reporter stated the details matter-of-factly as Alex absentmindedly mixed chemicals in a glass beaker.

The feature on the case, with a smiling photo of Kelly
in her construction hat, ended just as Alex's phone starting
ringing. With the beaker still in her hand, she dashed back
into the glass cubicle at the far end of the lab that served
as her office.

When the caller identified himself, she nearly dropped
the beaker. "Dr. Blake," he said. "This is Admiral Mason.
I've just been watching CNN and I think it's time we
talked."

Alex wondered if she should confess that she was
pretty much off the case. Instead, she was vague. "I'd be
happy to set you up with a meeting with Dan Wilson when
he returns from Groton, either here or at your office."

"No, let's keep this between us. Say seven P.M. at my
house? I'll have Mimi, my cook, make a splendid dinner
for us."

"Why would I agree to that?"

"Because I might just tell you about my son."

It was only 4:00 P.M. Alex knew that she should page Dan in Connecticut or at least call Barbara at home to discuss what she was planning. She also knew that they would never let her do it. They'd insist on backup, procedures, sending in someone else for a bad-cop/good-cop extravaganza.

Instead, Alex said yes.

"I believe you know the location," said the admiral, "from your last unfortunate visit."

Alex thought of the fiasco with the news copter and the car crash. "I'll come without the police escort this time."

After work, she went home and exchanged her black turtleneck for a red lace blouse. She took her hair out of the rubber band that held it in back, bent over with her head down, and brushed the inside of her curls. When she cocked her head back and stood straight again, her hair fanned out in golden waves across her shoulders. She added a dangling pair of scarlet earrings and lipstick of a matching hue. Now she definitely looked like the type for Red Roar.

Her next stop was a local liquor store, where she wandered the aisles, trying to figure out what to buy for him. Champagne was always nice, but seemed too much of a come-on. A port would be right. Suggests a man of discerning tastes, yet doesn't convey any particular desires or emotions. She asked the clerk for a recommendation of a knock-your-socks off port and left the store $150 poorer. She'd chosen the 1963 Fonseca vintage port, in part, because it was the same age as her car.

The admiral was right about the dinner, a cold lobster salad, followed by venison in wine sauce that the cook had put in the oven before she left the house. Alex launched in on questions about his son, but the admiral pushed them aside, making clear that he was in charge of the conversation. He was stringing the impatient Alex along, showing he was in control.

Alex retreated from her inquiries and took the measure

of the man. Despite his pale blue French-cuffed shirt, the first word that popped into her mind to describe him was *soldier.* Maybe even *mercenary.* He had focus, power, and raw energy, all of which were seductive, yet frightening. Primed. Ready for action. Every movement seemed weighted with multiple meanings. She could as easily imagine him stabbing an intruder with his fork as lifting a piece of lobster with it. Alex wondered if the admiral's sexual appeal arose from this duality, from never knowing what he'd do next.

After dinner, they adjourned to the den. He motioned her toward the couch, but Alex wanted some control over the interaction. She sat on a wing chair so that he couldn't sit down next to her.

He remained standing, still dominant. He opened her port, poured two glasses, and handed one to her. Then he picked up an ornate rectangular box from the sideboard and moved back toward Alex with it. "This box once held the pistols from the last legal duel in Virginia," he said.

He positioned it in front of Alex for her to open. She took a gulp of her port, set down the glass, and undid the clasp of the box, not knowing what to expect. She did it fluidly, without hesitation. She didn't know what game he was playing, but she didn't want him to score on her.

Her racing heart slowed a bit when she realized the contents were innocuous. Cigars.

Alex's mother took up cigar smoking after a trip to Cuba to write about the Black Panther revolutionaries who had settled there. Alex recognized his brand, a mythic one that smokers sighed about but usually could not afford. "Fidel's favorite, no?" she said.

He was impressed.

She turned down a smoke, but when he lit one up, she took it briefly out of his hand and tried a puff. "Not bad," she said. "What are they now, sixty or so dollars for one?"

"I treat myself well. I'm a man of large appetites."

She tried not to squirm in her chair. Some men mentally undressed a woman, but his look was so intense, she felt as if he were peeling off her skin.

She broke his stare with a statement. "I'm here to find out about your son."

His look became unfocused, distant. "This afternoon, I read the whole file," he said.

Alex was surprised.

"The Office of Homeland Security has access to about anything you can imagine," he said. "Certainly more than—what was it that Channel Two called you folks?—a ragtag military gestapo."

He moved the other chair so he could face her. Then he sat, his knees just a few inches from hers. He put his cigar in an ashtray and put a hand on each of the arms of her chair, effectively boxing her in.

"You're not going to let a sixty-dollar cigar go to waste, are you?" Alex asked.

"My focus is elsewhere at the moment."

He took his right hand off the arm of her chair and started unbuttoning his pale blue shirt.

"You're not my . . ." Alex began. She swallowed the last word, *type,* when she saw his tattoo. It was the eagle the killer was carving into the women. Rather than being drawn closed, one of its eyes was obliterated by a deep scar.

"The day after we buried his mother, my son hit me with a fire poker, right here." The admiral ran his finger over the scar. "I broke his jaw.

"The next year, Francis tried to burn down the house. That got him a year in a juvenile detention center. He came out, threw his clothes and books into an old duffel bag, and ran away."

The admiral walked over to a desk, a walnut rolltop. He rolled up the wooden bonnet and picked up a silver picture frame, then carried it over to Alex. "It's the only photograph of him I kept. I'm sure you'll need it for the investigation."

Alex took it from him and instantly realized why this

photo had been saved. The ten-year-old boy wasn't the focus of the portrait at all. Despite her curiosity about him, Alex hardly noticed the young man. Her attention was fixed on the slender, ephemeral woman. A beautiful apparition. A thin golden-haired angel in a cream-colored dress that was almost as delicate as she was.

"Your wife?"

Mason stared at the photo. "She was this extraordinarily fragile young girl, heartbreakingly pretty and afraid of her own shadow. She was nineteen when I met her. I had the audacity to think that I was good for her, that I could protect her from the demons that haunted her."

"You really loved her."

He nodded. "And then she gave me a son. A future Navy SEAL."

"What happened?"

"When I went to sea, she'd just shut down."

"She suffered from depression?"

He shrugged his shoulders. "I'm no doctor. I didn't realize how bad it had gotten until Francis was eight. I was commanding a submarine for six months. When I came back, I learned she had pulled him out of swimming lessons, hardly even sent him to school. *He* was taking care of *her*.

"I tried to get everything back on track. Took him to the officers' club with me to work out, but the kid almost drowned in the pool. He was afraid of water, afraid of leaving her side. I didn't know what to do. I told him he wasn't allowed to be at home on weekdays before five P.M. No more ditching school. No son of mine was going to be a mama's boy."

"Did you try to get her to counseling?"

The admiral looked at her as if she were crazy. "The service is like politics. People don't trust you to run a ship if you can't run your family. What goes on at home stays at home."

Alex's heart broke as she thought about that poor woman, that poor little boy.

"I tried to get him to shape up, to make me proud," Mason continued. "But he seemed to have gotten the worst of both of our traits. Afraid like his mother, but aggressive like me."

"Do you have any idea where he might be now?"

He flicked his wrist as if batting away an insect. "I haven't thought about him in years." He grabbed a file folder off the bookshelf and took out some photos, arranging them on the end table to the right of Alex's chair. "Then I saw these."

Alex saw they were pictures of the dead women's tattoos. The admiral sat down and put his right hand back on the arm of her chair, boxing her in again. "There were details in the file that you hadn't released to the press," he said.

"Yes, details about the women."

Alex could sense the pulsing anger behind Mason's measured exterior. "That little monster is trying to egg me on," he said, pounding the arm of her chair, causing her whole body to shake. "He's killing women who mimic the affairs I had at each base."

He then moved his arm and slumped back in his chair. Alex let out a breath, relieved that the heat of his body was not flaming so close to hers. "What do you mean?"

The admiral looked at her with a boastful jut of his chin. "I screwed a waitress in Galveston, started a long affair with a businesswoman when I was stationed in San Diego, had sex with my buddy's daughter in Norfolk, but she was begging for it, I tell you." He smiled. "Luckily, these were just the ones he knew about. If he were as frequent a killer as I was a cocksman, you'd have a real bloodbath on your hands."

Alex excitedly moved to the edge of her seat. She put her hand on the arm of his chair. "And the Pentagon? Who was your little woman there?"

He gave her a bemused smile. "Be nice to me and I might tell you."

She locked onto his gaze. "I think you are going to tell me anyway; that's why you asked me here."

"Yeah, I'm going to tell you. And then I'm going to handle the situation. You're going to find him, and I'm going to finish him off."

Alex gasped. "You'd kill your own son?"

"I take care of my messes," said the admiral. He picked up his cigar. It had gone out.

"He's not going to stop," he said, almost to himself.

Alex touched the admiral's arm, forcing his attention back to her. "He's your *son*, not some special op gone awry. Help me find him and maybe he can still be saved."

CHAPTER 39

THE AIR IN THE TASK FORCE ROOM WAS stagnant, tinged with the scent of failure. Too many late nights with tense men, turkey sandwich remains, and dusty files of suspects who, through some quirk of fate, had come within the Task Force's radar. When Jillian was away on assignment, Dan would sleep there, head down on the conference table. He'd shower in the health club on base, the only time he'd ever darken its door. His taut muscles came from fieldwork, not workouts.

"I tell you, I am not going to allow it," said Dan, who was seated next to Grant and across from Alex at the conference table. He shook his curly hair in a firm no.

"I appreciate your concern, but I want to do it," said Barbara. She was standing, and as she spoke, she collected empty Coke cans from the table and walked them over to an already overflowing trash can.

"Never argue with a woman whose mind's made up," Grant said.

Wiatt entered the room. Barbara sat down and Alex filled him in on her conversation with the admiral. They were a hundred percent sure now that Mason's son, Francis, was the Tattoo Killer. The women who were killed were like the ones his dad had cheated on his mom with. He was branding his victims with a copy of his father's tattoo. And Rick Baer's analysis of the samples from the hotel room had shown a clear match to the one flake of skin from the bathroom at Great Lakes.

The Task Force was pulling out all stops to find where Francis had gone, but they were coming up empty. His trail ended a few years after he ran away. His W2's showed some low-paying jobs when he was eighteen and nineteen.

"And then what?" asked Wiatt.

"The underground economy, most likely," said Dan. "Work a little construction, serve as a busboy, mooch off passersby. We're interviewing his grandmother, other kids from the juvenile detention center, and his landlords from the days he had reported income."

"But we might not get leads soon enough, so we want to set up a target for him," said Alex.

"What have you got in mind?" asked Wiatt.

"Put someone in his next posting, the Pentagon, who meets the description of the lover Mason had there," Alex said.

"What did she do?" Wiatt asked.

Barbara interjected. "She was a JAG lawyer."

Alex thought about how Mason had described it. "I wanted to sample a little dark meat," he'd said.

"And she was black," continued Barbara.

Dan went on to voice all of his concerns. Barbara countered them point by point. She'd gone through basic training before going into the JAG Corps. She'd won a medal in hand-to-hand combat. She didn't need to be at home, because Lana was already living at Gallaudet. She could wear a wire so that her backup team would know what was going on at any point. "If I so much as take a pee, they will be in on it," she said.

Dan was exasperated. She seemed to be anticipating his objections even before he voiced them. "It's almost as if you can read my mind."

"Well, my great-aunt was a voodoo priestess."

While Dan, Grant, and Wiatt argued about the details, Alex whispered in her ear, "Really?"

Barbara smiled and whispered back, "Hell no, she

worked the panty-hose counter at Macy's. I just read Dan's lips down the hall when he was telling Grant why he wouldn't let me take the job."

Barbara finished the last of her own soft drink—a diet root beer—and tossed the can into the trash some ten feet away. Alex applauded. "Now I know where Lana gets it."

Dan made one last try. "The D.C. police have some good undercover operatives. Why don't we put one of those women in?"

"The kid's not dumb," said Barbara. "He's managed to create a silent identity, evade us, and create a virtually clueless crime scene. You have no idea when he might strike. Could be weeks. No one could keep a cover that long."

Wiatt interrupted. "What if I need you on the Devon case?"

Barbara had already thought of that, as well. "E-mail. I'll be detailed to the Pentagon legal department, where I'll be using my own identity. But once I'm there, I can just continue to work on our stuff. If you need a warrant, I can write it up, have one of the boys here run it over to Judge Kline."

Wiatt considered the matter. He turned to Dan. "What do you think the level of risk will be for Lieutenant Findlay here?"

"Inside the Pentagon itself, virtually no risk," he said. "If the attack comes, it will be at her home or on the drive to the office."

"I'll make a call and get her into some Pentagon housing. You can control the risks from top to bottom there," said Wiatt. "But nothing obvious. This is a stealth mission. We don't want to scare him off."

Grant held up a pair of women's glasses. "We can send her in with these. They broadcast continuous surveillance. We'll receive the image at a unit within the Pentagon and have a backup team in the housing complex in radio contact with us so that they can roll within seconds if the guy shows there."

Barbara tried them on, and what she was looking at

through the glasses showed up on the screen on the wall. "They go into my pocket when I enter a ladies' room. Your group gets enough jollies without learning the color of my panties or looking at other women."

"But—"

"Relax, Grant," said Barbara, "we're gonna get this guy."

CHAPTER 40

BARBARA'S IMMEDIATE TRANSFER TO THE PEN-
tagon left a gap in Alex's life. She thought of calling
David, or maybe even Luke, but she had some serious
thinking to do first about what she wanted out of a relationship, and what she was willing to put in.

Since scientific puzzles had always comforted her in the
past, Alex tried to concentrate on her work with Rosie. She
looked again at the renderings of the protein from the
Spanish flu. An image of Larry helping her open her locked
car flitted through her mind. Now, why was she thinking
about that?

Then it came to her. The protein was shaped like the
metal strip that Larry had used, with a little elbow at the
end. That was how it unlocked the entrance to the cell. In
a single elegant flash, Alex realized how to stop it. A vaccine could be designed to sever the bend.

Alex walked to her inner office and sat in the chair,
feeling suddenly exhausted. She now knew the way to develop a vaccine to immunize soldiers against biowarfare.
This insight was a career maker, an amazing accomplish-
ment, but she couldn't allow herself a moment of self-
congratulation. Her best friend was in the path of a killer.

THE NEXT MORNING AS SHE DRANK COFFEE
in her living room, Alex wondered if she should skip that
day's subcommittee meeting at Sissy's office on Capitol

Hill. She scrutinized her multiple reflections in the mirrors and wondered if she could face David. What would she say? What would he say? How awkward would it be?

Alex looked around the room. She had reminders of Luke everywhere—an amp, CDs, a funky lamp they'd bought together, but no traces of David. She hadn't cleared a spot for David's clothes in her closet, nor had she put a photo of him next to the bed. She hadn't offered him her key. She wondered if he'd been right about her unwillingness to commit to him.

But she did commit to her work, she told herself when she got into her car, which was why she decided to grit her teeth and point the T-Bird toward Sissy's office.

TRAFFIC WAS A NIGHTMARE AND SHE AR-rived ten minutes late. She entered the room with her heart racing and looked at the assembled group—the two other consultants, plus Congressmen Quiller and Sissy. No David. Perhaps he'd looked into his mirror that morning and come to the opposite conclusion.

At the end of the meeting, Alex lingered so that she could be alone with Sissy. The older woman read the question in her eyes. "He's with the little girl. Since her mom's in custody, they're waiting for her grandmother to arrive from Colorado."

Alex nodded absently. So this was how her relationship with David was going to end. Not with a bang, but with a whimper. She took a deep breath. Then she remembered the newspaper photo of Rayna clinging to David at the *Nutcracker* performance. Rayna needed David far more than she ever would.

"I'm sorry," Sissy said as Alex left.

AROUND 3:00 P.M. THAT AFTERNOON, ALEX took a break and headed to the machine room for her usual AFIP snack, Cheetos and Coke. On the way back, she passed the conference room and walked in, as she had done several times already that day, to get an update on

Barbara. Dan was red-faced and swearing. Someone—presumably the Tattoo Killer—had tried to access the Pentagon employment records that afternoon, but he was shut out before he could get anything. Turned out the Pentagon IT people had updated their virus protection and cut off access to the clever false trap that Dan had previously set.

Chuck explained to Alex how they'd erased Barbara from all government databases and created a separate file for her at the Pentagon, so that if the Tattoo Killer was looking for an African-American lawyer there, he'd see her photo and her new address in Pentagon housing.

Dan was on the phone with his contact at the Pentagon now. They assured him that the digital route would be reopened immediately. But maybe it was too late. Maybe the killer would have given up, moved on.

"What's the next posting Admiral Mason had?" Dan asked Chuck when he hung up the phone.

"A base in Maine."

Dan paced. "We need to put a few guys in place there."

"What about Barbara?" Alex asked Dan.

"I'll just send one or two, keep the rest focused on the Pentagon."

Chuck was still on-line. Now that he had learned which Internet café the inquiry had come from, he could trace the other Internet sites Francis Mason had visited that afternoon. "So far, I don't see any travel plans for Maine. He visited news databases . . ."

"Son of a bitch was probably trying to read about himself," said Dan.

"Looked at a movie review."

"Blood and gore?" asked Dan.

"No, romantic comedy with Hugh Grant."

Alex shook her head. Go figure.

"Wait, wait," said Chuck. "Here's something else. God he's clever. He went into a credit union database for government employees."

Chuck read further as Dan and Alex anxiously awaited his report. "Bingo. He found Barbara."

Alex gasped. Her skin tingled.

Dan was all business. "Shit. Has it got the old address?"

Chuck smiled. "No, we've got him hooked. Looks like she took out a small loan for her daughter's summer camp. The monthly bill is now being sent to the Pentagon."

Alex could see nothing to smile about. The Tattoo Killer now had Barbara in his crosshairs. "How are you going to warn her?"

Chuck explained that they had agreed upon a signal. He immediately sent Barbara an E-mail from a fake Web site for women's cosmetics. It said simply, "Your order is ready."

Alex felt a pang of fear. They had practically painted a target on Barbara's back.

Dan looked at her, reading her thoughts. He nodded. "It is risky, Alex. But we've got a continuous feed from her, as well as combat teams at full readiness a minute from where she works and lives."

"A lot can happen in a minute, Dan." Alex thought about the San Diego coroner describing the killer as a phantom. Marilyn Mayne's trachea had been crushed in seconds.

He looked at Alex's white face and put his arm around her. "You have my word on this one. Nothing's going to happen to Barbara. Whether he strikes tonight or weeks from now, it's going to be all right."

Alex nodded feebly, without confidence. This guy was smart. Much smarter than Grant or any of his gadgets. She had the foreboding feeling that it wasn't going to be all right at all.

CHAPTER 41

AS SHE HEADED BACK TO HER LABORATORY with the disturbing news about Barbara, she ran into Harding, who asked her how her work was going. When she explained the vaccine principle, he stopped short. "Alex, that's amazing. Why aren't you out celebrating?"

She couldn't tell him about Barbara. The reason for her posting was known only to the Task Force. Even her daughter, Lana, thought she'd merely been assigned to the Pentagon to help with some dreary legal case.

"I've got an idea," he said. "How about a sail?"

Alex thought for a moment. "May I bring a friend?" He nodded. Alex picked up Lana at camp, and an hour later, they boarded his thirty-two-foot sailboat. Alex felt a need to be close to Lana, in case—no, she wouldn't let herself even think about that possibility.

Neither Alex nor Lana had been on a sailboat before, and Alex's mind was distracted from her dismal fears when she felt the first swish of the sails. Harding, as helmsmen, pulled the tiller toward him to turn the boat away from shore, and off they went. Alex was amazed at how much work it was to get the boat to seem to glide effortlessly. Not to mention all those utterances from Harding, seemingly in a foreign language. "Ready about." "Hard-a-lee." To change course—"tacking," Harding called it—the three of them had to sit on one side of the boat, practically dangling their butts over the Chesapeake

Bay; then Harding did some magic with the tiller and mainsheet, and Alex had to pull and tighten the line to the so-called jib sheet. Harding shifted positions suddenly, until the sails began to fill out again, with Alex and Lana moving carefully to the opposite side of the boat to balance it.

Alex was grateful when they dropped anchor, and Harding took them on a little tour of the boat. It had a teak deck and, below, a compact sleeping and dining area, complete with a DVD player and laptop computer with a wireless modem. On the built-in couch was a small pillow that must have been embroidered by Harding's wife. It was lettered, in Scrabble style, with the word *smitten,* each letter showing its point value.

Harding served snacks in the downstairs galley on a small square table with a bolted-on Scrabble board. He challenged them both to a game, but Alex decided she'd rather sit on the deck, put a fishing rod into the water, and contemplate the waves. She left Lana and Harding to set up their tiles, ventured back up, and collapsed in a canvas chair. Alex was a perpetual motion machine, so it took a few minutes to let the warmth of the sun and the calming rhythm of the waves wash over her. She reached into the bucket of minnows, put one on the hook of a fishing rod, and wiped her hands on her jeans. She leaned back and felt, for an instant, like she didn't have a care in the world.

This relaxing stuff isn't so bad, she thought. Maybe I should consider doing it more often. A playground sign from her childhood flashed through her mind. The NO LOI-TERING admonition outside a Chicago playground had been badly translated in Spanish to PROHIBIDO MAL GAS-TAR EL TIEMPO—"You are forbidden to spend your time badly." She must have subconsciously adopted that as her motto. She was always racing about, working hard, not wasting a single moment. One of the appeals of Luke was that she could work a full day, until 9:00 or 10:00 P.M., and then still have the semblance of a carefree social life, going out late at night to a club to hear him or one of his musician friends.

She sat happily for the next hour. Then clouds blew in and the temperature suddenly dropped. The winds gusted and churned the waves. Alex went belowdecks. "Guys, the weather's coming up; we'd better go."

"Hold on, Alex," Lana said. "We're almost done."

Alex looked at the magnetic tiles stuck to the table. She could tell exactly which types of words had been placed by whom. Medicine and music, courtesy of Harding. Sports and popular culture, Lana's contribution. Alex made a mental tally. Harding was ahead by a good thirty points and Lana had seven tiles left.

Lana smiled at Harding after he put down a word with an *r* in it. She put her seven tiles above it: P-L-E-A-T-H-E. "Bingo," she said, "that's thirteen points for the word and an extra fifty for using all my tiles."

"Pleather," said Harding. "That's not a word." He reached over for a well-worn dictionary and turned to the *p*'s. *Pleasure* was there, but not *pleather*. He held the book open and showed Lana.

Lana flipped to the inside title page which showed the publication date, 1990. "This book is older than I am," she complained. She reached over to Harding's laptop and went on-line and called up the Web site for the latest Merriam-Webster dictionary. She turned the screen toward him.

Pleather: a plastic fabric made to look like leather. Entered into the dictionary in 2004.

Harding's eyes lit up at finding a worthy Scrabble opponent. "Lana," he said, "you're welcome here anytime you feel like teaching an old dog new words."

That salty dog then went upstairs and got them back to shore safely, just as the clouds opened and the rain poured down on them. On the drive back to Gallaudet, Lana bubbled over about Harding, recounting how he'd joked with her and asked about her classes. Alex realized that Lana had few older males in her life. Her dad had disappeared before learning Barbara was pregnant. Barbara's father, Lana's grandfather, still lived in the Bronx and rarely made it to D.C. Finding ways to get Lana and Harding together would delight them both.

IT WAS JUST PAST DUSK WHEN ALEX PARKED a block away from the Curl Up and Dye. She plucked her boots and briefcase from the trunk, sloshing through the rain in the sneakers she'd grabbed for the sail from the gym bag she kept at the office. She keypunched the code, NJDC, and when the metal gate moved back, she thrust her shivering body into the dark passageway. A figure wearing a hooded cape stepped out of the shadows.

Alex tried to slam the apparition with her briefcase, but the figure pulled back the hood. "I was desperate," said Gloria Devon. "I made David give me the code. I pleaded with him for Rayna's sake. He knows it would destroy her if I went to jail."

"Don't come any closer to me. Put your hands in the air." Alex walked over and patted Gloria down. She was carrying keys and some cash, but nothing else.

"How did you . . ."

"I was released on bail this afternoon. Apparently, the judge didn't think I was a flight risk."

"What do you want?" Alex reached up to screw the lightbulb back in properly. Gloria had loosened it to darken the hall.

"You're the only one who can help me."

Alex looked at the petite blonde in the dripping black cape. Her hair was wet and her makeup was running. Alex realized she was taking a certain amount of satisfaction in Gloria finally looking her age.

"I'm not on the case anymore," Alex told her.

"Just listen to me for a few minutes," Gloria pleaded. It's not often, thought Alex, a Senator grovels at me. At the Curl Up and Dye, no less.

She relented. She opened the inner door and invited

Gloria inside. Gloria stepped into the main room, her eyes taking everything in. She looked at the posters in the salon room, then craned her neck to see the bedroom. She seemed as curious about Alex as Alex had been about her.

"No wonder he fell for you: You make him feel young," said Gloria. "Washington's most eligible bachelor can hardly be with a woman in menopause, can he?" She pulled a Kleenex from her pocket and began to wipe the mascara from under her eyes.

"From what I heard, you dumped him," said Alex. "But now the big roadblock, Ted, has been removed."

"Ah, Ted," said Gloria, fingering her hair back in place. "I was nineteen when I met him. Smart woman, foolish choice."

"He was about to go public with something that would have ruined your career. He called you that night to tell you about it."

She turned from the mirror to face Alex. She seemed more confident now. "I've weathered bad press before."

"Ah, yes. The *Nutcracker* incident."

Gloria nodded. She looked more together now, almost elegant. Alex was acutely aware of her own salty, sweaty smell, the odor of fish bait on her clothes.

"I've been thinking a lot about this," said Gloria. Her expression was softer now. "When Ted called that night, he didn't sound like himself. He sounded stressed. Yes, he accused me of blowing the case. He threatened me with the affidavit. But he was confused about the facts, couldn't answer my question. He hung up right after that."

"What are you saying?"

"I think someone was forcing him to make the call, maybe at gunpoint. I was so pissed at him, so focused on the swearing-in the next day, I didn't pick up on it like I should have. I think he was trying to send me some sort of message."

"How?"

"Right before we hung up, he said he would say hello to my dad for me."

"So?"

"My dad's been dead for fifteen years."

Alex didn't know what to think. Gloria could easily be making this up.

"Alex, I was a prosecutor. The evidence doesn't lie. Wiatt sent me your opinion as *Brady* material. There wasn't even a one-in-a-million chance that there would be an even spread of blood under the nails. Unless, of course, somebody planted it there."

Gloria dropped her cape to the floor. She pulled her sweater over her head. She was standing in her bra, her eyes clenched in embarrassment.

Alex peered at her smooth pink skin, the slight scar from an appendectomy.

Gloria recovered her poise and turned so that Alex could see her back, as well. "If he scratched me that deeply, I'd still be marked. And if I was in that apartment, why didn't you find any hairs or any other trace of me? How likely was it that I could go in and out of there and leave only blood?"

"You've got a defense attorney who can raise that as reasonable doubt. You don't need me."

"Sure, I might be able to argue reasonable doubt, show that the prosecutor can't completely prove his case. But my reputation will be ruined. I need to do more than get off on some technicality. I need to find out who did it. That's where I need your help."

"Why should I help you?"

Gloria sat down in one of the hair-dryer chairs, still in her bra. "Because whoever did this is toying with you, too. And you're like me. You're not going to let that slide."

She reached over and started turning the nail polish rack around while Alex thought about it.

Alex picked her sweater off the floor and handed it to her. "Put this back on and I'll make some coffee. If you were framed, we've got to figure out where the murderer got your blood."

Gloria dressed and then followed Alex into the kitchen. "I've already racked my brain about it."

"Let's start with the easiest," said Alex as she took two cups from the cabinet. "What could have been in your garbage? Did you injure yourself in any way? Any blood on bandages?"

"Maybe I cut myself slicing bagels."

"Wouldn't be enough blood. What about your period?"

"That stopped two years ago."

"Where do you go for health care?"

"Usually, Colorado. On rare occasions, here. Two years ago, Rayna and I both got chicken pox, and we were treated at Walter Reed."

"A lot of hospitals save the blood samples. Call your doctor in Colorado and see what the policy is there, and whether there is anything missing from their pathology lab. Meanwhile, I've got an idea of my own."

CHAPTER 42

AFTER ALEX SHOWERED AND CHANGED, HER first stop was the morgue. "Well, you guys are taking chain of custody to new heights," said Jeanie Nash, who was performing an autopsy on a pregnant thirty-year-old who had been stabbed by her accountant boyfriend. "First, you come by to look at the corpse, then Rick Baer does, then here you are again. I know this is a high-profile case, but isn't this a bit of overkill?"

"I'll just be a minute. I only need one quick sample."

"Far as I'm concerned, you can dump the whole body in your car and ride off with it. He's taking up space while bodies are piling up down the hallway."

"I'm surprised the old boy is still here, actually," said Alex as she took scrapings from under Ted's nails.

"We're waiting for a legal opinion from the District's lawyer about who to release him to. Gloria Devon can't take him because she's charged with his murder. The daughter's a minor, so she can't authorize release."

"What about his people back in Colorado?"

"We called his brother and he refused to get involved. Said he didn't want to be stuck with the cost of a funeral."

"Some family."

Jeanie nodded and went back to her work.

BACK AT HER LAB, ALEX RAN A FORENSIC DNA print on the fingernail scraping. Like Rick Baer, she found that the profile was definitely Gloria's. But if her hunch was correct, there was more to get out of the sample.

She teed up her sequencer to run the infectious disease program that she'd used on Rosie. That type of analysis could provide the sequence not of Gloria herself, but of the genes of any infection in Gloria's blood.

While she was waiting for the results, Alex flipped through the autopsy photos of the women in the Tattoo Killer case and tried not to imagine Barbara's face on them. She thought of her father, reread all the articles about him, told herself she couldn't take another loss. Then she felt angry at herself. *She* couldn't take another loss? What about Lana?

Fifteen minutes passed and then the computer spit out its work. Rick hadn't found this because he hadn't thought to look. Neither would Alex have, had she not talked to Gloria.

Alex looked down at the results again. *Varicella zoster.* Chicken pox. The blood under Ted's nails showed the sequence of the pox. Alex had seen Gloria's chest and back just an hour before. No little red dots. Someone had stolen an old blood sample from Walter Reed, taken when she'd had chicken pox two years earlier, and planted it on the body. Gloria Devon had been framed.

Alex thought about everything Dan had taught her about forensics. Who else had a motive? Who would benefit if she were out of the picture?

Alex could only think of one person who stood to gain big. Jack Wiatt.

There was already talk of him getting the FBI job now that Gloria was under a cloud. The White House was floating that idea through plants in the *Washington Post,* information that they claimed to be leaks. Wiatt's recent meeting with the President, where he'd claimed they were closing in on the Tattoo Killer, had put him back in the administration's favor. Once Francis Mason walked into the AFIP trap, the FBI job was as good as Wiatt's.

Motive, for sure. Opportunity, too. Anybody could breeze in and out of Walter Reed from the AFIP. Larry and the other day workers did it all the time to bring Alex materials she needed, or to take pathology samples from Thomas Harding to labs at Walter Reed if he didn't have the right equipment in his lab here.

Wiatt was a soldier. Hadn't he talked about stealth missions? She thought about the Fort Bragg paperweight in his office with "A Warrior's Ethos" inscribed on it: "I am an American soldier. I will always place mission first. I will never accept defeat. I will never quit."

As Alex paced her lab, her heart flopped oddly, as it did when she'd had too little sleep or too much stress. Shit, she thought, I practically gave Wiatt a blueprint for this—telling him about how old blood samples were stored at Walter Reed.

Alex wished she could talk to Barbara. But with the listening device, anything Alex said would be broadcast back to command central, with Wiatt able to listen in. E-mail was out, too. If Alex sent her something over the Internet, the magic glasses would convey it to the three-foot-high screen in Grant's command post at the Pentagon. No, it was too dangerous to call Barbara.

Alex briefly considered talking to Dan. She could remind him how suspicious it was. Wiatt had taken Dan off the Devon case, then her. His right-hand man on the case was now Grant Pringle, who'd wanted to bury the Senator from the beginning.

But Dan would tell her she had no proof, that she was letting her imagination run wild. Although Dan was miffed about being bounced from the Devon case, he'd probably argue that it made sense to have him focus on the more complicated Tattoo Killer case. Devon had rapidly seemed like an open-and-shut deal.

There was only one place Alex could think to turn. Someone who had had the best interests of AFIP in mind for a long time. Someone who wasn't beholden to Jack Wiatt.

CHAPTER 43

"THAT'S QUITE A STORY," SAID HAL AFTER Alex told him what she had surmised. "There may have been some bad blood between Wiatt and me in the beginning, but even I can't believe he's a murderer."

Alex had been thrilled to find Webster still in his office this late in the evening. His wife and kids were visiting her parents in Florida that week, and he was catching up with work. His computer screen was on and his desk was uncharacteristically littered with faxes, which he had neatly placed in a single pile and stuck into his drawer when Alex had entered and asked to speak to him.

"The DNA shows chicken pox all right," said Alex. "I don't have proof yet, but I bet we'll find evidence that Wiatt planted the blood."

"That's an ingenious use of DNA testing," said Hal, whistling under his breath. "First-class detective work. I had no idea that sort of thing could be done."

"I bet we can find a witness who saw Wiatt go over to Walter Reed, or even some evidence that he was in the pathology lab where the samples were kept."

"Maybe there were other people in on it," said Hal.

Alex nodded. "Who can we trust? We can't tell anyone about it until we figure out what to do. We can't take the chance of tipping him off."

"Alex, we're in an extraordinary situation. You could

very well be at risk. Do you want me to assign a couple of soldiers to watch over you?"

"No," said Alex. "There's no way you could do that without Wiatt finding out."

Hal stroked his chiseled chin, thinking it over. "I'm worried about you, Alex. But I guess you'll be safe for one night. Just go straight home and meet me back here in the morning."

She nodded, a slight shudder racking her body.

ALEX LEFT THE BUILDING AND BEGAN THE drive home. But a few blocks down Georgia Avenue, she began to worry that the next morning might be too late. What if the coroner told Rick she'd been to the morgue again and Wiatt suspected that she knew? She needed to find out about the Walter Reed lab as soon as she could.

For the second time that night, she left her T-Bird in the lot at AFIP and walked past the guard inside the reception area. "Can't get enough of me tonight?" the young recruit asked.

She knew he was still embarrassed about having to send her to Wiatt's office the other evening. "Yeah, I'm simply wild for a man in uniform."

"There're only about four thousand of us here in the complex."

"Ah, so many men, so little time," she said, smiling at him as she passed.

She walked down the corridor until she was out of his sight. Instead of turning toward her lab, she headed down a flight of stairs into the tunnels below. She now knew the route to the museum by heart. Getting to Walter Reed was a whole other challenge.

Luckily, the hospital was busy, Visiting hours were just ending and there was a lot of movement in the hallways when she popped up one of the staircases. Once she was in the main hospital, she followed signs to the pathology laboratory. As an M.D. at AFIP, she had access to the patient database so that she could render second opinions.

Two night techs were working in the pathology lab, but since she looked like she knew what she was doing, they didn't question her as she put Gloria Devon's name into the computer and her medical record came up. Alex copied down Devon's patient ID number and then walked to the sink, pulled on a pair of latex gloves from the bulging dispenser, and took a small specimen-collection bag from a pile on a shelf.

Alex used her shoulder to push open the door to the inner repository where the blood samples were stored. She used the number 516-49-993 to try to locate Gloria's blood from her bout with chicken pox. The holder was on a lower shelf in a refrigerated unit, requiring Alex to kneel down to look for the right space. But the holder was empty, the blood tube gone.

Alex looked closely at the space where it should have been. There was a short dark hair stuck to the rack. She took tweezers from her fanny pack, pulled out the hair, stuck it in the small evidence bag, and pushed the bag into the pocket of her jeans. She had followed protocol exactly—gloves, tweezers, evidence bag. When she got back to her lab, she'd log this evidence in so, if it were useful, it could be used in court.

She headed down the nearest staircase. The tunnels below were dark, with only a flickering light. The route from the AFIP entrance to Walter Reed had been straightforward, but finding her way back to her lab underground would be more complicated. She hadn't been in this stretch before.

Her shoulder muscles ached from pulling up anchor and helping Harding maneuver the sailboat back to shore. She thought of herself as in such good shape, but tasks like "tacking" obviously challenged body parts she didn't normally tax.

Alex patted the pocket with the hair in it. The hair was dark brown. Like Wiatt's, she told herself. Then she could hear the imaginary voice of Major Dan Wilson in her head. "And like half the men in D.C.," he would have said.

That's why she was rushing back to her lab. She needed to sequence the DNA in the hair. Then she'd think of some way to see if it matched Wiatt's.

A rat raced past her, not the least bit perturbed by her presence. Before she even rounded the bend in the tunnel, she knew what the rat was after. The nauseating smell of garbage choked her.

The tunnel opened into a one-hundred-foot long room of overflowing Dumpsters, where the garbage was kept until pickup day. Alex shivered as the rat joined its buddies, creeping along the rim of a Dumpster, then up the mountain of garbage. The frenzy of the rats as they searched for leftover food from the hospital trays caused the peak of noxious items to tip to the floor, spilling used syringes, feces-flecked plastic undergarments, and all manner of disgusting hospital detritus.

Alex held her breath and tried to figure out where she was by listening to the sounds above her. The noises one floor up receded as the last family members left the hospital at the end of visiting hours. Then she heard a louder set of footsteps. Someone must be wearing a helluva set of boots up there, she thought. Then she heard running. She started to turn her head just as the blows began. A sharp crack on the back of her head flattened her facedown on the ground, right next to a Dumpster.

The rats atop the Dumpster scattered at the sound, knocking garbage off the pile and onto her head. One rat raced past her cheek, tail thwacking her eye. She turned her head toward the ski-masked figure above her, just in time to see him raise his foot and stomp her on her back. The searing ache in her right kidney was echoed by a symphony of pain as her ribs crushed against the cement.

She pushed herself up slightly with her right hand, but a discarded IV bag under her palm slipped, causing her to crash back on the cement, cracking a tooth. Her nose was bleeding, as was the inside of her mouth. As she lay there, her assailant took a step back and kicked her squarely in the head.

The figure took a knife and sliced her fanny pack, pulling it away from her. Then he started to lower the knife toward her neck.

"No!" yelled someone, running clumsily from the direction of the AFIP end of the tunnels. The masked figure took off in a flash toward Walter Reed.

She was dizzy and in pain, but she still managed a smile at her rescuer. "Larry," she said. Then she passed out.

CHAPTER 44

ALEX WOKE UP WITH A BLURRY RAINBOW IN front of her. Larry must have carried her to his hideaway, put her on an air mattress there. She tried to sit up, but the kidney pain flattened her. She reached up with her hand to touch her face, then used the sleeve of her turtleneck to wipe the blood from around her nose and mouth. Her tongue probed the jagged edge of her broken incisor and the cut where she'd bitten the inside of her cheek. She longed to go back in time to a few hours earlier, when her only bodily concern had been the ache in her shoulder from working the jib. A searing pain flashed through her head, dulling her brain back into unconsciousness.

She awoke later to a light tickle on her face. With one half-opened eye, she saw that Larry was gently blotting blood off her cheek with a damp towel. As her mind came back on-line, she began to focus on what she could remember about her assailant. He was taller than she was, but that's all she knew. He'd had her on the ground so quickly, it had been hard to judge anything about him. Her eyes had been focused on the knife.

She thought momentarily of reporting this to the guard, but who knew who was in on this thing? If it went all the way to the top of AFIP, whom could she trust? Would it even be safe to walk past the guard on her way out? Was the killer waiting next to her car to finish her off?

Larry looked nervous.

"Wad's wrong?" she said, the blood in her mouth and nose causing her to speak like she had a deep cold. She took the towel from Larry and spit the contents of her mouth into it. Then she tried speaking again. "Are you afraid he'll come back?"

"Can't be late. Truck's here." He motioned toward a cart. He must have been on his way to take the laundry to the back, where the truck would pick it up.

"Larry, could you give me a secret ride to the truck?" She put her arms on the floor, grabbed the sides of the air mattress, and pushed herself up to a half-sitting position. The cart had long metal shelves, looking almost like a bilevel autopsy cart. Fighting the pain, she half pulled, half rolled herself onto the bottom shelf, shocked at the animal-like moans that were coming from her lips.

From the lower shelf of the cart, she reached up to the top shelf and pulled some dirty hospital sheets over the side to hide her body.

Larry pulled back the fabric. "Carnival ride!" he said.

"No!" said Alex. "Gently!"

He respected her wishes and pushed her slowly through the tunnel to the service entrance. The laundry truck was waiting, its driver puffing a cigarette alongside of it.

While the driver used the sole of his shoe to put out his cigarette, Larry reached under her, lifted her out of the cart, and held her up like a rag doll.

"What the fuck!" said the driver.

"It's okay," said Alex, "I just fell down the stairs."

"Ugh. What'd you do, fall down the stairs and land on a meat cleaver?"

"Just clumsy today."

Alex stopped leaning against Larry and took a step forward. The effort made her nauseated. "Any chance you could give me a ride into town?" she asked the driver.

"Company policy, no passengers."

"Think of it as a mercy gesture."

He wrinkled his nose at her smell as she came closer.

"All right. But you have to ride in the back. Don't want anyone seeing I'm breaking the rules."

The back was fine with her. Last thing she needed was to be chatting with a truck driver.

As they bounced along, she tried not to yelp in pain. She surveyed her situation. The assailant had her fanny pack, which had her wallet, cell phone, and the keys to her house and car. With great effort, she reached inside the pocket of her jeans. She had three singles and some change, which she'd put there as exact change for a frappuccino. It was enough to get her a ride on the Metro, if she could bear it, but where would she go? Whoever was after her might think to look for her at her house.

The truck driver dropped her off at Metro Center. In the ladies' room, she used wet paper towels to wipe the sticky IV fluid from her right hand and tried to mop the rest of the blood and gore from her face and hair. The area on back of her shirt where the garbage had landed was beyond hope. Her next stop was a pay phone. She dialed a number and asked if the person on the other end would accept the charges.

Twenty minutes later, she stepped off at a Blue Line stop in the section of Arlington known as Little Vietnam. Snatches of the Southeast Asian language tickled her ears as she followed directions down a side street, then buzzed an apartment. A few minutes later, a familiar figure let her in.

"Thanks, Luke," she said.

CHAPTER 45

LUKE HOVERED OVER HER LIKE A MOTHER hen. He drew a hot bath for her in his old-fashioned claw-footed tub, and once she'd cleaned up, he offered her an oversize shirt. He then put hydrogen peroxide on the cut on her scalp. The places where she had been stomped and kicked were starting to bruise. "You look like you had a run-in in a mosh pit," he said.

She tried to sit comfortably on his couch, but every position made her grimace.

"Do you want me to take you to a hospital?"

She thought for a moment. Wiatt was probably checking ERs for her right now to finish the job. "Mainly what I need is a painkiller."

He walked to the bathroom, opened the medicine cabinet, and then came out with a pill bottle in each hand. "You've got a choice of Bayer aspirin or some of the Tylenol with codeine that my dentist gave me when he pulled my wisdom teeth," he said. "Or I can run over to one of the clubs on Arlington Row and score whatever street drug will cure what ails you. It's our local equivalent to the twenty-four-hour Walgreens."

"The codeine will do it."

He put some tap water into a *Brady Bunch* glass and gave her two pills. "Do you want to tell me?"

"Nah, I came here to get away from it."

"Is it a guy?"

"Oh, Lord no, not in the way you mean. It's about a case I'm working on."

"I never thought I'd see the day where you'd be the homeless one and I'd be giving you shelter."

"It's a great place," said Alex. She meant it. The old wooden floors of the apartment Luke had recently rented had a comforting warmth. Luke had taken some of his things out of storage, like his collection of 1970s TV-show lunch boxes, which were displayed on shelves in the living room. Luke had been born in 1980, but he was fascinated with the 1970s. His salt and pepper shakers were characters from *I Dream of Jeannie*.

"Looks like you're planning to be here for a while," she said.

"Yeah, go figure. Live music is making a comeback in the District. I've got a gig a few blocks from here, at the Galaxy Hut."

"How come no tour posters?"

"I didn't want to feel like I was living in a Hard Rock Café."

He gently helped her up from the couch and led her to the bed. "You're in no shape to chew the fat right now, Alex."

Luke tucked her in and sang a quiet little song, his mouth close to her ear. While he stroked her hair, she fell asleep.

ALEX WOKE AT 6:00 A.M., BUT A HAZE OF pain engulfed her. Her moan woke Luke from his slumber on the couch, and he brought her another two codeine tablets. When she opened her eyes again, the clock read 11:00 A.M. Shit, Hal would be wondering where she was. She dialed his home and office numbers, but he didn't answer at either place. She didn't want to leave a message, in case it reached the wrong ears.

"You're keeping musicians' hours," Luke said. He had used the washing machines in the basement to launder her clothes.

"The shirt is ripped, but you can borrow one of mine."

"Omigod, Luke, you didn't wash the jeans, did you?"

He reached over to his dresser and held up the evidence bag of hair from the Walter Reed pathology lab. "Don't worry, I didn't wash this."

She grimaced as she sat up in bed. She dangled her legs over the side of the bed, assessing which parts of her hurt the most. She desperately wanted another codeine, but she knew it would interfere with what she needed to do. "Could I have two aspirins and get the codeine to go?"

She stood up and dressed slowly.

"You're in no shape to go anywhere," he said.

"I have to," she said. "Can I borrow a little money and the van? It'll just take a couple of hours."

"Have I ever denied you anything, Alex?"

Alex looked at him, remembering their time together, and how she'd kept him at a distance. "No. Mainly because I never asked for anything."

"Well, ask away," said Luke. He gently put his arms around her, lightly touching her so that he wouldn't hurt any of her sore spots. He put his cheek close to hers. "Alex, I missed you."

She didn't say it, but she had missed him, too.

ALEX TURNED INTO THE PARKING LOT FOR the Department of Defense DNA Repository. She pulled her curls forward so they covered some of the scrapes on her face, then practiced talking to the rearview mirror with her lips close together so that her chipped tooth didn't show. Inside, she said hello to Lieutenant Colonel Frank Middleton, who had helped her on the Tattoo Killer case, and told him she had one more sample to retrieve. "Slipped through the cracks for some reason," she said.

For once, she was grateful for the expressionlessness of a military face. He regarded her momentarily and, without a question, escorted her into the freezer. She'd used Luke's computer to find Jack Wiatt's bio and had figured out which base he'd been at in 1992, when the Department of Defense started collecting DNA. Middleton pulled out one of the samples and put it in the box she had borrowed from the clerk. She thanked him and took it to the van.

Alex now had to compare the hair from the pathology department at Walter Reed, where Gloria's sample had been snatched, to the DNA from Wiatt. If they matched, then Wiatt had framed the FBI director.

She wasn't ready to go back into AFIP to run the test. That was too dangerous. But she knew of a place that had a whole lot of sequencing power she might be able to use. She began thinking of how she might explain all this in court, if it came to that. The hair in her pocket hadn't exactly made it through a normal chain of custody. Yeah, it would be a little hinky to explain going to Luke's, sleeping, and taking codeine, all while the hair was in her custody. But she'd worry about that when the time came.

THE RECEPTIONIST LOOKED MIFFED AT THE warm welcome Trevor Buckley gave Alex, and the way his eyes lingered just a tad too long on the contours of her body under Luke's oversize shirt. Trevor looked at the bruises and scrapes around her eyes.

"Are you okay?" he asked. "Is there anything I can do?"

She basked for a moment in his clucking concern.

"When I was here, I noticed that your sequencers are a generation more advanced than the ones I use at AFIP," Alex said. Still dizzy, she was using one arm to balance herself against the reception desk.

"Of course. I had them built to my own specs," he responded.

"I'd like to take them out for a test run. I've got two samples that I'd like to compare."

Trevor seemed flattered. "No problem. We're running way below capacity. That political appointee running your place is queering my deal with Webster about access to the Department of Defense DNA Repository."

This was news to Alex. She hadn't realized that it had gotten that far.

Trevor continued. "Webster told me he's got a few more tricks up his sleeve, so I'm sure we'll get them soon enough. Those samples will be a great boon to medical research."

He led her into the lab and pointed her to two sequencers on the end. Then he pressed a few keys on the first one's keyboard. "This will allow you to use both at once and speed up the comparison."

"I'll need to extract DNA from the samples."

"No worry. Put it through the robotics. You'll love how fast it goes."

She removed the label from the DOD sample and stuck it in her pocket. Trevor pulled over a chair for her and she handed him the specimen bag and the blood sample, both of which were unidentified. After the robotic arms took a sample of DNA from the hair and blood, Trevor carefully placed the bag and vial in a small box and handed it back to Alex.

They made small talk while the samples ran. He spoke of his work to find a gene related to juvenile diabetes, and how it might help kids like Hal Webster's daughter, who'd needed insulin shots since she was eight. She mentioned her work with the Spanish flu, taking care not to drift into the classified portions, which had to do with her theory about the cell receptors. Talking about her work calmed her. Science was always the place where she could escape from pain.

Then the colorful quilt pattern of DNA appeared simultaneously on the two screens. She looked at it closely. In each place where there was a red rectangle on the first screen, there was a red rectangle on the second. Same with green, blue, yellow. And it wasn't just a matter of eyeballing it. The computer proclaimed that both were identical.

This wasn't some low-level forensic test that compared five different genes to each other. In record time, Trevor's sequencers had generated a CD-ROM with all three million base pairs, the entire genome, of the person who had stolen Gloria's chicken pox sample. They were a match, letter for letter, with the DNA bank's sample labeled with Jack Wiatt's ID.

CHAPTER 46

ALEX STOPPED AT A DUANE READE PHAR-macy, wrote a prescription for a stronger painkiller for herself, got herself a new fanny pack, and bought some thick makeup to cover her scrapes and disguise the bruises that were beginning to circle her eyes. She wanted to get back into the AFIP without anyone thinking there was anything wrong.

Once there, she went straight to Commander Webster. He shut his office door behind her. He looked panicked, disheveled, and genuinely relieved to see her.

"Where have you been? I thought Wiatt had found out and you were floating in the Potomac," said Hal.

As she got closer to him, he saw the extent of her injuries. "Are you okay?"

"Just barely," she said, "but I nailed the case."

"How?"

She laid the hair and DOD sample on the desk. She explained that the DNA was a precise match.

"Alex, that's great," he said. "We need to move quickly, before something else happens to you."

"Where do we take it from here?"

"I'll turn the DNA results over to a prosecutor I trust in the U.S. Attorney's Office. I called him last night and said that we had evidence of a high-level crime. I'll get back to him now and have him meet us at my house in an hour." He wrote his address down on a piece of paper and handed it to her. "Take a cab, but don't go straight there. Switch a few times to make sure no one follows you."

Alex nodded. Even that hurt.

He came around his desk to walk her to the door. "Walk right back out of the AFIP, before Wiatt or anyone realizes you are here."

Hal patted her on the shoulder as he opened the door for her. "This will all be over soon," he said reassuringly.

Alex looked down at his shoes as he left. He was always so spit-and-polish. His shoes were newly shined. But there was a definite marring on the toe of the right shoe. As if he had kicked someone.

Alex's hand was shaking as she went down the hall to her lab. Once inside, she reached into the pocket of her jeans and pulled out the label she'd taken off of the DOD specimen. It was Wiatt's ID number all right. She'd memorized it.

But as she felt the label, she realized that something was not quite right. The adhesive back was very sticky. Wiatt had entered the military during the Vietnam War, so his sample would have been one of the earliest samples taken, when the DOD DNA bank was first established in 1992. The back of the label should have been dry and flaky by now.

She looked at the back of the tape. There seemed to be a little piece of paper, no more than an eighth of an inch long, stuck to the tape. In her lab, she used tweezers to pull it off.

It was stuck too hard. When she pulled, she only managed to shred it. Shit.

The tiny paper was wrecked, but all was not lost. The impression of the ink from it was visible, slightly and backward, on the sticky side of the label. She could make out a four and an eight. She looked again at Wiatt's ID number. Wiatt's ID number did not have a 48 sequence in it. Someone had pasted a label with Wiatt's number onto the real killer's DNA sample. Someone had framed Wiatt for framing Gloria.

Alex thought about Hal's shoe. Could he have been the one who attacked her? Or was her imagination out of control?

She sat down, opened the bottle of Vicodin painkillers, and popped one. She wondered how she could get a sample of Hal's DNA.

Then she thought about how knowledgeable Hal was about Norfolk when the Tattoo Killings were being discussed. He'd obviously been stationed there at some point in his career. That meant that his DNA sample had been analyzed as part of the hunt for the Tattoo Killer. It was locked away in the lab next door.

Alex knocked on the door to the forensic lab. Luckily, Rick was there. He looked at her quizzically, waiting for an explanation of her bruises, the chipped tooth.

"I fell down my stairs last night," she said, cursing herself for having to lie. But that fib greased the way for a second. "I know I'm off the Devon case, but I need to double-check something for the Tattoo Killer case."

"Sure, no problem."

She was dizzy, so she pulled a chair up to the computer listing the DOD samples. She sat for a moment, holding her breath to stave off a wave of pain.

She waited until Rick returned to his own work, then put in her access code and typed in Hal Webster's name. His ID number came up 23624827. She told Rick she just needed to pull one of the DOD samples.

"New theory?" he asked.

"Something like that. Thanks a ton, Rick."

"It's an honor, Dr. Blake, and, uh, you should take better care of yourself."

She smiled. "So true."

She went back to her lab. She had given the hair from the Walter Reed pathology department to Hal, but she had the CD-ROM she'd borrowed from Trevor to copy the sequences.

She ran Hal Webster's sample from the Tattoo Killer investigation. The sequence matched perfectly the DNA from the hair from the shelf next to Gloria's chicken pox sample. But then her computer spit out an additional result: Hal's DNA matched the hair left at Ted's house the night of his murder. Hal was Male Three.

CHAPTER 47

BEFORE ALEX LEFT THE BUILDING, SHE MADE one stop—Grant's grandiose research center. He was out at the Pentagon, monitoring the video transmissions from Barbara. But there were a few things that she wanted. Then she drove the Cattle Prods van to Old Town Alexandria, about eight minutes south of the District. She parked it and, with some difficulty, walked half a mile to Hal's house. He had about two acres of land around a stunning turn-of-the century farmhouse.

Hal opened the door. He was wearing jeans, along with a faded Naval Academy windbreaker over a plain gray T-shirt. She'd never seen him dressed so slovenly. Even his hair was a mess. "Did anyone follow you?"

"Nope, I switched cabs several times, just like you said." She didn't want him to think she'd had any time to do anything but get over here since they'd last talked. "Where's your prosecutor buddy?"

"Oh, he's going to be about twenty minutes late. Why don't we have a drink in the dining room?"

Alex didn't know much about the military, but she knew that a Grade 5 commissioned officer couldn't afford the type of furniture and art that this house held. Hal pressed a button on a remote, and the music of the Navy Band flooded the room from the Bang & Olufsen speakers. Alex was a bit surprised. Hal seemed like the type who would at least feign a taste for classical music. This CD's main feature seemed to be a loud percussion section.

In the dining room, Alex sat in the Philippe Starck chairs surrounding a beautiful marble-topped table. Hal stood across the table from her, next to the family of Baccarat crystal decanters on the mahogany sideboard. He set the stereo remote down as he prepared to pour. "What can I offer you, Alex-ah-an-dra?" he said, his voice betraying his Southern roots.

"I think I'll pass," she said, observing him carefully. "The Vicodin's about knocked me out."

He filled his glass with an amber fluid, then lifted the drink in his left hand up in a toast to her, letting his other arm fall casually to his side. "You did a remarkable bit of detective work," he said. He looked at her, uncertainty in his eyes, and took a hearty gulp of his drink. "Take off your dark glasses so I can look at you."

"No, I've got a shiner from my beating last night."

"Yeah, how do you think Wiatt got wind that you were onto him?"

Alex chose her words carefully. "Well, now that I think back on it, the person who attacked me couldn't have been Wiatt."

The air seemed to compress in the room.

"What do you mean? Your DNA test proved it."

"My attacker last night wasn't tall enough to be Wiatt. He was closer to your height."

Hal jutted his chest out, standing straighter. "How can you tell? It's dark down in the tunnels."

Alex hesitated a moment before responding. "Hal, I didn't mention before where I was attacked. How did you know about the tunnel?"

Hal's eyes narrowed into slits. He reached inside his windbreaker, pulled a .45 from a holster, and aimed it at Alex's chest. "Such a pity, Alex. You were going to be the cash cow for my Gene-Ease deal. Now I'll have to find someone else to handle the samples."

Alex stood up from the chair and spoke calmly. She moved slightly so that she was squarely in front of a Remington bronze statue. If Hal tried to kill her, he was at least going to have to take out one of his more valuable possessions. "You framed Gloria Devon for killing her husband, because you knew that when she was booted out of the FBI, Wiatt would get that job. And you—"

"Wiatt stole my job," said Hal, his lips pursed, which turned his otherwise-handsome face cynical and ugly.

"And Wiatt screwed up your deal with Gene-Ease," added Alex.

"Guys like him got it easy. Yale. Lots of promotions. I had to claw my way through Officers' Training School, endure cracks about my being from Mayberry or East Butt Crack. He just lucked into it all."

"You took two-year-old blood of Gloria's from Walter Reed and put it under Ted's nails. And when I found out that someone had framed her, you switched your sample with Wiatt's at the DNA bank so that I would think Wiatt was the killer."

Hal beamed, as if Alex had congratulated him on some achievement. "It was easy enough to do last night after I'd flattened you. I'm in and out of that bank a couple of times a week, making arrangements for the Gene-Ease deal."

He wrinkled his nose, as if merely being in the room with Alex was distasteful. "You almost wrecked everything."

Hal put his drink down on the sideboard and used his left hand to pump up the volume on the Navy Band CD with the remote. A thin band of sweat appeared on his forehead. He steadied the gun in his right hand, which remained aimed directly at her heart.

Alex's body tensed and she tried to muster up the strongest voice she could. "Put down the gun."

Hal laughed. "You fool."

"Hal, you're not going to kill me here. You're much too neat to splatter blood on a Persian carpet."

"Don't you get tired of always being right?" He motioned with the gun toward the hallway. "Walk."

In the hallway, he stayed close behind her. She winced as he poked the gun into her sore kidney. Tears of pain rolled down her cheeks. She tried to slow her panicked breathing. This was not going at all like she'd planned.

He prodded her toward a door at the end of the hallway. He ordered her to open it. As they descended the old wooden staircase, she could smell the damp dirt of a root cellar. They passed through a utility room with a washer and dryer, then entered a larger room with a dirt floor. The far half of the floor was covered with a plastic tarp. "That's where you're gonna die," he whispered from his position behind her.

He pushed her toward the tarp, but, on the uneven dirt floor, the gesture caused him to lose his balance slightly. Alex turned suddenly and ran back past him. She'd made it only a few feet when he shot her point-blank in the back. She fell forward with a thud, landing facedown in the black dirt.

"Shit," he said, then turned toward the tarp. He started pulling it up meticulously and moving it over to her limp body. He dragged the tarp and floated it over her back, then reached down to roll her over. As he did so, her arm stuck out and paralyzed him with a Taser.

Then she heard the front door being blasted open and the voices of Dan and Grant as they burst through.

CHAPTER 48

"I WILL NEVER MAKE A CRACK ABOUT BOYS with toys again," said Alex. She was sitting with Dan, Grant, and the rest of the Tattoo Killer strike squad in their Pentagon office. It was the morning after Hal's arrest for the murder of Ted Devon. The day before, Alex had grabbed a few goodies from Grant's lab before confronting Hal—a pair of transmitting sunglasses, one of the new bulletproof vests, and the high-voltage combat Taser.

"You were a fuckin' pro, Alex," said Grant. "You can be the poster girl for our whole line."

"Will I get the same pay as Catherine Zeta-Jones gets for her phone ads?"

"Not until you get your tooth recapped," Grant replied.

He and Dan had been mesmerized the evening before when the screen at the Pentagon, on which they were watching Barbara, split in two and Alex began transmitting on half of it. When they realized what was going on, they told the rest of the strike team to keep Barbara under surveillance, then raced over to Hal's house. Luckily, Alexandria is within spitting distance of the Pentagon.

As they continued to congratulate her, Alex's thoughts turned to Barbara. "What's he waiting for?" she asked Dan.

"He's a planner, Alex. There were at least eighteen days between each murder, and it's only been eight since the Groton kill."

"You're going to count on the logic of a psychopath?"

Dan put his arm around Alex to comfort her. "We've got her covered, day and night."

Alex sighed. "How does she seem to you?"

"Well, we don't see her on the video, but we see what she sees. Her voice seems normal; she's okay."

"I can hook into the feed here if you want," said Grant. She nodded.

Dan spoke to Alex firmly. "She's a soldier. It's hard for a civilian to understand. She made a deal to give her life for her country."

For a brief moment, Alex grew angry. "Lana didn't sign on to that particular deal."

Grant flashed the feed up to a large screen. Now Alex could see what Barbara was viewing and hear what was going on around her. The images danced in front of her on the three-foot-high screen. Alex was moved to have this little connection with her friend. It relieved her to see that Barbara was going about her ordinary life.

"How did you swing this?" she asked Grant. "Isn't the Pentagon worried about its secrets being broadcast?"

"She's only got the lowest level of clearance. She won't be in any highly secure areas, and she's promised to tilt the glasses back on her head if she is looking at any confidential documents. I sweetened the deal by promising them a prototype of the microchip we use in the glasses."

Every once in awhile, a black line would encircle one of the people in her field of vision. Grant explained. "We've fed a physical description of Francis Mason into the computer. The program compares similar men to see how close a match they are."

"Are you still checking construction sites around the District?" Alex asked Dan.

"Yeah, D.C., Virginia, Maryland. We've got men at a couple of sites right now. It doesn't help that we're in a building boom."

She turned back to the screen and watched her friend Barbara walk down the hall in the Pentagon. Maria Con cepción, a young Hispanic lawyer who had attended one of Barbara's JAG training lectures, greeted her in the hallway.

"Is Grant Pringle still working at AFIP?" Maria asked.

The blurring image indicated that Barbara had nodded her head.

"He goes to my health club. I think he's hot."

Grant broke into a lecherous smile, thrust his left arm out, and made a muscle.

"I don't think he's your type, Maria."

"What do you mean?"

"He's—how do you say it in Spanish, a *mariposa*?"

Alex laughed, but Grant's grasp of Spanish didn't extend that far.

"He's gay?" said Maria.

"Shh. Don't breathe a word of it. He's one of my best friends at AFIP and I certainly wouldn't want him booted out."

Maria nodded seriously and left. Barbara's vision lingered on the young woman's cute butt and long legs, just to give Grant a sense of what he would be missing.

Grant was talking to the image on the screen. There was no return audio. "Barbara, I am going to kill you."

CHAPTER 49

ALEX PULLED THE T-BIRD INTO THE PARK-
ing lot of the Gallaudet dorm. It was the third Sunday in
June, Father's Day. Hal wouldn't be spending it with his
kids. He was still being held without bail. The chilling
full-color video of him trying to kill Alex to cover his
tracks had been enough to convince a judge that perhaps
Hal was not the poster boy for the presumption of inno-
cence.

Alex had told Lana they would be having an un–Father's Day dinner.

"Sort of like the un-Cola," said Lana.

Alex was Lana's guardian angel while Barbara was off
on her assignment. The day before, Alex had spent the
morning at the dentist, getting her smile back, then had
taken Lana to the Smithsonian to see an exhibit about the
golden age of Hollywood. Alex and Lana had giggled as
they bought each other Father's Day gifts from the museum shop. Alex had hinted that she wanted the cherry
blossom soap. She had been sure to pick something within
the price range of a fourteen-year-old.

For once, Alex felt lucky about her dad. At least she
had those five years of memories. She knew he really
loved her. Lana had never known her father. He'd dropped
out of high school and drifted west before Barbara even
told him she was pregnant. Barbara never saw him again.

As Alex slammed her car door, she marveled at how,

for the first time since her beating in the tunnel, she could move without triggering a cacophony of aches and pains. Her face still looked like something from a grade-B horror flick, and she'd cut her hair a few inches to rid it of some sticky hospital adhesive from her roll in the garbage, but she was beginning to feel like her old self.

A few boys were exiting the coed dorm. They held the door for Alex, so she didn't need to buzz the dorm head to be let in. Alex bounded up the steps to the third floor. She overheard snatches of conversation about a dance the night before.

As she walked up the stairs, her cell phone rang. It was Dan. Alex stopped, frozen on a step.

"Is she okay?" Alex asked, panicked about Barbara.

"Yeah," said Dan. "But the admiral just called. When he went outside this morning, there was a picture taped to his door. It showed seven pieces of the bird."

Alex gasped, counting the six familiar bases: Galveston, Norfolk, Beaufort, San Diego, Great Lakes, Groton.

Dan continued. "There was a new piece of the eagle, one we haven't seen before. A tail. We think he'll make his move today."

Alex expressed her concern, and Dan again promised he wouldn't let anything happen to Barbara. She stood for a few moments on the stairs, letting students pass her. Then she composed herself and solemnly approached Lana's door.

She pressed a button next to Lana's door, which caused a flashing light to go on inside to let Lana know she had a visitor. No answer. C'mon, thought Alex, don't stand up your surrogate dad. Not today, of all days.

Alex turned the knob and was surprised when it opened easily. The room was a mess, not at all the orderly sanctuary that Alex had visited the previous day. A lamp was thrown against the wall. The desk chair was broken. Unthinkingly, she reached down to right the chair. On the chair's leg was a small smudge of baby powder.

She snapped open her cell phone and sent an instant

message to Dan's whole team. "Get a crime scene team to Residence Hall C, as in *crisis,* on the Gallaudet campus. Someone's kidnapped Lana."

Alex didn't wait for the techs to arrive. Within minutes, she was back in her car, flying down Florida Avenue. She was on the phone with Grant as she pressed the accelerator. He gave her the information she requested from the file of Carolyn Duvalier—the JAG lawyer who'd been involved with Kenneth Mason.

Admiral Mason answered the door on the first ring. She pushed him aside and entered the house. "Why didn't you tell me that Duvalier had a daughter?"

"Kitty? I didn't touch her. She was in high school, for Chrissakes."

"Francis kidnapped the daughter of a JAG lawyer."

Mason went to the closet and got a knife and a Glock 18. "I think I know where they might be."

She and Mason got in the T-Bird and drove off. Dan was already on his way to Gallaudet when she called him again. "I'm with the admiral and we're headed to the groundskeeper's shack at Rock Creek Park. His son used to go there with Duvalier's daughter. How soon can you send backup?"

"We can be there in fifteen minutes by copter. Wait, I repeat, wait until I get there. Grant will meet us with the SWAT team."

Alex had no intention of waiting. She'd jogged the park alone and with David and knew right where the shack was. She zigged the car toward the park's entrance and glanced guiltily at Mason, who, unlike her, had not buckled his seat belt. She slammed on the brakes, causing Mason to pitch forward and strike his head on the dashboard of the old car.

She grabbed Mason's gun, flung open her door, and started to run. She hoped that Mason would be too dazed to follow and that at least her problematic passenger door would slow him down. She didn't want to take the risk that he'd go after his son and get Lana killed in the process.

She looked like a maniac as she ran. Her long blond curls were flying in all directions, her new leather fanny pack bounced against her waist, and she was holding a gun. After one family with a small kid freaked, she realized she'd been waving it like a madwoman. Luckily, it was dusk in the park and most of the families had already gone home.

IN THE HUT, FRANCIS WAS SITTING CROSS-legged, a sturdy, intimidating hunting knife in his hand. His duffel bag lay open on a nearby table. Lana was kneeling in front of him, trembling. Her hands flapped impotently behind her, the cold metal of the handcuffs gagging their movement.

"Don't look at me like that," he squawked.

Her breath came in horrified gasps.

He calmed himself and began to stroke her hair. She closed her eyes, fighting back tears.

He scooted closer to her. "You let your hair grow, Kitty. It looks nice." He reached out and began stroking it.

"I'm not Kitty."

"Oh yeah, I forgot. Now that you are all grown-up and turned sixteen, you want to be called Katherine."

He fell silent, just staring off into the space behind her. She looked out of the corner of her eye, sneaking a few peeks at the cabin around her. It was dark and scary, with just a single lightbulb hanging above them. The angle of the light made his face look drawn and long.

"I'm not going to hurt you, you know," he said. "I just want to talk."

She looked at him with a terrified gaze, biting her bottom lip raw. She took a deep breath and spoke. "The handcuffs hurt. Can't you please, please take them off? I won't move." She looked at the knife.

He shifted up on his knees and yanked her arms roughly to the side. He put the knife down for an instant while he used a key to pop open the cuffs. Then, in a split second, he had the knife pointing at her throat. "Keep your hands behind you. If you move one inch, I'll cut you with this."

He left the cuffs in back of her in case he needed to bind her once more. Then he settled back into a sitting position in front of her. He began whistling Chemical Brothers' "Elektrobank."

At the end of the song, his hand moved to stroke her cheek. "Maybe it's a good thing my dad's banging your mom. We can be brother and sister." He reached down and started unzipping her sweatshirt. He used the tip of his knife to cut the front of her bra in the middle, exposing both breasts. He pinched one roughly. A tear ran down Lana's cheek.

"We could live in the same house and I could visit your room anytime I wanted," he said. "Maybe I'd even do to you what he does to your mom."

Francis was getting aroused. His penis pressed against his jeans.

He put his knife under her chin. "Stand up and take off your slacks."

He stood up first.

Lana grabbed the loose handcuffs from the floor behind her and vaulted up. She swung at the lightbulb above them and knocked it out, then ran into the kitchen. The shack was now completely black. She was next to the refrigerator. He came after her, plunging the knife in her direction. She spun around and the knife hit the wall, chipping the paint.

She pulled her sweatshirt sleeve down over her watch, afraid that the luminous dial was giving off enough light to pinpoint her. Lana stood next to the refrigerator, holding her breath. She couldn't hear him, but her eyes were better than his and she could sense his vague silhouette. He came near her, and she opened the refrigerator door, slamming it right into him. He groaned and dropped the knife. She flung open the door of the shack, and ran out. He was only a few steps behind her.

"Francis, let her go," Alex screamed as the two of them came into view.

But instead, he closed the distance and put his hands around Lana's neck and squeezed.

"Stop or I'll shoot," said Alex, pointing Mason's Glock at Francis. She'd never held a gun before and the weight of it pulled on her wrists.

Francis closed his hands tighter around Lana's neck. "Drop the gun and step back, or I'll kill her."

Lana's eyes were bulging out and she was struggling to breathe. Francis's thumbs were moving toward her trachea. Alex couldn't get a clear shot at Francis. He was holding Lana as a shield.

She dropped the gun.

"Step back with your hands in the air," he said.

She obeyed, moving back one step.

"Keep going," he ordered.

When she was about ten feet farther away, he walked forward toward the gun, pushing Lana in front of him, hands still around her neck. Then he pulled the back of Lana's unzipped sweatshirt up over her face so she couldn't see and kicked her legs from behind so that she fell to the ground. He reached down, picked up the gun, and cocked it. Then he pulled Lana to her feet, keeping the gun aimed at her head as she rose.

"Stay right where you are," he said to Alex. "Or you're both dead."

Alex pleaded with him. "Let her go. Take me instead. I'm the one you want."

"You're nobody!" he yelled. "You're not on the list."

"I'm the woman who's with your dad now."

Francis seemed confused by this new bit of information.

"He showed me his tattoo. The one where you burned him, you naughty boy."

"He deserved it," Francis said angrily. "He killed my mom."

"And you want to punish him?"

Francis nodded.

"Take me, then. Take me."

"Nooooo!" yelled Lana.

Francis was mesmerized by Alex. "Do you want to see the merchandise?" she asked as she took a step closer. "Do you want to know how your dad likes to fuck, what he let your mom rot away for?"

"I know how he likes it. He likes to hurt women."

"Like you. Just like you."

"No," he screamed. "I don't hurt them when we make love. I put them to sleep first." He was rocking back and forth on his feet like a little boy, gun still aimed at Lana. Then he wrapped his left arm around Lana's neck and aimed the gun at Alex.

"Please, Francis," said Alex. Then she remembered the conversation with his teacher. "Please, Sam."

He seemed confused. Alex kept talking. "Sam, let the little girl go. She's not part of this. Let's go in the cabin together, you and me. Just Sam and Alex."

"Shut up," he said. "Stay right there."

Just then, the loud din of the AFIP chopper registered overhead. Alex and Francis both turned to look. But Lana hadn't heard it. When Francis slackened his grip, she bit down hard on his right arm. He recoiled suddenly and dropped the gun. Alex charged at him and hit him low like an NFL linebacker. He fell down and Lana kicked him in the ribs. Alex then sat on his chest, her legs straddling his arms, pinning them to his sides.

Lana turned away, digging through the grass with her fingers, trying to find the gun. The copter landed a hundred feet away.

A pair of hands grabbed Alex from behind and tossed her off Francis's body. She watched in horror as the admiral straddled his son and pricked a knife under his chin.

Francis gave a wail of a wounded animal. "Dad-dy," he cried.

The admiral hesitated, and Francis put his hand over the admiral's, battling for control of the knife. The sharp edge first came perilously close to the admiral's chest, then near Francis's neck.

"Freeze," yelled Dan, aiming his gun at the son, while

Grant, with considerable zest, poked his at the temple of the father. "Happy Father's Day," said Grant, cocking the hammer of his revolver and ordering the admiral off.

Dan addressed them both. "You have the right to remain silent. . . ."

Alex got to her feet and put her arms around Lana, who was shaking. She stroked Lana's hair and kissed the top of her head. Lana clung to her as minutes passed. Since Lana's head was buried in Alex's chest, there was no way for Lana to read Alex's lips. Alex just kept stroking and holding her.

When Alex could feel Lana's terrified heartbeat slowing to a more normal rate, Alex leaned back slightly so that she could pull the two sides of Lana's sweatshirt together and zip it properly. With Lana still clinging to her, she asked Grant to give her a flashlight.

Alex pointed it at her own face so that Lana could read her lips in the dusk. "You saved my life, Lana. Your mom is going to be so proud."

CHAPTER 50

TWO WEEKS LATER, ALEX KISSED LUKE AS she positioned the triangle of turquoise at the correct height on the black cords of the bolo tie around his neck. The turquoise matched the country-and-western stitching on his black suit. "Are you sure this will pass for black tie?" he asked.

"Luke Matthews! Since when are you worried about the fashion police?"

"Since when do I get invited to a Fourth of July State dinner at the White House?"

"Ah, the White House. Been there, done that. Maybe we can reprise our sex in the cloakroom there."

"Well, honey, I think I feel a song coming on. 'We got it on among the hangers, Burberrys askew. I got it bad for someone, and that someone is you—'"

"There seems to be more coming on than just a song." She rubbed her hand down the front of his pants. "Is that the neck of a custom-made Fender guitar in your pocket, or are you happy to see me?"

She kissed him dramatically, causing him to swallow at least one stanza of his new tune. Then he two-stepped her over to the bed. "Are you sure this is okay?" he asked as they started taking off the very clothes that they had just so carefully put on. "I don't want to make you late for the White House."

"I'm one of the guests of honor. They can't start without me."

PRESIDENT BRADLEY COTTER HAD INVITED a mix of people to the Fourth of July dinner—Big donors. Union officials. Hollywood celebrities. But the bulk of his energy and charm was focused on the crew from AFIP. Jack Wiatt had the seat of honor between Cotter and the First Lady at the head table. The rest of Wiatt's group was at table number two. All except for Dan, who was on holiday—which, for Dan, entailed joining his photojournalist wife in Bolivia, where she was videotaping a rebel leader. Some men golfed for relaxation. Major Dan dodged bullets and rattlesnakes.

"What, no burgers?" Grant said when the main course arrived, a salmon in a white wine sauce with an asparagus risotto. But the White House cook had a playful sense of humor. He delighted the crowd with a layered ice cream dessert disguised as a hamburger and cannoli mimicking hot dogs.

Alex sat between Luke and Barbara. She had persuaded Barbara to let Lana sit at the Hollywood table, next to the latest Leonardo DiCaprio clone. Lana was a celebrity herself these days after *Newsweek* had featured her on its cover for a story about the Tattoo Killer.

"Yeah, some friend you turned out to be," Barbara said to Alex. "You go and let Lana save your life, so now I have no excuse for not treating her like a grown-up."

"Maybe they'll do a movie of the week about her and she'll make a lot of dough," Grant said.

"Grant, tasteless as usual," said Barbara. "I'm just glad to have her back alive."

Grant smiled over at his date, Maria Concepción, the Hispanic lawyer who'd expressed interest in him. Barbara had fessed up that Grant wasn't gay. And even if he were, what gal could resist an invitation to dinner with the President?

Alex could tell Grant was happy. He was relaxed, sitting comfortably, not posing. Alex excused herself to find a bathroom. Barbara's eyebrows rose when she noticed Congressman David Thorne get up from another table to follow her.

David caught up with Alex when she came out of the powder room into the ornate hallway. "There's no way I can thank you for everything you've done," he said.

"Hey, no worries," she said. "I'm glad things are working out for you."

"And you, too."

He leaned against the wall, taking in the rare vision of Alex in a dress, a clingy royal blue silk sheath, tiny seed pearls visible for the first time around her delicate neck. With her high heels, she could look straight into his eyes.

"I wanted to be the one to tell you that we've decided to keep the museum in D.C.," he said. "It makes sense for the research. Plus, I can visit that old geezer's leg bone anytime I want."

She threw her arms around him. "But why would Congressman Quiller agree to leave the museum here?"

"All he really wanted was the money to build his bridge from Jersey City to Ellis Island. I cut a deal in Congress to give him that."

An honor guard walked by, and they disengaged from their hug.

David looked sheepish. "I'm sorry I gave the alarm code to Gloria without telling you. I couldn't imagine how Rayna would cope if Gloria was sent to jail."

Alex thought about the code, NJDC, for the two places they'd made love. "What did you tell her it stood for?"

He blushed. "Never Judge Dames Cavalierly."

Alex rolled her eyes. They both laughed and began walking back to their separate tables.

When she sat down, Luke pulled her close. He kissed her on the cheek and whispered, "You're an amazing woman."

Coffee arrived and Grant confessed to Luke that he'd heard him sing the previous spring. As they discussed the local music scene, Barbara leaned toward Alex and whispered, "Does it make you feel jealous?" Barbara tipped her head toward David's table. David was sitting with Gloria Devon and her daughter. David smiled fondly at Alex as he caught her gaze, and Gloria gave her a grateful wave.

"Nah, they're right for each other. And it's important for that girl to have a real daddy."

"I wonder if Gloria Devon's going to get the FBI job back," said Barbara. "The President forced her to resign when she was a suspect."

Wiatt and President Cotter ambled over to the AFIP table. "I want to express my gratitude to each and every one of you," President Cotter said. He gave them each a pale blue eight-and-a-half-by-eleven-inch piece of paper: Citations of Honor for their bravery in solving the two sets of crimes.

Luke whispered to Alex, "Where do I get the souvenir that says 'My girlfriend got a Citation of Honor and all I got was this lousy T-shirt'?"

The President continued speaking. "I want you to know that I offered my good friend Jack here a new post—as the director of the FBI."

"Congratulations," Barbara said. The rest of them nodded.

"Not so fast," said Wiatt. "I told our chief executive that the FBI is a mess. I like it just where I am. We're the definition of a lean, mean fighting machine. There's just one loose end I need to tie up."

Wiatt nodded his head toward Alex. "She's the one I told you about," he said to the President.

"Ah, Dr. Blake," President Cotter said. "Colonel Wiatt told me that he would like to make your position a permanent one. I'm hoping you will agree."

Alex paused for a moment as a series of images filtered through her mind. The glint of the charm bracelet on the librarian's severed wrist. The pieces of the tattoo that she helped stop Francis from completing. And the field of dandelions that she had blown and blown and blown. Maybe she'd found the place where she could settle down.

"I'd be honored, sir," she said.

"But," Wiatt said to the President, "we could use a little money to replace the day work—"

"Don't even go there," Alex and Barbara said in unison.

The President led the AFIP gang out to the Rose Garden and motioned them to their seats for some spectacular fireworks. It was a good 102 degrees in the July D.C. heat, even after dark, and Alex started folding her blue paper into accordionlike pleats.

"*Alex . . .*" Barbara said in dismay as she watched Alex fan herself with the former Citation of Honor.

"A girl's gotta do what a girl's gotta do," said Alex.

Then Alex grabbed Luke's hand and they doubled back inside. There was a certain cloakroom needing their attention.

CHAPTER 51

THE NEXT MORNING, ALEX WOKE EARLY. she showered quietly and put on a nice pair of pleated black pants and a pale blue silk shirt. She took two items from her dresser and put them in her fanny pack.

She left a note for Luke on the kitchen table. "Loved your fireworks last night. I'll be back in time for breakfast."

In the living room, she surveyed herself, front view, side view, back view, peering over her shoulder and tucking her shirt in more tautly. She took a ponytail holder out of her fanny pack and pulled back her hair. Again she checked all the angles and then impatiently tugged the rubber band out of her hair and fluffed her curls out naturally. She took a deep breath and left the apartment.

This morning, she was too impatient for the Metro, so she flagged a cab. There was no convenient parking place near her destination. Mercifully, the driver was the quiet type. She would have hated to put up with small talk now.

As she slammed the cab door at her destination, a sole jogger ran past her. She followed him with her gaze as he started running up and down the stairs of the Lincoln Memorial. D.C. was funny that way. The tourists treated the monuments with awe. The residents used them as their own private playground.

Alex veered to the left. The place was completely still. She walked with determination, moving so quickly, she seemed to be skipping like a child. This time she didn't stop at the statue, or at the directory. Instead, she headed directly to the black marble vortex.

The first black marble panel was 70 E the seventieth panel east of the center. She had a long journey to the one she sought, 1 W. The seventy black marble panels increased in height as they moved toward the middle. The tops of the panels were level with the grass on the plateau above, while the bottoms were level with the sidewalk and ridge along which Alex walked. From a distance, Alex had thought she'd feel like she was walking down into a trench, as the panels increased from the height of her waist to a few feet taller than she was at the apex of the monument. But despite inclining below the park's grass as she walked, she didn't feel as if she were descending into a foxhole, but, as the height of the marble grew, as if she were ascending into the clouds.

In the little ridge between the marble and the sidewalk, people stuck their offerings to the dead. A small flag here, a poem there, flowers farther on. Her journey was slow, as she stopped to read some of the letters and poems. Love letters to a high school sweetheart, a poem for an older brother. So many people had poured out their feelings through the gifts they left that a museum was planned to display them all.

Alex could feel tears forming as she got closer to the center. She passed 2 E, 1 E, then came upon 1 W. Line 130 had to be near the bottom, so she bent forward and started reading up from the last line. Elwood Eugene Rumbaugh. Andres Garcia. Danny Glen Marshall. Then she reached it: Alexander Northfield Blake. She pressed two fingers to her lips in a kiss, then touched those fingers to his name. She lingered, caressing the name.

Then she sat cross-legged on the ground, her eyes level with the eight-inch gash of carved letters that represented her father.

She took a moment to compose herself and then began to speak. "Mom's, well, still Mom, a little zany. Still trying to save the world. She really misses you. I guess nobody else measures up."

Alex stared at the letters, a little window into her father. She made several false starts at further conversation. "Uh, Dad . . ."

She used her right hand to wipe a tear from her eye, then reached forward, as if seeking his embrace.

After a deep breath, she said, "I think I've found my way." She smiled, a faint upturned ribbon of pink. "You'll never believe it. I'm working for the military, just like you."

She put her fan-shaped Citation of Honor in the crevice in front of the Wall. She closed her eyes for an instant, fighting back further tears.

Then she opened the carved Vietnamese box and let out the kiss five-year-old Alex had put there for her dad.

ACKNOWLEDGMENTS

The Armed Forces Institute of Pathology is a real institution, with dedicated scientists, soldiers, social scientists, physicians, and civilians. The flaws and dark sides I have introduced into my fictional AFIP characters shouldn't be taken to reflect badly on the amazing men and women who work for that fascinating organization. With wide-ranging projects that involve national security, forensics, historical analyses, infectious disease investigations, and much more, the real AFIP is more fascinating than any novel.

Many people contributed mightily to this book: Lesa Andrews, Richard Baer, Eric Goodman, Joe Terrence Gray, Gary Kubek, Christopher Ripley, Clements Ripley, Mark Rosin, Jim Stark, Liz Stein, and Darren Stephens provided boundless encouragement, as well as gracious and insightful comments on the manuscript. These are people who have enriched my personal life in countless ways.

As I ventured into writing about a geneticist, I was inspired by the integrity and intellect of various people in the genetics, policy, and forensic realms, including Joan Abrahamson, George Annas, Ellen Wright Clayton, Bob Gaensslen, Debra Greenfield, Nanette Elster, Charles Inlander, Hal Krent, Debra Leonard, Valerie Lindgren, Max Mehlman, Ellen Mitchell, Jordan Paradise, Gene Pergamaent, Laurie Rosenow, Mark Rothstein, David Stoney, and Nancy Wexler.

I also want to offer special thanks to my extraordinary

editor, Kelley Ragland, and the amazing St. Martin's Minotaur team—and heartfelt gratitude to Katharine Cluverius and Binky Urban for their many contributions to this book.

I began writing *Sequence* in San Sebastian, Spain, continued it while I was a visiting professor at Princeton, and finished it at the base of the pyramids in Cairo, Egypt. The bulk of it, however, was written during various stays on a California beach, where I experienced the hospitality of Francis, Rose, and Dominick Pizzulli—my love to the three of you.

READ ON for an excerpt from
the next book by Lori Andrews

THE SILENT ASSASSIN

Coming soon in hardcover from
St. Martin's Minotuar

PROLOGUE

THE TANK THAT ENDED THE VIETNAM WAR over thirty years earlier by crashing through the gates of the presidential palace provided cover for Huu Duoc Chugai as he strode to the War Remnants Museum in Ho Chi Minh City. At 2:00 A.M. the few people on the street were drunks or lovers, probably with little interest in the tall forty-year-old, but Chugai fell into the routine of keeping in the shadows, his head down. His pace picked up on Vo Van Tan Street, then slowed as he wove through the arsenal of captured American planes and bombs outside the museum. He swore under his breath as he clipped his knee against the rocket launcher attached to a rusting American helicopter.

He glanced around as he reached the door, saw no one, and let himself in with a key. Chugai was a man who made the most of opportunities. The ministry which had previously employed him oversaw the park system, including the museum. He'd hung on to a key to the museum, not knowing at the time how he would use it. His life was like the construction of the tunnels at Cu Chi. He believed in stealth, in collecting and manipulating information, in winning at all costs. Sometimes he couldn't tell if it was his birthright or the two years he had spent in the United States that had honed his resolve. But his planning was about to pay off.

He locked the museum door behind him, congratulat

ing himself on his choice of a meeting place. When the
general arrived, Chugai planned to walk him past the
photo of a smiling American slicing the head off a North
Vietnamese soldier. It would remind the man of his debt,
of how Chugai's father had saved his life during the war.

Chugai lit a cigarette, thought about the warm bed of his
mistress he'd just left, and smiled again at his own clever-
ness. He'd arrived a half hour before the proposed meeting
time and was looking out the window so he could let the
old North Vietnamese soldier in. Or maybe he would move
back through the museum, so the man would knock and
wait for a few moments, just to show him Chugai was running the show.

His thought was abruptly interrupted by an arm reaching around his neck and grasping him in a choke hold. His
cigarette fell to the floor as his assailant spun him around.
Chugai looked down in embarrassment at the general,
who was three inches shorter than he. How the hell had he
gotten in and crept up so silently?

The older Vietnamese man grinned, with a touch of
madness in the corners of his eyes. Chugai was sufficiently chagrined that he forgot his grand plan to walk the
general through the museum to seal his loyalty. Instead, he
thrust an envelope into the general's hand. The man didn't
even open it. Instead, he held his pointer finger up, signaling "one."

Chugai knew what he meant. He'd kill once more and
then he would consider the debt repaid. Chugai opened his
mouth to speak, but the man was no longer listening. Instead, the general had moved over to the French guillotine
that was on display.

The old man placed the envelope on the wooden bench
at the bottom of the guillotine and let loose the weighty
blade that had been used to kill prisoners of war. The
crushing thump severed the envelope in half, shredding
and scattering the Vietnamese and American currency it
held. As Chugai rushed over to see if the airline ticket was
still intact, the general disappeared out of the museum.

Screw it, thought Chugai. If the general wants to do it his way, so be it. Chugai put the mangled currency and plane ticket into his pocket. He didn't care how the general got to Washington, D.C., as long as he killed the bastard.

CHAPTER I

LUKE KNELT ON THE HAND-LOOMED RUG next to the bed and started zipping his guitar into its traveling case. The loud crackle of the industrial-size zipper brought Alex in from the next room. Her long, wavy blond hair cascaded over her black turtleneck and she still looked flushed from their lovemaking. She walked up behind him. "I heard the zipper and thought it was your pants coming back off."

He turned toward her, still kneeling, and faced the fly of her jeans. He reached his hand up to the snap at the top. "Dare me and I'll have you back in bed in twenty seconds flat."

She thought about how that might make him late for his flight to London, and how she'd probably lose her favorite parking spot at work. Then she smiled down at him. "Dare you," she said.

A flurry of clothes streaked across the room like the streamers from a New Year's Eve popper. She fell back on the bed and he joined her, licking her mischievously down her body, a favor she promptly returned. Then he moved up over her and they made love tenderly, gingerly, his face down close to hers, nose to nose, their sighs turning into gasps. As they were about to climax, they rolled across the bed, so that she was on top of him, almost seated, lifting herself up and down. Her hair shook like a horse's mane, but a horse that was riding a man.

She came first and the rolling motion caused him to climax and groan. She flopped over next to him and buried her head in the crook of his arm. Brushing her hair back from her eyes, she noticed the wristwatch she'd failed to remove before lovemaking. "Yikes, Luke, we'd better hit it."

She got out of bed, but Luke feigned exhaustion. She bent over to shake his shoulder and her cell phone rang. A tune by Luke's rock band, the Cattle Prods.

"Oh, Luke, you didn't reprogram this again, did you?" She was glad it hadn't rung like that in some high-level meeting.

"Alex Blake," she said into the receiver, as Luke continued to simulate a coma.

The familiar voice of Major Dan Wilson said simply, "You've got a date with a corpse at eleven hundred hours."

She hung up and addressed the body on her bed. "Up and at 'em, Luke, you're not my only stiff today."

A few minutes later, Luke and Alex were packing the trunk of her battered 1963 yellow T-Bird and racing to National Airport. She couldn't bear to refer to it by its new name, Ronald Reagan International Airport. Hadn't they named enough stuff after him? Was it true that every big city now had a Reagan Street, a Reagan School, probably even a Reagan Prison? Was anything safe from the creeping Reaganisms? She could imagine a day when they would start renaming people's body parts. Yes, my Reagan bone broke just above the Coca-Cola cartilage.

At the United terminal, Luke lingered to say goodbye. He handed her a CD of songs he'd recorded for her. She looked at this almost-handsome man as he shouldered his guitar case and gripped the handle of a meager duffel bag of clothes. He loved playing and writing lyrics so much that he'd do it for squat—and, in fact, earned only slightly more than that. But the music did provide him with an excuse to see the world. When an old bandmate in London offered to put him up in exchange for Luke helping the guy move his piano to his new flat, Luke jumped at the chance and the Cattle

Prods Second World Tour was born. After London, there would be gigs in Spain, France, and Denmark.

"I haven't taken any vacation. Maybe I'll meet you in Barcelona," Alex said.

Luke looked down at the ground, then back up at her. "That's not so great," Luke said. "I'm staying with Vanessa."

Alex's mouth gaped open before she could hide her feelings. And then the curbside skycap told Luke he'd better haul ass if he wanted to make the flight.

Luke stepped forward. "It's nothing. She's just a friend. I'll e-mail you once I land." He bent over to kiss her, but she turned her face and the smack landed on her cheek.

Luke ran into the terminal, and Alex started the old T-Bird. As she sped toward the George Washington Memorial Parkway, she pumped up the heater to chase away the chill she felt, a combination of the unseasonably cool December day and the icy thoughts running through her mind. Who the hell was Vanessa? Probably someone he'd met on the First World Tour, last year, after he and Alex had broken up.

The parkway was more like a parking lot that time of day. Alex used her time in traffic to pick up her messages at work. One from Dan, left before he reached her at home about the autopsy and another ordering her to meet with the head of the Armed Forces Institute of Pathology, Colonel Jack Wiatt, at 2:00 P.M.

As a civilian working at the AFIP, she bristled at the term *order*, especially when it came from Wiatt, with whom she'd tangled on more than one occasion. When President Bradley Cotter had appointed him head of the AFIP a year earlier—and not head of the FBI, which he'd wanted—he'd practically gone postal. But it turned out the AFIP suited him. Overseen by the U.S. Department of Defense, the compound functioned like a city, with its own fire department, police station, and hospital. The facility sat on 113 out-of-the-way acres in D.C. near the

Maryland border, four acres larger than the Vatican. Like the Vatican, the AFIP had a surprisingly wide reach, often working in mysterious—or at least sub rosa—ways. It oversaw forensic investigations in the United States and abroad involving the military and the Executive Branch—all without the close scrutiny that the public and Congress gave other institutions like the FBI and CIA. A high-testosterone soldier who'd led men in every war, incursion, altercation, and conflict since Vietnam, Wiatt was a man for whom rules were flexible. Running an institution where they could be bent suited him. But he and Alex often butted heads as she tried to do her job using genetics to create biowarfare vaccines and he pulled her into activities that took her away from her work.

Once she reached the compound—a frustrating forty-five minutes later—Alex nosed her car toward her favorite parking spot, but, of course, it was now occupied. The only space left was across the base from the main AFIP entrance. She walked to the door of the National Museum of Health and Medicine, which was connected by tunnels to both the AFIP, where she worked, and the Walter Reed Medical Center, where she often provided second opinions for prominent patients.

As Alex approached the museum, she was surprised to see twenty or thirty people outside, some holding placards. The museum was usually a sleepy place, with tours of third-graders staring at the microscopes and medical oddities like the stomach-shaped hairball from a teenage girl who constantly chewed (and swallowed) her curls. This was a much different crowd. Elderly Vietnamese couples in cream-colored flowing pants and denim-clad college students carrying signs with phrases like "Let their spirits rest in peace." A thin white guy in his early twenties with a megaphone blocked the sidewalk. He shouted into the mouthpiece, "Give back the Trophy Skulls."

He looked straight into Alex's blue eyes, at her beguilingly sweet heart-shaped face. His gaze traveled down her body, noting her beat-up, brown leather jacket and jeans, nicely taut over her lean, athletic curves. He handed her a placard to carry.

"No, thanks," she said. "I work here."

ON THE WAY TO HER LAB, ALEX STOPPED AT the office of her best friend, Navy Lieutenant Barbara Findlay, the African-American lawyer who was the AFIP's general counsel.

"So, what's with the crowd outside?" Alex asked. She folded her legs under her in the comfortable chair across from Barbara's desk and reached into the cut-glass candy bowl that was Barbara's way to get secretaries and generals alike to stop in and chat.

Barbara, poised and feisty in her crisp Navy uniform, leaned forward and pushed a *Washington Post* across her desk toward Alex. "Didn't you see yesterday's newspaper?"

Alex shook her head. "I was busy having good-bye sex with Luke."

"Break-up sex or tour-schedule sex?"

Alex thought for a moment. "Not sure yet."

"Frankly, Alex, your taste in men—"

"At least I'm taking a swim in the dating pool. You haven't even put on your suit."

Barbara laughed. "A teenage daughter and parking lot full of protestors keeps me busy enough."

Alex looked down at the front-page photo of a small hill with a pagoda-shaped pillar of five carved stones on top of it. She read the caption. "The Ear Mound?"

"Yes, the Korean Ear Mound in Kyoto, Japan. A five-hundred-year-old pile of ears that samurai warriors cut off of Korean soldiers."

"Why ears?"

"The samurai generals got a bonus for each soldier they killed in Korea. At first they sent back heads, but when the ships got too crowded, they started dispatching just the ears."

Alex looked at the mound of dirt as high as a house. "They must have killed tens of thousands."

Barbara nodded. "Recently, a group of Korean monks placed fifty Korean flags on top of the mound and began to negotiate for a return of the ears, at least spiritually, to Korea. That's what provoked the Vietnamese Ambassador to the U.S. to contact us. Some U.S. G.I.s kept skulls of North Vietnamese soldiers. Most of the skulls were confiscated when they tried to bring them back through U.S. Customs. And the skulls ended up here. We've never displayed them, though, because the soldiers shouldn't have taken them out of Vietnam. We just stuck them in a drawer."

"So what's the big deal? Give them back, let them rest in peace."

"It's not that simple," Barbara said, getting up from her desk chair. She motioned for Alex to come with her.

As the two exited the office, Barbara walked with the dramatic posture of a soldier, her body forcefully and efficiently slicing down the hall. The kinetic Alex commandeered more space.

They approached the storage area of the museum, and Barbara said, "Wiatt wants me to see if I can find a way to delay their return, some legal maneuver."

Alex wondered why Wiatt would care about sending back a drawerful of skulls. Sure, he'd fought in Vietnam, but hadn't the whole nation moved on?

"What's his problem?" Alex asked as Barbara approached a cabinet in the storage room.

"Well," Barbara said, "the U.S. soldiers added a few touches of their own."

Barbara pulled open a drawer, and Alex peered in. The skulls stared back at her. Some had grotesque faces painted on them, a few had their craniums lopped off so that they could serve as ashtrays. A half dozen had been painted neon colors and covered with graffiti, with holes drilled through the top and candles jammed in.

Alex's eyes grew wide and she shook her head. She'd

seen bodies and bones in all states of decay, disease, and disfigurement. But graffiti on someone's supercilliary arch? This was chilling and demeaning. "Who would do something like this?"

"Now you see. We can't let them go back like this."